The Wisdom of Wood

Volume 1

Hazelnut

ISBN-10: 1460907272
EAN-13: 9781460907276
LCCN: 2011902263

The Wisdom of Wood

Volume 1

Hazelnut

Mary L. Peers

FOR JOHN

ACKNOWLEDGEMENTS

THERE ARE MANY writers who have become enamored with the world of Glastonbury, England. Its blend of history, mythology, and mysticism is as entrancing as a palimpsest that draws one ever deeper into a world of the past. I thank each and every one of them for their willingness to step onto that winding road and share their findings with us. In particular, I would like to thank Nikolai Tolstoy, Geoffrey Ashe, Robert Graves, Dion Fortune, and John and Caitlin Matthews for their enormous efforts in shedding light on some very complex mythology.

I would also like to thank Carl Jung and Joseph Campbell for their outstanding work on symbolism in dreams and mythology. It was the concept of mythology as a social dream that opened my eyes to the process of myth as a vehicle for the evolution of consciousness and started my own journey into Glastonbury and this resulting book. Because I believe that mythology is a living energy, I have chosen to give it a voice of its own and not conform to the structure of the past.

Finally, it is those we live with, day-to-day, that share in our journey. And so, I thank, with all my heart, my husband John, for giving me the freedom to dream.

The Wisdom of Wood

ONCE UPON A time, there was a language. This was not a language of letters and words but of lines and notches carved into stone, and it told a story that was older than bones.

It was called the language of trees and spoke about something sacred that was buried in trees, as if there was wisdom in wood. But over time, people lost interest in the wisdom of wood, so a story began to spread about a maiden who used magic to bury a wizard in a tree. That was its way of returning the mystery to the wood, as there was no point in telling a story that wouldn't be heard.

And there it has remained, knowing that someday, when the time was right, a maiden would return to break the spell, and the magic would once again step forward and walk by her side.

That time is now.

THE OGHAM SHIELD

BASED ON THE TREE ALPHABET

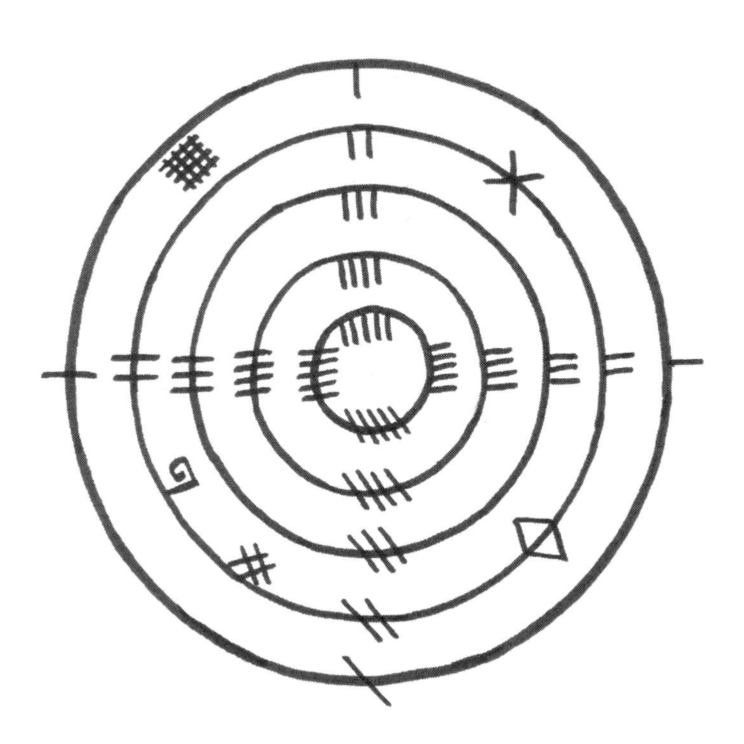

CONTENTS

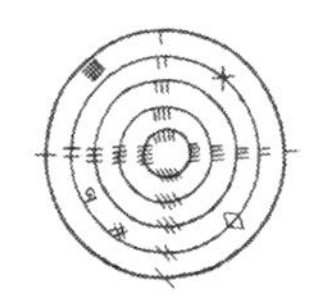

THE OGHAM SHIELD

STAGE TWO
DEATH

STAGE THREE
REBIRTH

SAMUEL ALEXANDER'S JOURNAL

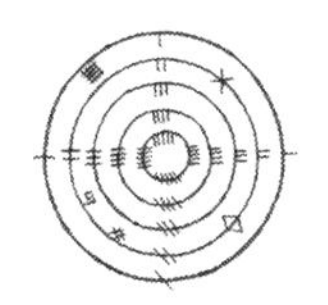

PROLOGUE

England
October 31, 1969
Samhain

"Samuel..."

SAMUEL ALEXANDER EASED into the stony arms of the cemetery bench. The pitted concrete, expanded from cold, had heaved open great gaps that bore nested lofts of moss, and earth pockmarked with the graves of fallow seeds. Samuel shivered as the bitter damp leached its way to his bones, passing through skin and cloth as if transparent. The crumbling seat provided the only remaining corner of late afternoon sun, and Samuel, who felt the chill of evening coming on, had hoped to garner whatever warmth he could.

Samuel was tired. He wasn't sure if it was the trip from America to Cornwall, to research his family heritage, which was so exhausting, or whether the ancient crosses marking the graves had laid their weariness upon him. Whatever the case, he had quickly nodded off.

As he slept, an elderly gentleman in brown slacks and faded tweed jacket appeared, his cap tattered and worn with the look of an old friend. He approached the bench and cocked his head in a quizzical fashion.

The back of the bench was high, and Samuel's head rested upon it. He was a good-looking man in his forties, with salt and pepper hair and clean-shaven. The old man stood off to the side and listened, a slight curve widening his lips.

"Bride's Well, Samuel..."

The words were faint, barely a whisper. The man nodded, dropped his head and stepped forward, snapping a stick on the ground. Samuel stirred.

"Good evening, Sir. Wasn't meanin' to be startlin' ye."

Samuel sat up and rubbed his eyes. "Must've drifted off..."

"Aye... 'tis common in these parts."

Samuel looked up at him questioningly.

"'Tis the graves...they're quite old. I've been tending them for some time now and often find the voices cross o'er."

"Voices?"

"Aye."

"Actually, I did hear a voice, now that you mention it. Someone called my name."

"Aye."

"It wasn't you?"

"Not when I wouldn't be knowin' it."

Samuel sat up and rubbed his hands to ward off the chill.

"You were whisperin' too, Sir."

"I was?"

"Aye. Bride's Well...you were talkin' of Bride's Well."

Samuel looked out across the sweep of green, peppered with crosses and stone graves. "Yes. I remember hearing that."

"It was you that be talkin', Sir."

"Well, I don't know anything about Bride's Well."

"Ye needn't. The graves know. And if they be talkin' to ye, I'd suggest ye do their bidding, Sir."

Samuel stared up at the old man and wondered if he'd scattered a few of his own marbles across the cemetery. He looked to be about seventy and was tall and straight, what Samuel's mother used to call a long drink of water. His tweed cap had molded to his head and he wore the usual English country attire; his clothing knew him well. But despite Samuel's concern the old man's eyes were sharp as tacks.

"Aye...ye'd be wonderin' if I'm a bit daft."

Samuel smiled and looked away.

"It's a different world we inhabit here, Sir. There's a bit of the faery in us all."

"Well. What do you suggest I do?"

"'Tis Saint Michael's line that connects us to Glastonbury. There's an energy that speaks when it wants to be heard. If the Well be callin', I'd suggest ye' go."

"Is that where Bride's Well is?"

"Aye, Sir, in Glastonbury."

Samuel felt a chill grip his spine. He shivered and stood up to shake it off. "I'd best be going. Thank you kindly for your help."

"Aye."

Samuel turned and started to leave.

"Another thing..." The old man's voice dropped to a whisper.

"Yes?"

"Just in case...sometimes the words don't stay... like mist. When you're not familiar, so to speak, it's hard to get a grasp."

Samuel stared, wondering what on earth he was trying to say.

"You're to dig in the water's edge at Bride's Well. That's where you'll find it. That's what they're sayin'."

Fog descended on the graves. Samuel shivered again and looked across the cemetery. "Find what?" he called out.

But there was no answer. And when Samuel looked back, the old man was gone.

The next day, Samuel knelt in the damp earth and stared across what had once been an inland sea: the lowlands spreading out from Glastonbury Tor, formerly known as Avalon. Bride's Well was more like a muddy pond filled with storm water from a nearby sluice, its pool rising out of the earth or sinking back, depending on the season.

Samuel dipped his fingers in the water. He was a practical man and not inclined to follow whims, but whatever was calling him appeared stronger than Samuel's abilities with reason. The old man at the cemetery had talked of Saint Michael's line, a dragon line that pulsed with earth energy and ran from Land's End east through England, including Glastonbury and the cemetery where the voice had spoken.

He reached deeper into the water, stirring up silt. Bride's Well honored Saint Brigit, although Samuel suspected there was older energy here. Saint Brigit was probably the Catholic manifestation of Brighid, the Celtic goddess also known as Bride. Samuel gazed into the muddy water; if Brighid was rising, she was making a hell of a disturbance.

Samuel grimaced and wrenched his hand out of the Well; something had stabbed him. Carefully, he reached back in till he felt a sharp object and pulled it out. As he pulled it up through the water, light hit the edges and Samuel saw what appeared to be a red stone. He cupped it in the palm of his hand, closed his eyes, and resurrected it from the Well.

"Dig in the water's edge," the old man had said. "That's where you'll find it."

He took a deep breath, opened his eyes, and gasped. Resting in the deep flesh of his palm was a ring: an old, double-banded ring with a triangular red stone. Goosebumps shivered up his arm, as he closed his hand, slipped it into the pocket of his trousers, and headed into town.

Glastonbury was a cobbled web of circuitous lanes slick with moss. Samuel meandered aimlessly till he noticed a storefront window displaying books on Glastonbury. He entered and picked up the first one he saw.

"That's a good one," a sultry voice said. "That is, if you're interested in the mystery."

Samuel looked over to the counter and saw a beautiful red head.

"Actually," he replied, "I was just thinking that I know very little about Glastonbury...except for all the Arthurian stuff."

"...Stuff?"

"Well...probably not the most eloquent description." He was somewhat taken aback by her penetrating stare. She was younger than he but not by much.

"You are an architect?" she asked.

"And you are psychic."

"I knew it. Don't ask me how...it just comes. The book you have in your hand would be of interest in that case, as it will give you a deeper understanding of..."

"...the mystery." Samuel finished her sentence.

"Yes...*Ynis Witrin*, The Isle of Glass, otherwise known as Glastonbury. There is much more here than meets the eye."

Samuel fished in his pocket for some coins, careful not to remove the ring. "I also need a small pouch, for carrying coins and the like."

The woman looked down to his pocket, cocked her head, then looked into his eyes. "You might try Merlin's Crystal Cave. I suspect the quartz he sells would often require a small bag."

"Merlin's Crystal Cave is a shop?"

"Yes, Merlin's Crystal Cave on Magdalene Street, where the Druidic priest meets the Christian goddess." The woman took his money and handed him the book, glancing once more at his pocket. "I suspect the owner will be more than happy to oblige."

Samuel found Merlin's Crystal Cave on Magdalene Street, just as the woman had said. It appeared to be closed, however, as the windows framed nothing but darkness. He clutched the rusty knob and turned slightly, surprised when it yielded, and the door swung inward; he bent low to avoid the massive beam. As he entered, the Abbey Bell Tower erupted in a cacophonous chiming that exploded into the room with him, its resonance intensified by the energy of hundreds of crystals. Samuel staggered, hit by the force of an ancient clanging that rocked him to the core, like a deep sorrow that made him want to vomit or sob. He hung onto the door, queasy with the sensation of being caught between worlds.

"Is there something I can do for you?"

Samuel peered into the dimly lit room and saw the outline of a man.

"Perhaps a glass of water?" the man continued.

"No, thank you. I'm all right. It's just the Abbey Bells...I've never heard anything like them before..."

Dust whispered up from the stone floor, as the man stepped forward. "Aye...they're thick with sorrow..." He was about Samuel's age but with a more powerful frame, one perhaps inclined towards the wild Cornish coast, or perhaps another era. He was tall, with a black beard and startling gray eyes that shone brightly in the shadowed room. He reached behind the counter, withdrew three feather dusters, and began to brush them over the tops of the crystals.

"'Tis the crystals...the Bells chime and the crystals answer. Talking stones is what they're called...just no one listens anymore."

Samuel watched as the man feathered different crystals with the dusters, and the ache that filled his belly eased. "What are you doing?"

"Some crystals are visionary. I use hawk feathers to calm them. Obsidian is the mother of all transformation, so I made one of swan feathers; seems to help them. I collect the feathers and create these to lighten their burden when the energy's too intense."

"Is that what the Bells do to them?"

"The Abbey Bells last rang in 1539 when Henry VIII took it upon himself to assault the monasteries of England. In 1536 there were more than eight hundred...and when Henry finished there were none. The Abbey was his crowning glory; he pillaged, ransacked, then hung and quartered the Abbot. He put himself above God and rained blood upon us. What you're hearing is an echo from the past."

"They ring the bells to honor the dead?"

The man stared at Samuel. "No one is ringing the Bells, Sir. There are no bells to ring."

"Then what am I hearing?"

"That which few are able to hear..."

Samuel released the knob, letting the door click shut. The man eyed him intently. "In fact," he continued, "I've never known anyone else that's actually heard them. It's been my own private world, to know their sorrow and that of the crystals."

"Why did I hear them?"

"That remains to be seen."

As his eyes adjusted to the dark, Samuel realized he was in a tiny cottage whose walls were lined with shelves stacked thick with so many crystals they covered floor to ceiling, giving the impression of a crystal cave. He wondered what it would look like if the lights were on.

"I keep it dark on purpose," the man responded. "It's easier on them...and me. If you've got the gift, they'll open your mind, but it's a hard task to close it again. And if you've got something on you that's wantin' to be heard, you can get caught in the crossfire and lose your way." He looked at Samuel's pocket then back into his eyes. "Is there somethin' I can help you with?"

"I need a small pouch...nothing fancy...just something to carry coins."

"Aye..." He opened the drawer behind the counter and pulled out a small green velvet bag embroidered with cherry blossoms.

"That'll do nicely." As Samuel stepped forward, he noticed a locked glass case on the counter displaying a very small crystal; the man cocked his head and broke into a wry grin. "That one's not for sale."

"Why's it here?"

The proprietor continued to examine the velvet bag, rubbing his thumb over the cherry blossom embroidery. "It's been in my family for centuries; I like to keep an eye on it. Might I ask how you happened into Glastonbury, and in particular, my establishment today?"

Samuel was mesmerized by the tiny quartz. "I'm visiting Cornwall, from America, researching my family heritage. The woman in the bookstore said you might have small pouches for carrying coins."

The proprietor nodded. "These bags are made by a woman who embroiders them with the leaves and flowers of trees from the Ogham Tree alphabet. Trees are an important part of our Druidic world. The letters, or *fews* as they're called, represent trees. Each tree has a lineage...a history of wisdom sacred to its own wood. This is the first bag she's done that's not part of the Ogham."

"You said they were cherry blossoms?"

"Aye...she will be fresh, as the dawn that rises from the east, and will come to release the wisdom from the wood. She will be new, as cherry wood is new to the Ogham. You've come because of your family heritage, but we are more here than just a bloodline, Sir."

"Is that a prophecy you just spoke?"

"Aye...take the bag with you...and take this with it." He printed a receipt, wrote a phone number down, and stuck it in the bag. "There are things being murmured in this room that you cannot hear. Someday, someone you love will return to Glastonbury in need of information. This number will help them find the way."

"You speak of things I do not understand," Samuel whispered.

"Aye...it will take you many years to crack our code. And when you do, it will be time to surrender that which belongs in this bag."

Samuel looked away. "How much do I owe you?"

"There is no monetary exchange required," he said, and then glanced again at Samuel's trouser pocket. "My only guidance is that if the goddess wishes to use you, let her have her way. She has a tendency to stir the pot when resisted."

Samuel took the bag and departed, his hand buried deep in his pocket, protectively cradling the ring.

STAGE ONE

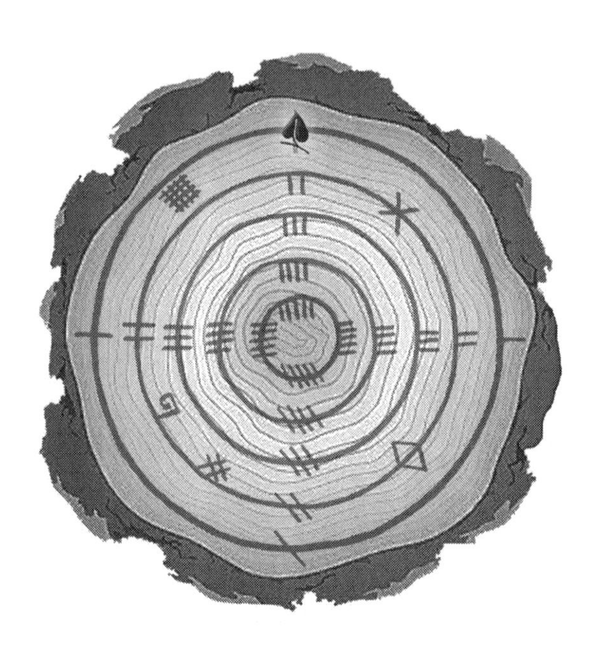

BIRCH

New Beginnings

18 years later
California
February 1, 1987
Imbolc

SAMUEL LEANED BACK and tossed his pen on the drawing sketched in his journal: a cross and a circle. It was always the same...a dead-end wall resurrecting, as if it were some mammoth headstone, obliterating all light, and yet it should be just the opposite.

The pages of his journal were splattered with the blood of his inkwell, pooled and smeared from eighteen years of research into the Glastonbury ring. It had become a mystery that had drawn Samuel deep into a mythic realm that, at times, drove him to the brink. And yet he'd come so close. He could feel it. The clue to unlocking the message of the ring and why he had resurrected it from the Well, was embedded in the numbers and geometric forms that surfaced repeatedly in the mythic landscape of Glastonbury.

He spun out of his chair and walked to the window, where he looked out at the adobe courtyard. As an architect, he had always appreciated the Spanish structures so prominent in many areas of California. Bougainvillea vines strapped the walls like tendons, releasing a profusion of crimson flowers that spilled across the dead gray of a slate terrace. He pressed his palms to the sill, dropping his head in frustration. Why couldn't he see? For eighteen years he'd been digging in a symbolic world trying to understand the riddles that continued to emerge anywhere they pleased: pagan and Christian.

As the morning sunlight slipped through the window, illuminating the crown of Samuel's head, a golden pendant slipped out from beneath the collar of his shirt. He squinted, as light splintered off the gold into his eyes. When he looked back to the terrace, a woman had appeared.

Samuel blinked and rubbed his eyes. The woman wore a diaphanous gown of white silk, and her long hair shone like spun silver, rendering an image of a fairy creature, formed from the illusion of shadow and light. Samuel blinked again.

"It's time, Samuel." The woman's voice was gentle and rose in his mind unbidden.

"Time?" Samuel's hand went reflexively to his neck where he grasped the pendant.

"Yes. You know what must be done."

His thumb caressed the gold chain. "But it's too soon," he whispered. "She's only a child. I need to understand more if I'm to help her...before I..." A breeze ruffled the bougainvillea fluttering shadows like butterflies.

"It's time."

Light fled the courtyard, taking the vision with it, leaving Samuel gazing into the shadows, while he gripped the pendant.

Slowly, he brought it forward and looked down. It was his Celtic cross. Samuel stared, as if he'd never seen it before. His eyes turned inward, and years of research raced through his mind with lightning speed. "Could it be...?"

His breath pumped as his heart raced to keep up with his thoughts. He clung to the cross and turned towards his desk but, before he reached it, spasms of pain ricocheted through his chest, snapping his head and buckling his knees. He pushed forward, collapsing onto the chair, gasping for air. Somewhere in the distance, he heard the muffled ring of a doorbell.

Samuel doubled over, grasped the desk drawer and wrenched it open, showering the room with paperclips. He shoved his balled up fist in, swinging wildly in search of something. Far away, down the dark corridors of his mind a voice was calling. He hauled his hand out of the drawer clenching the small velvet bag and dropped it on top of the journal. The voice ruptured in his ears.

"Dad!"

Samuel's eyes rolled in their sockets, as another spasm shattered his chest.

"Jesus! Son of a bitch what's happening, Dad!" Eleni Alexander bolted into the room and fumbled for the phone.

"Eleni..." Samuel's eyes were glazing over.

"We've got to call 911! Jesus Christ, you're having a heart attack!"

Samuel marshaled his strength and struck his daughter's hand, knocking the phone to the floor.

"What are you doing!" she screamed.

"Too late..."

"It's not too late...they can get here in seconds." Eleni slid to the floor and yanked the phone from under the desk. Samuel pushed it away.

"Sophie...must give...Sophie..." Samuel reached for the bag and journal sitting on the desk.

"Why are you talking about Sophie at a time like this..." Eleni's face contorted in fear, as her father rolled forward, tumbling onto the floor beside her. "Sophie!" he screamed.

Eleni kicked the chair aside and cradled him in her arms. "I need to call emergency...they can get here quickly...don't talk..." Samuel's lips were blue, and a gray pall was saturating his skin; he began to go limp.

"Don't leave me, Dad...hang on..." Eleni held her father and watched, as his right arm cascaded to the floor; his clenched fingers unfolded like a flower, surrendering the book and velvet bag. Samuel gazed into his daughter's green eyes and watched them pool like mountain lakes after a storm. It was too soon and too fast. He'd thought life would ease away slowly through the years...that he'd have time. Never had he anticipated this.

"Eleni..."

"Don't talk, Dad."

"...The cross...around my neck..."

"Dad..."

"...Must...listen..."

Eleni leaned closer to Samuel.

"The book...must read the book..."

"Ok...I'll read the damn book. Please stop talking!"

"Sophie..."

"Oh Lord, Dad..."

Samuel closed his eyes. "Had to be sure..." He reached out and dragged the velvet bag across the floor. "All these years..." he whispered.

"I don't know what you're talking about..."

Samuel's head slid into the crook of his daughter's arm. "I should have told you...so long ago..." his face contorted, as another searing blast cracked down his arm. “The ring belongs to Sophie...give it to her...help her...” Samuel’s breath was labored and his words faint.

“I don’t understand...”

Samuel nodded. “I know,” he murmured. “But it’s time... and now it’s up to you.”

Eleni bowed down, kissed his brow, and cupped her hand beneath the cross resting on his chest. The muscles of his face convulsed. He had no more breath to tell her how much it mattered, or to explain what he was seeing now from the other side. It was the cross...the cross was the key, and now it was too late. Too late to use his last breath to call out her name and tell her how much he loved her...too late to explain the journal and the contents of the bag...too late to help her understand. So many years, and now he would never be able to tell her that it was all too precious; his time was up. All he could do was pass on the journal and the ring. Life slipped away from Samuel with one final breath, within which he whispered one name to guide them on their way.

“Sophie...”

Then Samuel Alexander died.

Mr. Watson, the funeral director, rested his elbows on the carved oak arms of the office chair. “Your father was most specific, Mrs. Alexander. The headstone is to be changed.”

“Miss...”

“I beg your pardon?”

“It’s Miss Alexander.”

Mr. Watson lowered his eyes and nodded, his head slightly tilted to the left. “My apologies. It says here that you and your daughter are the only surviving relatives.”

"We are." Eleni's eyes were shot ridden with broken capillaries. "He wasn't even sick. Why did he make funeral arrangements?"

"It's not uncommon, Miss Alexander, when an individual has lost a spouse to make preparations for themselves in the event of an early demise. I spoke with Mr. Alexander on a variety of occasions. He often came to visit your mother's grave."

Eleni looked at the sheet of paper requesting the replacement of her mother's headstone with one larger headstone, with both her parents' names on it.

"He purchased the plot next to her years ago," Mr. Watson continued. "I believe it was, in fact, at the time of her death."

Eleni nodded. "I just can't believe he organized the whole thing, the type of stone, the engraving."

The funeral director was used to the difficulties that arose in such situations. "Many parents take charge of these things, to make it less stressful on the family. You have my deepest sympathy. I know this is quite a shock."

Eleni kept reading the sheet, outlining her father's wishes. "He even chose the time of day to be buried."

"Yes."

"I suppose none of this can be changed?"

Mr. Watson gently removed the paper from Eleni's hands. "We cannot bring your father back, Miss Alexander. We can only honor his wishes."

Eleni's hand fluttered up to her father's gold chain, now draped around her neck. "The headstone has already been prepared?"

"Yes. It was actually completed not too long ago. He brought us a drawing that he wanted cut into stone, a sort of etching. He saw and approved it upon completion."

Mr. Watson was a large man with a ruddy complexion. He was dressed in charcoal slacks and a blue blazer with a starched kerchief peaking neatly out of his breast pocket. Eleni had to admit that she appreciated, not only his composure and kindness—which one would hope was a component of the business—but his keen eye and human awareness, as well. It was almost as if he had a foot in each world, thereby understanding the manner of assistance needed on a multitude of levels. He sat beside her with a manila folder perched upon his knees.

"Do you still have a picture of the etching my father requested?"

He pulled a sheet of ochre parchment paper from the crisp file and held it to his chest. "Before I show you this, Miss Alexander, perhaps we could have a few words."

Eleni's brow rose in question.

"Your father had been working on something for quite a few years, a personal project. His funeral requests, which I will go over with you now, are connected to that project."

"And what was that project?"

"That is the unfortunate part; I do not know. Your father was apparently working on something—something symbolic I surmise—as he wanted an aspect of his research reflected here, at his grave. I believe he felt he was beginning to get the measure of that research. His plan was to present his findings to you and explain why he had incorporated certain aspects into his burial rites. From what I see in your reaction, that is not a conversation that has occurred. Is that correct?"

Eleni's thumb flickered over her father's cross. "We never spoke about it. But he mentioned something just before he died. Something about a book he wanted me to read."

Mr. Watson's gaze slid down to the pendant. "And he gave you his cross?"

She blushed and dropped her hand. "No. He never took it off. Ever since I was a little girl, I remember seeing it around his neck. I took it after he died." Tears spilled down Eleni's cheeks. "I can't believe he's gone."

Mr. Watson slid a box of tissues across the table. "Miss Alexander...it was not meant for me to be the bearer of certain information contained within this file. All I can do is advise you that your father was an exceptional man, with a deep sense of purpose and responsibility towards something. What that something is I cannot help you with, other than to say that he loved you and your daughter, his granddaughter, dearly, and that his guidance, here in this file, is meant to help."

Eleni blew her nose and wiped her eyes. "Show me the drawing."

Mr. Watson flipped the parchment paper over and placed it on Eleni's lap. It was a drawing of two interlocking circles, one above the other, with a tree growing out of the intersection of the circles.

"The interlocking circles, or rather the junction thereof, is an ancient symbol seen throughout history. In Christian terms, it is called The *Vesica Piscis*. He has placed the Tree of Life in the center, growing as, perhaps you might say, a seed, from the core of the drawing."

Eleni stared at her father's signature, seen so often in papers at his desk. "He was an architect," she whispered.

"Yes, I know."

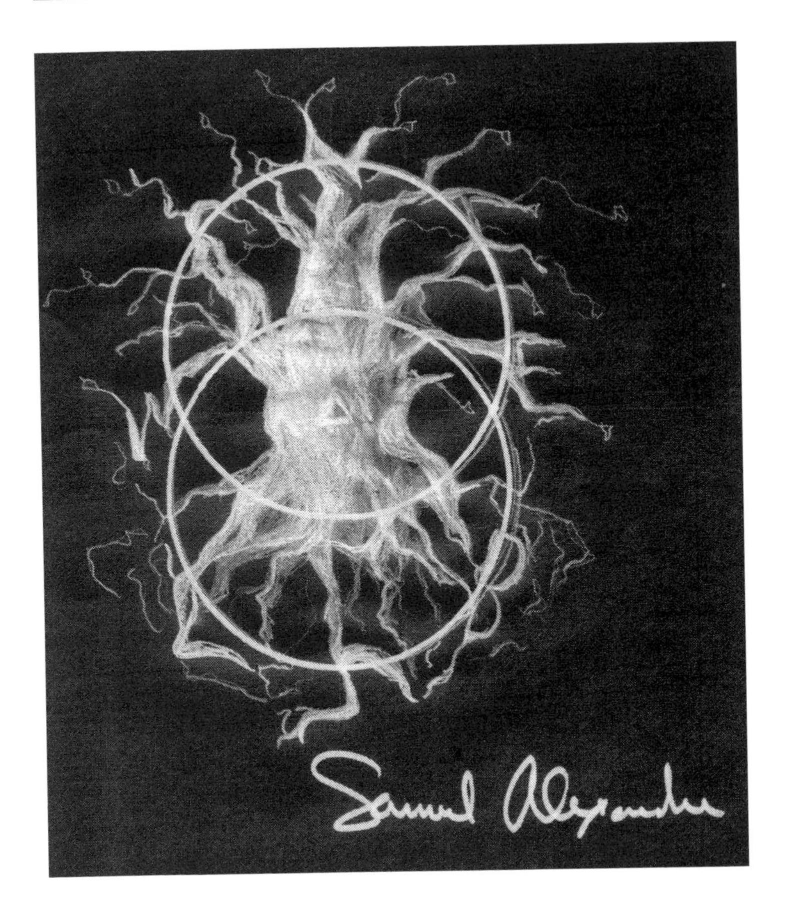

"Always interested in history and civilizations..."

"We have etched the drawing onto an unpolished slab of green granite. Your parents' names are inscribed, calligraphically, to the left and right of the symbol...along with the dates of their respective births and passing."

Eleni nodded.

"When you are ready, I'd be happy to show it to you."

"And you think this symbol has something to do with his research?"

"I believe so. But also, the fact that he is placing it here."

"On his grave..."

"Well..."

Eleni looked up.

"My own assessment, resulting from our conversations, is that its importance lies in the fact that it is on their grave...husband and wife. It mattered greatly to him that they be seen as one."

"He loved her so much."

"Yes."

"She died giving birth to me."

Mr. Watson sighed and looked away. Sometimes his business was burdened with sorrow that he was unable to soften, no matter how astute or caring. "So I was told."

Eleni slid the drawing onto the table.

"You may keep it, Miss Alexander. Perhaps it will help you someday."

Eleni reached for her purse.

"There is more, however..."

"I'm sorry. I thought we were finished."

"The burial is to take place three days after death, at 9:00 a.m. I will give you a copy of his requests for your records."

Eleni nodded.

"And..." Mr. Watson looked away and coughed, choking slightly on his words.

"And...?"

"Your father also requested that the ashes of your brother be interred in the coffin with him." The funeral director stared intently at Eleni, hoping that he would not see what, in fact, he was.

"I don't have a brother."

"As I said, your father's untimely death has left me in an awkward position."

"I don't understand."

"Your father has been coming to the cemetery for many years to visit the grave of his wife."

"Yes."

"But, also, to honor the unlived life of a child that was born dead...whose ashes are in our crematorium."

"A baby?"

The ruddiness drained from Mr. Watson's cheeks and a slight perspiration clung to his upper lip. "Your mother's first child was a son...apparently a healthy child who died at birth, strangled by the umbilical cord. The baby was cremated and placed here."

"Mr. Watson, I have a hard time believing that my father would keep something as important as that from me my entire life!"

"It was his intention to tell you."

"Why would he wait?"

"His first child died at birth, and then his wife died giving birth to you. What happened to your father opened a very painful door that he was unable to close. I suspect it is tied up in whatever research he has been doing and is connected to the drawing you have just seen. We do not always tell our children everything, Miss Alexander. Sometimes, we wait till they are adults, and perhaps there are those of us who keep some things private forever. I am sorry to be the bearer of news that should have come from him. I do know, however, of his deep love for you and his desire to share what he was discovering. I have watched him at your mother's grave for many years, and as of recent times, he has been different. I'm not fond of the word *feverish*, but for lack of a better one I will use it. I encourage you to read whatever it is he presented you with and incorporate into it what he is saying here."

"His funeral rites?"

"Yes. Write them down, Miss Alexander, and try to see them symbolically, as your father's final words."

Eleni watched light filter through the glass pane of Samuel's office window, illuminating his final handprint, the one that hit the wall of glass as pain ruptured his chest. She rested her own upon it, seeking the shadow that was gone. Behind the glass the courtyard sat in silence. The bougainvillea blossoms seemed less profuse, as if their brilliance had dimmed without the rapture of he who sought them. Eleni dropped her hand and walked to Samuel's desk where she eased into his chair.

On the desk was a sheet of paper with a drawing of a circle with an interior cross. An icy chill gripped her spine. She went to the window, jammed it shut, and scurried to the closet where she grabbed Samuel's old Oriental robe and threw it on. The worn fabric draped her in soft folds rich with that particular scent of seasons that permeates the texture of being without knowing where it begins or where it ends. It was the fragrance of her father: musty, woody, the soap of manly oils. It was a childhood scent of safety, and now he was gone.

Eleni slid to the floor and sobbed. She reached inside her bag for a tissue and brushed up against the leathery skin of Samuel's journal, pulled it out, and wiped her face with his sleeve.

"Did you see something in the courtyard, Dad, something that had to do with the cross?" She stretched out her legs in the posturing stance of a lost child and randomly opened the book, hoping to find the father who had left her far too quickly.

JOURNAL ENTRY:

Spirit: There is a woman frequenting my dreams. I call her *woman* although she is more spirit than flesh, if that can be said of anyone in a dream. She wears white, yet it is not solid, as white is on Earth. I suppose *diaphanous* would apply, yet not completely capture the transcendence of her gown, which seems to change with every visit and yet remains the same. Her hair is spun of moonlight and pours out of her cranium like spring water bubbling from the crest of high mountains, pouring down her back in a stream of consciousness to which I am not privy. Her voice is the gurgling of that stream, the whispered rushing of water, dipping and sliding over rocks. I strain to listen, yet the only word I hear is, "Samuel."

Eleni closed the book and wandered over to his desk. She began opening and shutting drawers, scanning contents like clues in a puzzle. Samuel was neat. Pens were in pen boxes and pencils were in little wooden containers labeled lead or charcoal. Paper of differing weights was in drawers coded by color tabs, and rulers had a drawer of their own.

She grabbed the top drawer, pulling it out so far it nearly unhinged. Items scattered to the fore, including a tiny leather folder, housing a pocket calculator. Eleni flipped it opened and pushed 'on'. It worked. Samuel didn't leave things unattended. The leather folder had a slim pocket on the inside flap. She slid her finger in and dredged out what appeared to be a neatly folded newspaper clipping, which she unfolded, careful not to tear the edges. It was the graduation announcement for Jack Harrington from Stanford University School of Psychiatry, dated 1979.

Eleni's brow furrowed. She read it again then stared long and hard at the photo of a man whose face she knew all too well. Eight years and she still couldn't forget. Apparently, for reasons unknown to her, neither could Samuel. She folded the clipping, slipped it into her pocket and went home...lost in thought and the memories embedded in the weave of Samuel's robe.

In the silent hours of dawn, eight-year-old Sophie struggled with bed sheets that twisted into a tight corkscrew, gripping her legs. Her flannel pajamas were moist with perspiration.

"Sophie..."

Sophie's cheeks flushed crimson, and her long auburn hair curled from a damp heat rising from the crown of her head. She stared inward, listening, then slid off the bed and walked down the hall to her mother's room. She tiptoed through the open door and across the room to the dresser where she stared down at the green velvet bag.

Eleni stirred. "Sophie?"

Sophie picked up the bag, turned, and left the room.

"What is it, Sophie?" Sophie was known to be a vivid dreamer, but Eleni had never seen her sleepwalk; she threw on Samuel's robe and followed downstairs where Sophie rummaged through kitchen drawers till she found a pocketknife and a tube of glue. She went to the patio door and slipped outside. Across the lawn was an old cedar tree with branches heavily laden, forcing them low to the ground. Crawling on hands and knees, she scuttled beneath and sidled up against the old trunk. Eleni followed, flinching, as Sophie opened the pocketknife and began digging a hole in the trunk of the tree. Her hands scraped against the bark, rubbing her knuckles raw. When the hole was big enough, she picked up the velvet bag, released the cord and tipped it upside down. Perspiration beaded on her brow, as the ring tumbled onto the earth. Eleni leaned forward.

The ring looked quite old and was an unusual shape: double-banded with a large red triangular stone. Sophie grabbed it and shoved it in the hole. She squeezed glue onto the wood chips, gathered sticky clumps, and shoved them in. Over and over, bits of wood and glue, earth, and moss went in, until the ring was secured and the burial site properly disguised. Then she crawled, unseeing, past her mother and returned to her room, and, hopefully, a dreamless sleep.

Eleni went to the tree, removed the ring from its wooden grave then returned to her room. Resting on her bedside table was

Samuel's forest green journal, the corners curled like peeling bark and gold-trimmed pages stained with oil from Samuel's fingers.

She flipped it open.

JOURNAL ENTRY: PLACE

Land, Sky, and Underworld: The Glastonbury ring was discovered in Bride's Well in the lowlands of Somerset, land once swamped by inland seas that rendered the hills into islands navigable only by boat. The watery world of reflection and mist gave Glastonbury its name: *Inis Witrin*, The Isle of Glass. Place was established and the aspects of land entered the story, setting the framework for the mythology of the ring.

Early nomadic tribes wandering these islands in search of food chose seven of them to become their route throughout the year. They chose certain islands because, when viewed from above, the formation was the same as the Big Dipper of the Northern Hemisphere. The islands became a mirror of the heavens, and Glastonbury was known as *Dubhe*, the pivotal star of the Big Dipper. Heaven therefore became anchored to The Isle of Glass, and heaven and earth also entered the story of the ring.

There are currents running beneath The Isle of Glass: magnetic and water. An energy pulse, known as a dragon line, connects Avebury with St. Michael's Mount. And subterranean springs, of individual source, provide an eternal flood of water: one runs red and one white. The mysterious world of earth energies and underground wells became part of the story, as well.

Eleni fanned the pages and watched drawings blend with words, and then she quietly closed the book. *You started this when I was ten*, she thought, *and I know nothing about it. And now, what am I supposed to do, Dad, if she doesn't want the ring?*

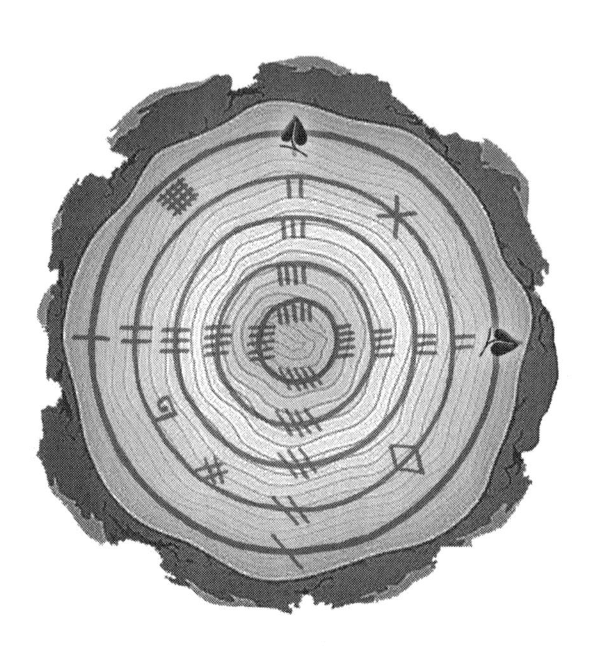

HAWTHORN

Fertility

ELENI SAT NEXT to a mound of freshly laundered, rumpled clothes. She picked up a shirt, rubbing fingers deftly over painted cloth, lingering slightly as she brushed against the wax of melted crayons or the brittle stain of ink. At about the age of five, Sophie had developed an incessant need to draw moons and stars; she drew them on her skin. From head to foot she was adorned with renditions done in vivid colors extricated from her box of crayons. And every night the bath water turned oceanic as a flow of salty tears went down the drain, along with the pictures that were such a potent part of her imagination. No matter how many times Eleni scrubbed them off, Sophie drew them on again.

Frustration inspired Eleni to create a wardrobe of cheap T-shirts and jeans, fabric paint, ink, and crayons. If she couldn't stop Sophie from drawing on her skin, she might at least be able to transfer the images to cloth. It was a quirk of fate, because the images saturating her daughter's shirts were the same symbols chronicled in Samuel's journal. A modicum of reading of Samuel's journal showed the images hearkened back to the order of High Priestesses, once recognized by a blue crescent moon, marking the center of their brow.

It appeared that Samuel had gone to Cornwall to research a family lineage that had remained unbroken, father to son, since 100 AD, and ended with the death, at birth, of his own son. As Mr. Watson had said, this, paired with the subsequent death of his beloved wife at a second birth, had turned Samuel inward. Sorrow, and something else, haunted him.

It took eighteen years of research for Samuel to begin to understand the story of the ring. After seeing the drawings that emerged on his granddaughter's T-shirts, he began to believe that she was part of that story. For beneath the faded drawings of crescent moons and five-pointed stars, Samuel had seen a triple spiral, the image swirling within Bride's Well. It was the symbol of Bride, the Triple Goddess, three-fold muse and keeper of the flame.

Eleni folded a T-shirt rich with patterns that had bled, one into the next, with washing: crescent moons, stars, spirals, and circles. She stared at it a long time then picked up the journal and continued to read.

JOURNAL ENTRY:

Trees: When the water receded, the Isle of Glass became a hill, and trees grew. The land became rich with oak, ash, elm, hawthorn, hazel, and groves of yew and apples. The marshes were thick with reed, willow, and alder. The branches reached up to the sky, and the roots went down to the underworld. The trees became part of their language and entered the story as a symbol that connected the three domains: heaven, earth and underworld.

She closed the book and tossed it on the mound of wrinkled clothes. "Then why," she mused, "did Sophie bury the ring in the tree?"

The trail leading to the old cedar, where Sophie had buried the ring, soon began meandering past it, towards the forbidden forest: a smattering of aged trees, entangled with the creeping limbs of the neighboring woods. It had been labeled *forbidden* by Eleni in recognition of Sophie's proclivity towards wandering, thus applying boundaries that forced the old cedar to become her regular point of destination. But the old tree that had so lovingly housed her imaginary world was now anathema to Sophie, so she turned a deaf ear to her mother's warning and wandered surreptitiously into the woods.

She rested against the ragged bark of an Alder tree and spread out her canvas: an old sweatshirt. Out of the pocket of worn jeans came splintered fragments of crayons, which she used to sketch upon the shirt, adding to the palimpsest of geometric shapes that were her fascination, and that layered the weave of fabric with lines and circles that had bled color and stretched images with every washing.

On the far side of the glen, a woman sat on the hollowed carcass of a felled tree, whittling away on a chunk of gnarled wood. She was draped in a long cloak and had amber hair that poured across shoulders and back like a great river reflecting the sun. Agile hands flicked the silver blade expertly, peeling bark to expose striations of white wood. She glanced up, as the child entered the forest, lingering for a moment to watch, as she settled to her task.

"*You know,*" the woman whispered, "*I don't blame you in the least.*" It was a low, sultry voice, full and rich with things beyond the imagination.

Sophie looked up. "...For what?" Something about the voice had engaged her curiosity.

"For burying the ring..."

"What ring?"

A sly grin elongated the woman's mouth. Her lips were moist, tinted the color of honey. *"Ahh...yes,"* she whispered, *"it was a dream. It's never real when it's a dream, is it?"* She continued whittling, turning the wood gracefully, as if it were a spun bird. *"The number one rule of enchantment, however, is that for every action there is a reaction;* an *unfortunate precedent, yet one that should have been presumed."*

She laid down the wood and raised her head to look at the young girl across the glen. Her cloak slid open, exposing legs clad in worn deerskin pants that hugged the curves of strong thighs. Sturdy leather boots spanned across her knees, where they were cinched with buckles, and a pouch of animal skins was strapped like a harness across her breasts. Her skin was translucent, like fine porcelain, and her eyes sparked with intelligence, beneath a brow marked with the faint sliver of a crescent moon. She stood up and began pacing in front of the log, a dark chuckle gurgling out of her throat.

"Yes...one would presume that reversal of an action would contain the necessary elements within its original prescription." She glanced at Sophie. *"That's where I was wrong."*

"I don't know what you're talking about," Sophie replied.

The woman lowered her gaze till it rested on the shirt spread on the ground before the child. *"I don't believe that's a true statement."*

"It's true. I'm just a little girl."

"A little girl who draws ancient symbols on her garments is not as little as she thinks."

Sophie looked down at the circles, triangles, squares, and stars that adorned her sweatshirt. "I like them."

"Obviously...but why?"

Sophie shrugged and tossed her crayon onto the shirt.

"Your body may be young, Sophie Alexander...but you...are very...very...old," she responded with a secretive whisper then chuckled and sat back down on the log.

"How do you know my name?"

The woman stared up into the trees, distracted with her internal discourse. *"You see...burying him wasn't really an act of vengeance. It was just so irritating of him to think that I would fall prey to his whims: exchanging lessons in his magic for the pleasure of my being. As if I didn't know that pleasure holds its own magic..."*

"How do you know my name!"

She turned slowly to look into the child's face, as if she'd forgotten for a moment that the girl was even there. *"Because you, Sophie Alexander, are the beneficiary of something I did...a very...long...time...ago."*

"Does that mean we're related?"

"In a sense... yes. Not physically, mind you. But in other ways, yes, we are related. You see I also buried something very special, once upon a time."

"I didn't bury anything."

"Yes, I understand. It's most unfortunate, but important to know, that certain actions are very good at giving birth to forgetfulness. So let us just pretend that you did bury a ring in a tree. Wouldn't it be important for you to know that it wasn't really just a ring and that you had no way of knowing because of what I did, all those eons ago?"

"What is it if it's not a ring?"

The woman leaned forward and whispered in a conspiratorial manner. *"It's a love story. But the Bride and Groom never made it to the wedding...at least, not at the same time."*

"Because of what you did?"

"Partly. But there were others involved, as well. And in the end, things just didn't go as planned. As I said, all actions hold within them a course of enchantment, and my action was one of silence. I silenced the story, and now you don't know who you are, or what it is you're supposed to do. And it is my obligation to help you undo what I have done."

Sophie's mouth hung ajar, as she contemplated the woman's words. "If you lost it, you should be the one who has to find it."

"I wish it were that simple."

"You're one of them, aren't you..."

"One of whom?"

"The voices."

"The voices in the ring? The ring you didn't bury?"

Sophie's little mouth tightened, and her jaw went rigid, like clamping the lid on a treasure chest. She gathered up her crayons and sweatshirt. "I have to go now. I'm not supposed to be here."

"Yes, I know. But I do hope to see you again." The woman smiled and, despite herself, Sophie smiled back. She turned to leave the forest then glanced back one more time. "Who are you," she inquired.

"Nimue...High Priestess of Avalon."

JOURNAL ENTRY:

The Goddess: The number nine represents the Goddess. Nine is a magical number, complete unto itself; all derivatives of nine reduce to nine. The Isle of Glass, a star that mirrored the heavens, was also an apple orchard: Avalon, home of the Goddess. Here she speaks through nine priestesses, each expressing a different facet of her character. She lives in all three domains, heaven, earth, and the underworld, as mother, sister, and bride: three faces of woman. Nine priestesses entered the story.

When Sophie left the wooded glen, a second woman emerged. She stepped out of the Beech tree and wore a gown that shone like a shifting wash of opalescence and silver, fragments of moonlight attempting to coalesce. Her face, pale and angular, bore the mark of the crescent moon, and her hair streamed in all directions, like lightning during a storm. She hovered over Nimue, studying hands that deftly carved a small block of wood.

"I trust you are using Alder." Her voice was the haunting cry of wind, as it bows the limbs of trees.

"You fear our silence has rendered me forgetful, Mother? Yes, it is Alder."

The silver woman slipped into the glen. "*Mother*?"

Nimue continued carving. *"Your spiritual mothering does not foster mortals alone. We too benefit from your wisdom, Argante. And yes, though long silent, I do remember. Draw from nature that which will facilitate the form. The Alder tree is resistant to water. Thus, I carve this little boat from wood that will serve its greater task: to float. But spiritual waters will need to be navigated, as well, and the spirit of this wood will lend strength and wisdom to the journey."*

"So…it's true," Argante mused, *"she has forgotten."*

"We have been silent too long."

Argante gazed through the shaded envelope of trees that swayed in and out of light, slim shapes, appearing and disappearing like a gathering of wraiths. *"As always, Nimue, it is my duty to guide her."*

"She is deaf to us, until she willingly reclaims that which we have buried." The aged wood in Nimue's hands slowly shed its gnarled weave, as she expertly peeled away its shape and gave it another: the hull of a tiny boat. She held it up in the palm of her hand for Argante to see. *"Like this, she is a new vessel formed from ancient wood, one that will need to navigate turbulent seas. It is not idle gossip that labels me Merlin's twin, yet even I will have trouble reaching her."*

Argante glanced through twisted limbs towards the house. *"Her bedroom faces north and is protected by a Birch grove, whose branches sweep the earth when winds blow. It is the time of inception, and that which is old must be new again. She is our link between death and life. The ancient weave is upon her and it will call her out."*

Nimue sighed. *"Until she reclaims the ring, we remain locked within these woods, trapped by our own sorcery. It is true you are the muse, our voice of guidance and protection. But it is I who must reopen the door, as it is I who closed it. When Merlin tempted me with lessons in magic, in exchange for love, he never anticipated that it would turn against him. His intended seduction had everything to do with sorcery and nothing to do with love. What sort of consummation did he expect?"*

"Yet he desired you, Nimue. That alone says that love of a higher order was awakening."

"Sorcery cannot be used to lay claim to love, Argante. Whatever is intended at the time of consummation will thrive in the elixir of the moment. We dealt in magic, and magic had its way. My sorcery trapped him...silenced him for all time. His seduction was thwarted, and now he remains locked within these woods. Little did I know that the magic would also silence us, High Priestesses of Avalon. Now the ring, whose time has finally come, has been returned to the woods, because the child inherited my very own silencing of the wisdom we represent."

"Yet the spiral turns."

"Yes, it turns! The girl may not understand the triple spiral, yet there is no doubt she carries its energy. Her childish drawings show she is consumed with it. We know it as a pathway... that when Bride's wheels spin, we are enlivened...weaving a web that unifies body, mind, and spirit, releasing elixirs of enlightenment. But Bride's wisdom lies dormant in the past. This new world demands a breaking of old ways, Argante; it is evolutionary. Machines disseminate knowledge more easily than a wizard's spell. The wisdom of the holy few is now a world of the past. If we are to meet our task, we must recognize that, although the spiral has begun to spin, the moment she reclaims the ring, we have no way of knowing how it will manifest."

Argante split through the trees like a shaft of light. *"Yet spin it will, Nimue, awakening first, as always, the elemental wisdom of the mother. Igraine, Kundry, and I...mothers of body, mind, and spirit, must be able to reach her...through dreams alone if that is our only avenue."*

Nimue inspected the gnarled boat resting in her palm. *"She draws circles on her clothes, yet knows nothing of their meaning. I told you, she is the product of our silence."*

"And her mother?"

"...another faded reflection."

Argante turned towards the glen, as the shadow of a woman appeared. She was tall, with the bearing of a queen. *"You speak of Igraine and Merlin's spell."*

"I speak of sorcery that, like an echo, repeats again and again, each time a little weaker, until the end when it will draw all semblance of itself into the grave with it! Merlin's spell allowed Uther Pendragon to wear the visage of Gorlois, Igraine's husband, and thus sleep with her to beget Arthur. This girl was conceived at Samhain, a feast now known as Halloween, when the veils of reality are thin. Whatever elements of mystery were present at the

moment of her conception, they remain unseen...a direct descendent of Igraine's blind conception. These people are unaware of the mystery and from whence it comes, just as Igraine was blind to who truly fathered Arthur. The ruse was necessary for Merlin to take part in the conception, yet no one asks why."

Behind them, tree limbs shivered, as the muddy image of a mule appeared with an old woman draped across its back. She dug her knees into the animal's bloated ribs, forcing it a few steps forward. The lady was dark and ragged, with eyes like lumps of coal. Nimue glanced at her and nodded respectfully. "*You've grown old, Kundry...*" she sighed. "*Does your beast still bear the burden of your wisdom?"*

The woman's head curled forward, a wizened knob on a gnarled limb of tree. "*I am not old, Nimue...I am ancient...and therein lies my strength."*

Nimue observed the three women, priestess mothers of elemental wisdom, ready to inform and guide the girl child they all knew was marked with the triple spiral of Bride. The child was their descendent...their salvation and resurrection... yet she was deaf to the ancient ways.

"*For now,*" whispered Nimue, "*we wait. In a few years, womanhood will be upon her, and the energy will awaken dreams. Who knows...maybe the old wizard's magic will be stirred within his oaken grave. One thing I've learned is that we are not one without the other. And just as we are eager to have our voices heard, I have no doubt that Merlin is ready to rise up from beneath his shroud of darkness."*

Sophie wandered into Eleni's room and sat on the bed, tossing her sweatshirt onto the pile of clothes her mother was folding.

"Been drawing?" Eleni looked at the shirt and back at Sophie who was looking decidedly pale. "Are you all right?"

Sophie nodded. "I need more paint."

Eleni picked up the shirt and examined the drawing. "What's this?"

"A tree..."

"A tree? I don't think you've drawn a tree before. What kind of tree is it?"

Sophie stared into the room, disturbed by her encounter. "It's not finished. I need pink paint."

"It's going to be a pink tree?"

"No...it needs pink flowers. It's a cherry tree."

Sophie got up and wandered out the room, glancing at the journal as she passed. Eleni watched then examined the imagery on the bed.

"I guess whatever you decided to bury in the trunk of that tree has no intention of going away," she whispered to herself.

Eleni leaned over and hauled a large book up from under the bed, flipped it open, and fanned the pages, scanning photos, until she came to a dog-eared corner and stopped. It was a picture of a young man, about twenty-one, with an inscription underneath: "Always and forever, Jack." Stapled to the side of the page was the newspaper clipping she had found in her father's pocket calculator. She rubbed her hand over the image, as if remembering the contour of his face, then quietly closed the cover of her college yearbook.

The years passed, and Sophie distanced herself from any longing to return to the woods. Eleni read, and reread, Samuel's journal, still confused as to what her father was trying to say. And Nimue maintained her vigil, assessing Sophie as she wandered past the woods, with hesitation, or a tilt to her head, as if listening. But it wasn't until Sophie turned sixteen that Nimue recognized in her the awakening of the full moon.

To the priestesses, it was known as the opening, when moon and woman become one; it was their dreamtime. But in Sophie's case, it became a sleepwalking nightmare, when strong dreams unseen by the dreamer are forced to animate the body. She began to wander during the full moon, draped in its silver webbing with eyes haunted by the unseen forces of the night, appearing more spirit than flesh.

The priestesses knew the dreams were rising, but their language was foreign, leaving Sophie little choice but to wrestle with confusion then succumb to sleep, disturbed from the chaos of undigested power. Thus, the moon that filtered between the thickened limbs of the forbidden forest grew dim, like beams struggling through rain, or light that diminishes as it passes through cloth.

On one particular night, it illumined the trunk of the sacred Beech tree, scattering images onto the earth that took shape. Nimue sat with her back to the tree, watching Sophie and listening to darkness rustle through leaves. Behind her, two shades emerged: one large and strong, the other a slim slip of smoke. The large one defined itself quickly; she was a full-bodied female of pulsing darkness; she glided past Nimue into the glen.

"*The passage of time does not appear to have weakened you, Morgan.*" Nimue grinned.

"*Do you really believe the goddesses' power to destroy and resurrect could be diminished? You question my ability to transform what lies prostrate upon your field of battle. Yet, just as you have learned to transmute worlds, it is I, the Raven Queen, who will feed upon the carcass that lies prone before us and bring it back to life.*"

"You have a challenge, then, as we are the dead carcass."

"I would not emerge from the Queenly Beech if I were dead." Morgan lingered, flexing dark muscles like a caged panther. *"She is at the age when the guidance of sisters must speak."*

Nimue pointed a finger towards the far side of the woods. *"Look across the glen, Morgan, and join the gathering of wraiths. Argante, Igraine, and Kundry sit in silence without the ear of she they were called to serve."* Then she spun around and looked beyond their wall of trees to Sophie, standing frozen on the earth, moonlight shimmering within dreamer eyes. *"You think she has called you forth? Do you see recognition in her eyes? No... the chasm between our cloistered woods and that young woman's world is greater than you think."*

"What is our wisdom worth if we cannot bridge the gap?" Morgan walked towards the edge of the wood and peered through knotted limbs towards Sophie. *"Stars, moons, pentagrams, and triple spirals do not speak of an uninformed female,"* she mused.

"Her mind is closed." Nimue sighed and turned away. *"And we have little time."*

"It is clear we are in her blood, and our blood is ancient," Morgan continued. *"Something will happen to turn the tide, and I assure you that, when she is ready, she will not back down. You may see the battlefield as prone to chaos, but is that not inevitably the nature of battle? We are shape shifters; perhaps this will be our greatest challenge."*

That a wraith could appear wan or suffering from loss of life's very blood was strange, yet that was the appearance of the second shade, as she emerged from the Beech tree. She stepped into the glen, the very image of a cloistered female who'd paid a heavy price for life's journey.

"And who shall bleed upon your battlefield, Morgan, when what we are is bloodless, having paid dearly to force the consummation of this sacred quest?"

"Dindraine..." Nimue stared compassionately as Morgan responded.

"Dindraine, you of all priestesses know the journey that lies before her. She will need your wisdom and belief that its culmination is the greatest destiny to mark the blood of any."

"The price is dear, Morgan, and we are late," said Dindraine.

"How can you denounce what was your life's purpose?"

Dindraine wavered in the moonlight, her gray and weighted cloth diminishing the form within. Morgan refused to give up. *"You are the warrior spirit that refused to relinquish the Grail quest."*

"I have nothing left to give."

"You have already given all. Now is your time of fruition."

Nimue blustered her way between the women, sweeping the earth with the trailing hem of her cloak. *"Enough, Morgan! Until the ring is borne upon her hand, we are of no consequence. And if she succeeds in reclaiming it, we will awaken in a mind that knows nothing of our past. We must each hold strong to the one thing that we possess: you to challenge, me to opening of the door, and Dindraine to her knowledge of the redemptive power of love. We are nothing but energy, energy that once held hope of telling a story. When the ring is reclaimed, the Brides of Avalon will step forth: Guinevere, Enid, and Ragnell. Who will know their stories, Morgan? Who will explain that there is a message in each destined to open the way? When the ring is reclaimed and the spell is broken, we will spill forth like the rupturing of an ancient dam. She will hear us like the cacophonous resonance of an unknown symphony."*

From the far side of the glen a voice gasped. *"We cannot merge at once,"* cried Argante.

"There is no way to stop it," said Nimue. *"What the girl chooses to do with it is beyond us. Her world will begin to shape shift as*

ours did over the centuries. We can only pray that she will have allies to help her weave the way."

Morgan shimmered in a shadowed cloak of iridescent blackness. "*She is our destiny.*"

"*Yes.*"

"*Then, like me, she is also the challenger...and the challenger always survives.*"

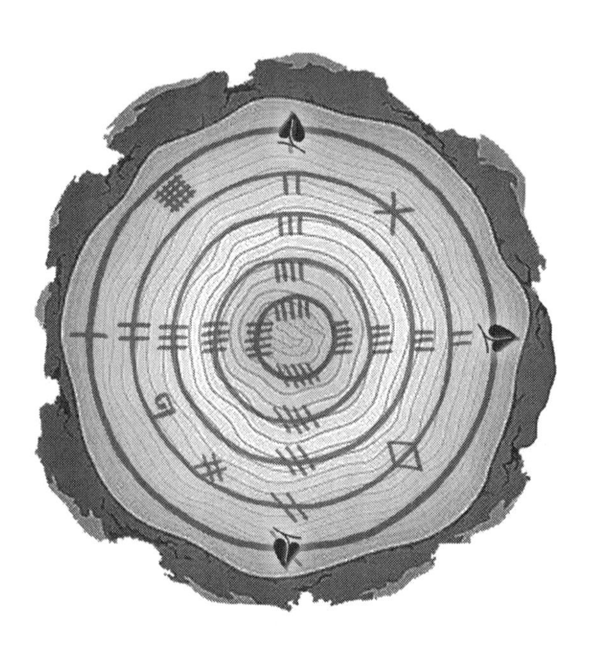

BRAMBLE

Crown of Thorns

California
August 1, 1997
Lughnasadh

DR. JACK HARRINGTON stood behind the long mahogany table and watched respectfully, as the four suited men filed by. The room was large and vacuous, and their heels hammered a hollow rhythm that echoed from wall to wall like a death march. Particles of dust floated in a slant of light shining through a ridge of windows that perforated the upper quadrant of the room.

The men positioned themselves across from him at a conference table that had four chairs, equally spaced, facing him. They wore dark suits in varying shades, and Jack thought their pallor to be suitably gray. The mahogany table in front of him was outfitted with five chairs all facing the same direction, towards the conference table. Jack positioned himself behind the middle chair.

"Dr. Harrington."

Jack Harrington was a tall lanky man with a strong jaw and sharp eyes the color of steel or slate. He wore moss green slacks and an open-necked white shirt and nodded slightly as they called his name. The men seated themselves and gestured for him to do the same. Manila files were stationed neatly in front of them and they folded their hands, as if in prayer, on top of the files and looked at him through somewhat caustic eyes.

"As you know, Dr. Harrington, the Medical Board is required to give you an opportunity to explain your actions before they come to a conclusion regarding the perceived unusual methods and procedures you have devised for the treatment of patients under your care." It appeared Dr. Clarence Moody was to be the ringleader.

Jack nodded. "I understand."

"There is no doubt that the practice of Psychiatry can be of inestimable help to those unfortunate enough to be plagued by certain types of disorders. The medical community is always seeking new avenues, through science and technology, to help. As stated in the brief, it has come to our attention that you choose to thumb your nose at the establishment and throw all procedure to the wind by advocating the use of new-age methods. This panel will listen as you defend your premise and determine whether or not to strip you of your credentials, thereby ending your career as Doctor of Psychiatry. According to our records, you have refused, as of the past two years, to administer medication or drugs of any kind. Is this correct?"

"If an individual, or patient, asks to be medicated, I refer them elsewhere."

"You turn patients away."

"I refer them elsewhere."

"You believe, Dr. Harrington, that you can help without the assistance of medication?"

"If you have reviewed my records, as thoroughly as you say you have, you should have noticed that, over the past two years, the rate of improvement for individuals under my care is decidedly higher than previously, when I administered drugs."

"Degrees of health are merely that, Dr. Harrington, especially in the field of Psychiatry. These individuals swing like pendulums, and what are they to do if they leave your care, thinking they are miraculously healed, only to be hit again without a method of retrieval? Relapses are common."

"Relapses are common because we haven't done our job."

Dr. Clarence Moody was highly regarded in the medical community, and his face, already somewhat pinched from years of service to the community, began to shrink back with a sour look of disgust. "Our records show, Dr. Harrington, that your 'job' now consists of two entire walls, in your office, dedicated to the self expression of your patients. I believe we used to call it coloring. Your patients are coloring on the walls. Is this true?"

"It is. Words are not accepted. The patient has to draw how he or she feels."

"And, am I correct in my understanding that you also sing?"

"Music is part of the therapy."

The medical examiner to the far left smirked, and a derisive laugh exploded from his belly. "Perhaps you'd rather start a new television show, Dr. Harrington." It was a dark, oily voice. "You know...a kind of Sesame Street for nuts."

Jack Harrington stared at the expanse of marble floor defining the space between them. "Meditation has proven that there is harmonic energy in the body. There is a tonal scale that resonates along the spine. When pain or sorrow is lodged in the body, it distorts the tonal scale. I use music to help track that disturbance. If a patient wants to do the work, I can help them.

If they don't, I send them to Doctors, such as you, for drugs." He turned to the doctor on the left. "But if I had a show for nuts, you'd make a wonderful contestant."

The panel stiffened. Loose pages from manila folders were shuffled back and forth across the table, as they murmured amongst themselves in agitation.

"Dr. Harrington, we are all past the point of popularity contests," Dr. Moody continued. "This is a matter of professional ethics. I have testimony from patients that list nothing but this tonal theory, singing, drawing, using one color one day and a different color the next, acting out dreams and nightmares. My God, Dr. Harrington, you're a professional doctor, not a gypsy. Patients even report that you use crystals."

"Yes, Sir, I do. It has been shown that quartz crystal is a conductor of energy."

"I do believe, Dr. Harrington, that there is a slight difference between silicon chips and crystal balls."

"Not really. Mankind is merely learning to harness what God creates naturally. I believe quartz crystal to be a powerful tool in many areas; that also includes healing."

"These people are not guinea pigs, Dr. Harrington. They are patients who come to you for help, and yet, you look into your crystal ball like some sort of ancient wizard, instead of the doctor that you are."

Jack Harrington cleared his throat, attempting to cool his response. "Dr. Moody, there is never one single method of treatment that works for all patients. Hopefully, we learn to assess where the disorder lies. I have a theory regarding certain patients."

"And what is that?"

"That they are gifted, not ill, yet they manifest disturbance."

"And you think you can heal them with crystals."

Jack dropped his chin to his chest. They would shut him down. Nothing he said mattered. They would ridicule him... make him the laughing stock of the medical community. "There is a schism," he whispered.

"Please speak up, Dr. Harrington. We can't hear you."

Jack looked at the four representatives of the Medical Board. "It is my belief that some individuals manifest symptoms of a mental disorder, but in reality are suffering from what I call a schism between body and spirit, and..."

"...Is that what this is all about Doctor? Is this some sort of messianic mission?"

"I am on a mission...yes. But I have no illusions as to who I am. There are fractured individuals who have the ability to heal themselves, if we were to treat them properly."

"Like your mother?"

Blood drained from Jack Harrington's face.

"Obviously you must have realized that we would check your background. Your mother was institutionalized when you were...let me see...I believe you were five. Yes. And she died while inst—"

"She died during a medical procedure in which pompous-assed doctors, like you, were attempting to lobotomize her! They believed that the visions she claimed to see were indicative of someone who lived in a fantasy world and that all they needed to do was cut them out of her brain, and she'd rejoin the rest of the group!" Jack Harrington stood up and leaned across the table, kicking his chair away from his heels sending it clattering across the floor. "You arrogant, overstuffed sons of bitches call yourselves doctors! What sort of humanity sets out to heal another individual life by removing part of her brain?"

Sweat dripped down Jack's brow into the creases around his eyes. All four men stared resolutely, unperturbed by his explosion. One by one, they picked up their pens and glanced at the files before them, sketching unrecognizable signatures across the bottom sheets. A look of righteousness and pity arose in their eyes.

"It is the recommendation of this board, Dr. Harrington, that the credential of Doctor of Psychiatry be stripped from your title. There is no need for further evaluation."

The men closed their files, stood up, and departed the room. As they clicked past, Jack whispered, "You are part of the sickness..."

"Excuse me?"

"...And you don't even realize it."

One of the medical examiners stepped forward and looked down at him with disgust. "Perhaps you might use your crystal ball to conjure up Merlin, Dr. Harrington. You could go into business together."

Jack closed his eyes and turned away, not wanting to look into the gloating face of defeat. After all these years, he had lost his battle.

JOURNAL ENTRY:

Enlightened Male: The tree is a conduit of the energies that converge on the Isle of Glass. Although all trees conduct and transform energy in their own manner, certain trees are more potent than others. The oak, known as Duir, is the doorway to enlightenment. It both attracts and is able to withstand the lightning strike. Oak is the most sacred of all trees, the shaman's tree. The body of information contained in the tree has been kept alive for centuries by the seer and prophet known as Merlin, the spiritual lineage that will soon awaken. The mystic must enter the story.

October 31, 2000

By the age of twenty-one, Sophie had retreated even further into the confines of her own mind. It was the age of responsibility, yet the ring was still hidden in a drawer in Eleni's room. She kept it hidden out of concern for her daughter.

The ring, however, was ready to awaken.

Samhain, October 31st, was the Celtic New Year, and marked the end of year as light and the beginning of the year as dark. It was potent, when time stopped and boundaries were breached.

For Eleni, it was just Halloween, when streets transformed, as if a great cauldron spewed spirits into the night. Turning the lights out was the only method of sandbagging the impending tide; Eleni's went out at 9:00 p.m.

When she went to close down on this particular night, she heard the musings of a familiar voice out on the lawn and saw the moon's illumination of a billowing sweatshirt. She huddled close to the screen and listened.

"You think I don't remember but I do...I remember your voice, and that it's your fault the ring was buried!"

Eleni stiffened. It was the first time she had ever heard Sophie mention burying the ring. She scanned the yard but saw no one except Sophie, talking to the trees.

"An old wizard keeps coming to me in my dreams...saying he's Merlin and that he'll die if I don't reclaim the ring. It's your fault! That's what you told me. But the wizard thinks I buried what was rightfully mine...that I have a destiny. I don't want your destiny! Stay out of my dreams...all of you! You buried it... you dig it up!"

She remained on the periphery of the woods staring into darkness. Her shirt filled with air as a night breeze wafted through, lifting her hair into a cloud of spun caramel.

Eleni gazed past her to the far side of the fence and the chaotic theater of the street then backed away from the window and wandered blindly to her bureau where she withdrew the green velvet bag. She collapsed on the bed and rolled the ring out of its velvet bag into her hand.

"How long are we going to do this, Sophie?" she whispered. "It's been thirteen years since Dad died and you're still haunted by whatever is in this ring."

She examined it again: one silver band and one gold band, with a red triangle stone at the junction. There were markings of some kind on the inside bands of crosses and lines.

"What am I supposed to do, Dad? Every year she grows more disassociated from the world. She sleepwalks and rambles incoherently in her sleep. Now she's talking to trees." Without thinking, Eleni slipped the ring onto the wedding finger of her left hand. Her body arched violently, snapping her head back, as she collapsed unconscious on the bed.

At the same moment, Sophie fell as the earth began to buckle and cleave from the force of a massive quake. On the far side of the fence, the street ruptured in a pandemonium of wildly swinging flashlight beams scanning the screaming faces of costumed children. Parents lurched to the ground, and the world went black from electricity outages.

Sophie swung open the gate and stared in disbelief. But it wasn't the heaving pavement or shattering glass that mesmerized her. It was the sound... like the rending of a great curtain.

For one fragile moment, it hung, the torn veil, exposing a world more horrific than the charade of parading costumes. She stumbled back, threw herself through the gate and bolted across the yard screaming, "Mom!"

Inside her cloistered woods, Nimue stood on silent ground and watched beyond the trees, the turbulent lurching of land swelling like roiling seas. It was not uncommon for Samhain to be the bearer of unusual events, just not this unusual. The air tasted burnt, as if tinged with fire. And when the veil split her spine stiffened.

"*We have a rupture,*" she cried out. The women in the glen stood as one: queen, muse, crone, warrior, and lover. "*If there is an opening, Nimue, use your magic,*" whispered Argante.

Sophie reached the house and exploded inside. The kitchen was a dumpsite strewn with shattered cups, flour, jams, and oatmeal that had catapulted from cupboards. The power outage left her in the dark, smashing into fallen paintings and chairs that had been tossed across the room like tinker toys. Terror gripped her, tightening her throat, as she clamored up the stairs.

She rushed past her room and into Eleni's where, barely visible in the dim light, she saw the pale form of her mother lying askew upon the bed. Sophie crumpled onto the floor, pushing aside cascading books from the nightstand.

"Mom...Mom, what's wrong?" She ran her hand across Eleni's brow and grabbed her wrist, feeling for a pulse. "Mom, there are people in the street screaming..." She rubbed Eleni's arm and tried to pry open her eyes. "It was like the world opened up, and I saw them...all their pain and darkness." Tears streaked through dust on her cheeks like rivulets in a desert. "It was like they were hollow shells without souls..." She doubled over and sobbed.

Her breathing punctuated her rib cage in sharp, stabbing spasms. She dropped her head onto her mother's arm. "It was like something robbed them."

The room shuddered from an aftershock, scattering tables and chairs. Perfume bottles tumbled onto the floor, shattering glass, erupting sickly sweet smells that bled into the carpet. "They looked like the walking dead," she whispered. When she opened her eyes she was staring at the ring.

In the dark recesses of the forbidden forest an icy wind began to stir. It whispered along the ground, scattering leaves and limbs, covering all with a hoary frost. Nimue sat on her log, listening, muscles flexing beneath their animal hides. A whirling wind of debris deposited itself at her feet, the leaves frozen solid with a cloak of black ice. She raised her head and looked back into the dark expanse of woods. A pale wraith appeared and wove a path resolutely through the forest, till it stopped in front of an ancient Yew tree. It was the spirit of Eleni Alexander.

"The Yew's journey is one of death and resurrection, Eleni Alexander," Nimue called out. *"It is not a path open to you."*

Eleni was wrapped in white gauze that clung to her limbs like a suffocating skin. *"But it is to her,"* she whispered.

Nimue studied the woman's form all the way down to the hand that bore the shadow of the ring. *"You are not the bearer of the ring. The decision must be hers. You cannot open a doorway she doesn't choose to enter."*

"How else will the spell be broken?"

Nimue cocked her head. *"What do you know of the spell?"*

"Only what the ring has told me."

"You propose to be the catalyst?"

"It is already done."

"You cannot take the journey for her."

"No...but I can lead the way."

Nimue paced the glen. *"The spell is too strong. She turned away from the ring and, now, in order to reclaim it, she will have to go to its source. The Yew tree will lead you there, but it is an ancient journey and requires great courage. I don't know how much of our wisdom lies dormant in her blood. It puts you at great risk, Eleni Alexander. Should she fail, your fate will be to remain in darkness forever."*

"Was I not already there, Nimue, High Priestess of Avalon, guardian of the door?"

Nimue stopped her pacing.

"The ring is using me," Eleni continued. *"I understand. I also understand that this ring is about love, is it not?"*

"Yes."

"Then love shall be her challenge. If she chooses to save me, she will follow. I will lead her into the darkness, for it is her destiny to bring light to that which has been dark too long."

"It is true the Yew tree is redemptive," continued Nimue. *"You can walk the path, but you will not know the journey. It is hers alone, as is the ring. Should she succeed, you will remember nothing. That is your saving grace."*

"There is a lineage of sacrifice in this ring, Nimue of Avalon. I do not need to know the story, but to recognize the price; we are all connected. If a rupture was needed to turn the tide, then let me be that rupture."

Nimue pulled the tiny boat out of her pocket and walked through the woods, placing it at Eleni's feet. *"This boat will seek its wood. Follow it, and it will guide you home."*

Eleni's eyes filled with tears. *"She sees the ring. Speak to her."*

"So be it."

The shaking ceased and the room stood still, and the groan of heaving building joints grew silent. Sophie gazed at the ring, unable to understand what she was seeing.

"What have you done?" Her words fell on deaf ears. Eleni was a limp rag doll with chalk skin.

"How did you find it? It was just a dream."

Her head swiveled, searching the room, as if there might be answers in the dark. She felt Eleni's neck for a pulse then looked back down at the ring; slowly, she unfolded her clenched hand and extended her fingers, reaching out to take it off.

"Don't remove the ring." The dark, sultry command froze Sophie on the spot. She stared at the triangle stone, flashing back thirteen years to the amber-haired priestess in the forbidden forest.

"It's you," she whispered.

"Your mother has created a rupture."

"She has the ring. It's what you want. You can take it back."

"It's not that simple, Sophie."

"What's happened to her?"

"She's entered the forbidden woods."

"Oh my God..." Sophie's breathing quickened and she reached again for the ring.

"You will lose her for all eternity if you remove the ring!" Nimue's command was a blow to the solar plexus; Sophie doubled over and gagged.

"I told you long ago that the ring is not an object. It is a story that spans centuries. You cannot just take it and say it's yours."

"You said I'm its destiny."

"Yes. And yet you proceeded to put it right back from whence it came. It has not been reclaimed because you know nothing of its story, nor your own."

"And whose fault is that, Nimue, High Priestess of Avalon?"

"So, you do remember our meeting."

"I remember. It's your fault that she's done this!"

"We don't have time to argue faults! The world is not as you imagine, Sophie Alexander. The ring is sacred, and you have been given a great gift to be the bearer of that ring. Your ignorance is our responsibility. But you will have to open your mind if you want our help."

Sophie reached out and touched the tip of the stone. "Can I save her?"

"Save yourself and she will be free."

The room shuddered from an aftershock, scattering glass across the floor. Samuel's journal slid from under the bed and flipped open to the drawing of the interlocking circles with the tree growing from its center. Sophie stared at the symbol. "What should I do?"

"Find a way to join her, without removing the ring."

"How?"

"That must be your decision."

Sophie looked at her mother. "I'm losing her...she's turning blue!"

"You are connected by blood."

Sophie stared at the triangle-shaped stone of the ring. Even in the night, its color was clearly blood red. She scrambled to the other side of the bed and lay down next to her mother, placed her right hand on top of Eleni's, and pressed down hard, piercing the tip of the stone deep into the flesh of her palm. Energy cracked through her like lightning. She jolted, as if electrocuted, then dropped back onto the pillow, mother and daughter, joined by the ring of Bride.

Within the forbidden forest, three more wraiths emerged from the sacred Beech tree, completing the gathering of nine. Together, they entered the glen and stood in silence beneath the umbrella of faded green.

"And now we pray," whispered Nimue. *"Pray for the one who can release us from our imprisonment within these cloistered woods. Pray for the soul journey of The 10th High Priestess of Avalon."*

The earth heaved again, snapping the journal's spine. An icy wind blew through cracks on the windowpane, whispered across the floor, and began turning pages, telling a story that went back in time, while the clock stood still.

Electricity arced through the room, pages sparked, and Samuel's diagrams were illuminated in lightning flashes upon the ceiling. The Big Dipper hung above the bed with the star, Dubhe, pulsing, as the story of Avalon unfolded. The interlocking circles burned onto the far wall then faded, leaving only the point of overlap, and the circle with the cross appeared and disappeared, with four concentric rings within it.

The wind murmured, pages flipped, and sweat spilled off Sophie's brow. Her legs jerked, and her cheeks flushed crimson then blanched white as ash, but her hand never moved from the stone buried deep within her palm. Eleni's body resembled the spiritless shell of the dead, yet she breathed and her heart beat faintly within her breast.

At midnight, the room shook, and the worn, green-leather cover of the journal clamped shut. Wind circled the room, gathering images of stars and crescent moons, wiping faded images from the walls. It gathered knowledge like decaying leaves and pulverized them into a fine dust, then blew it out the cracks around the windowpanes and followed.

The two women lay in darkness till 3:00 a.m., when moonlight entered the room. It slid across the floor and onto the bed. Eleni opened her eyes. She felt heavy, as if she'd gained a hundred pounds, or maybe just forgotten the weightiness of form. She sent a message to her legs, but they didn't respond; neither did her arms. She looked around, leaving her body to reattach itself when it was ready.

The room was in shambles. She'd lived in California long enough to know it was one of two options: she'd either been ransacked, or there'd been an earthquake. The strange part was she didn't remember either.

She peered into the shadows, seeing through occasional rivers of moonlight as it illuminated scattered books, toppled bureaus, shattered glass; there was also the smell of cheap perfume. She went full circle round the room and ended up staring again at the bed. Lying next to her was Sophie.

Eleni stared at her daughter's face, her pale cheeks with their dusting of freckles and heart-shaped chin, framed by an amazing mass of auburn hair. She studied the hair, glinting in the moonlight, flashing golden sparks that wove a trail in and out of strands curled on the pillow.

Consciousness trickled through Eleni's veins at a snail's pace. She couldn't wiggle her toes, but her right thumb began to bend at the crook and a tingling sensation was prickling up her right arm. Her left hand was dead as a door mouse. She kept staring at Sophie.

"What're you doing here?"

She raised her head an inch and tried to look more closely. Maybe something had hit her on the head and that's why she couldn't move. Staggered by the effort, she lay back down on the pillow and scanned the length of her left arm down to her hand. Resting on top of it was Sophie's.

As she stared at their two hands, moonlight shone along the bed to their arms, pouring over skin like liquid. The back of Sophie's hand appeared translucent. Beads of sweat reflected shimmering points of silver light, and the blood pulsing through her veins resembled a blue river snaking up her arm; her hand began to glow.

A warm circle of light emanating from the back of Sophie's hand pulsed and turned dark red. It beat like a heart and projected a shape, a triangle. At the base of her middle finger appeared the shadow of the red triangle stone, connected to a double-banded ring. Eleni blinked.

"It was the ring. I put on the ring."

The shadow took shape, gaining clarity and mass, till it possessed true physical form. Sophie wiggled her fingers and moved her hand, allowing Eleni to look at her own beneath, now free of the ring.

"My God...it moved all by itself."

Sophie rolled over and sat up in one jerky motion. Her jaw hung slack as she gasped air, trying to swallow the rising bile. It was no use. She doubled over and retched. Across the room, the digital clock blinked 9:00 p.m.; the power was on. She staggered to the bathroom, splashed cold water on her face and neck. In the mirror, hollow eyes framed with dark caverns stared back. She rested her hands on the countertop, watching, as blood trickled from her palm into the sink. She ran cool water and wiped it clean with a cloth.

Then she saw the ring.

It fit perfectly, secured to the middle finger of her right hand, as if it had always been there. The ruby stone was not too proud, as it connected low in the interlocking bands. In an odd sort of way, it looked rather modern, except that the gold was a richer gold and the silver had a shimmer she'd never seen before. She took a deep breath and looked back in the mirror. Staring back was Nimue.

"You have broken the spell, Sophie Alexander."

Sophie jolted, stopped, and looked into the face she'd seen so many years ago. The woman was more beautiful than she remembered, with long hair falling in rivulets around her shoulders and skin like pale apricots. But it was the eyes that captured her, like emeralds, or maybe the deep green of the sea.

"Nimue..."

"Our blood truly runs within your veins; you would not have survived without it."

Bile swelled in Sophie's stomach then subsided. She raised her hand and showed Nimue the ring. "I buried it in the tree, just as you said, but I thought it was just a dream."

"Dreams are not falsehoods, Sophie, nor will they lead you astray when viewed through the eyes of wisdom."

"Do you know where I have been?"

"You have been to the Tree of Life, the mythical tree that contains the wisdom of all wood, where the ring was buried eons ago."

"I remember you said that you were the one who buried the ring."

"Yes. But you must remember, Sophie, that the ring is an ancient story, a love story that never reached fruition. When the ring was buried, the story was silenced."

Sophie looked down at the ring. "And what will happen now?"

Nimue held out her hand. Cupped in her palm was a hazelnut. *"Our particular wisdom is contained within the hazelnut. Nine hazelnuts fell from the tree into the river of life, and were eaten by a Salmon. Thus, the flesh of the fish possesses powers of redemption. We, Priestesses, are those nine hazelnuts, each possessing a facet of that wisdom, whole unto itself, yet part of a greater story. We are each as different as the trees that comprise the forest, and yet we are one. Because you have broken the spell, we are released from our cloistered woods, and now will begin to tell the story of the ring, through you."*

"Through me?"

"Yes. Your first challenge was to reclaim the ring, which you have done. But now you must tell its story. And that will be your greatest challenge, Sophie Alexander, because in order to do that, you must become the story. You are the Chosen One, Sophie Alexander...the 10th Priestess. Let us tell our story through you."

"How?"

"It is unchartered territory. The mythical will enter your world and you will have to find your way. If you listen, we will guide you. Use our wisdom well."

Nimue faded into Sophie's reflection: pale, freckled skin and skewed masses of auburn hair. Her sweatshirt appeared as if it had been balled up for a century—creased, soiled, and stained with ink.

"Wisdom..." she whispered.

"Sophie?"

Sophie glanced once more at the mirror then returned to the bedroom.

"Who are you talking to?" Eleni's asked.

"Myself."

They stared at each other without talking, and then Sophie leaned down and brushed her mother's hair out of her face. "Why don't you sit up...I'll get something to drink."

"I can't."

"Why not?"

"I'm having a little trouble moving. I'll be all right."

Sophie's brow furrowed and she rubbed her mother's arm. "You're cold."

"Was there an earthquake?"

Sophie kept rubbing her arms, increasing the circulation. "I suspect it happened when you put on the ring."

"It's on your hand now."

Sophie nodded.

"I saw it move, Sophie, like a dream, all by itself, through your hand and onto your finger."

"That's all I ever thought it was, just a dream I buried in a tree."

"You were sleepwalking."

"But the ring was real."

"Yes. Grandpa left it to you when he died."

Sophie looked down at the leather journal. "Grandpa?"

"Yes."

"Why didn't you tell me?"

"Would you have listened?"

"Why did you put it on?"

"I never thought..." Eleni looked around the room. "When you saw what had happened why didn't you just take the ring?"

"There are voices in the ring. I did what I was told."

On the far side of the room, a pile of shiny black pebbles caught Sophie's attention; she walked over and dropped to her knees. "They're broken...all my records..." Shiny shards of forty-fives slipped like gravel through her fingers. At the bottom of the pile was one unbroken record: *North to Alaska*.

"My first record..."

"I'm sorry, Sophie..." Eleni began to wiggle her right hand. "My fingers are moving." She struggled to sit up. "Looks like I'm returning."

"I have to leave," Sophie whispered.

"What?"

"It's a spiral... the record is a spiral, like a medicine wheel; it's a sign."

"What are you talking about?"

"It's the circle and the cross. North...I have to go north, to Alaska."

"I don't understand."

"Maybe not all the way to Alaska," she continued. "But I need to go north. It's the north part that matters."

"You can't just head north. Where will you go?"

"Emily," Sophie whispered. "My first stop will be with Emily, in Oregon." She grabbed Samuel's journal. "May I keep this?"

Eleni nodded.

Sophie slid the record into the leather bound book and left the room.

JOURNAL ENTRY:

North: The tree, which spans worlds, is symbolically drawn as the cross. One version shows the cross within the circle, representing space, or directions, as North, South, East, and West within the dimension of time. The directions, defining the earthly plane, also describe psychological aspects of life. East, where the sun rises, is symbolic of enlightenment. North, the dark wintered night, is unchartered territory—that which remains to be seen. It is the aspect of the myth that is yet to be determined. North will enter the story.

Eleni Alexander stood at the foot of her parent's grave studying the symbol etched on their headstone. It had weathered well over thirteen years and was neither faded nor discolored from wind or rain. It was spring, and the cemetery gardens were beginning to bloom, which seemed incongruous to Eleni. Cemeteries were always tucked into glorious parcels of land, profuse with heady shade trees, ivy drenched rock walls, and creeping blossoms, yet all the inhabitants were dead.

The thirteen years since her father's death had been hard on Eleni. She looked tired and knew it, aware that her fair hair was withering with more than just a few strands of gray. She wore a light jacket and jeans and had her left arm draped in a cotton sling tied securely behind her neck. A stick snapped, and she cocked her head, listening as footfalls approached from behind.

"Good morning, Miss Alexander."

Eleni turned her attention back to the engraving on the headstone. "...As above, so below...good morning Mr. Watson."

Mr. Watson's ruddy cheeks had deepened over the last decade, lending credence to the supposition that he imbibed. Eleni thought that with a profession like his it was probably a necessity.

"Yes," he responded. "The Tree of Life...as above, so below."

"Thank you for coming," she whispered.

Mr. Watson nodded, smiling ever so slightly, as he noticed the strain pinching the corners of her eyes and the damaged left arm. "An accident?"

"Somewhat," she sighed, maintaining her focus on the headstone. "Did you know, Mr. Watson, that within the gnarled branches of this old Tree of Life are the twisted letters representing north, south, east, and west? You can see them at the four directions if you look closely."

"Yes. Mr. Alexander was very specific about those."

"You never told me."

"No."

"This is a rather meager conversation, Mr. Watson." Eleni's stress had tarnished her manners somewhat of late.

"My apologies...but as I told you at the time of your father's death, it was not my place to be the bearer of certain information. Your father was unraveling something. It was important that you discover, on your own, the clues he left behind." Although the tailoring had been updated, Mr. Watson still wore gray slacks and a navy jacket, and the handkerchief peeking out of his breast pocket was now a light shade of pink. He kept his feet out at a slight angle and maintained a look of thoughtful consideration.

"Mr. Watson, my father's journal didn't end with his death."

"I didn't think it would."

"These things that he was researching were not just ideologies that piqued his curiosity."

"Miss Alexander, you asked that I meet you here. How is it that I might assist you?" Mr. Watson was professional. He was formal, kind, reserved, and in control. Eleni wanted to ring his neck.

"Towards the end of my father's journal, the 'N' in the Tree of Life drawings began to be illuminated in gold. The drawing was pen and ink originally, and then, all of a sudden, he starts drawing the 'N' in gold. At first, I thought he was just highlighting the letters. But none of the other directions were highlighted. Eventually, I understood that he believed that 'north' was waking up. Do you know about north, Mr. Watson?"

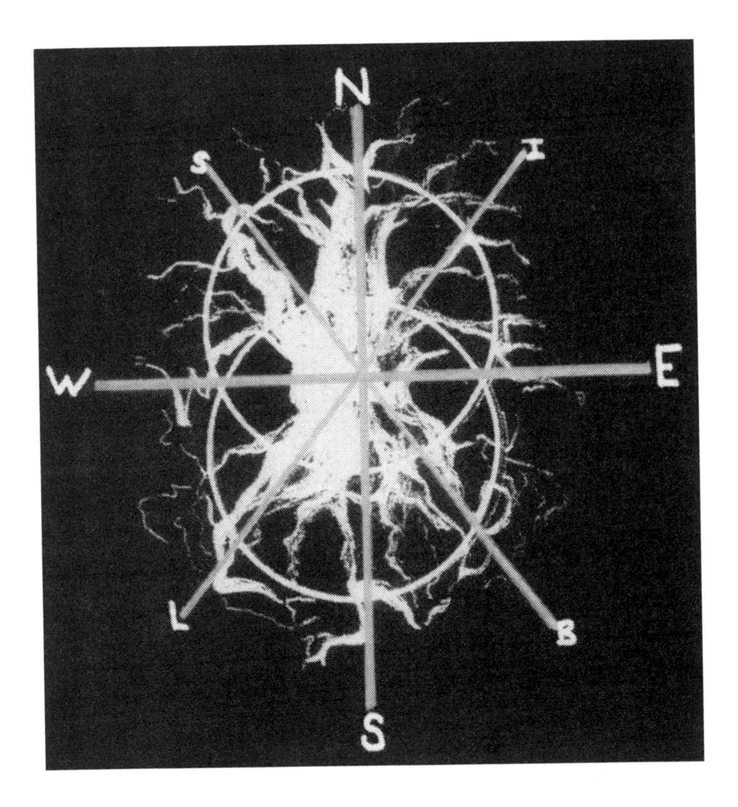

"I don't believe I do."

"North is an outward direction, but mythically, north represents the direction one takes to break out of an existing mold, stepping, psychologically, off the known path. To the Celtic people, it represented winter, night, or the unknown. The elders, in mythology, came out of the north. I guess it represents a journey into the unknown and, if you get to come back, you must have learned a hell of a lot!" Eleni, on the other hand, was not in control.

"And...?"

"After the earthquake last fall, my daughter left home. She went north. This symbol on my father's grave is like some sort of inner-outer journey that we appear to be embarking upon. It's like a map that represents something I am completely unversed in. You're the only other person who spoke with him about these things. I thought you might have some words of advice." Eleni's shoulders crept up around the knotted cotton at her neck.

"What happened during the earthquake that precipitated her move north?"

Eleni had no intention of discussing the ring. "All of her record collection was shattered, except for an old forty-five, *North to Alaska*. You might remember it. Ever since my father's death, she's been retreating further and further into herself. She draws on her clothes, and they're the same images my father studied in his journal. For the last thirteen years, I haven't been able to get through to her, and now she's gone north because of the title of a record. Don't you see? She's following a trail." Eleni rubbed her limp hand lying blue and cold in the cotton sling.

"You believe your daughter is connected to this in some way?"

"I know she is."

Mr. Watson shuffled his feet and stared down at the engraving.

"I have no place to go, Mr. Watson. Have you ever contemplated, in the last thirteen years, what my father might have meant by this drawing?"

"I have."

"Would you share it with me?"

"But surely, Miss Alexander, you must have gained some clarity from your father's journal."

"I need an outsider's point of view, and it's not exactly something one discusses with the pharmacist."

Mr. Watson lowered his eyes and looked away, bristling from Eleni's harsh tone. "Well, in my mind," he began, "Samuel placed the elements of a family—mother, father, child—in one grave, beneath an unpolished green stone, etched with an unusual symbol. The green stone mattered to him, didn't want black or gray..."

"...Go on."

"At first, I thought it was symbolic of the dying of his family name, as he had mentioned his concern over this with the death of his son." He looked to Eleni. "But you are here, as is his granddaughter. And you still carry his name."

"But the name, historically, is carried by the male."

"It has been, yes." Mr. Watson kept his eye on the stone, his back slightly slumped with hands plunged deep into trouser pockets. "But this was not just about Samuel," he whispered.

Eleni bent her head, listening. "Up until six months ago, I would have disagreed with you. But now..."

"Yes. I understand it must be very difficult. It is only my own intuition, mind you...upon reflection these last years...since you have asked..."

"Please continue."

"He has placed himself within the mythic structure he was fighting so hard to untangle. You must also remember, Miss Alexander, it was not his intention to die so soon. This premeditated burial rite was, in his mind, to happen at a much later date."

"I hadn't thought of that."

"Which, in my mind, lends it a greater sense of urgency...like a red flag waving in front of my mind's eye, and still, I don't quite understand."

Eleni pulled her jacket tight around her arm.

Mr. Watson continued. "In Samuel's life, the elements of family were fractured. His marriage was blessed but his first child—a son—dies at birth. Then you are born and his beloved wife dies. He is blessed with a daughter but loses a wife. Yet here, at his grave, husband, wife, and son are all together. You, in a sense, become the sacred witness, Miss Alexander, meant to bring this into the light."

"Bring what?"

"The holy family...they are emblematic, in my mind, of a holy family...or perhaps you might say that the family is holy. And he has placed this concept, like a seed, in the center of the *Vesica Piscis*, from which the Tree of Life grows. Samuel stepped into a mythic realm when he did this. He became part of what he believed was a living story."

"And what am I to do with it?"

"You have read the journal?"

"Of course I've read the journal. I've been reading it for thirteen years!"

"And...?"

"He's tracked, merged, and reanalyzed mythic images. He's joined things together that were originally separate, like this symbol on his grave. He believed myth wasn't meant to be static...that it had to evolve, if it was going to inform us."

"It was a large task Samuel took on." His gaze slid down to her left arm. "Would you like to tell me what happened?"

The cemetery lawn was slightly damp, wetting the soles of Eleni's canvas shoes. She shivered, as it worked its way up her spine.

"If I knew, Mr. Watson...I'd tell you in a heartbeat."

JOURNAL ENTRY:

Vesica Piscis: The convergence of energies on the Isle of Glass is described with the symbol of overlapping circles, representing the union of those energies. It is the image seen on the cover of the spring known as Chalice Well, where some believe Joseph of Arimathea placed the cup of Christ after the crucifixion. The point of overlap in the overlapping circles is called the *Vesica Piscis*, the union of opposites. When the trunk of the tree is placed within the *Vesica Piscis*, we enter the wood, or heart, of the tree. The wisdom of wood enters the story.

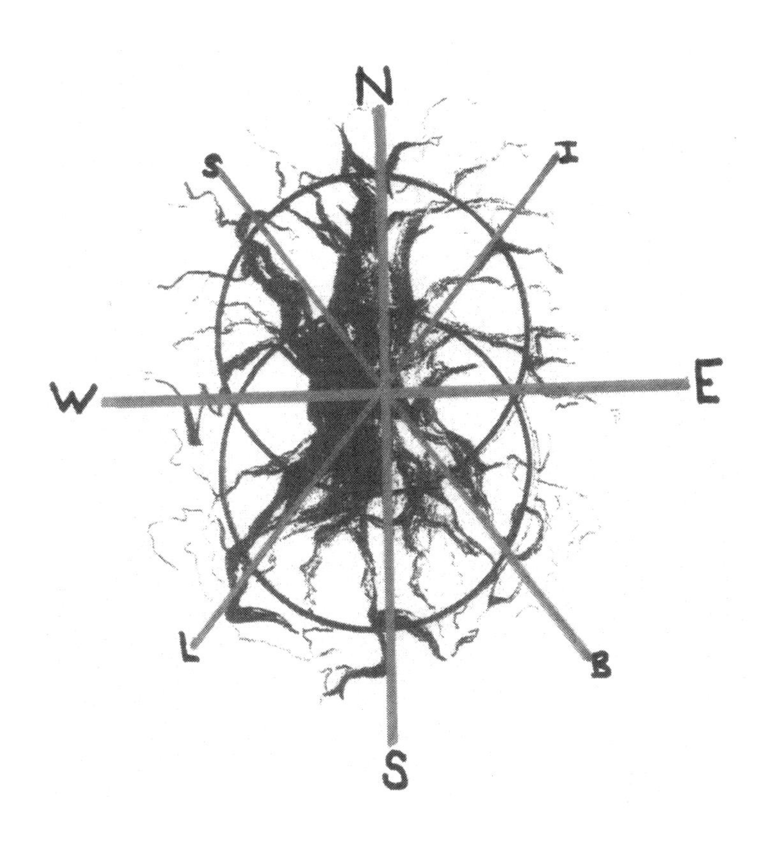
N
S
I
W
E
L
B
S

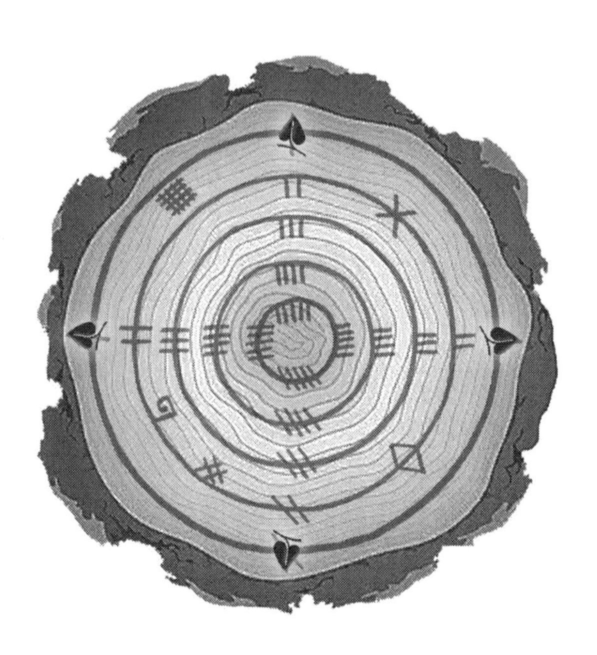

SILVER FIR

Divine Birth

Oregon
May 1, 2001
Beltane

MOONLIGHT CRASHED THROUGH the bathroom skylight. It hit the bath tiles and fractured into a million bends of light that scattered over her face and skin, reflecting translucent white in the mirror. She stood in silent abeyance, luminous hazel eyes and porcelain skin, with auburn hair falling in wild abandon over bare shoulders down the narrow spare back to her waist.

Opening a drawer, she removed an object and set it on the counter. It sparked a cold reflection in the dark room, as moonlight shattered off its edge. She clutched it firmly, and slowly raised her arm, reaching towards her neck. Bending forward she gathered hair at the nape and pulled it gently over her shoulder, the metal object flickering daggers of light onto her skin.

In murderous ascent, she sliced through her auburn hair one clump at a time, gracefully laying it on the ivory tiles. One handful at a time, she severed it from its source. Long, brilliant auburn hair coiled on the bathroom altar, devoid of all power.

The young woman stared at her reflection in the mirror then turned and looked up through the skylight at the moon, pouring silver light through the roof's eye and into hers, slipping over her pale body and down the white expanse of her arm to her hand, where it shone with ecstasy upon the red triangular stone of the double-banded ring. Then, seeing with the eyes of a dreamer, she turned and walked back to bed where she lay down and slipped reverently into sleep.

At 6:00 a.m., sunlight slid up the eastern wall of the cottage, exposing rotted wood and chipped paint, then filtered through murky windows onto worn sisal mats, where it began its journey across the room. Strewn upon the floor was a litter of books and Xeroxed articles. Light crept over them, up the iron legs of a single bed, and onto a faded patchwork quilt. On top of the quilt was a large book laying open to a photo of an old Well, its circular lid carved with a symbol of interlocking circles. Beneath the quilt was Sophie.

She opened her eyes, squinting from the light-reflecting photo, and scanned the room. Spare...just an old iron bed, dresser, and mirror. The walls were pine, painted white and rubbed back exposing the grain, probably a long time ago because, now, the white was yellow. She closed her eyes and nodded.

The cottage...

Color flooded her cheeks; it was greenish-yellow, the color of bile. She tossed her feet off the bed, bolted to the bathroom, and vomited in the sink. Morning light cascaded through the skylight, exposing the chalk of her skin and ribs that clamped down on a cadaverous torso. She hung her head and gripped the counter, her thin hands mapped with veins of blue webbing. When the vomiting stopped, she raised her head and stared in the mirror.

Cavernous eyes stared back, and in the periphery of vision she saw the butchered distortion of uneven clumps framing her sallow face and the disembodied hair placed on the tile counter. She inched her hand forward, brushing up against the auburn locks, then crumpled to the floor and passed out from shock.

At 6:30 a.m., she raised herself off the floor, picked up the hair, and returned to the bedroom. Out of the dresser drawer she removed a purple silk scarf, which she spread open on the bed. She laid the hair out and folded the scarf around it like an envelope. From beneath the bed, she dragged out a pile of wadded up clothing of jeans, sweatshirt, and underwear all carefully rolled into a tight ball.

Sophie sat on the bed and methodically unrolled the garments. Her hands trembled as she pulled on faded jeans, cinching the worn leather belt far past its allotted holes, tying a knot to keep the jeans up. The sweatshirt was a palimpsest of faded drawings. She dropped it over her head and stood up, its voluminous shape cascading to her knees. She slipped her feet into lace-less tennis shoes.

On the floor by the bed was a worn canvas bag stuffed with books. One by one, she removed them. At the bottom of the bag was a jet-black watch cap that she pulled down around her head. She placed the hair, wrapped in its purple scarf, into the canvas bag that she slung over her shoulder and silently left the cottage.

At 7:15 a.m., Margaret Clauson entered the elevator and pushed number three. The elevator shrugged beneath her weight, heaving once or twice, straining from a lifetime burden of carrying people's woes. The metal walls were faded past any coloration that had once been present, and although the janitor scrupulously scrubbed any graffiti scarring the walls, it always seemed to reappear, like magic ink that glows in the dark. She stepped to the rear and stared down at her shoes, even though no one else was present.

Margaret liked her shoes. They were beige and went with everything. Not that she had a lot. They were beige and flat heeled. Margaret didn't want to have to think about her feet or her shoes, and this particular pair brought a kind of serenity to her life.

She continued looking down, as the elevator climbed up. The ceiling light shone hard on her head, exposing thinning hair and a scalp slightly pink from too much home bleaching. Margaret didn't like to spend money on hairdressers.

For heaven's sake, she always said she was middle aged, single, and self- supporting. And although her psychiatry practice offered a modest living, like everything else, it was subject to fluctuations. It was important to be modest with one's life and not expect too much or get out of control. There were enough people in the world like that keeping people like Margaret in business.

No one would call Margaret a dreamer.

When the elevator door opened, Margaret stepped out and stopped. Standing in the shadowed hall outside her office door was one of her clients. At least the clothing appeared to belong to one. However, a black cap pulled low over the brow gave a new dimension to the individual and Margaret wasn't sure.

"Good morning, Margaret."

"Sophie?"

Sophie stared back, her mind a blank mask.

"I wasn't expecting you, Sophie."

"I know."

Margaret scanned Sophie's face then unlocked the door of her office. "Come in."

Sophie followed silently and watched, as Margaret went through her usual ritual: lights on, purse down, security off. Margaret looked at the blinking light on the answering machine. "I have half an hour before my first patient. Perhaps you'd like to tell me why you're here."

Margaret's desk was utilitarian with a pressboard table resting on file cabinets, the surface of which was anchored with all the necessary accouterments stationed in their appropriate places. Nothing ever moved. She stood behind it and stared. Sophie shut the door and walked up to the desk. "It's like the great wall of China, isn't it?"

"Excuse me?"

"This desk...it's the great wall separating sanity and insanity."

"Why don't you tell me what's happened, Sophie?"

Sophie reached in her bag, removed the purple scarf and gently placed the bundled hair onto the desk. She looked back at Margaret then slipped the watch cap off. Margaret stared. "You cut your hair."

"How long have I been coming to you, Margaret? Three months?"

"Approximately."

Sophie glanced down at the hair. "Do you remember what I told you when I started?"

Margaret sighed. "You were having dreams of an unusual nature...mythic...I believe you called them mythic."

"Priestesses."

"Yes. You said they were priestesses...nine, to be precise."

"Have you ever wondered, Margaret, why nine?"

"Sophie..."

'Have you ever noticed the drawings on my sweatshirts?"

"Yes."

"Why nine, Margaret...and why spirals?"

"These are ancient symbols, Sophie. You're obviously experiencing severe disturbances in your dreams. I've told you that already."

"They're not dreams anymore; they're taking over. I wake up in the forest at night with dead squirrels in my sack. I find weird clothes in my closet and strange food in my kitchen. I wake up naked with flowers in my hair. And now I don't even have hair." She rubbed her fingertips against the auburn locks. "If it weren't for Emrys picking me up and carrying me home time after time I'd probably be in jail by now. I doubt you even know the significance of his name."

Margaret started to mumble something.

"Last night, someone else awoke in me and very deliberately butchered my hair Margaret...laid it on the counter for me to find in the morning. This is a message; I intend to listen to it."

"Sophie, you need help. These episodes are just starting. I can give you medication to calm them down and we can keep working. You've obviously had some sort of trauma that's manifesting...in your dreams."

Sophie looked into Margaret's eyes and saw her for the first time—a sad little woman who had lost her own spirit a long time ago. "I wonder how many people in padded cells are gifted, rather than sick."

"Sophie..."

"I saw it, you know. I saw it but disregarded it, because you're the one with the degree, the trained professional. I'm not sure if it was the training that took you off course or whether you were never on course to begin with. You have no room for the non-ordinary, Margaret; your brain doesn't know where to go with it. That's why I've been getting worse. I put myself in the wrong hands and disregarded my own instincts. It's like going to the hairdresser for brain surgery."

"Sophie, you're overwhelmed with energies and dreams. You need to process them; it takes time..."

"I'm outside of time! You're working with the wrong map. You're so afraid of getting lost, you'd label me sick before following my trail."

Margaret jutted out her double chin and looked down her short, thick nose at Sophie. "The fact remains that disturbed energies are taking over your life, and you're out of control. Medication is very good in these instances. You need help."

"No, you need help; I need a guide. Your whole process creates illness, that's what this hair is all about. You've been causing separation, not healing it."

Margaret took a deep breath and dropped her chin to her chest, exposing her over-processed scalp. Sophie stared. "Have you ever wondered what hair is? Is it just something we comb and color and curl into oblivion? Is that all?"

Margaret's eyes fluttered in exasperation.

"Why my hair? Why do you think they'd do something as drastic as butcher my hair in the middle of the night?"

"There is no 'they' Sophie." Margaret's voice was a parched whisper.

"Hair is symbolic of the energy that flows through us. Some call it spirit. Despite your prognostications, I really don't believe I'm walking the boundaries of schizophrenia, Margaret. But I might if I keep listening to you."

Sophie wrapped the hair back up in its purple scarf and placed it in her bag. "You might want to stop bleaching the shit out of your own hair. It'd be a good place to start." She pulled the watch cap on and headed towards the door.

"Sophie?"

Sophie glanced back.

"Where will you go, Sophie?"

"The same direction that brought me here: North. Look it up."

At 8:00 a.m., Eleni hauled back the squeaky porch screen and pounded on the cottage door. When no one answered, she scurried down the flagstone path that connected the cottage to the main house. Eleni was tired. Her eyes were tinged yellow, and the furrow of her brow pinched as she observed the weeds cramping the beds at her feet, spilling across the walk. What looked like a once cascading splash of green had reverted to an unkempt field of overgrown dandelions. Emily's parents would have rolled over in their graves.

She slammed her knuckles against the kitchen door to no avail then scrambled around to the side of the house. It was an old farmhouse—a grand dame—full of character and the secrets of a bygone era. She stared at the vine-encrusted exterior, broken shutters, and sun-bleached paint and shook her head...such a pity.

A light was on in Emily's room, and raucous music seeped through the cracks of the cramped window. Eleni peered through milky panes at Emily, as she primped her overly lacquered hair and applied a shade of lipstick too bright for this early in the morning. Emily and Sophie had known each other since they were ten. Why they remained friends was a mystery to Eleni. One girl was consumed with an inner world, while the other by an outer. Eleni tapped on the window.

Emily looked up, surprised, then shoved on the pane attempting to break the suction of corroded paint and rain. It swung open with a jolt.

"Good morning!"

"I knocked but you didn't hear."

Emily switched off the music. "When did you get here?"

"Just now...took an early flight. Do you know where Sophie is?"

"Hang on." Emily disappeared into the dark house and emerged through the kitchen door, looking like a garden in full bloom. She wore a tight purple mini-skirt with matching jacket and three-inch heels—pale violet with pink flowers at the toe. Cobalt blue eye shadow, magenta rouge, and a neck choker of rhinestones and daisies topped her off. Eleni fought to keep her eyebrows down.

"I'm on my way to work...late as usual. I'll let you into the cottage."

"Work?"

"Receptionist. They don't open till nine, but they like the phones answered by eight. I can never finish getting dressed by eight!"

Eleni kept silent.

"I know she's here. I saw her last night." They headed up the path but stopped short at the sight of Sophie standing on the cottage porch. "There she is! What has she got on her head?" Emily whispered.

Eleni stared at her daughter's diminutive frame lost in oversized clothing, her pale face indistinguishable beneath a black cap. "She probably went for an early walk." She looked back at Emily. "She likes to walk."

"I know."

The two stood silently, staring at the girl on the porch. "You better get to work, Emily." Emily smiled and waved a manicured hand at Sophie, then trotted back down the path, leaving a cloud of vanilla fragrance in her wake.

Eleni's shoulders slumped, causing her arms to cascade limply and her chest to cave in. Her fair hair was parched, like corn too long in the sun or wheat fields without water. She gasped a breath of morning air, hoping its moisture would fill her lungs and buoy a posture that had begun to sag, like the aged wood beneath Sophie's feet. She smiled at her daughter, perched defiantly on the craggy porch.

"I didn't know you were coming," Sophie spat out the words like pellets from a toy gun.

"Nice to see you, too."

Sophie spun around and hauled on the rusty screen door and disappeared into the cottage. Eleni followed. The screen door stuck open, its joints too hammered from rain and wind to collapse anymore on its own.

"So, is there a problem or something?" Sophie continued.

"You tell me." Eleni's voice was calm, and she stared at her daughter without focusing on the cap.

"Usually you call and tell me you're coming."

"Usually you call and tell me you need help."

"Is this some sort of interrogation?"

"Take off your hat, Sophie."

"Why are you here?"

"Emrys called."

"How did he know where to reach you?"

"I gave him my number the last time I was here. I said if it got bad to call. He did."

"What right does Emrys have in my affairs?"

"I think you know the answer to that. How many times over the last six months have you awoken in bed not knowing how you got there? His sudden appearance next door was unusual enough...not to mention his name."

"My whole life is public property, isn't it! I asked you to stay out of this. Go home, I don't need your meddling. Leave! Get out!" She was in her mother's face screaming, when a cool firm palm blasted across her cheek with surprising force. "Wake up, Sophie Alexander!"

Eleni snatched the watch cap off and stared at her daughter's butchered hair. "When did this happen?"

"Last night."

She scanned Sophie's emaciated frame. "When did you eat last?"

"I can't eat...it just comes back up."

Eleni turned a trained eye on the kitchen counters. The linoleum, yellowed and stained with age, had been scrubbed and smelled of disinfectant. She opened the refrigerator; it was empty, except for one shelf stacked with canned fish. "Fillets of Anchovies...?"

"They eat them." Sophie was barely audible.

"I can't hear you."

"I don't eat them! They eat them. I throw up." She gripped the knitted cap and stared at the floor.

"They?"

"The voices in the ring, the Priestesses..."

"Where did you go this morning?"

"To fire my shrink. I wanted her to see what benefit her inestimable help had brought."

"Why on earth would you take this to a psychiatrist? This isn't psychiatric care. For Christ's sake, Sophie!"

"What do you want me to do? Lose myself more than I already have? I thought she'd be educated."

"What you're dealing with is beyond the comprehension of most people. Why didn't you tell me it was getting worse?"

"I almost lost you once. I can't let it happen again."

"You're not protecting me by not asking for help. The worse you are, the worse I am."

Sophie watched her mother turn and fill the kettle with water. "Your grandfather didn't exactly buy that ring at Tiffany's, you know."

Sophie looked down at the red stone that graced the middle finger of her right hand. "Six months ago my life turned inside out because of this ring."

Eleni opened her purse, withdrew the small green velvet pouch and slid the bag across the table. "Look closely at the embroidery beneath the cord."

Sophie grabbed the bag that had contained the ring for so many years, the velvet edges worn and frayed. She released the cord and looked beneath at the intricate needlework.

"Cherry blossoms," said Eleni. "Remember the cherry tree you used to draw on your shirt?" Outside in the yard stood a small cherry tree Sophie had recently planted. The kettle whistled and Eleni poured them each a cup of tea.

"You've been gifted with something, Sophie. It's up to you to decide just how it's to be lived."

"It's messing with my mind."

Eleni shook her head then dropped her forehead down and pressed it against the kitchen table. "Jesus Sophie, how long are you going to fight it?"

"I planted a cherry tree because of a message in a dream and now you show me cherries embroidered on the bag the ring was in. It never ends. The mythology of this ring isn't just about me, Mom!"

"It both is, and it isn't! I swear if you don't get it you won't make it through this. You'll wake up, and you'll wake up, and you'll wake up, and it'll always be someone different, until one day you realize you've mapped a pathway between them all, and you're no longer divided. They aren't just dreams, Sophie...

they're forgotten realities. Look in your Grandfather's journal! Even he said there were voices that needed to be heard. And I swear to God and to you, they will be your salvation, if you'll just stop resisting!" Eleni reached in her purse and pulled out a slip of paper that she laid down in front of her daughter.

"What's this?"

"It's the name and phone number of someone I want you to call."

Sophie looked at the piece of paper. "Who's Jack Harrington?"

"Do you remember when you were little, how Grandpa told you about the dream weavers?"

"He said they could knit energy the way we do wool." Sophie fiddled with the wool cap.

"When I was in college, I had a friend who was studying to be a psychiatrist, and we used to talk about the dream weavers, mystics who could bend reality, shape this world by going someplace deep. He decided to study psychiatry, because he believed that some types of mental illness were actually a result of spiritual disturbance...a disturbance our western world no longer understood. He believed that no one knew how to guide these people, so they were labeled mentally ill. I haven't seen him for years, but there were a series of articles a while back about how he'd been ousted by the medical community because of his unconventional beliefs."

"Jack Harrington."

"It took me awhile to track him down. He left the community and isn't practicing anymore."

"Then why would he see me?"

"You need help. You have a world of mythology rising out of that ring and into your life. You need someone who's willing to move beyond normal convention. I have a hunch he'll work with you."

"Where is he?"

"Campbell River, British Columbia."

"North?"

"North. Call him...ask him to talk with you. You can make the trip in a day."

The phone rang and rang. Sophie was about to give up when it clicked and a deep gravelly voice came on. "Yea?"

"Dr. Harrington?"

"Not anymore."

She hesitated. "Is this Jack Harrington?"

"Who wants to know?"

"Mr. Harrington, my name is Sophie Alexander...I was given your name and number by my mother. I think you knew her when you were in college." All Sophie could hear was the far off cry of seagulls as they filled the silence on the line.

"Eleni?"

"Yes. Eleni Alexander."

The phone went quiet again, leaving Sophie alone with the seagulls.

"Is she all right?"

"She's fine. Actually, I'm the one who needs help. She asked me to call you...see if you would speak with me."

"What did you say your name was?"

"Sophie."

"Sophie." He whispered it so quietly. "Perhaps your mother didn't know, Sophie, but I've sort of dropped out of society; I'm not working anymore. I assume that's what you were looking for...professional help?"

"No. Well...Mom knew what you just said." Sophie fumbled with her words. "Mr. Harrington, I know you're not practicing anymore. I need some help...of an unusual kind. I was just hoping you'd talk with me. Maybe you could steer me in the right direction."

"Sweetheart, I live on a rickety old fishing boat in Campbell River, British Columbia. How are you planning to bridge the gap?"

"I could make it there in a day. Maybe if you would just give me a little time, we could talk."

"Where are you?"

"Oregon."

"You'd come all the way up here?"

"Yes." The seagulls took over.

"Your mother was a good friend."

Sophie stayed silent.

"I'm not fishing tomorrow. The boat will be in all day. Can you be here then?"

"Yes."

"When you come into town, you'll see a large public pier on the right. Immediately after it, there's a marina for the old fishing boats. I'm in there. Just come on out."

Sophie could hear him readying the phone to hang up. "Wait! How will I know which boat is yours, Mr. Harrington?"

"Jack. Call me Jack, Sophie."

"And the boat?"

"*Dream Weaver*. Just look for *Dream Weaver*."

The phone clicked, cutting off the distant call of seagulls, their shrieking cries weaving around the creaking of wood hulls rubbing against taut ropes. Sophie stood paralyzed, hanging onto the receiver, listening to the dark silence, as if a tiny window had opened and blown a little bit of Jack Harrington down the line. She could feel herself reach out from turbulent waters and grab at the lifeline being tossed over the edge of his boat.

"Why don't you hang up, Sophie?" asked Eleni.

Sophie disconnected the phone from her ear and placed it in its cradle. "Want to help me pack?"

JOURNAL ENTRY:

Bride and the triple spiral: The Celtic Goddess, Bride, is the triple spiral. The triple spiral is like a maze that, when understood, shows how the inner life informs the outer life. Bride's Well, once filled with the rising tide of rain and sea, is the only Well on The Isle of Glass that is now dry. The ring emerged from the Well during a year of heavy rain. Bride has returned with the ring, looking for the groom. The Bride will enter the story.

The brass doorknob was rusty, worn, and rattled loosely in Eleni's hand, as she opened the closet. A panel of light slid into the dark interior, illuminating an army of outfits hanging in a tidy row. Eleni fanned her fingers down the fabric of a green velvet military cloak that looked like it would be more at home in a costume bank than the cottage closet. Battered storage trunks were stacked on the dusty floor. "These must be from Emily's family," she said.

Sophie hung back, filling the doorway with her baggy clothes. "They're mine."

"...Yours?"

She went over to the closet, reached in and rubbed her fingers against the velvet hide of buckskin jeans with cross-hatched ties at the waist. "Second-hand shops...something about old or strange or ethnic kept entering my mind. It's like I don't fit inside myself anymore."

Eleni slipped back and watched as her daughter grabbed a burgundy brocade gown with a high, jeweled collar out of the closet and threw it on the bed. "Anytime something got my attention I bought it. It's all I've done...just wander around weird shops and buy the most god-awful clothes in the universe. Leather and lace and velvet and...can't you just see me in this...wandering the streets at midnight? What a joke: Sophie the clown, Sophie the fool, Sophie the harlot...." She began tossing clothing into the room, screaming at the top of her voice. Eleni grabbed and shook her by the shoulders.

"Stop it, Sophie!"

Sophie buckled onto the bed. "I have worn them you know," she whispered. "Not during the daytime. I've never put them on when I can remember. But I wake up sometimes at night, and I've got one of these strange outfits on. God only knows where I go. Once there were pine needles and sap all over the skirt, like I'd been sleeping in the forest."

Eleni, struggling with her own emotions, reached for the closet door.

"Don't close it."

"Why?"

"I have to pack."

"You're not packing these things, are you?"

"If I'm going north to get help from Jack Harrington do you think I'm going to piss off these prima donnas by not bringing their clothes?"

Eleni blanched.

"What do I care if they each need their own outfit?"

Eleni scanned the bed littered with clothing remnants from another era. The nightstand was burdened with papers and dusty books left open to the pages last read. The shade had been knocked off the lamp and lay unattended and jammed between the nightstand and the wall. Even the clock had stopped time. She scanned the disordered room and ended up staring at Sophie's butchered hair. "Do you want me to even up the ends of your hair?"

"No."

Eleni collapsed onto the bed, feeling the give of rusted springs, and watched Sophie pack. One by one the outfits were laid out on the floor, where she pressed the fabric flat then folded arms and skirts into a narrow package that was rolled into a tight bundle and placed in her canvas bag; the meticulous, controlled movement of an individual fighting for order in a disordered mind. The garments were a parade of cloth characters: regal gowns, animal hide, cloistered prim, and weighted wool.

"We should leave around midnight to catch the early morning ferry. I think the crossing to Victoria takes about two hours," Eleni said.

"We?" Sophie's fingers, almost translucent blue, rolled the folds of a diaphanous floral gown.

"You can't go alone."

Sophie sat back on her knees and looked at her mother's left hand lying flaccid in her lap. "Your hand is still paralyzed."

"My hand is fine."

"Will it get better?"

"You can't take the chance of traveling alone."

Sophie looked at the ring on her right hand. "You should never have put it on."

"Well, I did," Eleni sighed.

"If you had just given it back to me when I was little, your hand would be fine."

"And what would you have done with it? Bury it again in some other rotten old tree? Six months ago, you came north because of a spiral in a record titled "North to Alaska." Have you noticed anything similar in Grandpa's journal?"

"Yes. The 'N' in the Tree of Life drawing became illuminated with gold towards the end of his book."

Sophie finished rolling up the gown, placed it in the bag, and began again. The veins on her hands protruded, making them look old, reminding Eleni of her father's hands. "Your Celtic lineage goes back a long way, Sophie." Black leather emerged from the closet. "My father's family ancestry has been traced in Cornwall as far back as 100 AD."

Sophie pressed and rolled the stiff black leather coat into a tight ball.

"It was a long unbroken line...till we came along."

"What do you mean?"

"The name has passed from father to son since 100 AD. Have you read your grandfather's journal?"

"Yes."

"Then you know where the ring came from, and you know what Samuel believed it to represent. And if you really read all of it, you know that I am not my father's first child," Eleni whispered. Sophie sat back on her knees and stared at her mother, the hollows of her cheeks showing too much definition for one so young. "There are strange things happening in our lives, Sophie. I'm trying to help, but you need to remember it's hard for me as well."

Sophie nodded. "Why didn't you tell me about Grandpa's journal before that night?"

"Mainly because you buried the ring, even though you were dreaming. But also, I guess, because I didn't really believe."

Sophie turned away and stared into the dark confines of the closet.

"Apparently we are the first to break a very long, male-dominated lineage. A family lineage, that went back to the time of Christ. My father believed there was significance in what had happened; that the dying of a son at the moment of his birth was some sort of mystical event. He went to England, he said, to research his ancestry. But he was looking for something besides solace. When he was guided to Bride's Well, it relinquished a ring that he believed was not only extremely old, but also sacred. But neither he nor I knew the extent of its power, nor what would happen when you put it on."

"I still don't understand why it was given to me."

"You're of Celtic blood, and that blood is old. There is information in blood. If you carry that within you, you become a seed, capable of bringing the ancient forward."

"Grandpa believed the ring was symbolic?"

"He believed the ring was mythic. It was delivered out of a Well that he was guided to by a voice in a cemetery filled with his ancestors. He passed the ring to you, as the firstborn of his daughter's womb; he believed you were its destiny."

"But why?"

Eleni looked down at Sophie's shirt. "Because of the geometric forms you have been consumed with since you were a child. The symbols are an ancient language; as he researched them, they surfaced in drawings on your skin and shirts."

"What about the green velvet bag."

"He purchased it in Glastonbury."

"It looks old."

"It is old."

"But it doesn't necessarily have anything to do with the ring."

"Are you referring to your dream and the cherries embroidered on the bag?"

"Yes."

"You're going to have to stop being linear. A mystical trail can show up anywhere it wants. The things your Grandfather studied and the conclusions he made require an enormous leap of faith. I didn't believe it either. Did I give it credence as mythology or something one reads in cultural history? Yes. But as a living, breathing energy as we've both now experienced? Good Lord, Sophie! I saw that ring move from my hand through yours and onto your finger. Whatever it's all about, it's not in our imagination. It's possible that the ring really does have some sort of lineage. But obviously, so do you. The ring is yours."

Sophie finished rolling the black leather and set it aside. "I'm going alone."

"You can't go alone! If you shift personalities along the way, God only knows where you'll end up."

"I need to do this alone."

"God help us," Eleni whispered. "All right...I'll take you as far as Victoria. You can get on a bus there that'll take you to Campbell River. At least when you get off the bus you'll be in the right town."

Sophie stared down at her hands; her nails were chewed to the quick. "It must be nice to be Emily. All she thinks about is whether her lipstick matches her nail polish..." She slipped her fingers beneath the folds of a worn, gray wool skirt and folded it over. "The bus sounds good."

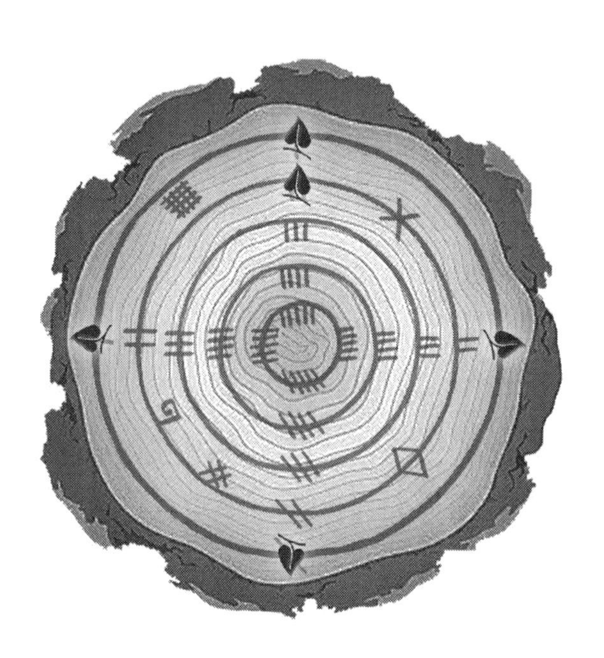

ROWAN
The Quickening

Campbell River, BC
May 2, 2001

AT 3:00 P.M. the next day, an Island bus stopped in Campbell River near the marina adjacent to Discovery Pier. One passenger stepped out. She stood on the walkway and turned her head towards the ocean breeze blowing in from the channel, ruffling her cropped hair. She closed her eyes and inhaled the scent of salty brine and seaweed. When she opened them again, they had changed color from hazel to green.

With a long stride and confident gait, the woman strode across the parking lot and down a wooden ramp to the marina, stuffed her duffel bag in a corner, and sauntered down the dock towards the fishing boats. When she reached the end of the pier she gazed long and hard at a vessel sitting low in the water.

"Is this the Avalon?" She swayed, as the dock navigated the ebb and flow of a changing tide. Above her, a man with weathered limbs stood at the boat's bow, his back squared to the wind blowing up from the south.

"No. It's the *Dream Weaver.*"

The woman looked down at the reflected letters floating in the gray water, then followed their reflection up to the boat's bow. Flecked paint peeling off the hull had scripted what appeared to her to be letters that formed a name beneath the blue painted *Dream Weaver.* The man had painted on the name *Dream Weaver,* but the salted sea air had stripped back the paint, etching letters to show the boat's true name.

"I don't think so. It appears you have incorrectly named your vessel. The sea says she's called The Avalon. If you expect her to work hard for you and navigate her seas, I suggest you adjust the name."

The man raised his head and stared out to sea a long second before turning and casting a curious eye upon her.

"Have you been catching any fish?" she continued.

"It's been a slow season."

"You do ask her to work for you, don't you? I mean you don't just make her rot her days away tied to the dock?"

Jack Harrington eyed the young woman up and down, noticing her butchered hair. Despite the twenty odd years since he'd seen Eleni it wasn't difficult to see the resemblance.

"A woman won't work for you if you don't know her true name."

"I thought *Dream Weaver* was a compliment," he continued.

She turned to leave then looked back. *"She's the weaver and the dream. Call her Avalon, you'll catch more fish."*

As she walked away, the dock shrugged under Jack's weight, as he jumped off the boat and followed. "Are you looking for someone?"

"I don't think so." She kept walking.

"Where are you headed," he bartered, casually, not wanting to lose her.

"I think I saw a little place in town that looked good for a meal, just up the road."

"Why don't I come with you? There's a better place farther along. The one you're talking about is kind of sleazy."

"I like sleazy."

At the end of the dock, she retrieved the bag, threw it over her head and across her chest like a harness, bounded up the ramp, and headed toward town. Jack had trouble keeping up with her. His untied sneakers flopped against his heels tripping him repeatedly, as he sprinted up the gang-plank. "Is that the place you're talking about?" he called out between huffs and puffs, pointing ahead to a scruffy building with no windows and a red lacquered door girdled with heavy bars.

"That's the place."

"Gemini Club," Jack muttered, "...wonderful reputation."

"The twins," she responded with a smile, *"it's the perfect place to start."* She turned and blew out of the sea air and into the dark, hallowed confines of the local dive.

Jack followed her in, stopping to let his eyes adjust to the dark. Ruby lights burned from table lamps through a fog of cigarette smoke. By the time he could see again, she was sitting at a corner table. "You adjust quickly to the dark," he said, squeezing into the booth.

"Yes. I move well between the dark and the light."

Jack fumbled with the menu, disturbed by the look in her eyes. "Would you like a hamburger?"

"Why don't you decide for me; I need a bathroom."

He pointed her in the right direction then ordered a double cheeseburger, fries, and a large glass of milk for the woman he was sure was Sophie Alexander.

After ten minutes, the bathroom door opened and the woman emerged. Jack looked up and caught sight of her standing on the threshold. The bathroom light streamed out from behind her and into the room, like streaks of sunlight across a cloudy sky. She had changed her clothes.

It appeared the oversized sweatshirt and baggy jeans had camouflaged a great deal. As she walked towards him, Jack couldn't help but admire the slim but shapely form approaching. A fitted velvet forest green cloak swept over her all the way down to her ankles. It had a stiff, military collar with gold buttons, cascading down the front that she had clasped only at the waist. Beneath it she wore what appeared were skin-tight buckskin pants tucked into suede boots. Her waist was cinched with a wide leather belt that held a pouch of animal skin and fur. And around her neck was a chain that held a pendant of two overlapping circles. She walked towards him with the unusual aura of an aggressive male in the seductive body of a female.

"You've changed," Jack said admiringly.

"It's not good to wear the clothes of others," she said. *"This is who I am."*

"And who might that be?"

"You may call me Nimue, Jack."

"You know who I am," Jack responded.

"We all know who you are. Her world is not hidden from us."

Jack stopped talking, as the waitress suddenly appeared out of the dark and placed food on the table. He waited for her to disappear, then watched as Nimue descended on the food. She was ravenous. He sat in silence, as she devoured everything on the table. He had ordered heavy food on purpose, wanting to slow down her body's energy. Nimue leaned back into the padded bench and closed her eyes. He stared at the pendant around her neck. It looked old.

"It is," she said. *"The ring belongs to her, she's earned it. But this is still ours. You won't see it unless we're present."*

Jack stared down and, for the first time, noticed the ring on her right hand. When he looked back, Nimue's eyes were heavy and beginning to glaze.

"The body is tiring, Jack. I must go. Look well at the pendant. It is the answer to the question. It is the answer and the question, and she has only you."

Nimue's head fell back and her eyes closed. Her body slumped down and leaned against the wall, slipping quickly into sleep. Jack dropped his head into his hands, and then looked up again at the young woman opposite him. The necklace was gone.

"What the hell have I gotten into?" he whispered.

Jack crossed the room to the bar and asked the bartender if he could use the phone. He dialed and held it to his ear while staring back at the table. Nimue was dead asleep. Slouched against the wall, her frame appeared smaller and more vulnerable in repose. He knew that situations like this were a terrible assault on the body, and he suspected she would sleep for hours.

"Hello? Hello...if you're not there I'm hanging up."

"Lilli, wait...it's me."

"Jack?"

"Yea. I need your help."

There was silence on the line, while Lilli pondered his response. "Are you in trouble?"

"No...but someone else is. Can you come down and pick me up? I need to get someone out to the boat and she can't walk."

"Drunk?"

"I wish."

"Where are you?"

"Gemini Club."

"Gemini? Shit, Jack, this is a small town. Maybe I should come disguised."

"Lilli, if you want to shape shift in and out of here, I really don't give a damn, just come get me!"

A bar of sunlight slid into the Gemini Club then got swallowed by the shadows. Jack could hear the shuffling of shoes across the concrete floor. When he looked up, she was standing next to the table, mounds of baggy denim and raven hair topped with a red cap that said "coyote" across the beak. "You always have this effect on women?" asked Lilli.

"I thought you were coming disguised."

"It's not actually me; it's coyote. He came disguised." She stared down at the woman and chuckled. "I asked all the others but coyote just kept jumping up and down screaming 'pick me, pick me!'" Lilli chuckled again. It was a deep clucking sound and emanated from somewhere dark. "Nice outfit."

Jack sighed and dropped his head. "Let's get her down to the boat."

They slid her out of the booth and threw her arms over each of their shoulders. Jack grabbed the duffel bag.

"Looks like she's planning to stay," smiled Lilli.

"Do you think everything's funny?"

"When coyote decides to mess with you, Jack, you better laugh cuz it can get real painful...you turn your back once and you're a dead man."

"That's funny?"

They walked her outside to Lilli's truck. "She's so light you could just hold her high and let the wind pick her up. You know she's gonna land on your boat."

"Just open the door."

"Why you always do things the hard way, Jack?" Lilli opened the door and helped slide the woman inside. Jack threw the duffel onto the floor and squeezed in, grabbing her just as her body slumped forward onto the dash. He put his arm around her and tucked her head gently onto his shoulder. Lilli watched, a wry grin sneaking across her face. "You sure she's not dead?"

"Look, Lilli, I can't tell you everything that's going on, because I don't know everything that's going on! She's not dead, ok? It's completely normal for a person to have this kind of reaction after going through what she just went through. She'll probably sleep twelve hours and wake up retching, with a class ten migraine."

"Well," Lilli continued, "I think all those people in the Gemini Club are dead. They look like the same ones that were there when I went in 1950."

"Lilli, you weren't even here in '50."

"How'd you know?"

"You're not old enough."

Lilli chuckled. "Maybe I was dead, too."

"Pull up to the dock." Lilli skidded to a stop on the gravel and popped out to help Jack.

"I can manage her," he said.

"I'll carry the duffel then."

"I can manage that, too."

"You pissed?"

Jack backed up, unfolding himself from the cab of the truck. "This woman's got problems, Lilli. I don't know how bad they are. It doesn't make me happy."

"Well, maybe you can help her. People don't just cross paths for no reason."

"I closed the door on helping people like this a long time ago."

"Looks like she just blew it open. It's coyote, Jack. Read my cap." Lilli's face split into a grin. "Give me a call if you need help. I've got lots of friends." She tossed her raven mane into the wind and winked at him before hopping into the driver's seat. The truck door slammed and she tore out of the parking lot leaving Jack holding the girl with one arm and the duffel bag with the other.

"Shit," he whispered.

Jack dropped the bag by the ramp and picked her up, cradling her like a baby. Scanning the dock to make sure the coast was clear, he sprinted down to the *Dream Weaver* where he slid her carefully onto the deck. He ran back, got the bag, and returned to the boat. Within five minutes, he had her resting on his bunk with a bucket on the floor by her head.

He grabbed a couple of blankets and tucked them around her, then stopped for a moment to stare. She looked a lot like Eleni, but the butchered hair was a blatant contrast around her face. She was actually attractive, he thought, pale and very gaunt, but good-looking in an unusual sort of way. He remembered thinking something similar about her mother.

"Jesus, Eleni."

Jack Harrington's boat was a fifty-year-old, stripped- down seine with a wood hull that he had repaired with planks of Alder to help it withstand the turbulent waters of Discovery Passage. The drums were tossed to make room for deck space, and the inside cabin scrubbed clean enough to inhabit, without stripping the stale smell of rotten fish. Jack had reconstructed it himself. Some said it showed.

It wasn't that the boat wasn't sea worthy; it was just hard to get home when the tide was running fifteen knots and he was moving against it, low in the water, pushing eight. The working fishermen looked at the boat and smiled. Some said it had character—others just grinned, understanding there were lots of reasons to immerse oneself in the sea that had more to do with life and a whole lot of nothing to do with fish. It didn't matter. They liked Jack and watched his back, if they saw his sagging stern make its way beyond the sea wall.

He was smart enough to know when to go and when to stay. If the tide was running as high as fifteen knots, and the wind was blowing that, or more, in the opposite direction, he kept his berth and stayed home. Even though they blew up Ripple Rock in 1958, Seymour Narrows still boiled with swirling tides on a bad day...or night. Some boats had had their sterns sucked down so hard, everyone jumped ship, afraid of the draw of a sinking vessel.

Some lived. Some drowned.

You had to know what you were doing, and no one doubted Jack's seaworthiness; it was his vessel that was limited; and if your boat didn't partner well, there was little you could do to make up the difference. Alder wood might help her float, but something more than that was needed to get her home. Don't put her in a situation she can't handle was all they said.

Jack agreed.

There were none of the familiar touches on Jack's boat that made a vessel a home. When he had left his former life, he reached out for anonymity. No window boxes with geraniums spilling out or welcome mat nailed to the dock for Jack. He had, in fact, worked so hard at obliterating any signs of human care that he downright blared himself trumpet-like across the marina.

He was alone, but they all knew he wasn't a loner. He was gruff but had a kind eye, and although not a big talker, he'd just as soon wish you luck fishing as turn the other way.

Jack had character, just like his boat, The *Dream Weaver*. So when they saw him change the name to The *Avalon*, everyone knew something was in the wind.

May 3, 2001

At noon the next day, Sophie rolled off the bunk and vomited into a bucket resting on the floor. She held it between her legs and vomited again...and again...and, in between, she noticed that her legs were clad in buckskin pants and suede boots and that the planks on the floor were old and weathered. The seagulls she'd heard on the phone were now screeching in the wind, and it sounded as if water was lapping the outside walls of the room. The smell of rotten eggs and seaweed permeated the air, and she vomited again.

She put the bucket down and stood up, only to fall back, as the floor shifted. Above the bunk there was a window exposing a soft gray fog breaking. Between the breaks, she saw a reflection of light across steel water, craggy coastal rocks, and weathered masts bobbing intermittently up and down.

She was on a boat.

She made her way into what appeared to be the main cabin and found her duffel bag. She flipped it open and rummaged around inside for her sweatshirt and jeans then disappeared into the head. She'd been through it all before. Remove the costume, scan it for evidence of any kind, and put it away. This was one outfit, however, that Sophie had never woken up in before.

She splashed cold water on her face and in her hair, rolled up the clothes and shoved them back in the bag, and put her tennis shoes on. A quick scan showed nothing else disturbed. Her purple scarf still contained two feet of auburn hair, and her money was still in her wallet. "Well, at least he's not a thief," she whispered.

"Good morning, Sophie."

Jack Harrington was tall. He looked particularly tall from Sophie's vantage point, squatted down on the cabin floor. He had that rugged look of men who worked by the sea. The skin begins to resemble the hulls of their boats: pitted, stripped, and covered with salt. You wouldn't say that he looked mad...it's just that he didn't look happy. "It's a good thing you look like your mother," he continued.

Sophie stood up, not knowing what to say. "Did you leave the bucket out for me?"

"Yes."

"Thanks."

He studied her through steel gray eyes.

"How'd you know I'd need a bucket?"

"Just a good guess. Do you drink coffee?"

"Yes."

"Why don't we go up on deck; I'll pour us a cup."

Sophie followed him up and looked around the marina. It didn't look familiar, but further away there was a pier. "I remember the pier," she said, half to herself. "I got off the bus and saw the pier."

Jack handed her a cup and gestured for her to sit down. "Why don't you tell me what's going on."

As Sophie raised the cup to her lips, light splintered off the ring. "Everything revolves around this ring."

Jack nodded. Seagulls shrieked, fighting over the carcass of a dead fish.

"It's hard to know where to start," she whispered.

Jack watched the seagulls shredding flesh. "Anywhere's usually a good place."

"I'm sorry for yesterday. I don't remember. I never do."

Jack nodded again. "Just talk."

"My Grandfather died when I was eight. He helped raise me, since we never knew who my real father was."

Jack's eyes flickered.

"He willed this ring to me...told mom it was very old."

Jack sat quietly, his back resting against the boat's railing, studying Sophie for any unusual behavior. "Your mother had never seen it?"

"No. Grandpa found it in an old Well in Cornwall."

"So what happened when you got the ring?"

Sophie felt that same wave of fear ripple through her, like a storm through water. "I was never actually given the ring. A few nights after my Grandpa died, I dreamt that a voice was calling my name. I sleepwalked into my mom's bedroom, found the ring on her dresser, and took it outside to an old tree; I buried it in the tree."

"You did what?"

"Mom woke up and followed me…saw that I was dreaming. I guess I got a pocketknife from the kitchen and went out back, dug a hole in the side of the trunk, and shoved in the ring."

"You don't remember?"

"No. I went back to my room and fell asleep. Mom dug the ring out of the tree and kept it hidden for years."

Jack began to examine the drawings that meandered up the sleeve of Sophie's sweatshirt. A trail of interlocking circles went up the right sleeve and a weaving of crescent moons and stars spilled down the left. The center of her shirt had a small, faded, triple spiral, framed with a square drawn in red, black, and white. Jack poured more coffee.

"Since the ring is on your finger now, what happened to cause its return?"

"Last October, California had an earthquake."

"I read about it."

"It was caused by the ring."

Jack looked concerned.

"On Halloween, Mom put the ring on."

"Why?"

"There are voices in the ring. I suspect they had something to do with it."

"Is that how you got it back?"

She flipped her hand over and exposed the scar. "The ring wasn't hers to wear."

"How'd you get the scar?"

"A voice told me that I couldn't take the ring off her. Mom became unconscious when she put it on. I was told that removing it would damn her to wherever she was wandering, and she'd never get back; I was supposed to follow. So I lay down at her side, grabbed her hand, and jammed the stone into the palm of my right hand. Energy shot up my arm, and I blacked out. That's how the journey began." Sophie rubbed her thumb across the scar on her palm. "When we woke up, the ring had transferred from her hand to mine. But her left hand...the hand that wore the ring...is still damaged from its energy." She looked out to an old tanker maneuvering the channel; it looked so burdened, you'd think it'd sink.

"There was a spell on the ring...the kind of stuff they make movies about, complete with voices and spells and ancient dying wizards. In my life it's real."

"And is the wizard still dying, Sophie?" Jack's attention was piqued.

"When I first dreamt of him, he was, Mr. Harrington. He was old as dust."

"Jack...call me Jack. Who was old as dust?"

"Merlin. He's part of the spell. Somehow, they're all connected. The journey I took, when I was unconscious, healed an ancient wound to such a degree that, not only is this old dying Merlin healed now, he actually became young again. They all did." Sophie cocked her head as if listening. "Well, Merlin is young, and the women are now in me...and I'm young."

"What women?"

"The voices in the ring, the nine High Priestesses of Avalon. Do you know the number nine?"

"Meaning?"

"Nine can never break out of itself. All multiples of nine reduce to nine; it's the trinity on three levels; it's the number of the goddess. Or at least it used to be."

Jack's gray eyes held the sharp glint of steel.

"The women were trapped in a state of stasis, held captive by their own spell. They've been waiting for the one who could break that spell and merge their voices into one entity. They were waiting for the tenth Priestess."

"There's another?"

"It's a new age. Nine must become ten. They were waiting for me...and now we're all together."

Jack's eyes mirrored the fog resting upon the sea. He stared hard at Sophie, his years of training kicking into gear.

"Why don't we take a break?"

Sophie disappeared into the galley, returning with the purple scarf. She placed it in Jack's hand.

"On the day I phoned you, I awoke to find that on my bathroom counter. It happened in the middle of the night and is a loud message that I've been on the wrong track. I need help, Jack Harrington."

Jack unfolded the scarf and found a long weave of auburn hair. "I wondered why your hair was so butchered."

"When you told me your boat was named ***Dream Weaver*** I knew you could help me."

Jack smiled; he looked weary. "It's not the ***Dream Weaver*** anymore, Sophie."

"What do you mean?"

"She's called the ***Avalon***. Let's go get some grub."

Sophie sat in a booth and stared down at two fried eggs swimming on the shiny surface of a green stoneware plate.

Stiff bacon jutted out to the sides, like masts on a ship, and the hash-browns were shaped into balls resembling the boulders separating the marina from the channel. She shoved the eggs this way and that with her fork, little round ships on a green sea.

"I thought you'd be hungry," Jack said.

"I'm sorry, it's hereditary. I don't like food."

"Is there something else to survive on?"

"Well, I eat, I just don't eat much."

"Yesterday, you ate a half-pound hamburger with double cheese, a plate of fries, and a large glass of milk in about two minutes. I was very impressed."

Sophie looked up, just as Jack swallowed a large mouthful of chili. "Maybe that's why I puked."

Jack threw his spoon in the bowl and wiped the chili off his mouth. "You know why you puked, and it wasn't the food. You're thin because you've been puking for months, and your body's beginning to reject any kind of sustenance the minute it hits your stomach. Don't give me any shit about inheriting a bird's appetite, Sophie. If you try and slide one more lie by me, I'll send you packing. I don't need it...understand?"

Sophie lowered her eyelids.

"Your mother's right...I can help you. But if I have to decipher between your lies and the chaos inside, I don't want the job!"

An attractive Indian woman with long black hair walked up to the booth and smiled down at Jack. "My, aren't we pissy." She looked at Sophie and turned back to Jack. "You going to introduce me, Jack?"

Jack kept eating his chili as if she wasn't there.

"Why you eat that shit, Jack? It always gives you gas and we can hear it all over the marina."

Jack glowered. His neck stiffened, and his face turned red.

"See?" she continued. "It's already starting." She turned to Sophie. "Hi, I'm Jack's sister, Lilli."

"You're not my goddamn sister, Lilli!"

"Well, I'm not your blood sister; I'm your spirit sister. I follow you around and piss you off. I stick gum in your fishing reel, clean your clothes, and put toads in your underwear drawer." She turned back to Sophie. "He's actually very fond of me, he's just mad because..."

"Lilli!"

Lilli smiled, obviously happy that she finally got his attention. "Like I said, aren't you going to introduce me?"

Jack dropped his spoon on the table and shoved back from the table. He glared at Sophie a long time, his gray eyes boiling with frustration. "Sophie, this is Lilli, a friend of mine. Lilli...Sophie."

Lilli leaned in and took Sophie's hand in hers. They were dry and calloused and held onto her fingers like minnows in a trap. But when Sophie looked into her eyes she saw a wonderful kindness. "Hi, Sophie...doesn't look like you're very hungry. Want some help?"

Lilli was about to lower herself into the booth when Jack coughed. "Sophie needs to eat, Lilli. She needs to eat and we're in the middle of a long discussion. Why don't you come by the boat tomorrow? We can all have coffee then. Besides, I've got a bag of laundry for you."

Lilli reached over and plucked something off the back of Jack's collar then flicked it on the table. "You got a raven on your back, Black Jack...better make sure you listen." She smiled at Sophie. "I get so hungry when I'm out to sea, don't you?" Lilli reached down and picked one of the potato rocks off the plate, popping it into her mouth as she turned to walk away. "Make sure the laundry's dirty. Last week you sent back the clean bag and kept the crap. Maybe that's why you don't smell so good."

When she opened the door, a gust of wind blew her denim clothes out behind her like a great cape and her blue-black hair flew out and around her cap giving the distinct illusion of a bird taking flight.

"She's got too much coyote in her. She won't fly...not today anyway." Jack's voice was barely a whisper.

"How'd you know what I was thinking?"

He shrugged, staring down at the object Lilli had set on the table. It was a large black feather. "Lilli has some unusual traits." He grabbed the feather and twirled it between his thumb and forefinger. "I have seen her fly, but she's got strong coyote medicine, and when it kicks in, you're more likely to see tail feathers than wings."

"Why'd she call you Black Jack?"

Jack stuffed the feather in his pocket. "Can you eat any of that?" He nodded towards the plate.

Sophie shook her head.

"Then I'll feed you back at the boat." He stood up, tossed some money on the table, and headed out the door, with Sophie following.

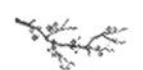

An icy wind blustered through Discovery Passage, churning white caps and chilling Sophie to the bone. She slipped her hands up the sleeves of her cotton sweatshirt and scuttled below to the galley.

"Who's Lilli?"

Jack rummaged around searching for something. "Lilli's a Kwakiutl Indian. Don't ever think you know her, because she can shift on you in a heartbeat. She's a good friend and a bad friend, because if she sees you need to learn something, she'll help make it happen, and you'll hate her for it, and then love her for it when you make it through. She turns life upside down just so you can see it inside out."

He stopped in front of the porthole, his attention captured by an old tug fighting hard to make progress against the tide. "Lilli wakes you up when all you want to do is sleep. Sometimes, you just have to turn her away because she never stops...never stops, till your mind's so tired and confused you finally stop thinking straight and that's when she goes to work."

He filled a kettle with water and placed it on the burner. "I guess, to answer your question, Lilli's a teacher. She's a good friend, and she's a bad friend...depends on how you want to look at it."

The galley was as tiny as a thimble. Cabinets did double duty, offering cups on hooks inside the door, as well as food on the shelves. He grabbed two cups, some instant coffee, and powdered cream. Sophie hated instant coffee.

"I came here to get away and ran into Lilli," he whispered under his breath. "That about says it all."

Jack handed Sophie a chipped cup with a thick lip with the words "Life's a Bitch" on the side. He poured the dark liquid in and tossed her the creamer. Sophie was so cold she decided she'd just about drink anything, as long as it was hot.

"Lilli calls me Black Jack because she says I'm like the Raven. I can fly in and out of dark places, bring back the goods, and not get lost along the way. I'm not so sure, though. She pisses me off a lot. But she does my laundry and shows up when I need her."

"She said she's your sister."

"Lilli says we're linked. Call it sister, I don't know. I don't feel like a brother." He continued ransacking the cupboards, till he found what he was looking for. "Are you old enough to drink?"

"Does it matter out here?"

"I care about your mother, Sophie. If she sent you to me I can at least be responsible."

"I'm twenty-one."

He grabbed the bottle of whiskey from the cupboard and poured a drop in her coffee. "It's a little early...but you're shivering worse than the mast on that old tug...probably in shock."

"It's just a little colder here than I'm used to."

He tipped the bottle a bit longer into his cup then set it down on the table in front of them. "Bullshit."

Sophie stared down at her "Life's a Bitch" cup. Bullshit was right. Wrapping her hands around the chipped crockery, she pressed it to her lips and drained the contents, wincing as the heat bombarded her stomach walls. "Are you saying that Lilli shape shifts?"

Jack nodded.

"I didn't think that stuff was real."

"Considering what you've been going through, it shouldn't be such a hard reach."

"What do you mean?"

Jack tossed his drink back and poured himself another. "The only difference between you and Lilli is that she's in control of the energy shift...doesn't make a squat of difference that her energy's animal and yours is high priestess."

Sophie clutched the cup for warmth. "No one's met one of them before, you know. At least, no one I know. When Emrys brings me home, I'm passed out. He lays me down in my bed, covers me up, and leaves."

"Emrys?"

"Yea, Emrys."

"Where have I heard that name before?"

"Ambrosius Merlinus, Myrddin Embreis, Emrys...immortal one, divine one...."

"Merlin?"

"Merlin, in my dreams and in my life."

"When did Emrys appear?"

"After I reclaimed the ring, I came north to Oregon to stay with my friend, Emily. That's when I started dreaming of Merlin as a young man in his crystal cave. Next thing I know, this Emrys guy moves in next door to Emily, starts showing up when I need help."

Sitting next to the sink was a dirty old Easter basket filled with individually wrapped cinnamon rolls. Jack grabbed two and tossed them down in front of her.

"Eat."

Sophie peeled the plastic wrap and unraveled the cinnamon wheel. "Another spiral," she muttered.

"What?"

"The Priestesses said that the ring represents a love story that never finished being told. Somehow, I'm supposed to tell the story. Maybe Emrys has something to do with that."

Sophie ate the cinnamon roll. "It's never happened during the day before. I thought for sure I'd be able to get here, as long as it was daylight. All I had to do was ride the bus from Victoria and drink lots of coffee. Just stay awake. That's all I had to do, just stay friggin' awake..."

"It's the ocean." Jack's voice was dark and warm, barely audible. He had turned to gaze out the porthole at the fishing boats bobbing up and down across the marina.

"What do you mean?"

"Why do you think we call our boats 'she'? They're vessels...helping us get closer...just a little closer to that great oceanic female that haunts our dreams." He stared at her with eyes that were far away, tormented, dreamlike. "You don't need to be schizophrenic to lose yourself out here, Sophie."

"I'm not schizophrenic."

"You're afraid that you are, though. How many other outfits are there in your duffel bag?"

Sophie focused on the cinnamon roll and its nut-brown spiral.

"How many?"

"Eight."

"Who's missing?"

"I have no idea who's missing, Jack. How would I know who's missing when I don't even know who wears what!"

"Nice of you to pack their outfits for them."

"What do you want me to do? Pretend this is all a joke? Just don't look and maybe it'll go away? I'm being flooded with your goddamn oceanic females and believe me some of them aren't very pretty. At least if they wear their own clothes it leaves me a trail. Whether its buckskin pants or brocade gown, at least I know someone else was here!"

"Calm down."

"And furthermore, Mr. Salt Sea Air, how do you intend to keep me here? Watch me twenty-four-seven so I don't untie the ropes and let us drift out into Seymour Narrows? That's right. I can read too. I'm a goddamn genius! Some of the worse tidal waters in the world are right there, outside our window. I'll show you oceanic, Jack. Just check the outfit before we sink and see if—"

Jack grabbed a glass of water and, with a quick flick of his wrist, splashed the liquid in Sophie's face. "Sit down!" Her legs buckled and she collapsed back onto the bench.

"When did you get that scar on your forehead?" Jack tossed her a towel; it was dirty and smelled like fish. She wiped the water off then explored her forehead, rubbing up and down with her fingers. "What scar?"

"Think."

She rubbed back and forth, feeling a slightly curved indentation in the center of her brow. "The only thing that used to be there was a thumbnail scar from the doctor when I was born. It healed quickly. Mom told me about it."

Jack disappeared into the head and came back with a mirror that he placed in front of her. "Look."

Dead center on Sophie's forehead was what looked like a crescent moon. It was blue, illuminated by the blood pumping through her head. "I've never seen it before."

"It might help us," Jack whispered.

"Why?"

"It was on Nimue's forehead, too."

"Nimue? That explains the buckskin pants."

"You recognize her?"

"She's the only one I've ever talked to...said she was partly responsible for the burial of the ring."

"More coffee?"

"With whiskey."

Jack poured the elixir. "Yesterday afternoon a young woman appeared on the dock and informed me that I had incorrectly named my boat. Although I'd painted *Dream Weaver* on the hull, she said its reflection in the water said Avalon, and that the vessel wouldn't work for me if I didn't call her by her true name. The woman, dressed in jeans and a baggy sweatshirt with severely butchered hair, had an uncanny resemblance to Eleni Alexander."

Sophie listened and sipped, following the heat trail down her throat to her stomach, where it radiated out to her extremities.

"The woman decided she was hungry so I followed her down to the Gemini Club where she preceded to use the bathroom to change her clothes. She said it wasn't good to wear the clothes of another. She also introduced herself as Nimue. What else do you know about her?"

"When I read about her in Grandpa's journal, I remember thinking she was actually very modern: intelligent, educated, independent, a huntress. She was also supposed to have been incredibly desirable to men."

Jack looked askance. "I noticed."

"But the main thing she's known for is silencing Merlin."

"So she's the one," Jack whispered.

"Merlin wanted her...sexually. So he kept offering to teach her his secrets, if she'd just sleep with him. Nimue kept one step ahead of the game, though, learning from him but never giving in. In the end, she used his own sorcery to trap him."

"...under a rock."

"There are various stories: under a stone, in a sarcophagus, in a hawthorn bush, or a prison of glass. Nimue said they were all trapped in the forest, and that Merlin was trapped in a tree."

"Look's like she's decided to let him out." Jack looked at Sophie's ring. "I hope he's ready." He grabbed a pad of paper and drew something on it, then shoved it in front of her. "Have you ever seen that symbol?"

Sophie stared at Jack's picture then went to her duffel bag, pulled out Samuel's journal, and flipped the book open to one of his early drawings. Jack looked at an ink drawing of the interlocking circles. On the same page were sketches of circles and triangles. He fanned the pages and saw a series of other drawings and commentary.

"That's my Grandfather's journal."

"What was Samuel up to?"

"You knew my Grandfather?"

Jack sighed and continued studying the drawing. "Yea...we met."

"My Grandfather found the ring in Bride's Well in Glastonbury, England. I guess that symbol is on the cover to the other Well...the Chalice Well."

"It's the *Vesica Piscis.*"

"He found the ring in 1969."

"And when did he die?"

"1987. I was eight."

Jack flipped through the book to the back where he found Samuel's drawing of the Tree of Life growing out of the center of the *Vesica Piscis.*

"That's the symbol he had etched on his headstone," Sophie said.

"He organized it before his death?"

She leaned over and flipped the pages to Samuel's last entry. "He placed the four directions in the limbs and roots of the tree and illuminated the direction north. He drew a cross on top of the tree, connecting the four directions. Then he died."

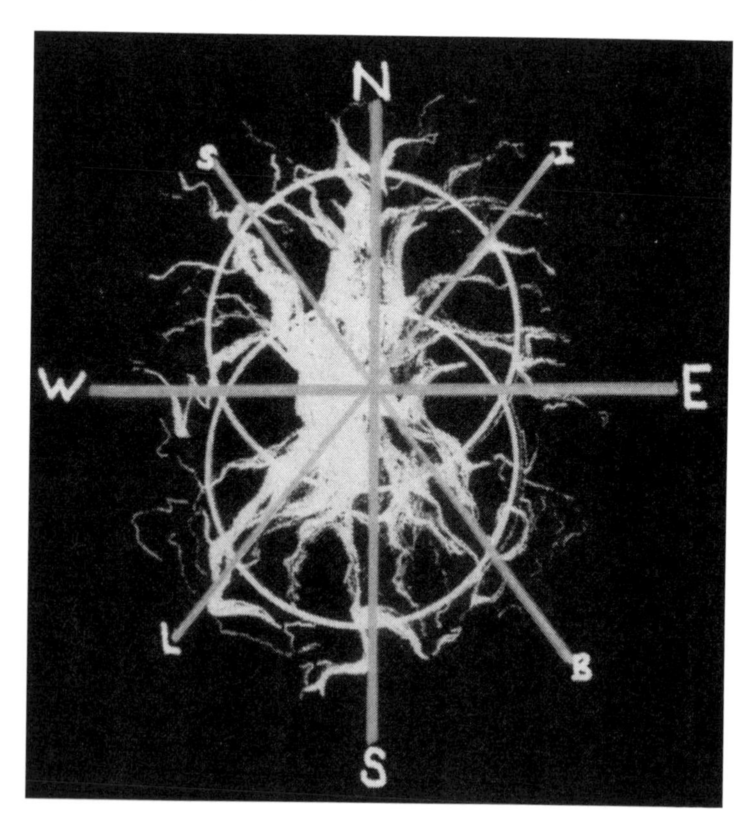

Jack turned the page. "But there are more entries."

"Those are mine."

Jack shoved back from the table and looked intently at the young woman, slight and frail with haunted eyes.

"Your entries?"

"I went north to Oregon because the only thing I had left after the earthquake was a record called "North to Alaska." It was my first spiral. Mom gave me Grandpa's journal when I left."

"The spiral in the record was a medicine wheel, pointing you north," Jack whispered.

"In my dreams, the first time I saw the interlocking circles was when I dreamt of Merlin. He drew them in the dirt, saying they represented the way to break the bonds of duality. The overlap—what you call the ***Vesica Piscis***—he called the void. That's where I was standing when I met him."

Jack studied Sophie's simple drawing of a Tree with a wizard superimposed over the trunk of the tree, all at the junction of the two circles.

"I wrote all my dreams in the back. That's when I flipped to the front and found that Grandpa had already been tracking the very same symbols."

"But you said he had this one carved on his headstone. You probably saw it there."

"It's possible. But it wouldn't explain everything else. Glastonbury is supposed to be the ancient site of Avalon. Beneath the hill there's a spring that's been bubbling since God knows when. People believe it represents the waters of life...healing waters. It was the domain of the High Priestesses, and the well cover is carved with that sign. My Grandfather believed their energy was connected to this ring. From all the things that have happened to me since the earthquake, I think he must be right."

"Nimue wore a necklace of two interlocking circles," Jack continued. "She said that the ring was yours—said you'd earned it. But the interlocking circles would only be seen when one of them was present. She said to pay attention to it, because it was the answer...and it was the question. When she passed out, the necklace disappeared."

"When my Grandfather went to England, he was trying to research his ancestors. When he was in the cemetery, he fell asleep and heard a voice that told him to dig in the mud at the edge of Bride's Well. It said there was something he needed to claim."

"As I recall, your mother's family goes back a long way in that part of the world."

Sophie nodded.

"You think your lineage is connected with the lineage of this ring?"

"I don't know. But if you read his journal you'll learn that my Grandfather had a son that died at birth. Up until then, his lineage was an unbroken line of father to son since 100 AD."

"Samuel had a son?"

"Born dead...strangled by the umbilical cord. Mom didn't even know till after he died."

Jack looked out the porthole to the gray water. "The end of a male dominated lineage...he was looking at it symbolically... that's why he put the symbol on his headstone..." His voice was barely a whisper.

"What?"

"He's analyzing the mythology as if it were a dream..."

"I don't know. I keep hoping I'll wake up and it will all have been a dream."

"That's what the Indians think." Jack turned back to her.

"What?" Sophie was tiring. Her eyes were at half-mast.

"Go to bed, Sophie."

Jack opened a drawer by the sink. It was one of those drawers filled with everything that's passed before your eyes when your brain was too muddled to allocate its destiny. He shoved the stuff to the back and found what he was looking for: a cat bell. "I'll tie this to your duffel bag in case you decide to change your clothes."

"What if you're asleep?"

"I won't be."

"But you might fall asleep. I mean you might not intend to fall asleep, but what if you do?"

"I won't."

"I'm serious, Jack. I don't want to wake up to find this boat being sucked down by an outgoing tide. You have no idea what you're dealing with here. Maybe we should call Lilli."

"You think Lilli doesn't know what's going on?"

"Well, you haven't told her anything yet."

"Lilli doesn't learn through words, Sophie. You'll be ok. I promise."

"How come everything's blurry?"

"Because you're drunk. You need to go to sleep." Jack walked over to a small desk and pulled out a cardboard box filled with books. "Your mother sent you to the right person. I've got a lot of reading to do. I also love coffee. And if it helps any, I rarely sleep at night—too much magic on the water." He grabbed a pair of glasses and sat down at the desk where he opened the box and started removing books. "Go to bed."

Sophie swaggered down the hall and collapsed onto the bunk.

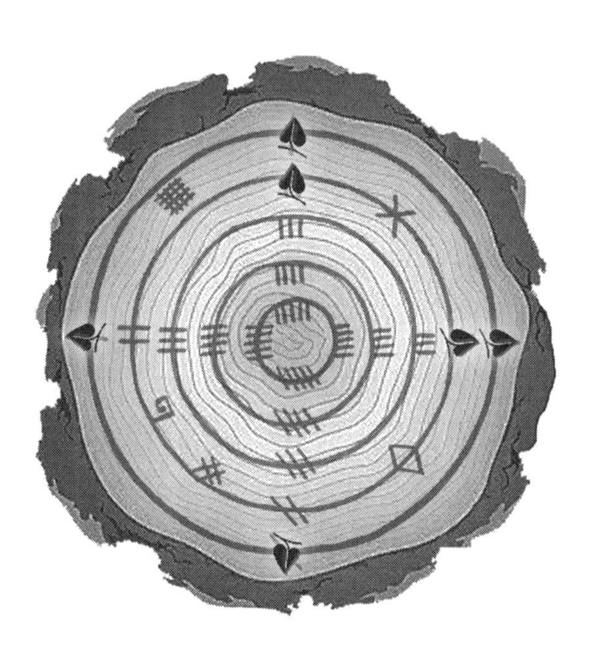

11

OAK
The Doorway

JACK'S MEDICAL BOOKS were buried in a box beneath his desk. On stormy nights, when the wind screamed down the channel, whipping the mast, he wondered why he kept them. Most likely he'd die from stepping on a rusty nail and rot in the confines of his water-born coffin, as he had no intention of ever going back to his former life. But for some reason the books had stayed. He just didn't notice them as much anymore.

Tonight, however, he raised them one by one out of their cardboard house, reading the titles as he went along. After five names, he went to the sink and took another swig of scotch, staring intently at Samuel's journal and wiping his mouth with the hem of his shirt. Lilli was right; it stunk.

He leafed through the journal, recognizing some of the symbols Samuel had notated. The circle represented the feminine—the eternal process of life. One of Samuel's circles was silver and one was gold, just like the bands of the ring. Silver was equated with the feminine and gold with the masculine. Samuel was using the circles to represent two separate worlds of thought.

The triangle was the trinity.

The number nine was written on the same page as the triangle. Mythology connected the goddess with the number nine: the trinity on three levels, just as Sophie had said. Glastonbury was like an archeological dig, only with mythic symbols. And Samuel was right...certain things kept showing up again and again through time...all on one tiny plot of land.

It wasn't as if, in the beginning, anyway, Samuel had been trying to prove anything. He just went out searching, hoping to meet his sorrow. Jack could relate to that. Only Samuel had found a magic ring. Jack couldn't even catch a fish; and here he was in a little village advertised as the salmon fishing capital of the world.

And even Jack knew that the salmon was the sacred fish of the Celtic people.

He swept his arm across the table, scattering medical books onto the floor. With his feet propped up he began to read Samuel's journal.

JOURNAL ENTRY:

Nimue: Huntress and prophetess sometimes referred to as Merlin's successor or twin. Her abilities and beauty aroused his desire, so he offered to teach her his wisdom if she would give herself to him. Nimue keeps one step ahead of the game while learning his magic, and in the end, turns it against Merlin, trapping him in a tree. She silences the enlightened man and returns the wisdom to the tree. Nimue, representing female enlightenment and equality, will enter the story and undo what she has done.

At 2:00 a.m. Jack's chin hit the table when the boat lurched from the force of a changing tide. He ricocheted back, overturning the chair, and catapulted onto the floor. With a wrench of his neck, he searched frantically for the duffel bag. Jack had fallen asleep.

The bag was right where he left it, zipped shut and secured with the cat bell. He pulled himself up, shrugged sleep out of his shoulders, and wiped saliva off his cheek. The boat rocked, causing books to slide back and forth, pages flipping open and shut. He stepped over them and glanced into the cabin, scared stiff that Sophie might be gone.

Moonlight poured through the porthole like some angelic flashlight onto her face. The room was dark except for her moon-enlightened countenance. Jack stared, transfixed, then turned and climbed the stairs to the deck outside. The boat was rocking wildly.

"What the hell's going on...tide shouldn't be shifting yet."

The moon was larger than usual and much too close to the water. He closed his eyes and rubbed leathery palms against his face, trying to wake up. When he opened them, the moon had descended farther, sitting on the edge of its reflection in the sea.

It kept dropping. One quarter, then half, then almost three quarter's of the moon immersed within the channel. As it merged with the sea, the water began to shimmer with silver nets. All across the channel the netting sparked and shifted, weaving moonlight threads closer to him.

"What the...?"

The moon was now completely immersed, its silver web skimming rapidly towards the *Avalon*. As it neared the boat, the netting shaped itself into a gown...and within the gown, a woman appeared.

"There are no earthly threads made of light, Jack Harrington."

Jack looked around, wondering if the voice was coming from the dock. "What do you mean?" he asked suspiciously.

"Where would Sophia find a gown representative of this?" She swept her hand through the water sending slivers of silver across the waves.

"The missing outfit," Jack whispered.

"It's not missing; it's just not earthly."

Jack shook his head and rubbed his eyes again. Maybe he was dreaming.

"Dreams aren't only visited when we sleep, Jack Harrington."

"Who are you?"

"I am Argante, spirit mother. Sophia has reclaimed the ring, which I must guard at all costs."

Jack watched as her form slid closer to the bow. As the figure shimmered, he noticed a crown on her head made of two interlocking circles, and beneath it, on her forehead, was the mark of an iridescent blue crescent moon.

"Sophia must not schism," she continued.

"I'm aware of that."

"She must learn to traverse different worlds successfully in order to join them. It is her only way to transformation...it is our only way."

Argante shifted into a reflection of cascading stars that glimmered against the bow of the *Avalon*, climbed the hull, and began pouring through the porthole of Sophie's cabin.

Jack scrambled down into the galley, tripping on books and ripping pages with the heels of his sneakers. He threw open the door and stared at Sophie's face, as the beam of moonlight poured across the room and into her. It poured and poured, till the room was empty of all light except for that emanating from within Sophie. Her pale skin had taken on a translucent cast, creating a halo around her head, in the center of which was the fading shadow of the two-circled crown.

"The tidal waters within are turbulent, Jack Harrington. You hold the key. Avalon must rise again."

As Jack stared, dumfounded, the vision started to fade. He turned and stumbled back through the cabin to the stairs, where he climbed topside, looking for the moon. The sky was completely black.

"No moon tonight, Black Jack! Good time for raven to fly."

He turned sharply and looked down into the water. Barely visible against the dark sea was the dull outline of Lilli's rowboat. "What are you doing out here, Lilli?"

"Delivering laundry. Ernie left a note in his pocket, reminding him of a doctor's appointment tomorrow morning. Thought I better get laundry back with note so he don't miss it."

"At 2:00 a.m.?"

"Chinese always deliver laundry early. You know that, Jack."

"You're not Chinese."

"How you know I not Chinese? Might have beautiful Chinese great, great, great, great Aunt, twice removed, on mother's side who did laundry. That's why I so good."

"You do everyone's laundry, so you can learn about them, Lilli. What they eat, how they smell. Maybe you find the smell from one person on the laundry of another. You're a snoopy Indian Sherlock Holmes and you should be ashamed of yourself."

"Indian's don't believe in shame...that white man's god. Besides, I'm doing it to help."

"And what do you smell on me, Lilli?"

"You smell like fox hiding in hole. Smell of loneliness. Lilli push fox out."

Jack shook his head.

"Besides, full moon called coyote out to sea. Might as well bring laundry."

"There's no moon tonight," said Jack, eyeing her suspiciously.

"Looks like it sunk. Lilli never wrong. Maybe I find it at the Gemini Club." Lilli rowed the oars through silky black water, gliding away from Jack. "Gotta go, Black Jack. Don't want Ernie to sleep in and miss appointment."

Jack watched as the boat's outline melted into the sea.

"I bring your laundry about noon. Ok? Maybe moon come up by then."

"Yea...noon's fine," whispered Jack, mesmerized by the shadowy frame of Lilli's hair disappearing into the water. He turned and descended into the galley.

On the table sat Samuel's journal, the page corners worn yellow from skin oils. Jack rubbed the edges, fanned the pages like a deck of cards then started to read.

JOURNAL ENTRY:

Argante: Foster mother to heroes, she provides guidance and often the ability to achieve impossible feats. Somewhat anonymous, she tends to appear as spirit, imbuing one with the mystery of life. She is the spirit mother that will enter the story and guide the ring and those connected with it.

May 4, 2001

At twelve-noon a bag of laundry flew up over the edge of Jack's boat, landing on deck. "Moon's up!"

Jack continued gazing out towards the ferryboat, lost in its watery reflection in the channel.

"Moon's not up, Lilli."

Lilli tied her rowboat to the dock. The boat was filled with laundry bags made from colored pillowcases. "Maybe we're not talking about the same moon," she replied. "Coffee ready?"

"What other moon is there?"

Lilli climbed on board, her red coyote cap pulled down snug to her head. "The one that's sleeping on your boat. I hope you behaved yourself last night, cuz that old moon can make some men real crazy."

"If you're talking about Sophie, she's asleep in the cabin."

"No, she's not."

"I've been sitting here all morning, Lilli. She's not up yet."

"She's up all right. She's in town riding a mule down Main Street. I recognized her, cuz she looks a lot like me, just uglier. Where's the coffee?"

Jack bolted to his feet. "She doesn't look anything like you, Lilli! What are you talking about?"

"You know, Jack, like sisters; she's the moon and I'm coyote. We call to each other. It's a different language. But she's a hell of a shifter man, cuz she looks like shit this morning, all bloated and dark around the eyes with a big old burlap bag on. Shit, the jackass looked prettier than her."

Jack scrambled into the galley and wasn't gone five seconds before surfacing again. "How the hell did she get off this boat? I put a bell on her duffel bag and I didn't hear a goddamn thing!" He pulled on his sneakers and grabbed a sweatshirt. "How did she get off this boat, Lilli? How did she get past me?"

Lilli stared at Jack and started talking seriously for once. "She's like me, Black Jack; she's full of magic. I smelled it the minute I went into the Gemini club. Only problem is she's not in control. If it flows in your blood, you move in and out of realities so fast you don't know where the hell you are. It's easy to be invisible. People get real sick from this shit. For all you know, that jackass could be her too."

"Does everything have to be funny to you, Lilli?"

"I'm not being funny. Whoever's inside her has a lot of faces. Some of them might have animal counterparts. If you ask me, the old lady and the mule are connected. But what would I know?" Lilli turned her red cap backwards on her head then winked at Jack. "Think I'll let coyote chase his tail."

Jack threw his sweatshirt over his head and scrambled off the boat. "I've got to go get her."

Lilli rocked back and forth as the boat rolled. "Jack."

"What?"

"I can help, you know."

Jack stopped but didn't look back.

"My truck is in the parking lot."

"What's it doing there?"

"I left it there last night. Thought you might be needing me."

Jack turned around and looked up at her. How could someone so attractive be such a pain in the ass? "Let's go," he muttered.

"Where do you think she's going?" Jack's voice was scratchy as a rasp.

"Well, I don't think she's going shopping. Although from what I've seen so far, she probably should."

"How did you know the moon would be up at noon?"

"Animal instinct. Besides, right now she's only part of the moon. Haven't you seen it yet?"

"What?"

"Blue crescent moon on her forehead."

"I saw it. I saw it at the Gemini club and then again yesterday, when she was angry. The blood flow must have illuminated it."

"Blood flow, bullshit. When the energy shifts, the moon appears. She wasn't angry, she was wavering, losing control, but she came back, and it subsided. When you see the crescent moon it's a sign. Kind of like the TV telling you a new program's about to start."

"Shit."

"Lots of crescent moons means full moon divided." Lilli grabbed her hat and turned it around so it was facing front. "Out there!" She pointed past Jack towards the shipping docks. The marshland around them was thick with tall grass that swayed with the tides. The ground was nothing but ocean soup. That's what they all called it, just a bog of mud and silt and seaweed that looked solid but would bury you to your waist and higher depending on the tide. "Dumb ass is headed towards the soup."

"She's not dumb, Lilli."

"The mule's the jackass! He's trying to head out towards the ocean, that's what's calling to her." Lilli turned sharply and drove her truck off road into the adjoining field, while Jack stared, dumbfounded, at the animal's rider.

"That can't be her," he whispered. The woman on the mule looked fat and old. Half her face sagged as if she'd had a stroke, and her head looked like a matted bird's nest.

"Major heavy duty energy in that one, Jack. Better do your homework."

Jack continued to stare as the truck screeched to a stop. He heard Lilli's door open and close and reached to open his but was startled by a low growling sound by the rear tire. He looked through the open window and into the bloodshot eyes of a coyote. Jack scrambled to roll the window up then watched, as the animal sidled across the field towards the mule.

The coyote crouched low, slinking its way furtively in and out of the marshy weeds. The mule's ears rotated back, then it stopped in its tracks and the woman swiveled her head left then right. The coyote moved, as if herding sheep, pushing the mule, till it turned and headed back towards land. They were closer to the truck now, and Jack could see clearly what appeared to be a very ugly transformation. The woman wore slovenly horsehair pants and heavy boots with what looked like a burlap shirt.

The mule, spooked by the coyote, picked up speed. It ran, slipped in the mud, coming down hard on its rear haunches, throwing Sophie backwards. It looked like her head hit the ground first, snapping her like a jack knife. Jack hit the ground running, hoping she wasn't dead.

The mule lay on its side, heaving from exertion. His belly was distended, saturated with flies and sweat. Sophie's body was tangled in the reeds, her arms and legs askew as a broken doll.

Jack ran over but stopped short, appalled at her hideous appearance; she was even worse close up. It wasn't just the clothing—the horsehair fibers thick with grease and dirt. It was Sophie herself. An ugly pall had draped over her skin, and her eyes were tinged yellow. She stared at him, not moving.

"Did you think you could escape us so easily, Jack Harrington?"

Jack stumbled back. Her voice was old and withered, even mocking. She opened her mouth to smile, stretching taught lips wide to expose a single tooth, decayed and brown. A derisive laugh erupted from her belly. It took everything Jack had in him not to turn away.

"From whom am I escaping, Lady?"

"Ahhh..." she breathed out, *"...chivalrous. It always helps. At least it carries the illusion of such."* She smiled and continued eyeing Jack up and down. Jack looked past her and saw that the mule had disappeared.

"*Fast...isn't he*?" she whispered.

"So it would appear."

"Appear, disappear, reappear...it's all so very interesting, don't you agree?"

Jack noticed that she had a mantle embroidered with turtledoves draped around her shoulders and that she wore a crown of interlocking circles and her brow was marked with a blue crescent moon.

"Illusion is everywhere, Jack...or hadn't you noticed."

Jack scanned her body, concerned that Sophie might have broken something. "Do you have a name, lady?"

"I have many names, and I have no name. It depends on how you wish to view me. I am surprised, however, that you would ask such a question. Have you really forgotten, Jack? Have you turned away from your quest and chosen blind solitude instead?"

Jack could feel her eyes piercing through him...challenging him...questioning his decision to live life out in peaceful anonymity.

"Your mother didn't abandon the quest, Jack. She carried the lantern to the very end."

Jack staggered back at the mention of his mother. The reed tangled round his foot, and he slid backwards out of his shoe, stepping barefoot into the slimy mud. "What do you know of my mother?"

The woman's eyes closed, revealing purple veins mapping a network across her lids. She raised her hand and beckoned Jack to come closer. He stepped forward. She motioned again, and again, till Jack was standing at her side.

Her eyes opened and she raised her hand, whispering for him to kneel. Jack's face was blanched of any seaworthy tan; he was white as a ghost. Timidly, he lowered down on one knee. "What is it, Lady?"

She opened her mouth and exhaled a great breath of air into Jack's face. It was sweet and smelled like a perfume of roses. Jack's nostrils flared as he breathed in the fragrance.

"Look past the illusions, Jack Harrington...it is the only way."

Her voice had lost its ancient cackle. It was softer, kind, even feminine. Jack closed his eyes, haunted by the velvet of her voice and the perfume of roses. When he opened them, she was gone. The transformation faded, as if the illusion had hung on the very bones, and beneath the glamour was the frail form of Sophie.

Out in the field, Lilli's truck started up. It rolled across the grass and eased to a stop. Jack raised his head slightly and saw Lilli sitting in the driver's seat, free of coyote's cap, wearing very dark sunglasses. He looked away. He'd learned the hard way about the sunglasses.

"Get her in the truck, Jack."

They drove in silence along the waterfront towards the marina with Sophie slumped between them like before, head resting on Jack's shoulder. "Do you think she's hurt?" He whispered.

"If you mean physically, no."

"She stinks."

"Marsh water."

"Maybe when we get to the boat, you can get her out of these things."

"You need to leave them on."

Jack was disturbed. He couldn't get the image of the old woman out of his mind. Sophie looked like a dead bird wrapped in a burlap rice bag. Her boots and hands were covered with mud, as was the back of her head. "Maybe you should make sure she hasn't damaged her neck or something. She hit the ground pretty hard. You're good at that stuff, Lilli."

"I'm so good, I know she doesn't need it, and you're trying to protect her from seeing herself. Can't do that, Jack."

"Did you see her, Lilli?"

Lilli pulled into the Marina lot and stopped. "She needs a trail...needs to see where she's been."

"I asked if you saw her," he whispered.

"Yea…I saw her. The Indians would call her Crazy woman—the bearer of wisdom, enlightenment."

"She smelled like roses."

Lilli stared at Jack, his skin white as chalk. "I can help you with the shape shifting, Jack; it's the moon ladies that are killing her. Too many of them."

"Moon ladies?"

"How many, Jack? Who are they? What's their energy and why are they here? You're gonna have to do your homework, cuz she's already skin and bones."

"There're nine of them, the nine High Priestesses of Avalon."

"Priestesses?"

Jack stared down the dock. "Ernie's up," he said.

"I pinned his note on the outside of the laundry bag. Must've worked. I'll go distract him while you carry her down." Lilli reached over and handed something to Jack. "Take this." Her hand opened up and a wad of mud and grass dropped into Jack's. The skin around her nails had tiny cracks with small tufts of animal hair coming out of them.

"What for?"

"Put it in a pan on the stove with sea water in it and keep it on low. It'll make the boat smell a little like the marsh."

"What's the point?"

"She has to start remembering. Don't go telling her what happened. Coax her. Take her for a walk to see Harry Swanson's mules. Are you keeping a list of the moon ladies?"

"Three so far."

"Six to go." Lilli watched Ernie climb into the galley and come back with a cup of coffee. "Break it down to three," she said.

"What do you mean?"

"Ernie drinks too much coffee."

"What do you mean, Lilli!"

"Nine, Jack! Three times three! Break it down. There must be something similar in each group. It's like a prism. It'll make it easier if there are only three to understand, instead of nine."

Ernie sat on the deck of his boat and pulled a candy bar out of his pocket. "That's why his clothes smell sweet," Lilli continued.

"Candy bars?"

"No. Diabetes. I can smell it on his clothes."

Jack sighed deeply and looked down at Sophie. Lilli reached under the seat and pulled out a couple packages of Twinkies. "Give her one of these when she wakes up, providing she doesn't puke too much."

"After what you just said about Ernie?"

"Different problem. You don't want to be particular when you shape shift. She needs calories but not too much information in her food. Her body's already working too hard. Those little snowball jobbies with all the pink flakes are good, too."

"Didn't think they made those anymore."

"She needs something else, too. I'll have to make it up and bring it over later." Lilli opened her door and got out. "The smell of the marsh water might keep her from puking. You're gonna need to weave one world into the next, Jack. Do something in your real time that honors what happened in the dreamtime. It's a thread. The marsh water is a thread. You teach her how to knit. You should understand that, considering your boat is called *Dream Weaver*."

"That's precisely why my boat's now called the ***Avalon***."

Lilli waved as she turned to go, and Jack noticed the hair on her fingers had disappeared. "Lilli?"

She glanced back. The sunglasses were gone, and her eyes were clear as a bell.

"Thanks," he whispered.

Lilli winked then trotted down the dock waving her arms at Ernie. Jack watched as she swung easily onto the boat and gestured for a cup of coffee, opening her package of Twinkies as they talked. When the two of them disappeared down below, Jack swung Sophie over his shoulder and walked quickly to the *Avalon*, the wad of muddy grass clenched tightly in his fist.

After tucking her into the bunk and heating the marshy water on the stove, Jack stared down at the young woman who, in two days, had turned his world inside out. The side of her face that had sagged was yellow and slightly blue, as if bruised from inside. He remembered reading about schizophrenics that had to have different sets of eyeglasses for each personality. The vision actually shifted when the energy did. Some personalities had illnesses, like diabetes, while others didn't, all within the same body. The energy inhabiting the system had the power to shift many things. He walked back to the galley and checked the pot on the stove. It stunk. But if it kept her from retching, who the hell cared?

Jack's hair had started turning gray last year. He rubbed his weathered palms through it and dropped onto the galley bench, taking a sideways glance at Samuel's journal sitting on the desk next to an old medical book. He stared at one then the other, went to the sink, grabbed the scotch, and took a long drink. Then he sat down and opened Samuel's journal and continued to read.

JOURNAL ENTRY:

Kundry: Dark woman of knowledge: ugly, prophetic, and the bearer of wisdom, often seen with a mule. She can shift her appearance to that of beauty when desired. Her wisdom is equated with that of the Grail, and her purpose to challenge awakenings. Kundry will enter the story and question those who seek answers.

Jack was startled out of his reverie when the boat lurched starboard. Someone had climbed on board.

"Here it is," Lilli called out.

"What?"

"That stuff I told you about. It'll help her. It stinks in here."

"What is it?"

"You sure you want to know?"

"I'm not giving her any powder in a zip lock bag if I don't know what it is, Lilli."

"Ok. Frogs eyes, lizard tail, and ground up salmon nuts."

"Salmon don't have nuts."

Lilli stared at Jack. "It's tough being white, isn't it, Jack?"

"I thought you said I was Black Jack."

"Yea, but you don't let him talk too much. They're hazel nuts. Haven't you ever heard of them?"

"It rings a bell."

"I thought you cared about the Dream Weavers."

"I do."

"But you don't know about the hazel nut."

"I told you it rings a bell! Perhaps you'd like to refresh my memory!"

Lilli made a disgusted grunt and turned to watch the seagulls.

"Look, Lilli, the medical community shut me down because I resisted their shock therapy and prescription medications. It sickened me that we were so far afoot we couldn't track the map these people were walking. I really want to help Sophie, but I walked away from that world, and now my mind needs refreshing. So be my guest!"

She crooked her neck and looked back. "These nine priestesses walk a Celtic map. Their story has its own medicine. It's buried in the puzzles they're laying at your feet. I'm not going to gather corn pollen and have Sophie do a painting, when that's not the language running in her blood."

"She's of Celtic blood," he whispered.

"That makes it stronger. It's in her genes. At the restaurant she had a shirt on with faded drawings. They were almost washed away, but I could see one was a triple spiral. The medicine has to match the map."

"Go on."

"These Celts believe that all wisdom is in the hazel nut. You can't eat it directly, though, because there's too much information and it'll blow your brains out. So they wait till it drops in the river and the salmon eats it. And then, they eat the salmon. The salmon digests and transforms the wisdom, so it doesn't blow their brains out when they eat him. I collect his nuts."

"You just said they were hazel nuts."

"Well, they were at one time. Just cuz they changed form doesn't change what they are. Why you having so much trouble with this shit, Jack?"

"Salmon don't have nuts, Lilli!"

"They do after they eat the hazel nut, not before...very special salmon, Jack, not easy to find." Lilli's eyes twinkled.

"What do you do, Lilli, sit by the side of the river and, when they swim by, bare your breasts to see if you can attract them like moths to a flame?"

Lilli lowered her chin and glared at Jack from beneath hooded eyes. "You still don't get it, do you?"

"What?"

"Why she entered your life."

"She's the daughter of an old friend."

"She's here to break you down so far, you'll forget your damn pretensions and start being who you really are. Until then, you're no help to her at all. You think she looks bad now? In a week, you'll look back and remember her as the picture of health." Lilli held the bag of powder out to Jack. "Mix a table-spoon of this in a glass of water, and make her drink it once a day. It tastes like crap and she won't want it. But she won't want it for more reasons than that. Something in her is fighting this. She says she wants help, but the truth is she's afraid of who she really is. Maybe she's a lot like you."

Jack looked at the powder. "Maybe I should take it too, then."

"Can't."

"Why?"

"You can only take it if you menstruate." Lilli grinned.

"Well, what have you got for me, then?"

"Everything that's happening is for you, Jack. Honor it. It'll transform you...might even grow salmon nuts."

"Does that mean you'll bare your breasts at me?"

Lilli tossed the bag in the air and turned a pirouette off the boat while Jack dove to catch the bag. "Damn you, Lilli! It almost fell in the water!"

"I'd be careful with these moon ladies, Jack," she called out. "It's a good thing you renamed your boat...might've sunk otherwise."

Jack gripped the zip lock bag and stumbled down the steps to the galley, where he tossed it on the table next to the journal then collapsed on the bench. "Damn woman." He pressed the bottle of scotch to his lips and leaned back, closing his eyes, as amber liquid trickled down the back of his throat. When he opened his eyes, Sophie was standing next to the table.

"Shit, Sophie!"

Jack shoved the bench back, crashing his head into the cupboard behind him. The cabinet flipped open, and an old ceramic coffee pot fell out, shattering a piece onto the floor. The chip that landed by his foot was painted with a dove. Sophie squatted down and picked it up.

She was still in the same clothes and, for a moment, Jack wondered, then looked at her forehead; there was no crescent moon. The side of her face was still bruised, but the skin had lost its bloat, sucking instead to the crevices of her cheekbone. Her eyes were large saucers, like one of those Keane paintings, and her skin had the waxy look of someone in a coffin. She looked down at the dove in her hand. "I didn't get sick."

Jack draped a worn blanket across her shoulders, sat her down, and lit the stove beneath the kettle. Sophie's eyes followed his movements like a butterfly following its shadow. When he reached for the bag of powder, Sophie saw the journal.

"You're reading it." Sophie turned the page.

Jack glanced at the open book. In the center of the page was a large drawing of a record with the title "North to Alaska," and an arrow pointing north.

"Yea."

"It's a medicine wheel, but it's making me sick."

The kettle whistled and Jack spun, half out of his skin. He grabbed the kettle and knocked off the lid, releasing steam, burning his hand. The pot dropped, boiling water cascaded onto the counter and a cup shattered into the sink.

"Did you find the bridle," asked Sophie.

"What?"

Jack mopped the mess with a fishy rag and turned to look at her. There may not have been a crescent moon, but she definitely wasn't present. "What do you mean by a bridle, Sophie?"

Sophie opened her hand, exposing the scar in her right palm and placed the ceramic dove on top of the scar. "The animal must be bridled."

Jack grabbed the powder and spooned some into a cup with warm water. "Drink this."

"Why?"

He stared down at her, a fragile bag of bones, yellow skin, and defiant eyes. His mind was a storm of scrambled words and ideas that might lend her some tiny reason to go against this unrelenting drive for self-preservation.

"Because, Sophie, it will help us bridle the mule."

Her eyes flew open, and her head swiveled to the left, reminding Jack of her movements when riding the mule. She stared up at him and, when their eyes locked, chills rocketed up his spine. She dropped the dove onto the medicine wheel, grabbed the cup and drank, her eyes never wavering from Jack. When the cup was drained, she turned and walked back to the bunk, lay down, closed her eyes, and descended into sleep.

Jack stared at the dove resting on the drawing of the record with the arrow that pointed north then grabbed a spiral notebook and a pen. On the left side of the page he started a list of the images that were emerging. The triple spiral, interlocking circles, triangle, and turtledove were added to the pendant, crown, and cup, all part of an ancient language surfacing in Sophie's mind. He picked up Samuel's journal and looked for clues.

JOURNAL ENTRY:

Bridle: Symbolic of control and direction: horse or mule without bridle emblematic of land without good leadership. A woman without a bridle is akin to a nag who becomes ugly in her need to force the desired outcome, the recognition of spirit. The priestesses' story is about the infusion of spirit into matter. Without it, we live in a wasteland, our spiritual destiny unharnessed. The Bridle will enter the story when the need for direction and focus is great.

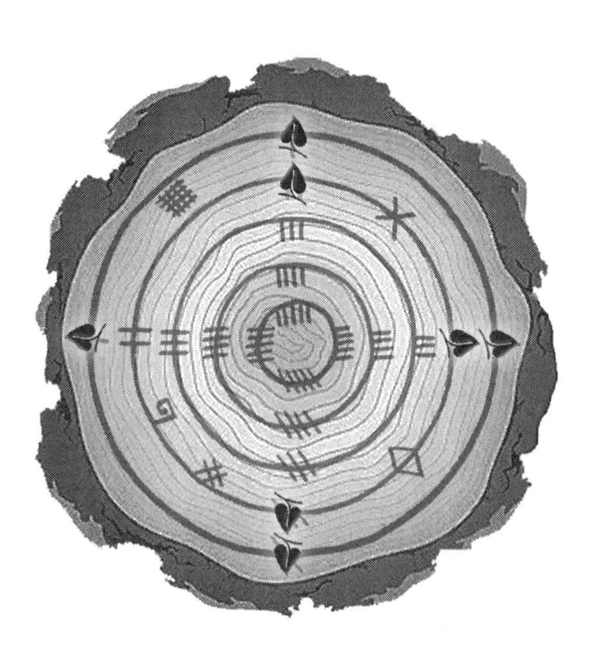

IVY

Resurrection

THE WATERS OF Campbell River spill down from the snow capped mountains above Strathcona Park. The snowmelt filters into crevices, sinking deep into the earth, where it follows subterranean chambers downhill, surfacing again in lakes and streams and carving deep pools out of granite boulders with its endless, unforgiving wash of time. Like giant stone bowls, the granite pools ladle crystalline liquid down the mountain, till it reaches the sea, where its icy blue crashes into salty green. It is here that the salmon thrive.

Nine pools, nine stone bowls, create the tributary known as Campbell River. The second bowl up from the sea is one of the deepest, and on its forested bank sits a diminutive shack comprised of corrugated metal and pitted siding. Someone cared enough to fill in the cracks that blow winter winds inside, and install a door roughly carved with totem images. The door-knob is lacquer red, and there's a small portico made from two-by-fours supporting a curved expanse of wood, which came from the side of an old boat hauled up from the sea and dried.

Light filters through windows, and sunflower cotton drapes, cascading patterns of saffron across the floor, where it lands on a tattered tweed couch stacked with colored pillowcases stuffed with laundry. The raw planked floor is swept clean and draped with an animal skin rug. Not just one skin, but bits and pieces from rabbits and bear and raccoon and fox and coyote and wildcat and god only knows what else, painstakingly stitched together, embracing one unified kingdom.

Lying on top of it was Lilli.

She held the red coyote cap in one hand and a book in the other. Weathered tree limbs spanned the ceiling, reminiscent of rough-hewn parlor beams; but these beams were real. Still encased in bark and dried sap they were anchored in place with torn fabric strapping nailed to the ceiling—four feet apart for aesthetics. Fishing line spiraled up and down each limb, and every two feet at the downward junction was a salmon hook—and from each hook hung a cap.

Lilli closed her eyes and tossed her coyote cap into the air. It fluttered towards the ceiling, righted itself, billowed out and attached to the one remaining hook. Standing effortlessly, she closed the book, pivoted, un-cinched a laundry bag, reached in and pulled out a phone just as it began to ring.

"Hi, Jack."

Silence filled the line.

"Jack?"

"How'd you know it was me?"

"It's your phone."

"It's not my phone anymore. I gave it to you."

"You gave it to me so you could call me."

"Doesn't anyone else call you?"

"No one else knows I have a phone."

Jack remained silent for a moment. "I need help, Lilli."

"Is she awake?"

"She didn't vomit."

Lilli stared up at all the animal caps staring down at her. Each had a name printed across the beak. There was porcupine, eagle, hawk, elk, deer, bear, snake, skunk, and more. Only one was missing: Raven. Raven had a purpose and had to come down. "That's a good sign, Jack."

"She wasn't completely here though...said we needed a bridle...wanted to know where the bridle was. She seemed upset about it. That's how I got her to drink your stuff."

Lilli walked back and forth beneath the caps, reaching up and feathering the beaks with her fingertips.

"I told her that drinking it would help us find the bridle. I don't know why I said that, but it worked. She drank it all and went back to sleep."

"You said it because it's true."

"Samuel's journal says the bridle is symbolic of harnessing the energy."

"He's right. It's symbolic, Jack."

"What do you mean?"

"She knows down deep that she needs to harness the energy...that's what the bridle's all about. It's not about the mule."

Jack listened.

"It's like wild horses stampeding; someone needs to reign them in." Lilli stared up at porcupine again.

"Can you come over?" Jack's voice was deep in his belly.

"You lonely?"

"I've got to read this journal. There's too much information in it. Samuel spent eighteen years researching something before he died; and where he left off, she continued. She's written everything in it...her dreams, the ring, the voices, even this underworld she says she traveled to. I need to know what's happened to her, Lilli."

"You want me to read to you?"

"Shit no, I can read! I want you to come and stay with her, so I can go somewhere for a few hours and read this damn thing uninterrupted! Every time I turn around, there's a seductress or a hag or a moonlight sonata staring at me! Just come and stay on the boat for a few hours. I'll go over to the coffee shop and read; they're open till midnight."

"She wasn't the seductress."

"That outfit looked pretty damn seductive to me."

"The chick in the Gemini Club was a huntress, Jack. She's a warrior, knowledgeable about animals and plants and probably the stars at night. She had on leather shoes and had an animal pouch hanging from her belt. Didn't you notice any of that?"

"Of course I noticed! I also happen to know who she was and, believe me, seduction is definitely part of the package."

"Don't make her into what she isn't. Her energy is strong... probably meet you as an equal. She'll meet you with her mind. Hell, she'll probably teach you a few things. She was the first to appear to you, so she's probably the guardian of the doorway. Her energy is wildly different than the seductress. The seductress embraces you with her thighs...she enlightens you with love. You haven't seen her yet."

"Great. I can hardly wait."

Lilli laughed quietly into the phone. "What's the matter, Jack? Scared?"

Jack grunted.

"Try to look at her like a dream, Jack. She's parading different energies; they represent something. She's a myth in the making."

"She's the daughter of someone I care about. I'm not particularly interested in seeing her as a seductress. Where are you learning all this stuff anyway?"

"I'm Indian. We grow up with it."

"I'm talking about the Celtic stuff, Lilli! Where are you getting your information?"

"Ernie's old girl friend wore T-shirts with Celtic knots screen printed on them. They smelled funny, like incense: sage, like the Indians use."

"You did her laundry?"

"Her stuff was in with Ernie's; you couldn't help but smell it."

"And..."

"She wore rings on every finger, more knot work, with crystal stones; used to leave them in her pockets."

"So how does all this help?"

"I asked Ernie where she got her things. That's all. There's a little store tucked behind the teahouse over by the theatre—lots of junk. But the owner likes Celtic stuff and she has books. I've been reading. You need help, Jack."

"I'm well aware that I need help. That's why I've got to read this journal. You could help me out by coming over."

Lilli tickled porcupine's cap. It quivered, causing a reverberation of the fishing line down the branch. She watched as all the caps wiggled in response till it landed on coyote. He lost his fragile footing and floated slowly to the ground. "Trust," she murmured.

"Lilli did you hear anything I said?"

Lilli picked up coyote, slipping him onto her head. "I'll be over in an hour."

When Lilli arrived the sun was setting. The lanterns on the boats flickered on and off in the eternal effort to hold the night at bay. She tied her boat to the dock.

"Hi, Jack!"

Jack looked up, startled. "Why'd you bring your boat?"

"Thought you might want to take it up to Sam's; it's faster than walking."

"What've you done? Put toads under the seat?"

"Just being nice...thought it'd be safer taking the boat at midnight than walking back."

Jack stared past her at the ferry pulling out for Quadra. "You're right, actually. Thanks. She's still asleep. If anything weird happens, call the café. What the hell...everything's weird; you know what I mean." Jack jumped onto the dock with Samuel's journal under his arm. "They close at midnight. I can't imagine finishing anytime sooner."

He settled into a booth at the rear of Sam's café, ordered a thermos of coffee, and asked the waitress to make sure he was left alone till closing time. After pouring a cup, he turned to the back of the journal, Sophie's part, and began to read.

SOPHIE'S DREAM:

The Tree of Life spans all dimensions; it can be anywhere or nowhere. What you find depends on where you are when you get there and whom you followed to arrive.

The Tree is filled with the songs of a million and one birds, each song embracing the wisdom of one particular branch from one particular domain of the Tree. The songs can be heard in your dreams. It is, however, the rare dreamer that chooses to follow the song; and rarer still is the dreamer who awakens and remembers.

However, there is one bird whose velvet wings carry him equally through all domains. Clear of all reflection, it is the Raven who holds within him a tiny piece of the void.

Jack's eyelids fluttered and his head dropped forward. He forced his body upright, shrugging shoulders and rotating his neck to get the blood in his brain. He hadn't even read one whole page and could barely keep his eyes open. He rubbed his palms into the hollow of his eyes, hoping to unglue the lids, and then he began again. When he looked down, all the words were backwards.

Ylno eht nevaR swonk woh ot evaew smaerd morf eht eerT fo efiL.

His head and shoulders cascaded down, and his arms splayed out across the table; his face landed gently on the open book where he immediately passed out. His jaw slackened, jutting his chin forward and leaving his mouth agape...just wide enough for Black Jack, the Raven, to take flight.

The predawn sky was a thick tangle of warped branches. Misshapen, gnarled wood fractured the heavens like capillaries in a body. A mist hung and twisted its way in, out, and around, forming soft sheets of gauzy fabric, now thick, now thin.

The raven extended blackened wings and rose up, maneuvering a pathway through the branches, penetrating veil after veil of diaphanous mist, till he reached the trunk of the old tree. He tucked his wings and glided down to land on the cracked bark of an ancient limb, looking down the massive trunk to the earth where lay a young woman with long auburn hair.

The raven cocked his head and listened, as the wind began to whip its way down the spine of the tree. It was a cold wind—cold as ice. The bird shrugged itself into a ball and hung on to the branch, as ice crystals and frozen leaves scattered down from above. It was the kind of wind that blows in the dead of winter when it's cold and the trees crackle and crisp leaves scuttle across the ground like scattering rats, the kind of wind that makes your hair curl.

The young woman below bolted upright and stared at the tree, having heard the whisperings of the wind. "Help me," the wind had cried.

Tears spilled from her eyes. "Help who?" she whispered, not knowing to whom she spoke.

"Listen to the tree," the cold wind blew. "It is he that is wounded. It is he who can no longer heal himself."

The woman stood and backed away, tripping over roots that rose out of the ground like giant gnarled knuckles, veins popping through cracked bark. Fear blanched her face, and she turned to run.

The raven's claws dug deep into the branch of the tree, but it began to shake and he fluttered to the ground. The tree shimmered and shifted and shrunk. All the ancient misshapen wood from branches, roots, and trunk shriveled down, smaller and smaller. Its cracking bark began to resemble skin, and fingers grew out of branches with arthritic bends, transforming itself into one lone diminutive figure. The woman turned her back to the tree and cried out, "Where am I?"

"Why, you are in the void, Sophie."

Sophie turned around slowly and saw that the tree was gone, replaced by the figure of a man that could only be described as a wizard. The man was small of stature, with a long white beard and hair and was draped in robes that bore the mark of faded opulence: their blue once brighter and golden threads no longer sparkling with the touch of sun or moon. He wore odd little slippers that curled up at the toes. The woman looked at the slippers

and wondered why someone who lived in the forest would wear brocade slippers.

"I am not affected by the same elements of wear as those more time-sensitive beings," he said in response to her thought.

She stared down at the feet standing lightly on the swollen earth, where the tree had been. "Are you Merlin?"

"If it will help you, I will be Merlin." The wizard clutched his arm to his side as if in pain. "Thank you for coming," he continued. "Although I must say, I never thought it would take this long."

"Am I dreaming?"

"No, Sophie Alexander, this is not a dream."

Merlin reached down and grabbed a stick, then swept the earth at his feet clean with his slipper. The raven sidled closer, where he watched Merlin use the stick to draw two interlocking circles in the dirt. "You have merely returned home. Whether you choose to stay remains a mystery." Merlin grasped at his side and winced. His skin, sallow with age, bled color, and his pale eyes receded.

"I don't understand," whispered Sophie.

"I know. The main thing though is that it's not too late. That would have been my greatest sorrow." He walked over to a tree and rested on the ground, his back against the trunk. "We have much work to do, you and I."

Sophie walked over to the drawing in the dirt of the two interlocking circles. "What is this?"

"In the world of duality, Sophie, there is always a mirror...thus, two worlds, two circles. It is the overlap of these worlds that is the place of mystery, where the image and the mirror become one. You have achieved consciousness in the realm where ideas form to create matter. Everything may look the same, but I assure you it is not."

Sophie stared at Merlin. He seemed to be shrinking before her very eyes.

"Yes, Sophie...I am dying."

"How can you die? I thought you were a wizard."

Merlin shook his head back and forth in sorrow. "Is it true Sophie? Have you truly forgotten?" Tears spilled down his cheeks, causing Sophie to stumble backwards in alarm. "Look into the forest," he whispered.

Doubled over in pain, his left arm held closely to his side, Merlin raised his right hand and swept it through the air, sending sparks of light in the direction of the forest. "Watch," he whispered.

The trees in front of Sophie began to shimmer. They broke into patterns of light and dark that scattered and shifted like a television screen gone awry, taking on a new form. Sophie watched as the forest disappeared, and the image of a small lawn bordered by a brick terrace appeared. To the left was the edge of a house. A screen door opened and a small girl about the age of eight came out and walked briskly across the lawn. Her cheeks were flushed and her mouth set in a tight line of determination. In her hand was a green velvet bag.

"Stop it," Sophie whispered.

Merlin stared through pale eyes.

"Turn it off," she continued.

"It's not a television, Sophie. It won't just go away."

The child was digging at the trunk of a tree with a pocketknife.

"Why are you showing me this?"

Merlin's eyes were pinched in sorrow. He watched the scene playing out before them then waved his arm through the air in an arc. The image faded back into the forest.

"The burial of the ring was a most grievous act, Sophie Alexander."

"I didn't...bury...anything! It was just a dream."

"The level of consciousness matters not, Sophie. It occurred within you, and thus it is so."

"The lady in the forest said it was her fault."

Merlin became deathly still. His head tilted back, and his eyelids drifted down, leaving the tiniest of slits through which he peered intently at the girl.

"What lady?"

"She said her name was Nimue."

Nothing moved...not the wispy strands of beard clinging to the edges of his thin lips, nor the brittle leaves beneath his brocade slippers; even the ebony tips of the raven's feathers acquiesced. "Nimue," he whispered. "And so the story begins...and they can't remember from whence it comes." He dropped his head and closed his eyes. "The ring is sacred, Sophie Alexander. You should have known. But we have all been silent far too long, and so, you turned away from, and buried, what was rightfully yours."

"She's the one that buried it. She told me."

Merlin's head hung in sorrow. "Yes. It is true. And there are reasons beyond your understanding. But what we are speaking of has a life of its own, Sophie, and it is destined to return. You see...you are afraid of the power within the ring...afraid of whether you can truly carry it in the light. There was a time, Sophie Alexander, when you were the abuser of that which is sacred. Our silence may have helped create that incarnation, but now it must be transformed. You must overcome your fear and face that which threatens your ability to wield this power wisely. You are our destiny, yet we are dying because of your neglect. If you are destined to be the bearer of that which is sacred, you must stand at the altar."

"And just what is it I'm supposed to do?"

"You must reclaim the ring. There is a battle being waged, Sophie Alexander, and the stone is beseeching you, crying out for the transformation, whose time has come. Power, trapped in the bowels of a decaying tree, wisdom trapped in the mind of a decaying wizard, must manifest into the light, or it will be drained back down into the bowels of hell and the Dark Ages will be upon us, again!"

The raven watched her eyes fill with terror.

"Your battle has arrived, Sophie Alexander. The time has come."

As Merlin talked, his eyes turned starry white, and light emanated from his mane of hair. He extended his arms out wide, fingers spread, and light shot out from the tips. Everything around him started to shimmer, and with the deep resonating voice of God, Merlin cried out:

"Sophie Alexander Henri Dumont, Awaken! Descendant of ancients and weaver of light, reclaim the ring before it is too late!" Merlin shattered open as a bolt of lightning ruptured his side. The air cracked with electricity, leaving the image of the ancient tree hanging in the sky. The raven fluttered off to a dark corner, where he watched in sadness as Sophie crumpled to the ground and wept herself to sleep.

Lilli sat on the bow of Jack's boat watching evening fade into the sea. The marina was thick with a corrosion of working vessels, peeled paint, and rusted hulls. The water's surface had a fine shimmer of oil, and it pushed the floating debris to the corners of the piers, collecting stuff like dust in hallways. She had left the lights off in the galley. Lilli wouldn't need a cat bell or the sound of shuffling feet to know when Sophie had awakened.

She flipped her cap off and looked at the name. Coyote had become Lilli's second breath. The Indian fathers had seen it in her as a child: the one who sees truth, forcing chaos and disruption to break a pattern, open a doorway. Lilli had always been able to see beyond the confines of normal reality. It wasn't that she thought about it; it just happened.

She twirled coyote's cap on her finger—coyote, the trickster. He'd chase his tail, catch it, and eat half his body before realizing he was almost gone. He played pranks and twisted the world into shapes you never knew before—made you wonder if you were seeing things—made you think different, act different. Coyote forced outcomes. He was funny and he was painful. And most of the time, he was good for you, unless you tried to resist and nail life to the ground. When that happened, it made coyote sad, because life wasn't supposed to be cast in concrete. A person could drown if they were concrete.

At 11:00 p.m., Lilli stood up, stretched, and then descended the galley steps through dim light. In the middle of the room loomed a shadowy figure in black leather, with leather boots, black leather pants split up the sides from ankle to knee, a shimmering black shirt that reflected light, and a long, lean leather coat fringed with feathers around the collar. Her hair was glossed down beneath a black cap, anchored tightly to her skull. On her forehead was the sign of the blue crescent moon, and around her neck the pendant of interlocking circles. She had a string of Christmas lights in her hand.

"They say I was sister, but I was fated as bride."

Lilli looked at the pendant around her neck, noticing that it seemed to strain at her throat. Sophie's face had become chiseled. The jaw was strong and jutted forward, ready to command. Her eyes were dark brown and snapped with intelligence, and they were focused on Lilli.

Lilli stepped back, instinct telling her that the challenger had arrived. The woman marched up the steps, boots clicking staccato commands into the night air. Lilli watched as she began to string the lights on Jack's boat.

"I must begin to light the way."

Lightning rods galvanized Sophie's frame, pressing sinew up against leather-clad legs, and when she reached to drape the lights her spine arched with muscular precision.

"Hell's Angel..." whispered Lilli.

"Hell has no angels."

"Well...this hell does...and they look just like you."

The woman bounded to the cabin roof. *"I am Morgan...Raven Queen of Avalon."*

She had draped the cord of lights over her shoulder and glared down in defiance. Lilli felt a vitriolic bolt of energy and staggered back. Morgan spun around and continued hanging the lights, her body pulsing with energy as lithe and supple as a panther. The lights were anchored, twisted, and secured around the upper masts and the rooftop of the cabin. When she finished, she stared at Lilli.

"We must start to create a pathway!"

Lilli kept her distance. "Where to?"

"Across the water. It is new...this Avalon, and the fog is only just lifting. She will create a new place. In as much as the mind must map new pathways for learning, I must help to define the territory for her. It will ease her burden." She looked out across the channel. *"It is as if a tributary must be created...thus engaged, through the mist to the new Isle of which she will be Queen."* A breeze blew off the water, slapping the leather hide against her legs.

"But she is flesh, Morgan."

"She is greater than flesh. She has accepted the ring."

A light sweat broke out on Lilli's brow. Jack's boat wasn't very seaworthy. "The place you speak of," she bartered, "it can be resurrected?"

"Avalon is timeless." Morgan exclaimed. *"It is a place of great knowledge and has been silenced too long; it is a place where terror and beauty reign side by side, as seen through the eyes of Kundry. The old woman and her mule speak of the great task required to achieve such a destination. She is wedded to the task, and her mule is strong-backed to bear the burden of her lessons.*

There is more beauty in Kundry than all of us combined. Avalon is a state of grace that requires honor."

The crescent moon on Morgan's forehead glowed, as did the interlocking circles around her neck. Lilli remained silent, recognizing the need for the woman to speak.

"If I must be seen as the vixen Queen, taking men to bed at will until another worthier comes along, it is because I challenge the worthiest. Yet it is not for myself, sister, but because the destination is not easily achieved. Avalon yearns for that which will seed and propagate the highest order of life." Morgan's eyes glowed like heated coals. *"We are creation's womb, and I am a challenger, because the journey I force is hard won."*

"If you are to see the true message of this story, know that it was not meant to solidify in the realms of your historic litany. Some have said that we are demon queens, but I tell you we are dreams, retaliating in anger, only when you choose to be blind and deaf...and I have no choice but to shrivel and die in my own oblivion or become the dark challenger who seeks to awaken!"

Morgan climbed down from above and cried out. *"Do your women understand the obligation they carry, sister? Any woman can rut like an animal, leaving nothing sacred behind. Do they not know the higher order of sexual congress, or are they merely girdled with lust, doomed to remain vehicles of darkness? Avalon cannot live without us, and neither can it be brought into your world without the sacredness of men. Yet men cannot find their way to Avalon alone; it is a world we bring to them. I wear black because of the battlefields I must roam and the death I fight to transform and resurrect, believing that there will come a day when my anger will be stilled. I pray that day has come. Release the ropes! We sail tonight."*

Lilli's black hair blew up and around her red coyote cap. She hesitated. "This is an old boat, Morgan. I'm not sure it's a good idea."

"Look to the image I portray before you. There is a Queen waiting to be born. One myth must give way to another. This vessel

must sail, and the lights it carries speak their message across the seas. You, of all, have the instinct to understand. Speak for us and aid what we are birthing. And remember, I have been trained in all manner of things, including physics and astronomy. We sail tonight!"

Lilli pulled the collar of her denim jacket up around her neck. "And the sea...do you understand the sea, Morgan?"

"I am the sea."

The *Avalon* slid out of its berth and onto the narrow channel that would take it out past the sea wall. Morgan plugged the Christmas lights in, illuminating Jack's boat with strands of starry lights. As they glided past the restaurant, she turned and stared through the café window at the sleeping man, draped across the table.

"He flies tonight," she whispered.

But Lilli didn't hear; coyote stood at the bow of the ship, mesmerized by the rising moon.

Morgan navigated the *Avalon* out past the sea wall, charting a course across the channel. The outgoing tide dragged the old fishing vessel north along with it. Morgan stood tall, the wind hurling leather coat tails around body and limb, but her skin began to pale.

Up at the bow, coyote marshaled attention towards a haze of light permeating the night sky above Seymour Narrows, the reflective glow of a cruise ship, heading right at the *Avalon*. The dog turned a wild eye to stern and ran to Morgan, who stared longingly towards land before collapsing in a pool of black leather.

With bared teeth, coyote bit the back of her coat and attempted to drag the now frail woman out of the cold, but the leather weighted her down, anchoring her to the deck. Coyote looked back to the lights on shore then trotted quickly down into the galley.

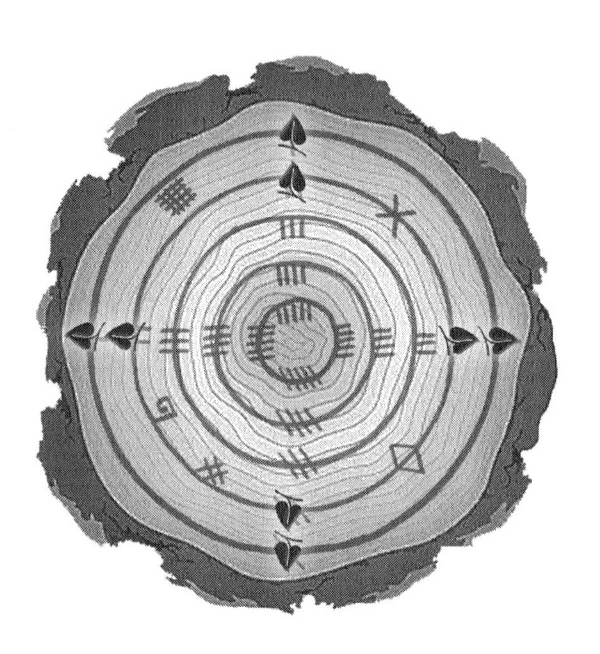

FURZE
Wisdom

AT MIDNIGHT, KATE, the waitress, sauntered over and jostled Jack's shoulder. "Closing time, Jack…time to wake up."

Jack's face was pressed against the journal, and his chest and arms sprawled awkwardly across the table. His left eye popped open in panic and stared birdlike up at Kate's looming form.

"I didn't have the heart to wake you sooner…been checking every half hour. Must be a hell of a story. You passed out within ten minutes." Kate grinned.

Jack unglued his cheek from the page and looked down at the last line he'd read; the words were now going in the right direction.

"You need a ride, Jack? You look white as a ghost."

He unfolded his torso, placed his hand on his stomach, and began turning green. "I've got Lilli's boat. Thanks, anyway."

"You sure you're all right? You're not gonna get sick on me are you?"

Jack slid out of the booth, swallowed hard, and shook his head.

"Well, if you're gonna take the boat back, the fresh air might help. Just watch out for those nuts out on the water. Must be filming another movie or something."

Jack fished in his pocket for some coins.

"No one in their right mind goes out at midnight with a storm due in, right? So, add Christmas lights to the boat, a woman dressed in black leather, and a wolf by her side, and all I can think is they're doing another movie like they did at Elks Cove. I hope it's a movie. Anyway, they just headed out towards the sea wall so be careful."

"A wolf?"

"Well, it's probably a trained dog."

Jack sprinted down the aisle, gulping air.

"Get some sleep, Jack!"

Jack waved to Kate then blasted out the café door. He hit the night air and broke into a run, jumped the rock wall, and dug his heels into the sand. Up ahead, he could see the shadowy form of Lilli's boat pulled up on the beach. Past it, out towards the sea wall, was the faint outline of a fishing boat strung with Christmas lights. Standing at the stern was a very slight figure, draped in a long, dark cloak. By her side was the animal Kate had mistaken for a wolf; it was a coyote.

Sweat dripped off Jack's brow. He reached Lilli's boat and collapsed in the sand, waves of nausea rising in his throat. He tossed the journal in and fumbled for the rope that tied the boat to the rocks, glancing repeatedly at the ***Avalon,*** as it disappeared into the silky, black waters of night.

"Shit, Lilli!"

The rope snagged between two rocks. He dropped to the sand and tugged at the rock. Bile rose from his stomach. His mind was swimming with images of ancient trees and interlocking circles drawn in the dirt with a stick from a dying wizard. Suddenly, he heard the muffled ring of a phone.

Jack stopped. It rang again, a muted bell emanating from the bow of Lilli's boat. He dove in and reached around blindly. Tucked under the forward seat was a laundry bag. He shoved his hand in and grabbed frantically for anything that resembled a phone. It rang again.

The bag was filled with something soft. Everywhere he reached it impeded his grasp, floating in, out, and around his hand. He turned the bag upside down and shook, unleashing a swirling cloud of ebony feathers that flew into the air around him while a heavier lump landed at his feet. The night breeze wafted feathers in his face and hair. The phone rang again. He reached down and grabbed what looked like one of Lilli's caps, folded over and tied with a cord. Inside, the phone rang insistently. He ripped the cord, grabbed the phone and enabled it.

"Lilli!" Feathers blew around Jack's back, giving the illusion of wings. "Son of a Bitch, Lilli!! I said to watch her, not take her for a ride!"

"Put the cap on," whispered Lilli.

"Do you have any idea what can happen out there, Lilli? Do you have a single, freakin' clue what those tides can do? It's an old boat! It can't maneuver the tides!"

"Put the cap on."

Jack looked down at the hat in his hand. Written across the beak was "Raven." He stared at it, confused, then noticed the feathers fluttering in the air around him. Obediently, he slipped on the cap.

"You followed her into the journal, into her dream world, didn't you?"

Jack's eyes shifted back and forth between realities.

"There's only one bird that can take you to those places and back, Jack. I knew if you read her journal, you'd have your chance."

He kept staring at the floating feathers. "Where is she?"

"Here. She just collapsed. I had to give her some lead."

"Can you bring her in?"

"Tell me what to do."

"Turn away from the tide...slowly. Let the tide push the stern around till you're facing more towards land. You can flip her if the tide is ebbing fast. Once you're turned, gas it as much as you can. There's a reverse tide that runs along shore. Get in it and ride it back."

"There's a cruise ship coming."

"There's always a goddamn cruise ship coming, Lilli! And they're not inclined to honk and ask you to get out of the way! Bring her in. I'll wait at the dock."

"Ok."

"Why'd you do it?"

"I have my reasons."

"It was a risk." Jack stared out to the boat strung with Christmas lights. "Why the lights?"

"That was her idea; she found them in the closet."

"Why?"

"Think about it." Lilli hung up.

Jack watched as the ***Avalon*** began to circle back towards land. Kate had said there was a storm due in, but it was clear as a bell; the full moon hung like a Chinese lantern in the night sky. Stars glimmered, and the surface of the water fluttered, like blackened silk caressed by a fragrant breeze.

It was a breeze from long ago.

It blew against the ***Avalon*** and tossed the strands of starry Christmas lights round and round, till the boat appeared to be escorted by tiny wings of light.

"Fireflies," Jack whispered.

"Wake up, Jack o' Lantern, there's something I want you to see." The smell of cinnamon spice floating in the night arrived before she did. She reached out, gently cradling him out of sleep and into her arms. "It's so beautiful, Jack o' Lantern...so beautiful."

Jack's mother believed he had the magic to bring light into the dark. That's why she called him Jack o' Lantern, Jack of Light. Jack swung his five-year old body into her arms, carried by her enthusiasm.

It was Christmas, and although the house was closed and dark it was not uncommon for his mother to sit up late in a room illuminated only by Christmas lights. She carried him silently down padded stairs, descending from darkness to darkness, passing the warm scent she'd left behind on the way up. Through narrow halls of wooded floors, her bare feet conversed with knots and creaking joints, confidently maneuvering twists and turns, till she reached the room at the back.

"You see, Jack? I carry you like a lantern in the night."

She opened the door, and a million stars exploded. At least it seemed that way to Jack, as if a million stars twinkled through the verdant green forest growing in their family room.

She sat Jack down on a large velvet pillow in front of the Christmas tree. The pillow was from India and had tassels on the corners and a border of tiny mirrors sewn into the seams around all four sides. The mirrors reflected the Christmas lights, making Jack feel like he was floating on a cloud of stars.

His mother sat down next to him and stared up at the tree. Jack watched how her eyes filled with light. He was sure if she opened her mouth a whole universe would pour out.

"I have something to share with you, Jack o' Lantern."

She stood up and walked behind the tree, reaching down for the cord that provided the Christmas lights with electricity. It snaked its way behind the couch, where it plugged into the wall. She crawled on her hands and knees till she sat right next to it. Jack watched.

"Sometimes Jack, magical things happen." She pulled the plug, but the Christmas lights didn't go out. She held her finger to her lips, gesturing silence.

"Watch..."

The lights began to glow brighter, and in between each one, spread a tiny tendril of light, which connected it to the next light and the next and the next, till the reflection of green faded, and all he could see was a massive tree of light. The tips of the branches glowed and began to vibrate so much that they popped off and spun around the tree.

"They're like fireflies," she whispered.

Jack watched, as the fireflies formed a spiraling cone that wrapped round and round the tree of light, finally exiting out the top, where the angel was, pulling the remaining tendrils with it.

Light filled the angel and gave it wings, then exploded into a million stars that rained down upon the tree, leaving them in darkness. They sat in silence, the lingering image burning white within their minds.

"It's real, Jack o' Lantern. Always remember that it's real...and not just a story."

It was a miracle she'd said. Eventually, she told everyone, and marveled at the raised eyebrows and subsequent doubt. Even when they carted her off to Doctor's to be tested, she was stunned by such obstinate disbelief. Perhaps they'd all been anesthetized. How else could she explain it? Finally, they drove her away to a place that she told Jack was for special people, people who heard things and saw things differently than everyone else. But Jack didn't understand why she had to go...because Jack had seen it too.

As the *Avalon* got closer, the Christmas lights grew bigger and bigger, reflecting in the water like a million stars.

"Just like fireflies," he whispered.

Lilli maneuvered Sophie's leather clad body down to the bunk, covered her with blankets, and sprinted back on deck. She navigated the *Avalon* into the tide, allowing the water's flow to turn the stern about and head her towards land. The reverse tide near shore was just as Jack had said and enabled the old boat to ride the current back to the marina.

As Lilli approached the slip, she saw Jack standing on the dock, the yellow lanterns overhead casting a sallow light across his skin; the Raven's cap was on his head. She tossed him the line and waited while he fastened it to a cleat then climbed on board.

"Where is she?" Jack's voice was dark and hollow.

"Asleep."

"What're you using to keep the trail going?"

"I'll go hang Christmas lights over her bunk. There's an extra strand. She'll see it when she wakes up."

Jack lumbered down the steps and tossed the journal on the table. Lilli followed silently.

"So, maybe you'd like to tell me what Christmas lights have to do with the *Avalon*?"

"You look pissed."

"I am pissed. I asked for your help and the next thing I know you're sailing off into the sunset together. I'm aware that you're quite an able woman, but neither you nor Sophie nor Nimue or whoever the hell she was out there could survive if you hit one of those sink holes past Brown's Bay."

"That's not what they're called."

"That's what I call them, Lilli! They're like spinning water tornadoes; they'll suck you down so fast you'll feel like Alice in Wonderland down the rabbit hole, but you won't come back. I've got to know I can trust you! Shit! If you can't control shifting when you're with her, get off the case."

"The case? Sounds like Scotland Yard."

"Look, you said you're able to hear her, that there's some sort of connection. If she's too powerful for you I'll change my plan."

"I didn't know you had one."

Jack glared.

"I already told you, Jack, I did it on purpose. When you cool off we can talk." Lilli walked to the bunk where she strung the remaining strand of lights around the bed and plugged them in. "It should help, but give her some more powder anyway." She headed up the steps.

"Don't go."

Lilli stood still, her back to Jack.

"Who was she?" he whispered.

"Morgan, the Raven Queen."

Jack pushed his cap off, stared at the name written across the beak. "What the hell's happening here?"

She slid her foot from the bottom step. "Indians call it leaving a trail: inner world and outer world are meeting. These women are manifestations of energy. People get confused...don't see the forest for the trees...get stuck on the myth or the legend and never pay attention to what it's really all about; looks like this myth plans to change the agenda."

"Go on."

"The energies are rising in Sophie...all of them at once. They're speaking to each other...trying to maintain a link...let us know they don't want to be divided. Morgan spoke about the old woman and the mule, a high priestess named Kundry. She's what I thought she was."

"Enlightenment. I read it in Samuel's journal."

"Enlightenment's a hard journey, Jack. The animal is portraying part of Kundry's story. Remember I said the old lady and the mule were connected? The mule bears a heavy burden, as does Kundry. She wants you to look deep, past all the ugliness, see if you can find the jewel in the dung heap."

Jack opened the journal, flipping through the pages till he found what he was looking for, a page of Sophie's drawings describing her doorway into the void. "That's where she went in her dream."

Lilli studied the diagram of two interlocking circles with a tree growing at the overlap. Jack flipped the page again. "All the elements are broken down over here. The point where the circles overlap is a place beyond duality, the mystic's realm. The *Vesica Piscis* is an ancient symbol. The point of overlap was the sign used by Christians. Samuel's calling the tree that's growing there the Tree of Life."

Lilli studied the drawing of the ancient tree whose core resided in the overlap, with branches and roots extending into the different circles.

"If you look closely," Jack continued, "you'll see letters representing north, south, east, and west in the branches and roots. They extend out into the circle. On the diagonal corners are letters representing the Celtic seasons. North is highlighted in gold. This is Sophie's grandfather's journal. He discovered the ring in Bride's Well in Glastonbury, England, in 1969, then spent eighteen years researching the symbolism. He was in the middle of discovering something when he died suddenly of a heart attack. This is one of his last drawings. He willed the ring to Sophie, believing her to be its destiny."

"She went north?"

Jack flipped the pages, again, to the drawing of the forty-five titled "North to Alaska" with an arrow drawn through it pointing north. "Most of her possessions were destroyed in that big California earthquake last year; one thing left was this record. The rivets in the record represent her first spiral, beginning of a medicine wheel. She followed the direction north and started using the journal to track herself."

"She's right," said Lillie. "It's shamanic."

"The earthquake?"

"Something cataclysmic always happens to wake the sleeping dragon. You can call him Shaman, Wizard, Seer...whatever. But if he's in there and if he's sleeping, something earth shattering has to happen to awaken him...or her." She studied Sophie's medicine wheel. "North is a hard place, even to the Indians. Everyone tells you don't go north. But it's the only direction you can go if you want to break out. If you can go and find your way back, you'll bring new wisdom for your people." Lilli looked down at the drawing again. "She went physically north, from California to Oregon. But she went north internally by stepping off a known path and following this clue—the record. She stepped willingly into the unknown."

Jack turned the page again. In the center of the next drawing, Samuel had squared off the area of overlap of the two circles. "There it is again."

"The eye of God," whispered Lilli.

"Yea, or the fish. It's Latin for fish bladder. But the Greek word for fish is *ichthys*, the acronym for Jesus Christ, Son of

God, Savior. The early Christians used it as a secret code, a way to identify themselves and avoid persecution. The overlapping circles are also carved on the lid of what's known as the Chalice Well in Glastonbury."

"Chalice?"

"Yea. Legend states that Joseph of Arimathea went to Glastonbury after the crucifixion and started the first Christian church. It's called the Chalice Well, because it's believed that he buried the cup of Christ there." Jack pointed to the overlap of circles. "That's where the Raven went in the dream."

"So what happened when he got there, Jack?"

Jack fiddled with the plastic wrap on a cinnamon roll; his hands were shaking. "It probably won't sound strange to you, being Indian, but it was as if that Tree, the one drawn in the center of the fish symbol, was calling to her. It sounded like that wind you hear sometimes at night...the one that makes your hair stand on end."

Color drained out of Jack's skin.

"Sophie stood at the base of this tree, looking up; the tree was enormous. No...it wasn't enormous, it was mythological. It was warped and gnarled with roots bigger than giant redwoods, rising like serpents out of cracked soil."

Lilli studied Jack through hooded eyes.

"Her hair was long. I just realized her hair was long. Anyway, this wind told her the Tree was wounded, and that she should listen to the Tree. But she was afraid, and when she turned to run away, the Tree disappeared. Poof! Just like that, and then it was gone. And when she looked back..."

"Merlin appeared," Lilli whispered.

Jack looked up, startled. "How'd you know?"

"Merlin's buried in the tree, Jack. Even I know that. He's part of the mystery."

"Well...you're right, he is. But he was an old, decrepit, dying, wounded..."

"I think I get it."

"I was surprised to see that he was dying."

"They're all dying, Jack. That's why they're calling her."

Jack slumped onto the kitchen bench and dropped his head towards his knees. "Even with all my training, if I hadn't seen it with my own eyes, I might have wondered if she was delusional. If I hadn't seen the necklace disappear, or the moon lady in the water...all my life I've wanted to prove that, sometimes, things happen that are beyond the framework of normal reality...and we don't know what to do with it so we label people sick."

Jack pressed his palms against the hollows of his eyes. "Why her? She looked so frail and small, as if you could snap her like a twig."

"She's got a lineage. They've been waiting for her."

Jack nodded. "Samuel was beginning to believe the same thing when he died. Maybe it's her Celtic blood. But the ring has a lineage, too, and it all started at Bride's Well."

"Saint Brigit," Lilli whispered. "She's in the book. The triple goddess is what it's all about."

"Yea...the triple spiral. I don't know...I'm a bit challenged by it all."

"That's what she does."

"Who?"

"Morgan, the Raven Queen."

Jack ran calloused fingers through his graying hair. "Fill me in." He took another swig from the whiskey bottle.

"Morgan's a challenger," Lilli began, "a challenger of illusion. She's testing your ability to see through their parade of stories...wants to see whether you're worthy or not."

"...Worthy of what?"

"Championing the cause..."

"I wasn't aware that was my role."

"It's not a coincidence that the Raven Queen showed up here, while you were flying as the Raven over there."

He stared down the neck of the bottle. "Everyone's heard of Morgan: half sister to Arthur, possible mate to Arthur, jealous bitch extraordinaire. But who is she now, in the midst of all this?"

"It doesn't matter whether she was real or not, Jack. Sometimes, a person becomes a legend, or maybe the legend gives birth to a person. What matters is that she's cast a long shadow that's darkened your door. She's a shape shifter and will use whatever form is necessary to achieve her goal."

"Go on."

"She's the Queen Raven. She transforms death, so she hangs around the battlefield. She's the black widow spider that'll mate with you then kill you with her stinger. She's a force of creation, and anything that powerful doesn't translate easily into our world. She'll challenge you to see through the illusion, and if you die, she'll go on to the next because she has to force the outcome."

Jack flipped open Samuel's journal. "Let's see what Samuel says."

JOURNAL ENTRY:

Morgan: Name means sea born, oceanic. A shape shifter, healer, and woman of enchantment. Most educated of all priestesses. Has a quest for power and challenges men by holding them in her grasp. It's important not to succumb to her enchantment in order to pass the test. Morgan is the principle of creation. She'll enter the story at a pivotal time, when the need to challenge its awakening is near.

"And you think that kind of energy can be assimilated by Sophie?" Jack asked.

"These women want to be reborn; this energy has a life of its own. It lies in abeyance when not heard…for a while. Then it rears its head, like a recurring dream that becomes a nightmare when the dreamer doesn't listen."

"This is big energy merging with Sophie's psyche. It could overwhelm her," Jack said.

"Not if the energy achieves its goal of creating one unified voice."

"How do you know that?"

"It's obvious; it's time for the myth to evolve."

"So, Sophie's gifted with the ability to hear beyond her own dreams…to hear a world dream."

"Sophie is a world dream." Lilli's eyes narrowed, her pupils elongating into tiny slivers of gold. "You just took a trip into someone's dream by assuming the Raven's form. You didn't read that journal."

"The last thing I remember? The words on the page were running backwards."

"You were already on the other side, looking back. We're just the tip of the iceberg. There's a whole lot of something underneath that's a bigger part of who we are. This myth is unresolved; it never finished. It's dying, and Sophie holds the key."

Lilli pulled a ratty, stained notebook out of her pocket. "Always knew I'd need this someday. Damned fruit jellies bleed…should've run it through the wash." She licked her fingers. "I've been doing a little homework of my own. I think the chick in the Gemini club was Nimue."

"Yea," said Jack. "She's the one that did in Merlin. Story says he wanted her, tried to bribe her with lessons in magic. She learned what she needed then turned it against him. Basically, he went back to the natural world. She silenced him."

"Well, that's why you saw her first. She closed the door, and there she waits. She's also called Merlin's twin."

Jack nodded. "The energy personifies itself...way of speaking. It isn't dualistic, but we are. I think she's called Merlin's twin because she's the other half of the story."

Lilli looked down at her notes. "Nimue wears the interlocking circles as a pendant, over her throat; it's a clue. The high priestess in the water wore them as a crown. Where the interlocking circles are worn, matters. The pendant is on Nimue's throat because she's a teacher. Her energy isn't that of a mother or a bride, but more like a sister. That's how she transmutes her particular wisdom into our world."

"Go on."

"The next one was Argante, Lady of the Lake, pure spirit, the one missing outfit."

"You don't miss a beat, do you?"

"She's the spirit mother. She's a muse that protects and guides. She wears the crown."

"Continue."

"I already told you what Morgan said about the old woman on the mule."

"Enlightenment."

"Kundry. The old woman on the mule is a Grail messenger, the black maiden, dark woman of knowledge."

"How is one human person supposed to embrace all this, Lilli?"

"Listen, Jack. You just said the energy personifies itself, so we can understand. The Grail has been symbolized as a chalice, a cup, a cauldron, and even, in very early times, a woman. The grail is a womb. It's not a thing...it's a symbol of transcendence. The mantle of turtledoves on Kundry's shirt is the symbol of the Grail. You saw them." Lilli grabbed the journal and started leafing through the pages.

"What are you looking for?"

"This." She shoved the open book in front of Jack's face. It was the page that showed the squaring off of the junction of the two interlocking circles. "This ***Vesica Piscis***, Jack, is a womb. It's a womb comprised of energy, male and female. The male energy is dying. Why? Because the myth of Avalon was not heeded! The female energy is expressing herself in nine voices: mothers, sisters, and brides. There are three representations of each, reflecting three levels of knowledge, heaven, earth, and underworld. One of those voices is dark, ugly, and unbridled. Remember, un-harnessed? All potential in the womb will die if it remains un-harnessed! Someone needs to finish telling this tale. Merlin wasn't dying because Nimue buried him but because he didn't understand the principles of union within the womb. The turtledove represents union. Merlin sent himself into oblivion, through Nimue! In a sense, they ran into each other, silencing Merlin and allocating the nine female voices into a state of stasis...until now...when civilization has a chance to transform it all and transcend! That's why Sophie's here!"

"She said it was the void. That place you're talking about...the place she went to in her dream. Merlin called it the void."

Lilli grabbed the book out of his hand and tossed it down on the table. "Well, maybe it wouldn't be a void Jack, if the story had continued to its end."

A creaking in the hallway startled them and they looked up simultaneously. In the galley entrance stood a woman with only a slight resemblance to Sophie. Her butchered hair had been plastered down with water, slicking it against her head like a helmet. She wore a long, gray woolen skirt with a white blouse buttoned up high around her neck. Draped about the collar was the pendant of interlocking circles.

She stepped into the galley with feet clad in worn military boots, unadorned and dirty. Her skin appeared more gray than white. Her eyes had changed color from hazel to white blue, and on her forehead was the blue crescent moon.

Jack and Lilli stared, shocked at the apparition.

"This sorrow rains tears of blood."

Her voice carried the dry wind of memory into the room and sent chills up their spines. Jack stood up, sensing the need to honor the woman before him. He just didn't know what to say. She stepped closer to him.

"You wonder who I am and why I mourn. I am none other than the sorrowful maiden. I am the virgin widow. I mourn the wasteland, even though I am her Queen."

Sophie turned and headed towards the steps.

"Wait," Jack cried. "Please, wait."

Lilli retreated into the shadows and listened, as the woman stopped, leaving one worn boot resting on the first step.

"Please tell me your name," Jack pleaded.

"I am Dindraine." Dindraine floated up out of the galley like a ghost. Jack followed, noticing the smell of pine coming from her skirt.

"Where will you go?"

Dindraine turned and looked out across the water. A breeze blew, ruffling the collar of her shirt. *"There is water in the wind,"* she whispered. When she looked back at Jack, there was a hint of bloom to her cheeks. *"I must go to the forest to bury my love,"* she said, then stepped off the boat and walked up the dock, her voluminous clothes anchoring her to the earth.

"Lilli!" Jack stumbled through the galley. "Lilli! We've got to follow her!"

Lilli emerged from the head.

"What're you doing?" Jack screamed.

"Smelling her clothes."

"She smells like pine," yelled Jack.

"There's blood in the sink."

"From what?"

"The price of honor."

"For cryin' out loud, Lilli, that's all fine and dandy but she's headed out to the forest to bury her love, whatever the hell that means!"

"I'll follow her," said Lilli. "I have her scent. You stay here."

"You think I'm going to leave her alone with you again? You know damn well you're gonna shift, Lilli! I can see it in your eyes!"

"The only way to follow her into the mountains and protect her is if I shift. You know that. I'll bring her back. I promise. I brought her back before, I'll do it again."

Jack stared.

"You need to honor this, Jack."

"Get going then."

Lilli slipped past then glanced back. "Jack."

"What?"

"Finish the journal."

"Are you serious?"

"Where is her enlightenment, Jack? Something's helping her take this journey. Go into the dream and find out what she had to do to reclaim the ring. It will help us help her."

Jack looked down at the open journal. "How will I know where you are?"

"You won't."

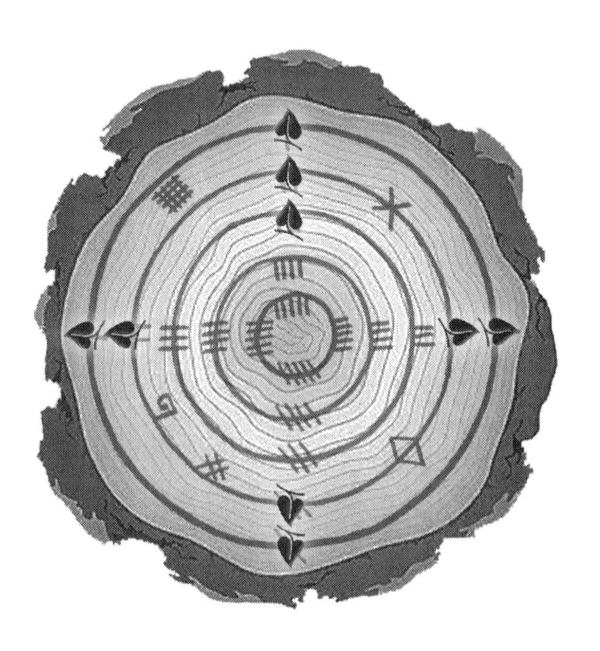

ALDER

Inner Strength

LILLI FOLLOWED DINDRAINE through the dark night, along the water's edge to the north of town, where she reached the mouth of the river. Dindraine crossed the footbridge then turned up a path that bordered the north side, following it till she reached the first stone pool. Spring water flooded the river, cascading waterfalls over the edges of rock cliffs. Dindraine raised her face to catch the spray and smell the scent of water in the air.

She turned off the path and headed into the dense forest, picking her way through brambles and green foliage thick with new growth. The ground beneath her feet barely made a sound as she walked lightly as a deer. When she reached a dark grove of trees, Dindraine sat on a rock and buried her face in her hands, allowing tears to flow.

"What greater sorrowful maiden than I, virgin widow, whose life must mirror a fallow land. I mourn you my dearest love, whose breath was taken from the very lips I longed to kiss. A fallow land

that mocks the sovereignty that gives it life has born the sorrowful maiden, and a king who rules a wasteland—I mourn you. The union that could have healed the Grail King's wound was not meant to be."

The coyote sat beneath the mantle of trees, watching Dindraine lament her sorrow to a lover that was not there.

Suddenly, a stick broke underneath the brush on the far side of the grove, and a young man stepped out of the shadows. He was strong of build, with long black hair and the keen eyes of a hawk. His skin was tanned, and he wore dark green shirt and pants. "Dindraine," he whispered.

Dindraine looked up, startled.

"Dindraine, the wound has been healed. There will be no more bleeding."

"Are you a ghost sent to torture me, my love? My eyes send daggers to my heart at the sight of you."

"Look at your hand, Dindraine."

Dindraine looked down at her right hand and saw the ring on her middle finger.

"The ring, Dindraine, is reclaimed. The ring is whole again."

Dindraine stared at the ring, confused. *"It is meant for two hands. Why do I wear both?"*

The young man stepped forward and held out his right hand to her. On the middle finger was a white line where the skin was not tanned, as if a ring had been worn. "Since the ring was reclaimed, my hand bears its spirit. I am marked with its presence. It is not long before it is worn by two, and not one."

Dindraine reached out and touched his hand. *"You are flesh,"* she whispered.

"You are no longer the sorrowful maiden, Dindraine. You have helped us to be reborn."

Tears spilled down Dindraine's cheeks, as she stared into his eyes. Her hand reached out to him again, wanting to make sure he wasn't an illusion. When she touched his skin, Dindraine broke out in sobs and collapsed, unconscious at his feet on the forest floor.

The young man slipped his hand around her waist and raised her to his side, where he tenderly held her. Eventually, he sat down on the rock, holding Dindraine like a child across his lap. He wrapped the folds of her gray wool skirt around her to keep her warm, rocking back and forth, till he began to see a hint of color return to her cheeks.

The coyote entered the grove and curled up at his feet, staring yellow eyes into the approaching night. They sat quietly, listening to the sounds of the forest and the distant rushing of the river. When it was time, coyote rose and lead the way out of the grove.

The young man cradled Dindraine in strong arms down the path along the river, where, with the guidance of coyote, he placed her in the bed of a red pickup then slipped away into the night.

Jack stared at the galley clock: 2:30 a.m. and he felt like hell. "Jesus, Eleni." He dragged his weary bones to the table and collapsed on the bench, rubbing calloused fingers over the journal. His nails were worn below the quick, and the skin was weathered by sun and sea, but his fingers were long and straight and his hands strong; he flipped the journal open.

"OK, Samuel...who's Dindraine?"

JOURNAL ENTRY:

Dindraine: Virgin widow. Union of love not consummated due to immediate death of knight/husband. Their love is equated with the Grail, spiritual love, yet not achieved due to the death of the groom. Dindraine must continue on alone to tell their story, completing the Grail journey she is destined to take. Seeking a male counterpart, she shows her kinsman, Perceval, the way. There is great loss of energy/blood in taking the journey as a woman alone. Although Perceval is with her, he is a kinsman and not a lover. She dedicates her life to showing the way and opening the doorway for others. Dindraine's entrance into the story implies the potential for manifestation of a higher love.

Jack scanned the entry then flipped the pages, passing diagrams, until something emerged that looked odd, misplaced. It was a drawing of a small cherry tree next to a sketch of five concentric circles with a line connecting them to the Tree of Life. Across the page was written: Tree rings = Wisdom of Wood.

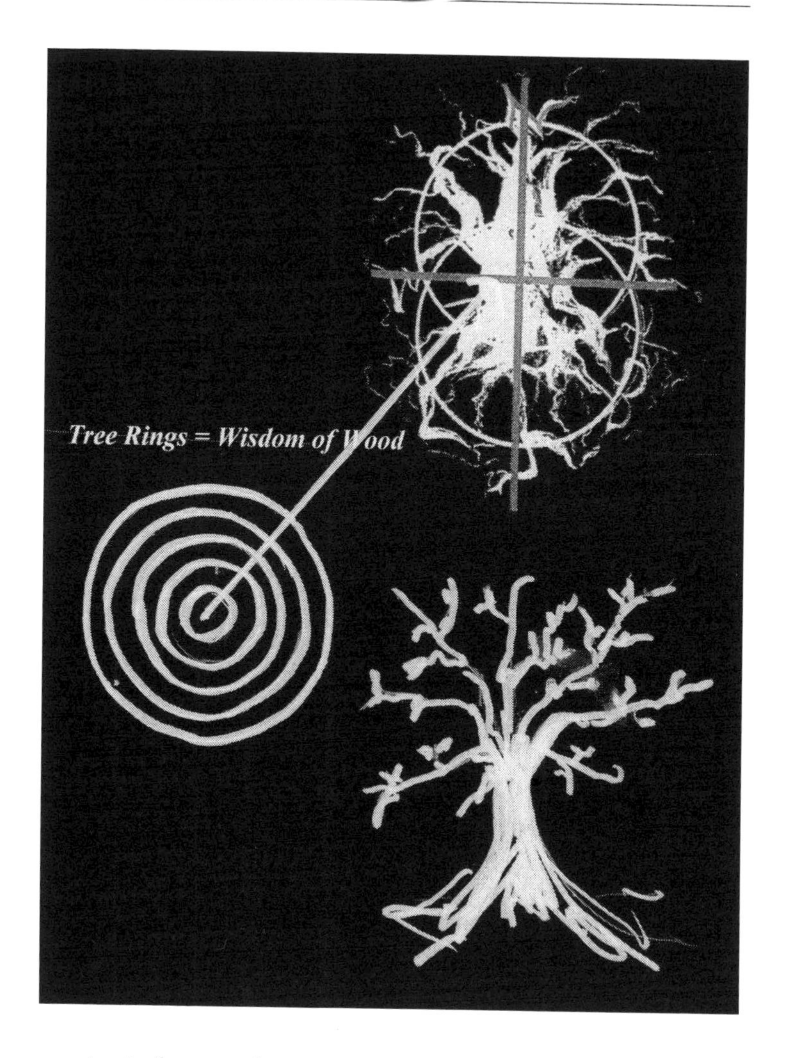

As Jack started to read, his shoulders slumped, and his torso cascaded across the table; his eyelids fluttered shut, and Black Jack, the Raven, entered Sophie's dream.

SOPHIE'S DREAM:

The raven's wings arched, feathers spread like fingers fanning the rush of air, as he descended out of the night. He glided into the forest and alighted on a low branch of a cedar tree. Below him on the ground was Sophie; lying in front of her was the dying wizard.

"You're almost dust," she whispered.

The wizard's robes were draped like parched skin over bones too old to remember, and his birdlike skeleton clung to the barest blush of skin. Sophie looked up at the moon; it was round and full as a pregnant woman, but its light reflected on nothing but Merlin's form. The illumination cast across the sky seemed to disperse and fade, as if night's reflection of the sun was being devoured by darkness. Merlin was the only receptacle—the only remaining mirror.

She moved closer, taking her place at Merlin's side. His hands were clasped together and rested beneath his heart; he looked frail, like a cadaverous bird. She reached out and touched his hand.

"Merlin, don't die. Please, help me."

The raven cocked his head, as she draped in sorrow over the spare bones of an aged wizard illumined with moonlight.

"Please..." Sophie gazed at the wizard's face, with gray crepe skin lying like dried flower petals over sunken eyes.

"There is still time, Sophie." The wizard's voice was barely a whisper.

The raven inched closer.

"You must find the ring and bring it back. Go within, Sophie...the energy of the ring abides within." Moonlight flickered, as the shadow of a night owl flew across his face.

"I don't know how. Why can't Nimue help you?"

"Nimue must work through you. She is a language from the past, a story whose ending rests with you. We cannot maintain a consciousness no longer embraced by all people. Can you not see that I am dying?"

"You told me there was still time. You can't die!"

"There is time. But time is waning, and you still resist the way."

"Why me?"

"That…is the essence of your dilemma, Sophie. 'Why' is a question that you should not ask. If I had asked 'Why me?' my destiny would not have been fulfilled. Your world is large, Sophie…enter it. But don't get lost in this world of dreams, as it is all just a reflection. The greatest pain of all is to lose your way. It is the great schism, the invisible sickness."

The wizard's form collapsed, like air leaving a balloon. The raven watched his shoulders drop, and a gray pallor saturated his skin. The lines in his face seemed to crack and cleave, and the ground shuddered underfoot.

"Don't leave me, Merlin!"

"We are dying, Sophie."

"We? We are dying?"

"Sophie Alexander Henri Dumont, find the ring…before it's too late."

"Why do you keep calling me that! It's not my name!"

The wind dropped. Nothing moved the wisps of gray beard or fading robes, just still, hollow silence and the remnants of a memory of mystery. The raven watched from the shadows.

"Why me?" Sophie whispered.

The raven shriveled into a black ball, as darkness closed around them. Sophie knelt on the ground, mesmerized by the disintegrating figure. One of Merlin's clenched hands slid to his side, opening as it fell. Out of it dropped a seed.

Sophie reached out to catch it, but the seed tumbled quickly to the earth, burrowing deep into the ground, and it started to grow.

At the base of Sophie's knees, a green tendril appeared. It unfolded, stretched, climbed, and thickened. Branches emerged. Out of the branches grew tiny leaves and a blossom of pink flowers. The tree stopped growing when it equaled Sophie's height, as she sat on her knees; out of it emerged the diaphanous vision of an Asian child draped in robes of purple and gold.

"I can help you," the child sang.

Sophie stared at the shimmering image. "No one can help me...it's too late."

The child's face appeared and disappeared, blown by a soft breeze in and around the cherry tree. "The tree was a reflection," whispered the child.

Sophie looked up. "It was just a dream...a tree in a dream."

"The story of the ring was buried long ago in a tree more ancient than any you know." The child's voice rang with the resonance of wind chimes.

"That's what the woman in the forest said. Why must I save what they've lost? Maybe the ring returned to the tree because that's what it knows."

"It is written that you are its destiny. Trees are bearers of wisdom... and that wisdom should not be silenced because you are afraid."

"I don't know anything about the wisdom of trees."

"That is why you must reclaim the ring. It is the only way. You must find the tree she buried it in; reclaim the wisdom...reclaim the ring."

"I told you I was dreaming. I buried it in a dream in my back yard."

"You must differentiate between the object and the story."

"I have to find the ancient tree?"

The child nodded. "Yes...the true tree...the Tree of Life. The story is buried within the Tree of Life."

"The tree within the circles," whispered Sophie.

"Yes."

"But how do I find it?"

"It is a more difficult path. You must go within."

"But how do I begin?"

"There will be a door; enter when it opens..."

Eleni Alexander sat in the pre-dawn light sipping green tea. Across the kitchen, the oven clock displayed red numerals in the dark room. Barely visible on the table was the green velvet bag; inside the bag was Jack Harrington's number.

Four days ago she watched the Island bus pull away from the station in Victoria and drive north with her daughter tucked safely inside. Safely? Even she knew that safety wasn't part of the equation. With shoulders hunched from tension, she had returned to her car to take the next ferry home.

Four days. Had Sophie found Jack Harrington or had she gotten abducted along the way? Or, worse still, had her mind shifted and taken her out to the forest to sleep in the folds of her ancient garb?

Eleni shivered and pulled the collar of her father's robe up around her neck, running her hand along the drape of worn fabric. She could still see him in her mind's eye, sitting at his desk, salt and pepper hair damp from the shower, wrapped in his robe, as he jotted notes and prepared for a trip. She rubbed the corners of the robe around her toes, and as she did, the fingers of her right hand slid into the hem where stitches were unraveling.

Inside the hem was a crumpled piece of paper.

She slid the paper out. It was a receipt dated October of 1969 and had an address stamped from Glastonbury, England. The numbers, worn and faded, appeared to represent the purchase of the green velvet bag. Samuel must have put the ring into the bag and sewn it into the lining of his robe. On the back of the receipt was a number: three digits, a dash, and three more numbers.

"It's a telephone number from Glastonbury," she mused aloud.

She studied the receipt, folded it carefully, and slid it into the green velvet bag, next to Jack's number. Then, clutching it firmly, she headed upstairs to her bedroom, packed her things, and headed north to Campbell River, British Columbia.

May 5, 2001

At 6:00 a.m. a horn bellowed across the channel, signaling the commuter ferry's morning service. Lilli stood on the deck of the Avalon and watched the cars line up, their idle engines puffing white clouds into the gray fog. People wrapped in bright mufflers with hands glued to paper cups of steaming coffee stood puffy eyed with sleep. She shrugged off the chill, descended the galley steps, and walked past Jack, face still pressed to the pages of the journal.

The galley sink was full of wild flowers from the forest. She arranged them in the chipped coffee pot—the one painted dark green with birds—the one missing the dove. Occasionally, she tossed a flower into a pan simmering on the stove, along with a little powder from the zip lock bag. When her arrangement was complete, she placed it near Sophie. It included flora from the forest to help her remember. Sophie lay on the bunk, hair strewn with needles from the woods, the skirt engulfing her in jagged mounds of gray wool like a swaddling blanket.

Lilli stared, remembering the woman who had collapsed in sorrow. She had placed Sophie's left hand on top of the right so as to feel the ring upon awakening and had left remnants of the forest stuck to the weave of her woolen skirt. On Sophie's cheek was a green thread; Lilli tied it around the stone of the ring then dropped her head, spilling waves of ebony hair onto her lap. When she looked up, the pale blue eyes of the previous evening had opened and returned to hazel.

"What's that fragrance?" asked Sophie.

"Wild flowers from the forest..."

A hint of blush spread through Sophie's cheeks. Lilli disappeared into the galley and returned with a cup of warm liquid.

"Drink this."

As Sophie took the cup and drank, she noticed the skirt scattered with flora and the green thread tangled in her ring. "Something's happened."

Lilli stared.

"Something's happened but I can't remember what it is." She sat up. "I need the journal...need to write...try and remember."

"The journal's not available right now," said Lilli.

Sophie looked at her, questioningly.

"Come." Lilli took Sophie's hand and walked her to the galley, where Jack slept. "I'd wake him, but I'm not sure how far he is and whether it's safe. He's been like this all night."

Sophie looked at the open journal beneath Jack's face. "It looks like he's reading my entries."

"That's just where he started. That's not where he is now."

"I don't understand."

"He's Black Jack." Lilli smiled.

"I still don't get it."

"Wasn't there a Raven in your dream?"

"Yes."

"Jack's not reading your journal...he's in it, as the Raven. He's not here right now. I always knew it would happen sooner or later."

"He's in my dream?"

"Jack wants to help, but he can't unless he knows what happened."

Sophie slid Jack's arm away from the journal, flipping his hand over, exposing the bleeding palm. "It's the stone," she whispered. "He's connected to the stone." She held her palm up, exposing the scar. "You can't enter the dream without absorbing the stone." She stepped back, mesmerized by the sight of Jack's hand. "Merlin called me out...Sophie Alexander Henri Dumont...reclaim the ring before it is too late. That was his clue...Henri Dumont...because if you don't know who you are, you can never gain access to the Tree."

She rubbed the green thread tied to the ring. "There is wisdom in wood. But the ring was buried so deep, the only way to get to it was total immersion in the Tree, and Merlin knew that if I didn't know who I was, I'd be annihilated, because the unknown always takes us down."

"And who are you, Sophie?"

"Dark and light, like everyone else. But my darkness was a part of their darkness, and it needed to be redeemed."

"The Priestesses?"

"The story was lost in time. I inherited ignorance, and ignorance begets darkness."

"You worried about Jack?"

Sophie looked down at his palm. "He must have his own connection to the ring. Let him see the story through the Raven's eyes. Don't wake him; he's in The Valley of Fear."

STAGE TWO

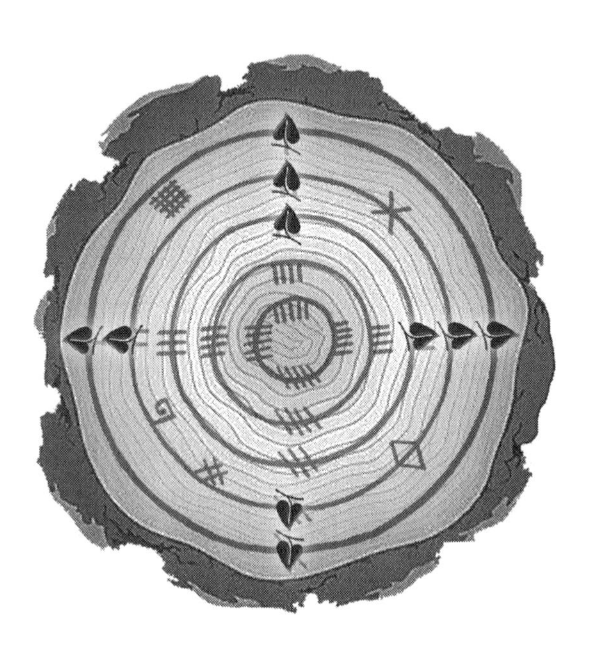

HOLLY

Holy

SOPHIE'S DREAM:

Into the dark night, the raven flew on wings heavy with ash, born of decaying life, through air thick with sorrow. He collapsed onto the cracked bark of an old tree, blinded by the night.

"You will know the success of her conquest by the lifting of the shroud."

A voice emerged out of the darkness, a voice that bore a melodious timbre, with that particular lilt known to people of India. It startled the raven, who jumped sideways, nearly stumbling from his perch. He cocked his head and peered into the ebony veil surrounding him, barely able to discern the faint outline of an animal sitting on the branch below. It had long, straight ears, a pudgy stomach, rather large feet, and appeared to be wearing a plaid jacket; it was a rabbit.

"Of course," it continued, "you are no more a raven than I a rabbit. I suspect you are new to the territory."

The raven's claws dug into the mossy limb. He hunched down and peered intensely at the creature, losing his balance and fluttering to the branch below.

"Yes, it is dark in here, and heavy with fear. I'm sure you can feel it," the rabbit said. "How do you do?" he continued. "I am Kitsym, her guide. Never mind trying to introduce yourself. Initially, transmutation of energy is disturbing in the least; speech is the last to come." He scratched his lengthy soles on the tree bark. "I have actually taken on many forms in my time. I suspect her particular analogy is to Alice in Wonderland. It matters not—the form that is—but only that she chose that which is agreeable and thus inclines her towards listening."

The raven's head bobbed left and right.

"The rabbit is new to me. I don't mind. Still, this incessant change of clothing is at times most bothersome. Every time our thoughts evolve, she puts me in another jacket. I'm sure it all appears rather odd to you, seeing you are a novice and all that. Where you come from, I suspect, rabbits don't sit in trees. But then, where you come from I am not a rabbit, nor are you a bird."

The raven stretched up tall, then squatted down, animated by the conversation, unable to speak.

"She has been challenged...called forth, so to speak. This darkness you see is the shroud of her fear. It is unfortunate; everyone thinks it to be a lengthy journey, yet it's all right here. She must find the Tree of Life. Transformation, they say. Something lodged deep within must be pulled forth. Yet you cannot remove it from the Tree without finding it within yourself...a painful endeavor... looking at oneself. She shall have to remove the splinter from her eye if she wishes to gain access to the Tree."

The raven began to notice a yellow tinge creeping up his claws and a hint of iridescence on the blue black of his feathers; light was filtering in. Kitsym began to take shape. He had shiny black fur and wore a red plaid jacket. The raven looked down at the ground, just as Sophie, gaunt and pale, emerged into the light. The rabbit moved quickly to her side. He was dressed in a somber gray woolen coat.

"Hurry, Miss Sophie," he cried. "There isn't much time! A Veil of Tears is approaching, trying to obliterate your entry to The Tree of Life!"

Sophie rolled gray wool into a tight bundle, stuffed it in her bag, and donned jeans and sweatshirt. She rubbed her hands through matted hair, splashed water on her face, and hesitated, resting a hand lightly on her cheek, wondering what it was that had been captured there. She tied another knot into the green thread and climbed the galley steps. When she surfaced on deck, Lilli noticed beneath the open neck of Sophie's sweatshirt was the prim collar of Dindraine's shirt.

"The Indians believe we walk many worlds," said Lilli.

Sophie glanced up the pier. "Do they catch fish out there?"

"Lots. Photo's on the bulletin board of salmon bigger than us hanging from hooks next to the beaming face of the fisherman."

"It doesn't please you."

Lilli shrugged. "Indians live in a different world. Don't need to take pictures of the food we kill. Might meet them in one of those other worlds and they'll be hunting us."

"I guess."

"It doesn't take a lot of imagination to know where you've been."

"I never remember where I've been."

Lilli stared again at the shirt collar. "I'm not so sure."

Sophie pulled her arms up her sleeves, wrapping her hands inside for warmth.

"We Indians have a place of fear, too," Lilli continued. "All people do; sooner or later, we all go there and get to see just how creative we really are."

Sophie smiled. "Have you gone?"

"On occasion."

"Fear is the doorway, isn't it, Lilli...the ultimate challenge?"

"It's your journey, Sophie, not Jack's. He won't be able to follow you all the way."

Sophie's eyelids began to droop.

"Go rest."

"What about Jack?"

"I'll watch him."

Sophie walked down the hall and collapsed onto the bunk.

Lilli grabbed Sophie's duffle bag and sat down on the planked floor; it was thick with dust. Scraps of food wrappers were scattered under the table. She ripped the Velcro, unleashing the flap of the bag and pulled back the opening, jerking back, as a cloud of fragrance wafted out.

Her eyes closed and her nostrils flared and sniffed, hunting the air. Her head bobbed and jerked, and a dark clicking sound emanated from the back of her throat. When she opened her eyes the pupils were slits of yellow gold.

The coyote stuck its muzzle into the bag and started pulling out clothing. She dragged Dindraine's nest of worn wool across the floor and pawed incessantly. She rolled in it, licked it, and peed on it, then stuffed in it a corner for safekeeping.

Coyote growled, pounced, and submerged her head in the bag. She pulled back, yipped, and went back for more, wrenching out a pair of calloused black leather pants. She chewed and snarled, ripping hems and hips with leather ties.

She nuzzled the bag and hauled out horsehair and burlap, like a favorite toy, dragging them to a corner where she rubbed her head and fur repeatedly with their musk.

Out came Nimue's forest green cloak and buckskin pants. She trotted across the floor with the pouch of animal skin and fur and nestled it into the horsehair bed.

The burgundy brocade gown and faded white dress were dragged across the floor. She rolled and peed and worked herself up with smells transferred from the oil of skin.

She clawed at the duffel bag, scattering garments in disarray around the galley floor: satin slippers, military boots, and red silk. And in the middle of it all lay a bridle.

Coyote bit the leather strap and dragged it to the corner, ripping pieces of cloth along the way—a torn square of black leather, a strip of floral chiffon, and the ripped hem of a soiled white dress. Round and round she dug in her bed, blending scents into one perfumed pillow. Then, exhausted, she curled up and slept, one paw resting on the bridle.

Beneath her pillow, tangled in the cloth, was a crumpled piece of paper.

JOURNAL ENTRY:

Igraine: Royal blood + Royal blood + Mystery

Igraine represents the myth's attempt to actuate and break into the earthly kingdom. Merlin, as mystic, impregnates Igraine, Duchess of Cornwall, via Uther Pendragon, King of Britain; the mystic enters the womb. The child of this union, Arthur, is raised by those knowledgeable of the mystery of life, Merlin and the Priestesses. His destiny is to bring forth the fruits of union into the Kingdom. The myth began to live at this point; but it failed.

The potential for a renewed union with the mystic enters the story via Igraine.

The *Avalon* rocked silently throughout the fifth day, as Lilli, Sophie, and Jack all slumbered in different worlds. But when night descended, moonlight slid down the galley steps and beamed across the chaos on the floor, illuminating the bare feet of a woman picking her way through the debris. Lilli heard a noise and opened her eyes to find herself curled up on a bed of clothes in a corner of the galley, looking out across the room at ankle height. Someone was walking around.

As her eyes adjusted, she discerned the pale shadow of a small, naked woman rummaging through clothing on the floor. Her hands rubbed fabrics till she found what she wanted. As she lifted the cloth up, moonlight glinted off something. She held it high over her head and draped what appeared to be a gown over her body. As it came down around her, the woman changed in stature, growing taller, filling out bodice and hips.

Lilli looked down into her bed and saw something glinting. She raised the torn remnant to her nose and breathed deeply, rolling a pearl in her hand. "Good evening, Igraine," she whispered.

"Your animal instincts serve you well, or is it your sense of smell?"

"They are the same."

"How do you know me, shape shifter?"

"By the smell of pearls."

"Wisdom?"

Lilli nodded, intrigued with the change in Sophie's appearance. "Yes. It's a white smell…the smell of pearls…like milk. You are the mother of all mothers; mystery entered your womb and Arthur was conceived.

"Yes, the wisdom of mothers. You are a good sister, shape shifter, to find your way through our chaos."

"It's not chaos if it's understood."

Igraine walked out of the galley and rummaged around near the bunk, finally returning with a bed sheet in her hands. *"There were markers in the bag."*

Lilli saw the crayons across the room, obviously of no interest to coyote. "I see them."

"The Avalon mustn't sail without a flag." Igraine walked over to them and picked up the crayons. It was the walk of a queen, the full-bodied presence of sovereignty. *"Clear the floor. We must prepare the flag."*

"Where will we sail?"

"To the Isle of maidens...to Avalon."

"Morgan said that Avalon must be resurrected. But the old Avalon is no more, Igraine. It's long ago and far away. It's merely a name for this boat."

"Avalon lives. It may be faded and weak, yet still it breathes," said Igraine, removing red, black, and white crayons from the box.

"This is another era, Lady Igraine."

Igraine looked sharply into Lilli's eyes. *"It is an era of rebirth, Talapas!"*

Lilli jolted out of her scented pillow. "You know my name?"

"As coyote explores us, we explore coyote. The Island lives."

Igraine used the crayons to draw two large interlocking circles joined down the center by a large sword while Lilli stared nervously at Jack, still draped across the galley table. "We can't sail yet."

"No, not yet. But we will, when he learns the inscription of the ring."

•

"The ring is inscribed?"

"The ring's inscription is the voice of two, not one. One inscription with two lives imbedded within it."

"Why don't we read it off the ring?" asked Lilli, looking down at the red stone glowing in the dark.

"The ring does not come off. It will never separate till both parties are present and together recite the words that bind them for all eternity. United, they will become the bearers of the ring."

"Jack?" whispered Lilli.

"No. He is the messenger, not the groom."

"So, it's true," whispered Lilli.

"It has always been the same, shape shifter. It is union that releases the waters from the well. But it is a journey that we have all but failed to bring to light. Woman is a vehicle of birth...of passage. Not just through her loins, but also through her heart, as spirit is also born through her. As Arthur was conceived within the arms of mystery, I gave birth to man and myth, to flesh and spirit."

"Because we were condemned to silence, Avalon faded into the mist. But the ring has been reborn and we have a chance to speak. Understand that we, each of us here, nine high priestesses who wear the different faces of our Goddess, are not sovereign in our own right but are reflections in the water of one greater than us all."

Suddenly, the boat heaved from the weight of someone climbing on board. Igraine had risen to her feet and stood proudly with the flag draped across her arm. Lilli, squatted on her knees, snapped to attention with the sound of footfall on the deck. The moon cast shadows down the steps and a voice followed.

"Sophie?"

"Who is it?" replied Lilli.

"I'm sorry to bother you, but I heard a voice that sounded like my daughter's; I'm looking for her. Is Sophie Alexander on board?"

Lilli looked up at Igraine.

"It is fate that we meet."

Eleni Alexander descended the galley steps and stared across a floor strewn with tattered clothes and moonlight. A beautiful Indian woman with long black hair was kneeling at the feet of a woman who bore little resemblance to her daughter.

"It's late and I'm very tired," Eleni continued. "I must be mistaken. Excuse me for disturbing you."

"Eleni Alexander is well known to us." The pearl encrusted collar of Igraine's gown seemed to stand to attention and the crescent moon on her forehead glimmered opalescent blue; the circled crown reflected moonlight. *"We are the same,"* Igraine continued.

Eleni stared at the woman in the burgundy gown. Scanning it quickly, she remembered seeing it thrown in a tirade onto Sophie's bed. But the woman wearing it seemed taller and more robust than her daughter.

"Was not Sophie Alexander conceived in mystery?" Igraine continued.

Eleni took another step into the room. "She was conceived during Samhain, if that's what you mean."

"It is part of what I mean. Who was her father?"

Eleni was unnerved by Sophie's appearance. She stared at Lilli then scanned the chaos in the room. "To whom am I speaking?" she asked quietly.

"I am Igraine, mother of Arthur."

"I know who Igraine is," she spit out. Eleni stood with her paralyzed left hand held tightly to her side; Igraine stared down at it.

"Your hostility is understood, Eleni Alexander, but it serves no purpose here. We are indebted to you."

Eleni continued staring at Sophie. Neither clenched jaw nor rigid neck could stop the tears that streaked down, saturating the breast of her shirt.

"Why have you come, Eleni Alexander?" Igraine whispered.

"To help..."

"Then try to remember the night of your conception. You were given a gift. But someone else was given a gift, as well. Too many years go by and we forget to remember that the greatest wound can be healed with love. If we are given a challenge, we must always know that it holds within it our enlightenment."

Igraine staggered. Lilli reached out to break her fall, but she buckled onto the floor, where Lilli cradled her in her arms.

"I am redeemed because of your love for your daughter, Eleni Alexander. We are all redeemed because you did not give up."

Her head dropped forward, and Lilli felt Sophie's body deflate, as if air were leaving a balloon. She shrunk to half her size, the dress bagged like excess skin, and the crown disappeared. Eleni stood paralyzed.

"What's happened?"

"The spirit's left her body."

"Is she all right?"

Lilli looked into Eleni's tired eyes. The marina lights cast a sallow glow across her skin, shadowing the hollows of her face. She was fairer than Sophie, but Lilli saw the resemblance. She nodded and looked back at Sophie. "Why don't you grab the bottle of Scotch on the table over by Jack and help me carry her to the bunk."

Eleni turned and saw Jack for the first time, passed out, doubled over, amid scotch, Twinkies, and dirty cups. She followed the moonlight's trail across the room as it illuminated torn clothes tumbled and strewn in disarray. Lilli sat in a bed of piled skirts and shoes with Sophie draped across her lap.

"Who are you," Eleni demanded.

"Lilli."

Eleni shook her head. "Dear God, what did I send her into?"

The two women raised Sophie and carried her down the hall. Eleni looked up at the Christmas lights randomly strung on the ceiling over the bunk. "She's lost more weight," she said. Lilli tucked a blanket around Sophie.

"Take the dress off first," said Eleni.

"I can't."

'I'll do it then."

"You can't do that, Eleni."

"Look, I don't know who you are...you obviously think you know me..."

"A lot's been happening around here. I learn quickly." Lilli smiled.

"Well, maybe you'd like to share a little of it with me because from my side of the fence this place looks like hell! What do you and Jack do? Sit around drinking scotch and ripping apart her duffel bag? I sent her here thinking she'd get help. Look at her! She probably weighs all of ninety pounds, her hair is dirty and filled with grease, her skin's yellow, and you may as well have rubbed charcoal under her eyes!" Eleni turned to walk out.

"Where are you going?"

"To pack her things..."

Lilli grabbed the back of her shirt. "By the way, Eleni, who is her father?"

"It's none of your business."

"I'm not an enemy," Lilli whispered. "The clothing's on the floor because we're making progress. You went through it with her. You know what I'm talking about."

Eleni glared.

"The dress stays on because it's part of the trail. She needs to know where she's been and who was present. When you're in the middle of it all it looks like crap, but it's worse if you try and hide."

Eleni stared at her daughter. "That's the same thing she said."

"Yesterday, she got dressed and forgot to take off Dindraine's shirt. She put her sweatshirt on over it."

"Dindraine."

"Yea, Dindraine. They're starting to become part of her. She's weaving the dream."

"I was told this boat was named ***Dream Weaver***."

"It was...until Nimue told Jack he'd incorrectly named his vessel...that, according to the sea, she was called the ***Avalon***. She told him it was important to know a woman's true name."

Eleni slumped on the side of the bunk and touched her daughter's hand. "Nimue..."

"Merlin's twin..."

"What's happening to Sophie?"

"She's evolving, faster than the blink of an eye."

"She's always been ahead of everyone else. Just didn't want to be."

A slow grin worked its way across Lilli's lips. "It's perfect!"

"What's perfect?"

"Can you stay with her till she wakes up?"

"Yes. Why?"

"You're her mother, that's why. It'll keep her from getting sick."

Eleni looked up surprised.

"It's not a joke. Elements of the dream need to be mirrored in her life, to help her remember. That burgundy dress stays on to help her remember. The clothing scattered on the floor stays out to help her remember. You are her mother, and Igraine was

Arthur's mother. ***Mother*** is the active principle that's being absorbed. Don't tell her what happened. Let her talk. Let her undress, and let her get dressed. See what she does. Let her see the bed of clothing in the corner of the galley...and let her smell it."

"Where are you going?"

"I have some laundry to do."

Eleni shrugged. "God help us."

Lilli turned to leave then spun around. "Oh yea...Jack's not drunk."

"...Could've fooled me."

"It's been kind of hard on him...flying all over the place, trying to help Sophie. I'm not sure how much longer he'll be out, but don't be too hard on him when he wakes up. He cares a lot."

"Right."

"I'll be back."

"I'm sure you will."

Lilli went into the galley and wandered round till she found what she was looking for, her coyote cap. She tossed it in the air, catching it deftly on her head, then walked over to the table and stared at Jack: His cap had slid onto the floor. Lilli picked it up and placed it back on his head, tucking it firmly in place.

She stared for a moment at the bridle on coyote's bed then went up on deck, jumped ship, and trotted off into the night.

SOPHIE'S DREAM:

The rabbit disappeared down the path, and Sophie ran after him, following quickly as he flurried through the trees. She ran and she ran and she ran, and the raven flew behind. She tripped and fell and scraped her face. She tumbled through scrub brush and fell over exposed roots. Circling a large evergreen, she stumbled again and collapsed at the foot of a very large felled tree. Sitting quietly upon it was the rabbit.

Tears and sweat poured down Sophie's face. She stood facing him, trying to catch her breath, while the raven disappeared behind a tree.

"Kitsym!" she cried out. The rabbit stared past her. His somber expression frightened Sophie. "I did it, Kitsym. I found my way through the Valley!"

Kitsym's coat was buttoned high around his neck. He remained silent, an expression of sorrow washing his face.

"Kitsym, what is it?" Sophie whispered.

A large tear welled up and rolled out of one of his eyes. He nodded for her to turn and look. As Sophie turned, she started rubbing the palm of her right hand. The raven peered out from beneath the branch to see what he could see.

Sophie looked across the clearing through something that looked like mist. Kitsym had called it a Veil of Tears, but it looked like a heavy rain, and through it she could see a very large tree; it was the Tree of Life.

Sophie and the raven scanned the Tree from the top down. Their gaze glided over limbs and down the gnarled trunk, looking for something that might explain the tears in the rabbit's eyes. Down the warped base they scanned, all the way to the ground, where roots writhed like serpents; it was there that they saw her. At the base of the tree, behind the veil, stretched out against root and trunk, was a white form.

"It isn't her, is it?" she whispered to Kitsym. "Please tell me it isn't her."

Kitsym turned and looked into Sophie's eyes. "You have very little time."

She broke into a run towards the Tree and screamed out, "Mom!"

"Stop!" commanded Kitsym.

The raven walked up and down the branch in an agitated fashion, unable to show himself, unable to help, only to watch and listen. Sophie stopped.

"You cannot penetrate the veil," continued the rabbit. "If you touch it, you will be annihilated...and so will we all."

"Why?"

"The rain of sorrow is powerful, Sophie. You cannot just run through it."

Sophie stood in agony, staring at her mother's spirit trapped in darkness behind the Veil of Tears. "I thought I conquered the Valley," she whispered. "I thought she would be saved if I conquered the Valley of Fear."

"You have conquered the Valley...but you have not yet reclaimed the ring. She is still in peril. Come here," said Kitsym.

She turned and walked back, as if in a trance.

"Sit down."

She sat.

"You must listen closely, Sophia, as you have only one chance to save your soul."

Sophie looked up confused. The raven cocked his head.

"Yes, you have made this journey out of love for your mother. She was the catalyst, I know. But she cannot be saved if you cannot save yourself. There is only one way in, Sophia."

"But there is a way in."

"Yes. But I cannot tell you all that must transpire for you to achieve it." The black rabbit started to look pale: He was fading.

"What's happening to you, Kitsym? I'm losing you, just like Merlin! You're fading out on me!"

"The Veil of Tears, Sophia, is preventing the light from reaching the Tree of Life. The rain of tears is killing us all. The voices of mystery are fading."

"You cannot die, Kitsym!"

"Yes, Sophia. I can die."

"What are you saying? Are you and Merlin one? Are you Merlin in disguise?"

"There is only one mystery, Sophia, but there are many faces." The rabbit turned and headed into the forest. His somber coat had disappeared, and he looked like a normal rabbit, hopping into the woods.

"Don't leave me, Kitsym."

The rabbit stopped.

"Is this my fault, Kitsym?"

The raven stepped back, staggered by the question.

"It is, and it isn't," the rabbit said quietly.

"Can I end this rain of tears?"

The rabbit sat for a long time facing the woods. Finally, he turned. "It matters not that the action is of the one or of the many, Sophia. As I said before, it is a nested universe. You are, as a drop of the sea, containing individuality and the resonance of all at the same time. Every action is both insular and multiple. You cannot project yourself in a linear manner, if you are to understand what you are facing." The rabbit got up and walked back towards her. "Do you wish for guidance?"

"With all my heart..."

"So be it."

The rabbit's words were barely audible, his energy draining because of his close proximity to the Veil. "You have reached a place of great mystery, Sophia. That, in and of itself, is for you a great awakening. Under other circumstances, perhaps it would be a time of great flowering, a time of enlightenment. But your awakening has arrived at a moment of potential imbalance and presents you with a challenge greater than most." The rabbit paused to get his breath. "The voice of the mystic...the voice of God...is faint. I...am diminishing before your very eyes...and may...or may not...be able to reach you...to guide you in this final battle."

"Then tell me now before it's too late."

"There is normally protection around The Tree of Life. The darkness that is spreading is contained behind this Veil of Tears. There is still a border on the outside, before you reach the forest that has not been touched. Where we stand now is protected. Your battle must take place here, if you want added guidance. If the Veil spreads too deeply into the forest, you may lose your way, Sophia."

"Why are you calling me Sophia instead of Miss Sophie?"

"You must know yourself by what you are to become, if you wish to succeed; it is my way to guide you home."

Sophie sat quietly, listening.

"Also, in this domain, this Valley of Truth, which is the abode of The Tree of Life, there can be no untruth in your heart. When battle is engaged, you must know with all clarity and love that you stand in truth. Only then will you gain access to the Tree of Life...to the Holy Grail."

"But it's the ring that I seek."

"The Tree..." Kitsym's breathing was labored. "The Tree...it is the doorway, the fountain of mystery. It is the grail...the cup of life...drink from it, Sophia...drink from it and wear the Ring of Truth."

"What else?"

"Look to your left, Sophia. Do you see the tendril of root reaching to you beyond the Veil of Tears?"

"Yes."

"The veil is spreading. It grows closer and closer to the forest wall and soon will embrace all of the Valley of Truth. But one tendril of root still extends under the ground and emerges in the light. Do you see?"

"I see."

"You must make contact with the Tree at your time of battle. That root is your only access. If the veil extends past it...there is no hope." The fur was sagging from his skin, as if the fluid

had been sucked out, leaving him frail and unprotected. "There is...one...more thing."

The rabbit raised his paw, as he sat folded over in the dirt. He raised his paw slowly and music began to play. It was soft, beautiful music. "Tell me what you hear, Sophia. Listen closely, and tell me what you hear."

The raven cocked his head and listened.

"I hear pain," she whispered.

"Mmmnn," he nodded. "What else?"

"Sorrow. I hear pain and sorrow, and, great beauty. I ache with its beauty."

"Transformation," whispered the rabbit. And the music stopped. "There is wisdom in this wood, Sophia. There is transformation in her rings of light. I can tell you no more."

Sophie's face streaked with tears. "I will not fail you, Kitsym."

The rabbit nodded, turned, and hobbled into the forest; the raven watched, every nerve standing to attention.

"I will not fail you," she whispered.

The raven fluttered to a lower branch just as something buzzed quickly through the trees. It was small, like a hummingbird or a very large bee. It circled Sophie three times, then stopped and hovered in front of her face. It had a tiny round body and a big head with two very large eyes. It stared at her suspiciously then cried out, "The Veil of Tears the Veil of Tears! We are all dying from the Veil of Tears!" It took off, buzzing frantically, then went back and hovered in front of Sophie.

"Who are you?" Sophie whispered.

It hovered up and down, its large eyes opening and closing, listening. "Ah..." it said quietly, "...it is you. I am a fairy in the Valley of Truth. We were many, but now we are one."

The raven stared down at the Veil of Tears, as it kept inching towards the exposed root, Sophie's only access to the Tree. The fairy kept watching. Her voice was high pitched and gentle, her large eyes the color of midnight, and her wings were gossamer light.

Suddenly, she darted off again, flying in terror, screaming out, "The Veil of Tears, the Veil of Tears!"

"Help me!" screamed Sophie.

The fairy stopped and hovered again. "Our voice is fading," she whispered.

"Help me while you still can," Sophie pleaded.

Suddenly, the fairy's eyes opened large, as she looked past Sophie then back into her face. "Reach into the light," she whispered before flying off in terror.

Behind Sophie a twig snapped. The raven scuttled to the end of the branch but still couldn't see. Sophie kept staring at the rain of tears and her mother's sleeping form trapped in darkness. Another stick snapped behind her. Sweat began to wet the hair that curled at her temples. Slowly, she turned to face what she knew would be her final adversary.

The raven staggered, as he watched Sophie's face ease. Joy flooded her skin, like a dam breaking, and tears spilled from her eyes.

"Grandpa!" she cried out.

The raven watched, as a man emerged from beneath the shaded woods. His beard was flecked with gray, and there were crow's feet crinkling the corners of his eyes, brimming with love. Although he was older, the raven saw an uncanny resemblance to Sophie.

"Sophie!" The man took a step towards her and stopped. "You have grown, my little Sophie. You are so beautiful!"

His voice was velvet and would have caressed the weariest of spirits, as it did Sophie's. The raven watched, as she raised a foot, ready to run to him. He could see the longing in her eyes, the longing to fall into the arms of her grandfather, someone who could lift this heavy burden from her shoulders. But her foot wouldn't move. Sophie looked down and saw her right foot planted firmly on the root.

"You have done well, little one. Come let me see you."

Sophie kept staring at the root, confused. Her grandfather held out his hand. "Come here, Sophie, it's been a long journey."

Sophie looked past him to the forest wall. "I'm not finished yet, Grandpa." Her voice was small. "I can't come see you. I buried the ring you gave me, and now I have to get it back. You were right. You thought I was its destiny, and you were right. But I was afraid, and so Mom started the journey for me. Now I have to bring her back, as well."

Her grandfather dropped his hand and looked at her compassionately. "Let Eleni go, Sophie. She's with me now. I'll take care of her. You can't get her back."

"I will get her back."

"It will hurt her, Sophie. She's suffered from a journey that was meant for you, not her. Leave her where she lies...with me."

The raven watched anger boil in Sophie's eyes; her spine stiffened. "Leave her where she lies...with you...in darkness?" Recognition enlivened her face. "Why don't we all just stay here, Grandpa?" Sophie reached behind her, towards the approaching rain of tears.

"Don't touch that, Sophie." Her grandfather took a step. Sophie reached her hand closer. "Why?"

"I wouldn't do that if I were you," he said more loudly. "It will hurt you."

"Yes, the rain of sorrow will hurt us all, won't it, Grandpa? We will all be annihilated."

The raven inched his way up and down the branch, severely agitated. Sophie turned to face the Veil and raised her other hand up as well, but she kept her foot on the root. "Why don't we all stay here, Grandpa?"

Sophie's grandfather broke into a run, bolting out of the shadows. She heard his foot land behind her, and she looked up, just as a ray of light split out of the sky. As she turned to face him, she reached into the light and grasped an object.

Her grandfather twisted her towards him, and within the angry passion of his face the raven saw another; there was flickering arrogance in the eyes and a jaw clenched by facial muscles that slithered down his neck.

"They are deceiving you, Sophie." The voice was dark and oily.

Sophie's face became a ravaged battlefield of emotion. The raven staggered back, shocked at the rage, hatred, bitter sorrow, and despair that blew through her skin.

"Your disguise is a greater deceit," she said. Their bodies became entangled in a dance of attraction and disgust.

"You know me?" He asked mockingly.

Sophie's head slid backwards, exposing a white throat dripping with sweat; her eyes darkened with despair. "Henri Dumont, alchemist and user of women's souls..." The words were strangled with fear and recognition of the man who held her in his arms.

"Don't let them take you in, Sophie. We have all the power between us...we need no one...."

He was mesmerizing; his eyes tempted and tormented at the same time. Sophie was weakening.

"You abused the sacred...." She could barely speak. "I abused the sacred..."

"Yes. We are one...the spirit rose within us...at another time...it can again. You have power, Sophie...don't let them tell you how to wield it..."

Suddenly, music filled the air. Sophie looked back at her mother then stared into the terrifying eyes of Dumont.

"There's only one way out of this nightmare," she whispered. "Embrace the darkness, Sophie Alexander."

At that, she looked up to see a sword of light still clasped in her wounded hand. Locked in the embrace of darkness, she turned her hand inward and stabbed the long blade of light swiftly through the back of Henri Dumont and into her own heart.

With the blade of truth joining them, they fell. With her one foot still connected to the root, they descended, as light and dark, and entered the Tree of Life.

The raven cawed and cawed and fluttered to the ground. But they were gone. They had entered the Tree, and the Tree was gone, and the white shroud that was Eleni Alexander had vanished.

So did the raven.

Some screams can wake the dead, predatory screeches across a night sky. At first, that's what Eleni thought it was...the cry of a wounded bird. She knew it wasn't a seagull, neither a hawk. It was too near to be a hawk.

At 4:00 a.m. she heard it again. When it broke the silence, she staggered to her feet and looked out the porthole. There was nothing but dark sea bearing splinters of moonlight. She turned and walked down the hall. Halfway to the galley the bird's wounded cry rolled into guttural choking sounds, like blood gurgling in a throat, gasping for air. She trotted the last few steps into the galley just as the bird's cry died into words.

"...Eleni!"

Eleni stood still in the dim light, staring towards the sounds emerging from the galley. "My God, Eleni...where have you gone?"

She stared as Jack raised his torso off the table, doubled over, and retched blood onto the floor. "I tried," he whispered.

He continued to gag, cough, and wipe his mouth on the back of his sleeve then gazed down at the journal. "I tried, but

I couldn't stop them. I couldn't do anything...just sit in the shadows and watch her terror...your terror." He slid his hand beneath the book and flipped it closed, but his wounded palm stayed open, staring at him, as if it had a life of its own.

"What kind of journey is this, Eleni, that I share your daughter's blood?" He grabbed the edge of his shirt and wiped his palm, hoping to remove the wound. Eleni remained motionless—a shadow in the shadows.

"At least I know she succeeded and that you aren't destined to Dante's inferno for all eternity."

"Do any of us really know that, Jack?" Eleni whispered.

"Perhaps not..." Jack looked towards the darkened hall, still lost in his dream world. "Although one would like to think there were merits for one's actions." He reached for the missing scotch bottle. As he did, moonlight slid from behind a cloud and illuminated the room littered with clothes. "Oh God...Lilli..." Jack stood up and walked around, avoiding boots, slippers, and balled up velvet. "It smells like you peed on everything. I suppose that's supposed to help us track her." Suddenly, he raised his head and released a bloodcurdling scream. "Eleni Alexander what have you wrought on me!"

"Who else would I turn to, Jack, other than you?"

"You're gone and still you speak and dreams spill from one world to the next...your voice haunting me from God knows where. Weave the dream, she says! Well, you goddamn weave the dream, Lilli!" Jack kicked at coyote's bed, lost his footing and fell to the floor; above him stood Eleni.

"It's not as easy when you're living it, is it Jack?"

Jack blinked. "It's holy terror...you should know."

"I was saved. I don't remember."

The boat rocked, as they stared into each other's eyes. "You're real, aren't you..."

Eleni stepped into the light.

"So many years... Eleni."

She reached down to help him, but Jack rolled onto his knees and stood up. "When did you arrive?"

"A few hours ago."

"And this?" Jack waved his hand around the room.

"You're asking the uninitiated. Although I suspect it was in process when I got here."

"Sophie?"

"Asleep."

"Lilli?"

"Left to do her laundry."

Jack laughed. It erupted out of his stomach like air too long contained. "Lilli's Chinese. She does everyone's laundry."

"She looks Indian to me."

"Yea, well, looks can be deceiving."

"She looks terrible."

"Lilli?"

"Sophie! I thought you'd be able to help her. Do you have a single clue what you're doing?"

"I seriously doubt it...although Lilli seems rather confident."

"This isn't a joke, Jack! This is my daughter."

"She's more than your daughter, Eleni...or haven't you noticed yet?" Jack slammed his fist on the table knocking a cup to the floor. "I didn't ask you to send her here you know! I didn't call up and offer my professional opinion and send an hourly rate. She goddamn walked down the pier and spun us into her web."

"Us?"

"Yea, us! Me and Lilli!"

"Is she your girlfriend?"

"At this particular moment in time, I haven't the slightest idea! Who the hell knows what went on here for the last twenty-four hours while I was passed out, flying around as a raven in your daughter's dream. Maybe we had a hell of a good time! How the hell would I know?"

Eleni didn't budge. "Then who is she?"

"She's a friend, a shape shifter...Coyote medicine. Her people didn't even have a name for coyote because there weren't any on the island; that's how unusual Lilli is." Jack looked around the room again. "Coyote probably did this...smelling out the energy." The light fluttered, as clouds blew across the moon.

"Why is your palm bleeding?"

Jack looked down at his hand. "You know, it's not like I do this every day." He rubbed his thumb into his palm. "It's the same wound as Sophie's. I can only suspect it's because I entered the dream. The only way to follow was to absorb the energy."

"I can't lose her, Jack."

"I never even knew you had her," Jack whispered. "Why didn't you tell me you had a child?"

"It was difficult."

"Well, maybe it was difficult for me too. You just walked out of my life. No call, no letter, no nothing. Twenty-two years later, a young woman named Sophie calls and says she needs help. Why didn't you tell me? I could've helped you."

"I didn't want to."

"Who is her father?"

"I don't know."

"How can you possibly not know?"

"I didn't come here to discuss her parentage, Jack! Some other time."

"When?"

Eleni picked up one of Sophie's T-shirts from the floor, tracing her fingers across the drawings on the shirt. "She's been doing this since she was five...drawing forms, circles, shapes...strange notations. At first, it was on her skin. I tried to stop her, but she cried when I washed them off in the tub."

"So you bought her T-shirts and crayons."

"How'd you know?"

"It's in the journal." Jack stood up and walked to the sink. "Have you seen a bottle of scotch?"

Eleni walked out of the galley and returned with the bottle. "How long have you been living here?"

"Two years. Drink?"

"Yes."

"Did you ever marry?"

"No." Jack handed her a drink, holding onto the glass a moment before releasing it into her hand. It was a cheap glass from the grocery store with pink flowers painted on the side. "Perhaps you can enlighten me as to what a cherry tree is doing in the middle of all this Celtic mythology."

Eleni downed her scotch and held the glass out for more. "Did you know that she planted one?"

"No."

Eleni took her drink to the table and sat down. "It was part of another dream. The cherry tree was a seed that fell from Merlin's hand, buried itself in the earth at her knees."

"I know."

"She planted one to keep it alive...move it from the dream state to reality. Sophie is the cherry tree."

"But Avalon and the High Priestesses are connected with apple trees," said Jack.

"I know."

"The Isle of Women is nothing but apple trees."

"The energy that's spinning is in the process of rebirth: new consciousness. The triple spiral is emblematic of the power of creation. Bride equals union. Sophie is the vehicle for the unification. She has to transform them. The cherry tree and the

Asian child symbolize the east. Out of the east comes enlightenment. It's all about rebirth."

"I've missed you, Eleni."

Eleni looked away.

"I'm sorry your father died."

"It's been a lot of years."

They both stared at the journal lying squarely on the table. Suddenly, they heard footfalls down the hall. Eleni stiffened visibly, as she looked up to see Sophie standing in the shadows still dressed in Igraine's dress.

"She's shifting," Jack whispered. "See the crescent moon on her forehead?"

"What do we do?"

"Watch."

Sophie stepped forward, as the moon slid behind a cloud, drenching the room in darkness, leaving Jack and Eleni to listen, as she shuffled through clothing on the floor. She stepped and dragged, stepped and dragged, reading textures and fabrics with bare feet, till she found what she was looking for.

When the moon reemerged, it lit the galley and the woman still clothed in the burgundy gown. The crescent moon shone blue across her brow, and on her arm was draped a floral gown of sheer silk. Her eyes were glazed, staring toward some distant shore only she could see.

"Igraine speaks that we have failed, but I say she is misguided, for are we not pieces of a whole, reflecting back the imagery meant to lead?" She continued to stare into the night, unaware of her audience. *"This gown I wear speaks of your queen-ship Lady Igraine. I am not unaware of the price you paid, as a result of dame fortune's random wheel. We have, each of us, paid dearly for our story. But the story has not ended."* She shifted her narrow shoulders, allowing the gown to slip to the floor. *"Would that shedding our past be as simple as removing thy gown."*

She held the floral dress up and watched, as moonlight passed through. "*The union of the grail will only occur when all parts are in proper alignment. You, Igraine, bore Arthur, under the guise of mystery. But was it fate or was it manipulation by someone who willingly paid a price to have you? Do they think otherworldly parentage alone is enough to turn the tide? Arthur was advised against his marriage to me, advised by Merlin, no less. Yet Arthur, as well, listened to his own desire, disregarding the very realm that held the power to heal his kingdom.*"

Then, tossing the floral dress into the air, she reached up and allowed the gown to slide over her tiny frame. As it slipped along, her skin started to shine. When the hem reached the ground, she lowered her arms and bared her shoulders, leaving the silk to rest low upon breasts already grown full and round like moons. Her cheeks fleshed out like ripe peaches and colored her skin the same.

Draping low upon her hips was cinched a leather belt embroidered with flowers. It joined together at her pelvic bone in a clasp of two interlocking circles.

"There it is," Jack whispered.

Eleni raised her brow in question.

"The interlocking circles," he responded.

"How were we to complete a story whose time had not yet come? If heaven is to be wrought on earth, are we not all to pay homage to that which gives life? I did not whore nor prostitute myself, but merely reflected the world as it was. We are all dreams, living for the day when the dreamer will awaken."

Moonlight hit the ring and sparked a red glint into her eyes. "*But the ring has returned, Lady Igraine, and now our sorrow shall be redeemed.*" As she turned and stepped towards the galley steps, Jack called out, "Guinevere!" She stopped and cocked her head. "Where will you go, Guinevere," Jack asked, not wanting to lose her.

"Is that not a question I should ask of you, Jack Harrington?"

"Me?"

"Yes. It is you that must go and return...as you are also fated with a part in this play of transformation."

Tears flowed from Eleni's eyes, as she watched her daughter.

"Return where?" Jack asked.

"Why do you think you are here, Jack Harrington?"

Jack stared, uncomprehending.

"There are no mistakes, Jack Harrington. You are not an inconsequential piece in this puzzle."

"What am I to do?"

"The inscription on the ring must be resurrected. It must be carried from our past into your future."

"I don't understand."

"You must fly back, Raven, and bring forward the words required to unlock the ring. You are the magic that can find it, and pass it on, to He that bears the mark of the sacred ring."

Guinevere's gaze shifted to Eleni, whose lips trembled as she struggled against the convulsions in her stomach. The eyes staring at her were dark brown, the head carried a provocative tilt, and the lips were full and red. How could a being change so drastically by the energy contained within?

"Your daughter will indeed return to you, Eleni Alexander. She is a Queen, harnessing us from her chariot on high. We will gladly do her bidding."

Eleni couldn't stop the tears.

"You have earned a million stars in your crown, Eleni, for retrieving the ring and following a path for which you had no rules." Guinevere lowered her head and bowed. "*We are Mothers, Sisters, Brides...and although I am Bride, I bow to you as sister, in love and admiration.*" When she raised her head, the color had left her skin, revealing signs of the fragile creature beneath the bones.

"You will not see me again, Eleni Alexander, except within the eyes of she that you have borne." Guinevere slid to the ground and passed out. Jack and Eleni dove to catch her, tumbling in a mass of bodies on the galley floor, where, together, they cradled the fragile body of Sophie Alexander.

JOURNAL ENTRY:

Guinevere: The myth's failure hinges on Guinevere. Mythically, she is fated to Lancelot, yet marries Arthur. Merlin warns Arthur of this, but Arthur is swayed by earthly passion; spiritual union is aborted. Guinevere is a warning to listen to the rules that dictate...the same rules that trapped Merlin in the tree: flesh must honor spirit. Guinevere is a red flag, a warning not to repeat the same mistake again.

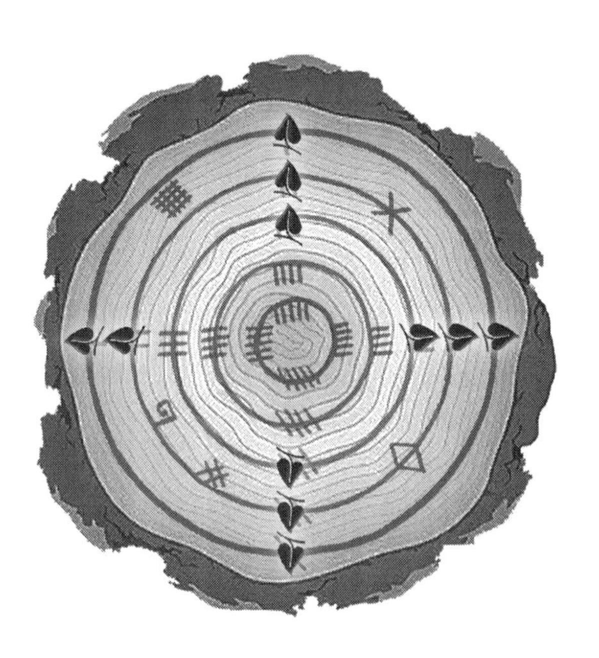

REED
Royalty

VARIOUS PATHS ZIGZAG through the forests of Campbell River. The more obvious ones are human, maintained by hiker's feet and ranger's hands. Less conspicuous are the smaller tributaries, marked by broken limbs and the scent of fur left in clumps on thorny leaves.

Coyote trotted sure footed through tangled brush and wooded groves. Moonlight rarely split the dark canopy of evergreen, but the yellow eyes saw everything. She reached the river at shallow water and waded across where she ascended the hillside, sending a fall of pebbles to the water below; up above stood the cabin. As she neared the shack, Coyote dropped low, sidling along with ears tipped forward and muzzle high, hunting the air. The scraggy fur along her spine jacked up. When she rounded the corner, she was face to face with a magnificent stag, reflecting white in the moonlight. It stared at Coyote then turned and bucked powerful thighs, bolting into the forest, where it quickly disappeared, leaving only the sound of pounding hooves and a powerful scent to follow.

Coyote ran, barreling through shrubs and limbs and hurdling fallen trees; spittle sprayed the sides of her jaw. The red glint of a fire emerged in the distance, red chili sparks flying into the night. Coyote slowed to a trot till she reached a small precipice overlooking a wooded glen in the middle of which was a pit filled with burning embers and a grill supporting a large salmon.

On the far side of the grove, the stag disappeared behind a tree—a mammoth oak split by lightning. The center was blackened, having been blown open, leaving a small cave. Out of the cave emerged a man.

When he stood up, the firelight played tricks with his hair, giving him the illusion of antlers that faded as he walked towards the fire. The stag was nowhere to be seen.

The man was dressed in animal hides, and his hair, hanging loose to his shoulders, was a glistening mane of black water. His skin was tanned and his eyes reflected a piercing blue in the firelight; and the middle finger of his right hand bore the white shadow of a ring waiting to be born.

Coyote turned and padded furtively to the other side of the grove, watching, as the man stoked the fire and poked the salmon with a stick. He took out a cloth and dipped it in a bucket of water then wiped a flat stone by the fire's edge. The stone hissed, and steam rose off the surface. Using two sticks, he lifted the salmon off the flames and placed it on the hot rock where the skin sizzled and snapped.

He whittled a stick into a sharp point, cut a small portion of the salmon with his knife, then stabbed it with the stick and ate it. When he'd eaten the top half of the fish, he put the knife away and rinsed his hands in the bucket of water.

Behind him, a fallen tree had been chopped in half, lengthwise, and raised off the ground, resting on two tree stumps, as if they were legs to an altar. The core of the tree had been hollowed, resembling a boat.

The man reached into the fire and grabbed a handful of burning embers. Coyote shimmied closer. He carried the handful of coals to the gutted log-altar, and deposited them in the core of the tree. The man's hand wasn't burned.

He then went back and removed the salmon's head and carcass from the flesh and placed the carcass on top of the embers, fanning his hand across the top to intensify the heat.

He dropped to his knees.

"The salmon's wisdom will be transformed to ash tonight, dear Lady, and the rains will wash it deep into the rings of this tree, and I will pray for thee. May it give you strength on this journey that brings you ever closer to me." As he spoke, the fish bones dissolved to ash and a light rain began, sending the ash into the vessels of the tree.

He stood and looked back at the remaining salmon flesh, still simmering on the rock then walked back towards the old oak. "We meet again, Coyote," he whispered into the night. "Please accept the Salmon as a token of my friendship."

Bending low he entered the tree. "You know, Coyote," he called out, "it was the wind that guided my Lady back to the Tree. And now, the Tree has a message for you."

Coyote stepped out of the shadows and walked towards the firelight.

"Tell your Raven to listen to the wind. The words he seeks cannot be found in the confines of another's dream."

Coyote sidled closer to the Salmon.

"And give him this." The man tossed a small object at the feet of Coyote. "It has inspired others...perhaps it will work its magic again."

Coyote stared at the object in the dirt then up at the Salmon. She took three steps and sniffed the flesh still warm from the fire, lowered her head and licked only the juice from the base of the rock. Then, she picked up the gift with her mouth and departed, disappearing back into the night.

The red lacquered knob on Lilli's totem door had more than a few scratches across the surface. Coyote leapt up, hit it hard and forced the knob to click open, allowing her to enter. The door had been hinged to close itself.

She trotted across the animal skin rug and jumped up on the old couch, dropping the item she had retrieved from the forest into a cup on the floor. Turning in circles, she scratched at upholstery worn thin and ragged from sharp nails and muddy paws, till the cushions conformed to the appropriate shape. Then she collapsed into the welcoming form and drifted off to sleep.

Jack and Eleni stared at Sophie, dwarfed by blankets and pillows. Jack had lifted her in her nest of floral silk and carried her to the bunk, where he tucked woolen blankets and plaid fleece around her, high enough to ease his fear.

"When did you speak with her last?" Eleni's voice was small and far away.

"She is in there, Eleni. They're not going to swallow her up."

Eleni was lost behind her daughter's eyes.

"Right after she got here," Jack answered. "It was the first and the last time we spoke...she hasn't stopped shifting since."

"She can't go on like this."

Jack stared.

"When did she last eat?"

"You can't keep food in her while this is going on, Eleni. She's moving too fast."

"She'll die."

"She won't die."

"How many women have presented themselves so far?"

"That's one way of phrasing it."

Eleni went still, like the silence between notes in a song. "Are you listening to them, Jack? I mean, really listening? You're being given a gift, you know. If Sophie dies they all die. If she can't find a way to map them together their voices will fade into oblivion, just like before. And when, I wonder, will they be heard again?" She looked out the porthole. "Why didn't you come back?"

"What?" Jack watched the outline of her brow against the dark sky.

"That night...so many years ago... You went to get wine and candles and never came back."

"How can you say that, Eleni?"

"I must have fallen asleep. I don't know how else to explain it."

"Eleni..."

"It was Samhain, remember? We were celebrating with candles, but they burnt down and you went for more. And then you just left..."

Jack reached out to take Eleni's hand but she pulled away. "Explain what, Eleni?"

"The vision...like waking up when your body's still asleep and watching a different world take place." Eleni looked into Jack's eyes, the soft gray of a sea fret turned to steel. "The room was dark. The door opened and unearthly light spilled in, blinding me. I heard someone enter and shut the door."

Jack kept silent.

"I knew who it was, even though I couldn't see, a spirit so long gone you forget just to ease the pain. I was ecstasy and I was despair, because I knew it would be as fleeting as a heart-beat."

"Eleni..."

"I made love with him, Jack."

"Eleni, I came back."

"The veils between realities lift during Samhain, Jack. Remember? They lifted, and he walked right through and into my room...and I conceived."

"Eleni..."

"No...listen! Sophie was conceived in mystery. Even I couldn't explain it. Something happened."

"I came back, Eleni!"

Eleni focused her eyes again on Jack, forcing herself into the present. "What are you saying?"

"I thought you didn't want to see me again because of what happened."

"What are you talking about?"

"You'd always said that you wanted to remain a virgin till you married."

"Yes, I did."

"But your arms were open, welcoming me into your bed."

"What are you saying to me, Jack?"

"I'm saying that I went back into a darkened room to a woman I loved, who offered herself to me in love and I didn't resist! That's what I'm saying! I made love to you, Eleni. And all these years, I've thought you hated me because of it."

Eleni's green eyes glazed, as she shifted back and forth through time. "You came back?"

"I should've known something else was going on. It was almost as if you were drugged. Hell! I felt drugged by you! I couldn't stop myself."

"It was a vision, Jack."

"They were all visions Eleni, but they had a human vehicle! Merlin! Arthur! All their births were the result of divine intervention. I understand what you're saying!"

Eleni kept looking at Sophie's laceless tennis shoes in the corner, then down at Jack's feet, clad in the same thing.

"Eleni, for twenty-two years I've missed you and hated myself for taking advantage of a situation that hurt the only person I've ever loved."

"She's yours?"

"But how could I hate what I'd done when it was done in love? How could I have misunderstood you and us to such a degree that one incident would send you out of my life forever?"

"Merlin placed a spell on Uther Pendragon, so he'd look like Gorlois, Igraine's husband. That's how he was able to make love to her," Eleni whispered.

"I know."

"Did someone put a spell on you, Jack Harrington?"

"The only one who put a spell on me in my entire life, Eleni Alexander, was you. I knew whom I was making love to. You, on the other hand, opened your arms to someone else."

"It was divine intervention, Jack."

Jack's gray eyes clouded over, dark smoldering storm clouds rising from the sea. He turned his back to Eleni and walked away. "Yea, well, I'm glad it makes you happy."

Eleni followed, lost in memories of divine light. "Where are you going?"

"To get drunk..."

"Did you hear what I just said?"

"If you need help, call Lilli. Her number is on the board."

"Don't you realize what this means, Jack?"

Jack spun around and glared down at Eleni. Her face was full of wonder, her eyes as green as the forest that spills into the ocean's reflection at land's end. He stared into them, feeling himself falling into all the years of loneliness he'd come here to forget. "It means, Eleni, that although I made love to you…you never made love to me."

"Jack."

"Just another vehicle of insemination…"

"She's your daughter."

"And what, precisely, does that mean, Eleni? She's also the daughter of whatever divine light inspired you to spread your thighs. Whose daughter is she, anyway?"

"After all the hours we spent discussing the miracle of life you say this to me?"

"You set me up…sent her to me. God only knows what might have happened."

"She's yours for a reason, Jack. It's not a mistake."

"Well, maybe I'm not interested, anymore." Jack grabbed the bottle of scotch and climbed out of the galley. "I'll be back in the morning. I'd appreciate it if you'd both clear out by then. Lilli's good at this stuff. See if she can put you up…help Sophie find her way."

Eleni bolted up the steps after him. "You heard what Guinevere said, Jack. They need you to resurrect the words that will unlock the ring."

Jack stepped off the boat and onto the pier, leaving Eleni rocking in the dark. He opened the bottle and took a long drink. "You know, maybe I don't give a damn. Ask Lilli where the inscription is. She's a real magician."

"It has to be you."

Jack took another swig. When he opened his eyes, the moon had slid out from the clouds, illuminating the name painted on his boat. "Screw ***Avalon***. Go find someone else to steer your ship. I'm tired of being used." He turned his back and walked away, but moonlight poured his shadow across the dock.

Jack watched as it marched bigger than life up the gangplank in front of him and into the parking lot where the moon sent it flying onto the "COYOTE" license plate of Lilli's truck.

"Shit, Lilli. Leave me alone."

May 6, 2001

The sun rose out of the east. Eleni took consolation in that one constancy—the ebb and flow of time, marked by moon and sun and stars, measuring space with astrological symbols, guiding mankind towards the heavens. Dear God...sometimes she felt she was going insane, believing in the unbelievable, embracing the immeasurable, giving birth to a daughter whose life ripped the fabric of normal reality to shreds.

She sat on deck, shivering, in jeans and a thin cotton sweater that absorbed the moisture from the fog like a paper towel, fog that crept out of the night to rest upon the water just as morning's light descended. It was pink light, and slid across the channel like rose Chablis—dreamy pink wine water and cottony fog.

And now he was gone.

Eleni was tired. No, she wasn't tired. Tired was for normal people. She was so far strung out, Jack's words were still reverberating. She was like taut strings of a violin, old and out of tune. She couldn't quite hear the song he was singing to her. Why did it sound so sour? Something in her said it was a beautiful melody, but she couldn't play it anymore.

Shivers ran up her spine, and she clutched the buttons of her sweater with her right hand. The left remained flaccid in her lap, cupped like an old claw. Eleni was battle weary and the battle hadn't ended.

She stood and shrugged the memories out of her shoulders, readying herself for whatever the day would bring, then she descended the steps into the cabin. In the middle of all the chaos, ripped clothing, peed on woolen, chewed boots, and broken pots...in the middle of it all...stood Sophie.

They stared at each other across the torn remnants of a life, across the torn remnants of many lives, and the boat rocked. Eleni looked at her daughter's forehead, frightened to lose her to the crescent moon, but it wasn't there.

"I heard your voice," Sophie whispered.

"My voice?"

"Yes. It's like swimming in a dark ocean with lots of voices calling to me, and I wonder if I'm going to drown. And I know that if I drown, I'll take them all with me into one huge watery grave."

Eleni stepped into the room, her fair hair frizzy from the sea air and her skin yellow with sorrow.

"They keep reaching in, pulling me to the surface, searching for the light." Sophie looked around the room littered with clothes purchased in second-hand stores, shoved in a duffel bag, and dragged onto a bus. She hardly remembered a thing, except getting sick into a bucket that first morning. How long ago was it?

"Sometimes the voices are familiar. I swim toward them, as if they're lifesavers in a stormy sea. I swam toward your voice this morning. They were all there with me, but all I could hear was you, looking up through sea-green water and praying it would pour me into your eyes."

Eleni couldn't move; she was a thin rail of icy metal, dripping water from her eyes. How could she go on?

"But I can't remember who you are."

"Sophie..." Eleni's voice shriveled with pain.

"I longed for your voice," Sophie continued. "I heard it and knew I had to get to it. They don't stop me. Somehow, I think they want to help. But it feels like I'm drowning in the earth's womb."

Eleni stepped forward.

"Are you Jack's friend?"

Eleni nodded. "Yes. We're old friends."

On the ground at Sophie's feet was a mantle, embroidered with turtledoves. She picked it up and draped it around her shoulders then started looking for something to put on. She slipped out of the dress made of floral silk, letting it fall to the ground like petals in a breeze. "I remember buying this," she said as it dropped. "I remember it felt like blackened spring, and I hoped I'd never have to wear it. Now it's too late."

A white shirt with a round collar caught her eye. She slipped it over her head, draping the turtledove mantle around its collar. Her jeans were balled up in a lump by the sink, next to a pair of leather pants. She pulled on the jeans and kicked the leather pants to a pile of clothes that smelled like dog pee. In the corner of the room was a burgundy gown with a pearl-encrusted collar half torn off.

Eleni watched as Sophie sifted through the garments, assessing, rejecting, and picking out the ones she felt associated with enough to put on. "Would you like your sweatshirt?" she asked.

"Do I have one?"

Eleni slipped into the bunk and grabbed Sophie's old worn sweatshirt, then returned to her, hoping the familiar smell of her own clothes would help.

"Did Jack ask you to stay with me?"

Eleni handed her the shirt and watched as Sophie's fingers rubbed quickly over the worn fabric. "Yes."

Sophie was taken with the pearl collar on the gown. She walked over and ripped it off the dress, wrapped it around her neck and buttoned it in back. She stood quietly for a moment, listening, then unclasped the back and held it to Eleni. "This is for you."

Eleni stared at the collar torn from the gown of Igraine, mother to Arthur, mother out of time. She looked at the pearls and remembered Igraine's eyes and the blessing of redemption, and knew the pearls were from her. Eleni reached out and accepted the gift, knowing full well that Sophie didn't quite understand why she was passing them on, but the fact that she did was good.

"Thank you, Sophie."

Sophie looked down at the sweatshirt. "This sweatshirt has drawings on it. Did I do these?"

"Yes, you've always drawn on your clothes."

"You act like you've known me a long time."

"I think I've known you forever."

"The women beneath the sea have known me forever too. Do you know them?"

"I've met some of them."

"Maybe when I go back, I can ask them about you; maybe they will help me remember."

Lilli's words stormed through Eleni's head, screaming orders of what to do and not to do. Don't tell her what happened; let her search, let her reach, and let her discover. Eleni wanted to cry out "piss on all of them!" She wanted to fall at Sophie's feet and reclaim her daughter, to wipe the invading schism out of her mind, and hold her to her breast. "They will speak to you of me, I'm sure, Sophie."

"Jack loves you, doesn't he...?"

Eleni stumbled over and collapsed onto the kitchen bench. "Why do you ask?"

"When I heard your voice, I heard his too. Not the words. The words don't actually matter. I heard love in his voice...and sorrow."

"And what did you hear in mine?"

Sophie looked at the woman with incredible green eyes and knew that she couldn't get past hearing her own desperate need for her. Why couldn't she remember who she was? "Salvation," Sophie whispered, "but I guess I was wrong, because I'm still under water. Have you seen my tennis shoes?"

Eleni went into the bunkroom and returned with Sophie's laceless shoes, watching as her daughter slipped them on just like Jack. When Sophie stood up, her jeans fell to the floor, having grown baggier with her decreasing weight. She hauled them up then took the turtledove mantle and wove it through the belt loops, pulling it snug, so the jeans rested low on her hips, tied tight with a sash of winged birds. She looked at the sweatshirt a long time then tossed it in a heap on the kitchen bench and started hunting through the clothes, till she found what she was looking for—a long, green velvet coat with high military collar, gold buttons, and a tight waist. She put it on over Dindraine's white shirt, buttoned it, and then went down to the head to wash. Eleni picked up the sweatshirt, folded it neatly, and placed it on the table. When she looked back up, Sophie was standing in the doorway.

"How do I look?"

Sophie had washed her face and run wet hands through her hair, pulling it out from her scalp. Her jeans sagged around floppy tennis shoes at the bottom and exposed her tiny belly at the top. The white shirt was frail cotton and all but hid beneath the elegant sweep of velvet green that topped the whole outfit; running down her thigh was the soft swirl of the turtledove sash. Eleni stifled her own thoughts, knowing that, indeed, this was progress.

"You look good."

Sophie scanned the room till her eyes landed on the bridle, jammed beneath the bed of clothes in the corner. She stared, haunted by something she was unable to reclaim. "Let's go; I think I could eat a horse."

"Where are we going?"

"There's a fair in town today. It started this morning."

"How do you know?"

"I know things," Sophie said and shrugged.

Eleni nodded. This she didn't doubt. She looked down at the pearl collar still clenched in her right hand. "Would you help me put this on? My left hand doesn't work very well."

Sophie walked over and clasped the pearls around Eleni's neck then turned her around and looked at her. They stared into each other's eyes for a moment. "They look pretty," Sophie said.

Eleni, shivering from more than the cold, reached over and grabbed Sophie's sweatshirt, threw it on, and followed her outside. Halfway down the dock Sophie stopped. "I've forgotten something, I'll be right back."

She boarded Jack's boat and disappeared below where she retrieved her purse. Turning to leave, she noticed the white powder at the kitchen sink, hesitated, then walked over, tossed a pinch in some water and drank it down; as she turned to leave, she again caught sight of the bridle on the floor.

It was a normal bridle, with headgear, bit, and reins—no distinguishing marks. She picked it up and, as she did, a tangled garment came with it, a white dress made of woven cotton. It was a sturdy working dress, slightly yellowed with time and sweat. It had a simple round collar and buttoned down to a low waist where the skirt banded into soft pleats.

The inside of the dress was lined with red silk.

Sophie stared at the dress, then detached it from the bridle, folded it, and stuffed it in her purse with a pair of white ballet slippers that were pinned to the hem. She set the bridle down and returned to Eleni.

"I forgot my purse."

Jack sat on an old wood bench staring out across the channel to Quadra Island. The bench was wet from morning dew, soaking through his thin pants to his legs. On the back of the bench was a brass plaque dedicated to the patriarch of a loving family, engraved with the words: "The time has come, the Walrus said, to talk of many things—Of shoes, and ships, and sealing wax, of cabbages, and kings—And why the sea is boiling hot, and whether pigs have wings."

Jack sat with his arms outstretched over the back of the bench, the bottle of scotch held in his wounded right hand. He really didn't give a damn if pigs had wings. He did, however, believe that the sea was boiling hot, and at the moment, he was drowning in it.

Jack's mother had died on the operating table one month after she was institutionalized. They were performing a lobotomy in hopes of erasing the magic she persisted in upholding and which everyone else believed was concrete evidence of her distorted reality. She apparently decided on which side of the line she wanted to fall, slipping away to her nether world, leaving the doctors confounded as to why their surgery had failed.

His father never remarried, choosing instead to honor and care for the one product of the union he had had with the woman he cherished and adored: Jack. He kept household and holidays going as much as he could, putting money aside to make sure Jack's education would be the best. But Jack's education had already started at the age of five, when he glimpsed something beautiful, then watched as the world tore it to shreds.

Years passed before Jack was old enough to talk with his father about what had happened. He learned more clearly how his mother's world had shifted and changed, and what had mattered before became insignificant. Jack's father had gone to counseling with her in hopes of integrating her experience into their lives, but she was put on medication that only made her worse. He never knew whether it was what had happened to her that made her sick or whether it was the lack of belief from a pragmatic world that offered no sanctuary.

Whatever it was, she retreated to the confines of her own mind and the belief that there was something incredible about to happen, of which she had been blessed with a tiny vision. Gradually, she withdrew from the world, leaving Jack's father no choice but to institutionalize her. He wasn't surprised that she didn't last long.

It wasn't until Jack was twelve that he told his father he had seen it too.

Jack pressed the bottle of scotch to his lips and took a long drink, wincing from the burn of alcohol, searing the open wounds inside. It wasn't that he'd forgotten that he'd seen it. At the age of five, a lot of things get mixed up; a lot of life is imaginary.

Jack reached in his pocket and pulled out a small bag of nuts and set it on his knee.

His father hadn't believed him at first...thought maybe Jack had imagined it, as children are wont to do. But Jack insisted, retelling the whole story of how she'd come to get him, smelling like warm cinnamon, carrying him like a lantern in the night through dark halls to the Christmas room. He told him about the Indian pillow with mirrors that reflected light and how his mother had crawled on her knees, shushing him to keep still, till she pulled the electrical cord out of the socket.

Jack believed. His father wanted to believe.

Jack opened the package of nuts and started picking through them one at a time, examining them in the light, tossing them on the ground. Peanuts, cashews, almonds...on and on he looked, picked, and discarded. Finally, he held one nut up. He let the bag drop off his knee, scattering its contents on the walk for squirrels and other scavengers. He rotated the nut between his thumb and forefinger and stared. Maybe Lilli was right.

It was a hazelnut.

Jack had got his degree in Psychiatry from Stanford University. It had become his life's quest. How many people out there had touched on something bigger than they had the ability to handle? How many people learned the hard way that the world had rules and regulations and that it wasn't wise to rock the boat? How many people were forced into solitude and silence, and how many became artists and musicians in an effort to speak a language that wouldn't confine them? It was his private war.

He didn't discuss it in school. He studied, memorized, and regurgitated. He graduated. And then he set up practice.

Many clients just needed help with what Jack called daily disorder. Some were traumatized at varying stages of life. There were a few that thought they'd seen Christ, and one who thought he was Christ, complete with a twenty-foot cross in his garage. Jack told him that the problem with being messianic was that one usually got crucified and suggested he buy nails.

The patient never came back.

He started disregarding conventional treatment. He encouraged clients to keep track of their dreams, and he made them act upon them, doing something in everyday life that responded to their dream life. He used music and song, playing symphonic pieces, till they elicited a response, resonating with sorrow or fear, unlocking energy lodged in the body. He had a whole wall in his office designated for coloring, paints, and crayons; in truth, the very accusations made by the Medical Board.

He never prescribed drugs, and he never told patients that their world was false. He let them weave their dream. And Jack's patients started getting better.

But the more the Medical Board heard of his unconventional approach, the tighter they cinched the noose, until the end, when they had taken away his credentials. So Jack had closed up shop and disappeared into a world that possessed its own kind of magic: the sea.

He held the hazelnut up, letting the pink haze of morning light fall upon it. Lilli had said that the Celtic people believed all mystic knowledge was contained in the hazelnut. It was potent. You couldn't have contact with it directly...couldn't eat it whole. Too much information would blow your brains out. That's what she'd said...blow your brains out.

The nut had to move into the water, into the salmon. The salmon flesh would then translate the information into something more palatable for us to digest. He rolled the nut around in his fingers. The one thing Jack had always wondered about was why his mother had gotten ill, and he hadn't.

A tug emerged out of the fog, pulling a barge piled high with logs. Jack shifted his gaze from the nut to the barge, his gray eyes lightening with the reflection of pink across the water. Eleni knew that his mother had been institutionalized. She knew what his mother had seen and what it had done to her. She knew that the whole experience had planted a seed from which Jack's life emerged. What she didn't know was that Jack had seen it too.

Jack held the nut up to his lips. It wasn't that he'd been afraid to tell her. He'd just been waiting for the right time.

But she went away.

And now she was back.

And now there was Sophie.

And he knew he couldn't turn his back again.

Looking at the hazelnut, as if it were manna from heaven, Jack opened his mouth and popped it in. As he chewed on the mythological nut, he stood up and turned towards the marina, ready to go back into the fray...back to help the woman he loved. But as he did, his untied shoe slid on the wet walk, twisting his ankle, throwing him sideways to the ground. The bottle of scotch catapulted out of his hand and shattered on the concrete. As Jack came down, his head hit a rock lining the path, and his shoulder folded beneath the weight of his fall. He was found an hour later in a pool of blood, scotch, and broken glass.

Sam's café was open 7:00 a.m. till midnight seven days a week, and Kate had worked the night shift for five years. She liked the locals that trickled in after work, some to catch a breather before entering the chaos of family life at home, others with no one to go home to. Fishermen drank beer to wash away the salt that clung to the back of their throats and talked about the tides, weather, or the ship that ran smack into the rocks on Maude Island and sunk. Captain must have fallen asleep they'd said, knowing that the sea could lull the most seaworthy. You had to watch your back and your front. And you didn't drink if you cared about your vessel and all the others out on the water. Kate liked them.

Morning shift wasn't her thing, but someone had called in sick, so Kate volunteered. What the heck, it was a beautiful morning, and it wouldn't hurt her to see the sunrise once in a while.

Kate looked across the channel, admiring the morning mist sitting low on the water. A soft breeze blew in her face, the kind of breeze that lapped moisture against her skin. She began to turn and tend to her duties, when a figure lying on the path that bordered the water's edge caught her eye. Kate sighed. Even if it was a bum, she should still report him. Besides, she felt sad for people who ended up caring so little about life and themselves, as well.

As she approached the body, Kate was surprised to see that the man on the ground looked tan and strong, and his clothes weren't those of a vagrant. There was broken glass everywhere...shattered hard, like it had flown up in the air and crashed down into a million pieces. It was the broken glass of a booze bottle. Kate recognized the brown glass, and there was a portion with a label stuck in the ground at her feet.

The man's face was pressed to the dirt so she couldn't see him well. But a chill ran up her spine, when she noticed there was a pool of blood by the head. Kate leaned down and touched his arm, cold as ice. And on closer inspection the profile stood out loud and clear: Jack Harrington.

Kate ran to the restaurant and called emergency. Jack liked a drink as much as the next guy, but no one ever accused him of being a Whiskey Jack, the obnoxious, in-your-face bird that hounded everyone. No. Everyone liked Jack, and everyone had noticed that he wasn't himself of late and that, although they didn't like to pry, it wasn't a secret that a young woman of indiscriminate character seemed to be staying on his boat. Kate didn't like the thought of foul play. But, sometimes, foul play was just a twist of fate and didn't have anything to do with someone wanting to do you in.

Emergency arrived, loaded Jack carefully, and rushed off with their siren piercing the morning calm. Kate tried to compose herself. But before opening up, she knew there was one more thing she had to do. She picked up the phone and dialed Sally Swanson up on the hill. Sally was older and wouldn't like being woken up so early. The phone rang six times before it was picked up. At first no one said a word.

"Sally?"

Sally wouldn't talk if she didn't like you. Kate knew the gap of silence was Sally's attempt to determine who the caller was.

"Kate?"

"Yea, it's me. There's been an accident."

"Who?"

"Jack Harrington."

Sally was quiet, probably not fully awake. "Bad?"

"I don't know yet. They took him to the hospital. He's unconscious."

"You need Lilli?"

"Yea. Can you help?"

Sally was quiet again. "I think Agnes is still running Haig-Brown house."

"Can you call her?"

"Yea. She'll be pissed I woke her up."

"I didn't know you used that word, Sally."

"Keep it that way."

Kate smiled and hung up.

Sally Swanson was eighty years old. She lived alone on the hill above Campbell River in an old house that was too cold in the winter and too hot in the summer. She kept a bottle of rum in a knitted vest used for hot water bottles on a hook by her bed and took a nip anytime she felt like it. Sally figured she was past the age of concern with proper standards of behavior, preferring to live however the hell she liked.

Sometimes, she fished on the pier, just to watch the tourists flop around with lines tangled in the seaweed below. That was how she had met Jack. She caught him spying on her once. When their eyes met, he winked and walked away.

Sally liked Jack Harrington.

She turned the light on by the bed and grabbed the rum. A little nip in the morning loosened her joints and eased her arthritis...not that she had any. She opened the drawer by her bed and pulled out an old address book, the leather binding torn and frayed. She opened it to 'H', for Haig-Brown, and dialed.

It seemed to ring for an eternity. She had another nip and waited. Agnes didn't have an answering machine. If you let it ring long enough, she'd finally get pissed and answer it just to tell you to go to hell, which she did.

"Who is this!" Agnes's voice was froggy; she obviously hadn't spoken yet this morning.

"It's Sally." Sally was enjoying herself. She and Agnes were of an age. They didn't always get along, but they had too much history to disregard each other.

"Have you been drinking?" Agnes's voice was warming up real fast.

"Of course I have. When am I not?"

"Well, what are you calling me for? Call the store and order another bottle instead. I'm sure they'll be happy to oblige." Agnes began to hang up and Sally screamed into the phone. "We're trying to reach Lilli!"

Agnes put the phone back to her ear. "Is something wrong?"

"It's Jack. Been hurt. In the hospital."

"You never were one for eloquence."

"Piss off, Agnes. Kate just called from Sam's. Jack's been hurt, and no one knows nothin' yet. He's unconscious."

Agnes was quiet a long time.

"You still there?"

"I'm thinking," Agnes replied.

"That's a change."

"Sally, you were a pain in the ass when you were little and you still are."

Sally chuckled and took another nip. She decided that she actually rather liked Agnes. "Well?" she continued.

"I like Jack," said Agnes.

"Good for you."

"Shit Sally...go to bed!" Agnes hung up. Sally put the receiver down, tucked her feet under the blankets, and turned off the light. She had one more nip of rum before hanging it back on its hook. "I like Jack too, Agnes."

Agnes ran the Haig-Brown Historical Site located on the south side of Campbell River. It was the original home of Roderick Haig-Brown, local sports fisherman and nature conservationist, who had published over twenty-five books immortalizing the area; it was also a bed and breakfast. Agnes loved to have a chance to share the history with people who cared. But if they didn't, she sent them across the river to the travel lodge. Agnes didn't tolerate fools well.

She went to the kitchen and pulled out her file of business cards. The travel lodge was on the top. She didn't care for their type of hotel but, in a small town, it wasn't wise to go looking for strife. She told them she sent people over when she was tiring from the work Haig-Brown house required. She worked hard for a woman her age and felt she had a right to back off on occasion. The fact that she picked what and when and who was no one's damn business but her own. The phone rang twice.

"Good morning! Campbell River Travel Lodge, Salmon fishing capital of the world. May I help you?" The voice was as cheesy sweet as usual and always made Agnes want to gag.

"Good morning, Christine."

"Agnes?"

"Yes, dear."

"Hello Agnes, how nice to hear from you. Is everything all right?"

"Well, there's been a little mishap in town and Jack Harrington's been hurt. You haven't by any chance seen Lilli, have you?"

"Lilli? Oh Lilli! Why heavens no. Lilli never comes around here. In fact, although you've spoken of her before I've never even met her, Agnes."

"For heaven's sake…is that so?"

"Yes, indeed."

"Well, excuse me for calling so early, Christine. I'll call Sally Swanson. She'll know what to do."

"Sorry Agnes. Hope he's all right."

"We all do, Christine." Agnes put the phone down and waited. She knew Lilli well, saw her regularly walking the paths along the river…in both forms. Didn't believe it at first. But if you lived long enough in one place, you'd begin to learn the truth of things, and Agnes knew that Lilli did a world of good for everyone. Including the time she ripped the pants off a burglar at 3:00 a.m. right outside Haig-Brown House, sending him screaming half mad, "Coyote! Coyote!" all the way down the road. Everyone laughed, because he got arrested for vagrancy and potential damage to a historical site, and because they all knew there weren't any coyotes in Campbell River.

Agnes smiled. She knew Christine didn't have even a speck of a clue just who Lilli was, or where to find her. It didn't matter. You just needed to make the phone connection across the river and say her name and Lilli would hear. It was one of those little oddities some of them knew, like Kate and Sally. If enough of you called her name down the telephone line and across the river and back, you could be assured that Lilli would hear. She always did.

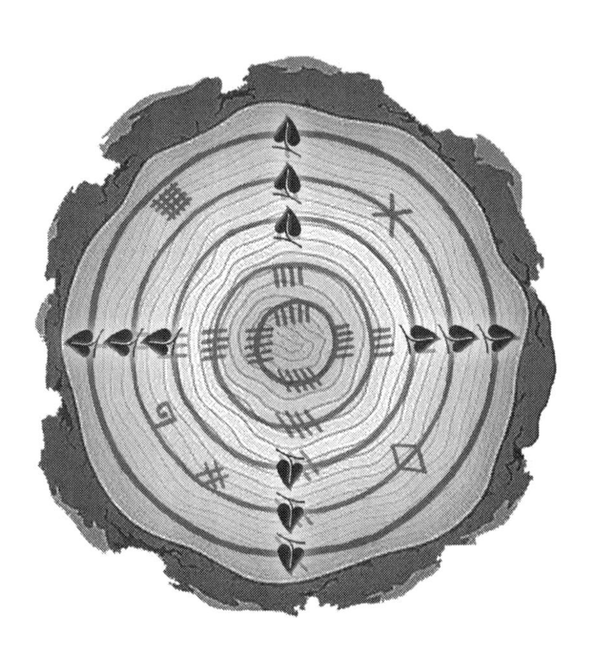

HEATHER

Spiritual Passion

LILLI FELT THE slap of dawn hit her face. It wasn't muted, softened by the passage through sunflower cotton drapes; they hadn't been closed the night before. This morning's light bore a particular intensity.

She lay curled on the tattered couch and tugged the saggy knitted blanket around her bare shoulders; there was panic in the air. Her arm slid over the cushion's edge to the floor, where she stuck her fingers in the chipped cup and removed the gift from the forest man: a tiny crystal. The edges were cold, faceted, and occasionally sharp; it had a mind of its own and it was telling her she needed to find Jack.

In the corner of the room was a laundry bag of many colors, stained from assorted washes. She reached in and grabbed blindly for pants and shirt. They were all denim, so it didn't matter which came out. She slipped her narrow feet into deer moccasins, tugged her cap down around her mane of hair, and was out the door, treading lightly into the dawn.

She arrived at the marina and stopped, abruptly, at the end of the pier, staring down the dock to the *Avalon*. Her eyes narrowed. It wasn't so much that the lights were off in the boat but that the energy was off. The *Avalon* looked hollow—discarded—like when life leaves a body and you see it for the shell it really is.

Lilli padded softly along the pier, allowing her senses to open, then climbed on board and descended into the galley. The three people she'd left there were gone; something had blown up in their faces, scattering them in different directions. The chaos on the floor had changed.

There was a silk floral gown in the middle of the room she hadn't seen before, and some of the clothing was missing: Nimue's long green cloak and Dindraine's shirt. The journal was open next to a pool of dried blood. She scanned the journal page.

JOURNAL ENTRY:

Inscription: The ring is inscribed with letters from the Ogham Tree Alphabet. All trees, as conduits of energy, possess information. In order for the wisdom within the trees to manifest, there must be a return of an enlightened male and female, the bearers of the ring.

Lilli flared her nostrils, breathing in the chaos. There was a lot of life trapped in the weave of clothing on the floor but its scent was old. The smells she was picking up were fresh. The anger was fresh. It was bitter and ran rancid down the back of her throat; and it was male.

She went back to the bunk. Eleni's overnight case had been tossed in a corner of the room, her purse at its side. People had left here without thinking. Too much emotion had painted worlds they wanted to run from. She returned to the galley and stuck her finger in the pooled blood then raised it to her nose.

"Jack," she whispered. "She's opened Jack's wound."

She trotted up the galley steps, leapt onto the dock, and came down to the end of the pier where her boat was tied. Lilli started the motor and headed towards Sam's café, where she pulled up on the beach and climbed the rock wall to the path. In front of her was the Fischer family bench. On the ground in front of it was a stain of blood, and the smell of whiskey was thick in the earth.

She walked quickly back to her boat, returned to the marina, got in her truck, and drove to the Campbell River Medical Center. On the way, she passed a park where a fair was going on. Her head swiveled. She made a mental note then sped her way up the hill to Jack.

Not everybody in the community knew Lilli. She was what some called a river rat, surviving on the edge of water and land, this world and the next. Anyone who inhabited the borderlands knew her. But the medical community was framed by civilized society; she took her hat off and combed her hair before going in. A stern woman with gray eyes and thick-rimmed glasses sat at the front desk.

"Was a Mr. Jack Harrington admitted here this morning?"

The woman looked up suspiciously then checked her book. "He was admitted this morning...yes."

"I'd like to see him."

"And you are?"

"I'm his sister."

The woman's eyebrows arched. "It says here that he has no family."

"All he has is me; I'm his adopted sister."

"The file doesn't say anything about a sister. Critical care is very careful about visitors. Besides, he's white."

Lilli eyed the woman. "You think an Indian family wouldn't adopt a white boy?"

"The words never escaped my lips."

"I adopted Jack Harrington a year ago. He's my brother, and I intend to see him, so you can either point me in the right direction or I'll find him on my own...which I'm very good at."

The woman looked down and sighed. "Critical care unit—East wing, third floor. There are no visitors allowed, so talk to the nurse at the station."

Lilli stood in the hallway of the critical care unit and watched as nurses scurried with medical boards clutched to their breasts. Suddenly, her eyes lit up.

"Irene!"

A woman about forty with buzzed hair and a small, discrete tattoo on the inside of her arm looked up from her position monitoring the desk.

"What'd you do to your hair, Irene? You look like the back end of a wet duck."

"Lilli!" The woman's smile bridged the cavernous gap between medicine and magic. "God, are you real?"

"Depends on your definition..."

The two women embraced, their laughter echoing down hollow halls.

"He's in a coma, Lilli." Irene wasn't partial to small talk.

"Anyone know what happened?"

"Chart says he was found outside Sam's café this morning...looks like he fell and hit his head on a rock; shattered glass and whiskey in his clothes."

Lilli nodded. "Can I see him?"

"I'm not supposed to. We're monitoring him. Don't know yet how serious it is."

Lilli looked into Irene's eyes and remembered the time Coyote pulled her father out of the river, where he'd almost died. He lived a long life after that and was around to share many years with his grandchildren. Irene scanned the hallway. "But since it's you, I think I can break the rules. Make it quick, though." Irene checked to make sure all was clear then ushered Lilli into Jack's room and closed the door.

The room was small and dark. Jack was hooked up to various machines, monitoring his vital signs. His head was bandaged, and a bruise spilled down the right side of his brow.

Lilli scanned the lines in his face, recognizing the trauma to be other than the fall. Jack had been hit hard with something on the inside. That's where he'd fallen. The broken glass and booze were inconsequential.

She let herself shift so that she was somewhere between human and animal. It was hard to do and she didn't do it often, but Lilli sensed there were two wounds here and she needed extra help. The one on the head was a big-time wake-up call. It was good. She'd told Jack a long time ago he should've been named "Running Bear," because he thought his boat was a place to hide from the world. This hit on the head was all about that.

But there was another wound.

Lilli's vision penetrated Jack's body. She moved down from his head to his neck, chest, and limbs. There was a constriction in the throat and a lump in his chest, like a black cloud, and it radiated down to his bandaged right hand, the wound of Sophie.

She pulled the tape off Jack's hand, and from her pocket withdrew the item she'd been given in the forest. She held it up, letting the small amount of light in the room reflect off it; she wanted to be sure. There it was. A perfect triangle etched into one of the six facets of the quartz crystal. She had felt it this morning, barely visible to the naked eye, but an indentation not to escape the sensitive searching of her fingertips. The ancient universal trinity, the third eye, etched so small it was almost beyond perception. It was the Record Keeper, one of the most sacred of crystals, with the potential to reveal ancient knowledge. She placed the crystal in the center of the wound on Jack's palm, grabbed the bandage tape off the table and began to wrap his hand.

"Sometimes, Jack," Lilli whispered, "people need to be stopped in their tracks in order to take a journey." She wrapped the tape expertly. "They need you, Jack. They need you to go someplace. This crystal will help take you there."

She finished her nursing but held onto his hand. "The wound on your hand is linked to your heart, Jack. Your throat is blocked and you're afraid to speak. The scar on your hand is an imprint; let it guide you. Sophie carries the ring for two, and it's a heavy burden. She needs you. You're the Honor Guard, Jack, the Raven King. You can help the transformation by retrieving the words needed from the past and bringing them into her future...to all our futures.

"There is a man in the forest who bears the horns of a great stag, and a white stain on the middle finger of his right hand. But he's paralyzed until you return."

Lilli rubbed the crystal gently through the bandage. "There isn't much time, Jack. The priestesses are leaving their mark on Sophie. She's doing it. She's integrating them. But when she's ready, we have to be, too."

She set his hand, palm down, on the bed and draped the blanket over it, then ran her fingers through the silver hair at his temple. "And Jack..." Lilli leaned over and whispered in his ear, "I know who she is."

Eleni and Sophie stood at the edge of a large field, bordered at one end with food kiosks and, at the other end, with camouflage tents crammed with hunting paraphernalia of guns, knives, and tracking devices. It was a hunting and fishing fair, and in the center of the field there was a demonstration regarding appropriate response when confronted with wild animals; Sophie chewed on an elephant ear.

Men of varying ages rallied around the booths, hefting rifles, checking sights, and admiring knives.

"Would you like a hotdog?" asked Sophie.

Eleni looked at the girl who had suddenly become a stranger. Sophie had eaten a corn dog, an elephant ear, and a bag of nuts. Eleni's stomach was too twisted to navigate food. "No thanks."

She watched, as Sophie got in line at the kiosk, then turned her attention to the demonstration. When she looked back, Sophie was gone.

"Oh, God..."

Eleni scanned the field for any sign of green: parkas, sweaters, and blankets. But there was no forest-green, ankle-length velvet cloak to be seen. Eleni was weary to the bone, beyond clear thinking; she didn't know what to do.

"They do battle and yet there is no war."

She turned sharply and looked into Sophie's face, marked clearly with the crescent moon.

"Most men do," Eleni responded.

Sophie had slipped away and changed into a plain white dress and slippers. She carried the coat and jeans on her arm. The dress, although plain, hung close to her body. It sat low on her waist, and a belt of braided leather with interlocking circles girdled her hips. She looked beautiful; an uncommon woman in common garb. Men began to stare.

"It is easy," she continued, *"for women to be enamored of being enamored...but in so doing, love turns in on itself and becomes self serving, and neither man nor woman can be carried to higher ground."* She seemed taller...and graceful, as a swan.

"Who are you?" whispered Eleni.

The woman looked down at Eleni's neck. *"You carry the pearls of wisdom."*

"They were a gift."

"They are never a gift but are hard earned. They are the milk that feeds us, so we might arrive at the destination of which I speak. I am Enid, Bride of Erec."

Eleni's hand floated up to the pearls at her neck, seeking sustenance.

"You are as Igraine," Enid continued, *"mother of life. And I am bride, learning lessons of love, and how it should be served."*

"And how is that, Enid?"

"By love alone..."

A young man, his bronzed skin pungent with the vigor of the outdoors turned a lusty eye to Enid. Eleni stared him down, and he walked away. Enid stared out at the men in the field. *"It is as Morgan said. Unless those who love possess their own sovereignty, higher union will not flower. Even in my lowly garb, Erec granted me this, showing no disdain for that which to some might have appeared common."* She lifted her skirt and fluttered the hem, exposing the red silk lining. *"He saw a queen beneath the peasant girl."*

"And where is he now, Enid?"

Enid turned a keen eye to the men checking gun sights and weighing the heft of knives. *"Erec seeks to find what all men seek, his manhood. But in his journey, he forgets that he need not battle for what is already won. How long must he journey? I do not know...except that I will wait for all eternity, as therein lies my honor of the very sovereignty he seeks. What he has granted me in love, I also do for him.*

"Erec is my love, and I have learned that I cannot usurp that love, nor drink too deeply of its intoxication. I wait to learn of his honor in battle, or whether he still battles for honor. But he is long gone, now, and I fear his death, and a story that speaks again of a failed dream."

The young man with unkempt blond hair and brawny arms reappeared. He carried the smell of a hunter, of unwashed sweat, the smoke of logs, and stale beer. He leered at Enid. "That's a real pretty moon tattoo you have there, sweetheart."

Enid turned and stared. His muscles ripped out of his flannel shirt, demanding attention, having been in the wilds too long. She turned away.

He stepped in and turned his back, closing Eleni out of the circle, resting a hand on Enid's narrow hip. "That's a real pretty dress too." His hand slithered up and down her back. Enid stepped back, but he grabbed her, pressed her up against his chest. Eleni grabbed his arm but he shook her off like a fly. People began to stare.

"Leave her alone!" screamed Eleni.

The man looked down. "What are you, her mother or something?"

Enid's struggle was spare. She began to bleed color from her face, fading into ashen gray. Her eyes slid shut, and her head dropped back, revealing the supple bend of a white throat. In one movement, her jaw split open and, from the caverns of her belly, erupted a shrieking cry. The man dropped his hand and stepped back, shaken by the wrenching grief that ripped out the sides of her throat. She screamed again...and again, and again. And they all stood still.

"Good god, woman...you trying to wake the dead?" The man blustered, trying to shake off his surprise and reached for her again. A blood gurgling growl emerged from behind. He turned and looked down into the wild eyes of Coyote, yellow splinters of hate, and lips curled tight exposing fanged teeth.

"Be careful," cried a man from a booth. "We don't have coyotes out here. The dog might be rabid. Better get a gun."

Enid raised her head and opened her eyes, white with venom. ***"Step aside,"*** she whispered.

"I'm not moving, lady, till someone shoots that thing!"

"Step aside," said Eleni. "The animal's with us."

"I don't think so," he said. "She's a bitch in heat and needs to be taken down."

Enid walked past him and reached down to Coyote's neck, soothing her for all to see and motioned Eleni to follow. They flanked the animal, preventing a clear shot, and walked out to the parking lot, where Coyote ran ahead to a red truck and jumped in the bed. Eleni checked for keys in the ignition and helped Enid in. As she walked around to the driver's side, she noticed the license plate on the rear of the vehicle. By the time she got in, Enid was passed out cold.

Deep in the forest, the shrill cry had bolted out of the morning sky like lightning, shattering down the trunk of the old burnt out oak tree, striking hard the young man still waiting in its hollow cave. He bowed his head and wept. "The cry that wakens the dead...and time is waning for the Raven King."

Eleni maneuvered the truck with her right hand, pulling into the marina parking lot. The rearview mirror showed that no one felt they were dangerous enough to follow. Coyote had remained curled low in the bed.

She threw the pickup into park, turned the ignition off, and stared at Sophie. Her skin, grayed beyond the soiled white of her dress, had shrunk back, having lost the energy of another. Her head rolled to the side in sleep. Eleni slid over and wrapped an arm around her.

"Remember, Sophie?" she whispered. "Remember all those years ago when we learned about Enid and Erec...?" Eleni shivered and held her daughter tight, hoping to generate warmth. "Erec came back to Enid, Sophie...he heard her cry...the cry that wakens the dead...that's what they called it. He had almost forgotten...was almost dead...but Enid's cry brought him back to life..."

Eleni closed her eyes on the rising tears. "Remember, Sophie...Erec rose...like Lazarus from the dead."

Lilli awoke in the bed of the truck aware of the sun warming her. She lay still with eyes closed, swallowing bile rising from her stomach. Too much shifting; it was making her sick.

She opened her eyes and winced, as light stabbed into her pupils. She could feel the yellow slits recede. "Too slow," she whispered. When her eyes had adjusted, she stared at her hands. Her fingertips were pads of gray leather. She blinked. They were still there.

Lilli remained in the truck bed, curled in a fetal position, for an hour. The sun warmed her skin, and the sounds of seagulls and water lapping against hulls helped, but she knew that, soon, she was going to have to enter the forest and not come out for a while; it was too much of an assault, even for her. They didn't have much time.

When she was fully recovered, Lilli climbed in the cab, started the truck, and reached beneath the seat for food that wasn't there. She felt gray, her energy trapped between worlds. Eleni and Sophie were passed out, slumped against each other like sacks of rice.

Lilli headed up the hill to the medical clinic, parked the truck, and got out, looking back at the women; it didn't seem likely they'd waken soon. She walked to the third floor of the east wing and slipped into Jack's room.

The blinds were closed, and the blanket still draped across his bandaged hand. Nothing had changed. Lilli went to his side and sat down on the bed. She reached up and turned her coyote cap around, then looked down at the skin beneath her nails; it was turning yellow.

The door opened and Irene walked in. "Thought I saw you," Irene said.

Lilli nodded. "Any changes?"

"Not a thing. Seems peaceful. Vital signs are stable. The Doctor will check him tomorrow morning."

Lilli looked back at Jack.

"You can't stay, Lilli. I broke the rules, earlier, but I have to ask you to leave this time."

Lilli nodded again. "Just give me one minute, Irene. I'll be right out."

Irene lowered her eyes and disappeared out the door.

Lilli scanned Jack's brow. "We've reached critical mass, Jack: too many worlds are blurring together. We need your help." She reached under the blanket and rubbed his hand. "There's only one priestess left. But if you're not ready to help us, a breakdown will occur. Not just for Sophie...for all of us." She raised her head and looked around the room. "It's already starting on me. And Eleni looks like hell."

She reached into her pocket and pulled out a feather. It was soft and gray, not too big. "I collect these. Sometimes, I'm lucky and have just the right one. You've got to find your way on your own, Black Jack, over and back. I hope this helps. It's from a turtledove."

Lilli tucked the feather into the bandage around Jack's head, ran her fingers lightly through his hair, then tiptoed out the door and headed down the hall.

Eleni opened her eyes; everything was blurred. The sign in front of her was double lettered. She blinked, and the letters merged. It was a medical clinic.

Sophie was draped across her like a rag doll. Eleni shifted her weight, nudging Sophie against the door. No one was around. The keys were still in the ignition, but the truck had obviously been moved, and it was two hours since she'd pulled into the marina. Lilli must have driven them here. She stared again at the medical sign.

"Jack," she whispered.

She slid out of the truck, shut the door, and looked at Sophie. Eleni hesitated. "I've got to go, Sophie...I've got to see if he's here."

She walked to the entrance where a stern-looking woman sat, deflecting traffic. The woman looked up at Eleni and grimaced. Eleni's hair was matted to her head on top and frizzed out on the sides from the sea air. She wore Sophie's oversized sweatshirt that was smeared with layers of crayon, ink, and painted lines. Around her neck was the choker of pearls from Igraine's dress, and she looked like she hadn't eaten for a month.

"Emergency's at the rear of the building," the woman said.

"It usually is," Eleni spat out, infuriated with the woman's insolence. "I'm looking for a Mr. Jack Harrington. Could you tell me if he was admitted? He probably came in through emergency."

The woman looked up, over steel-rimmed glasses. "He was checked in this morning."

"I'd like to see him. I'm his...wife."

The woman's brow rose and she held her gaze a full minute without blinking. "His wife?"

"Yes."

The woman nodded. "His sister was here earlier to check on him...said there was no other family."

"Well, he does, he just doesn't know it. You said his sister?"

"Yes."

"He doesn't have a sister."

"She said he didn't have a wife."

"He hasn't seen me for quite a while, that's all."

The woman stared.

"But he definitely doesn't have a sister. What'd she look like?"

"Attractive Indian woman...lots of black hair."

"Jack Harrington's not exactly Indian."

"She said he was adopted."

"...An Indian family adopting a white boy?"

The woman smiled. "She said she just adopted him last year."

Eleni's cheeks turned crimson with rage. "What ward is he in?"

"Critical care unit—third floor, east wing; talk to the nurse at the desk. No visitors are allowed."

As Eleni approached the critical care unit, a door open and Lilli stepped out. Eleni shrunk back into the hallway, waited for her to pass, then entered Jack's room. It was dark; the monitor glowed blue and green, and tubes ran into his arms. He had a bandage around his head with a feather sticking out.

She stared at his bruised face. Jack was handsome—rugged—angular. He'd actually gotten more angular than she remembered and Eleni thought it was probably all those years alone that did it. Her eyes darted back and forth, analyzing the bruise and small cuts to his head.

"Jack, I don't know if you can hear me, but I've got to hope you can. We're spiraling...big time. The priestesses are merging with Sophie, but if we don't get the inscription in time, the whole thing will turn in on itself. Sophie doesn't even know who I am..." Eleni stopped; her lips trembled. "But we can do it with your help, Jack," she whispered.

She touched his temple and wiped away a bead of sweat. "I lied to you, Jack. I said I didn't remember anything that happened when I put that ring on. That's only partially true. I was the catalyst, and for that I was granted the gift of forgetfulness; but the gift doesn't always hold." She stared at Jack's lips then turned way.

"You asked if I'd noticed that Sophie was more than just my daughter. Yes, I know who she is, and my pain is that, along with it all, she is still my daughter...and yours."

Eleni leaned down and kissed Jack's brow. "I don't know what happened to you, Jack. But we need you; don't recede into darkness. Please come back to us...and to me."

Eleni reached under her shirt and pulled out the gold chain and pendant. She slid it over her head and draped it around Jack's neck. "One of the things I remember is that on the inside, the Tree of Life grew in rings of light. When my father died, he was in the middle of something. He was drawing rings and crosses. Somehow, it's all connected." She leaned down and kissed him on the lips. "They say metal holds energy, Jack. If that's true, maybe this will help." She turned and quietly tiptoed out of the room. Around Jack's neck hung Samuel's Celtic cross.

Sophie rubbed her fingers along the worn weave of cloth draped across her legs. She opened her eyes and looked down, lifting the hem, feeling the silk.

"Erec," she breathed.

Down by her feet were the green velvet coat and her jeans. Her purse was jammed under the seat, stuffed with balled-up clothing. She pulled the jeans up under the dress, tucking in as much as possible and slipped the green coat on top. She slid her feet out of the ballet slippers and into her tennis shoes. She got out of the truck and looked around.

The sign in front of her said Campbell River Medical Clinic. She stared at it a long moment, whispered "Jack," then headed towards the entrance. A stern looking woman with steel-rimmed glasses and lacquered gray hair sat at the desk.

"Do you have a Mr. Jack Harrington here?"

The woman threw down her pen and stared up at Sophie. Sophie's pants were hiked up as high as possible, with her dress tucked in, balled up around the waist. The jeans were tied with the turtledove sash. The green velvet coat was incorrectly buttoned, one side riding higher than the other. Her tennis shoes were half off, and her butchered hair lay flat on one side and stuck out like a bush on the other.

"And I suppose you're his daughter?"

"At the moment, ma'am, I haven't a clue who the hell I am."

The woman nodded. "I'm not surprised…CCU, East wing, Third floor. Talk to the nurse at the desk."

As she entered CCU, Sophie saw a woman slip quietly out of a room; she looked familiar. She watched the woman disappear down the hall, then Sophie entered the room.

The blinds had been closed to keep out the sun; Sophie opened them. She went to Jack's side and assessed his head wound. There was a feather stuck in his head bandage and blood pooling down the side of his face. She cupped her hand beneath the pendant resting on his chest; a glimmer of recognition flickered in her eyes.

She pulled back the blanket and took Jack's hand, lightly palpating the lump beneath the bandage; she turned her own palm up and stared.

The crescent moon on her forehead flickered, not enough to stay, just a shimmer, now here, now gone, as whisperings in her mind. She untied the turtledove mantle and wrapped it around Jack's head, careful not to disturb the feather.

"It's your dream now, Jack. Maybe this will help you weave a trail." She placed her hand on his heart. "Just remember that the wound of man is here. This is where you must enter." She leaned over and kissed him on the brow then departed the room.

Lilli and Eleni's faces eased when they saw Sophie approach the truck. Without a word they climbed in.

"Do you know what happened?" Eleni asked.

"Only that he was found outside Sam's Café in a pool of blood and whiskey...looked like he fell and hit his head." Lilli glanced at Eleni. "I think we should head back to the boat."

STAGE THREE

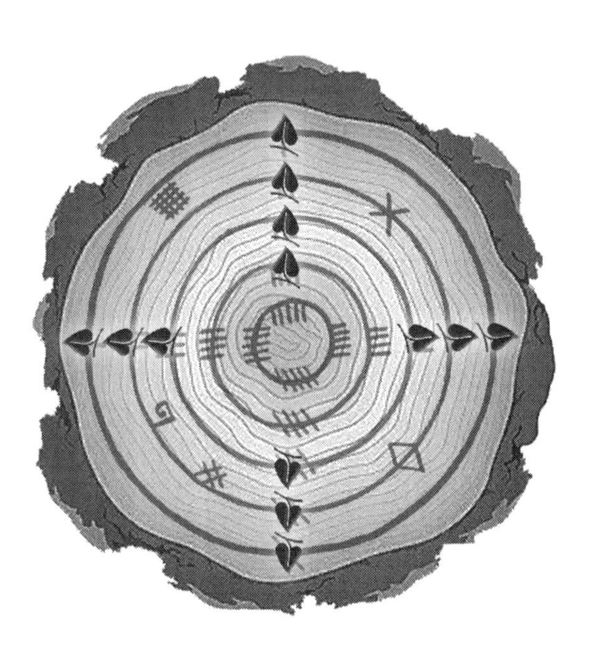

WILLOW
Enchantment

SOPHIE STOOD IN the galley, her feet tangled in clumps of gray wool, horsehair, and floral silk. Her back was hunched, and her arms hung loosely by her sides. Lilli studied Eleni as she scanned the chaotic scene, a nightmare moved to day. "She doesn't know you, does she?"

Eleni looked away. "No."

"It's just temporary."

"Maybe..."

Sophie explored the clothing, dragging articles around with the soles of her feet. She smashed the brocade gown into a large burgundy pillow and jumped in it.

"She's getting worse." Eleni's eyes were dark, like hollow caves. She turned on Lilli, trying to call forth some fire or resentment, but she was too tired to fight. Lilli grabbed the basket of cinnamon rolls from the counter and put them on the table.

"Eat," she said.

Eleni turned back towards the girl sitting down, gathering clothing around her like a giant donut. "I suppose you're going to tell me this is good."

"Biggest mistake people make," Lilli said, "is getting scared when things get crazy. Nobody likes crazy." Lilli unraveled a cinnamon roll. "...Nothing wrong with crazy."

"That's easy for you to say."

Sophie wandered around the galley, rifling through drawers, till she found a pair of scissors. Eleni flinched.

"People like to know what everything means," continued Lilli. "Dress a certain way, talk a certain way. Don't know what to do when someone breaks the rules."

"I think this is a little different than just breaking the rules." Eleni scrutinized Sophie with the scissors.

"You've got to let her go," Lilli whispered.

Eleni stiffened.

"See all those clothes?" Lilli went on. "She's in the middle of one steaming pile of chaos...right in the middle. She doesn't know you because she can't know you right now. Not if she's going to find her way."

Sophie started to cut the clothing. She cut the silk floral gown on the bias from hip to thigh, making it tunic length, then folded it over and set it aside.

"I'm an impediment?"

"You're her mother; you reflect back the known. The known has to die to give birth to something new."

Sophie held up the plain woven white dress and started separating it from its red silk lining.

"I can't watch this." Eleni turned and stared out the window at the ferryboat crossing to Quadra Island.

"You can't watch it because you don't want to let her die, don't want to lose her." Sophie held up the red silk to the light, folded it, and placed it on top of the floral tunic. "But you won't lose her."

"How can you be so sure?"

Eleni watched Sophie cut and patch the clothing. The pile grew, as she studied the elements they represented. She moved the cloth, tearing, sorting, and shifting parts of one outfit to that of another. Some garments were marked with crayons, some weren't. She cut some of the fabric into what looked like patches to be applied to other garments. She worked in a world of her own, unaware that anyone was watching.

She threw the shoes in the corner.

Sophie stood up and retrieved the discarded duffel bag. She unzipped it, as if something inside had caught her attention. She stuck her hand in and rubbed fingers over soft threads then took the bag to the berth.

When she didn't return, the two women looked in and found that she had drifted off to sleep, the bag secured beneath her head.

Lilli wandered around studying piles of cloth.

"Thank you, Lilli. Back there...at the fair...I didn't know what to do with that guy."

Lilli rubbed her hand on the woven white dress. "You should eat something."

"I just kept thinking that Emrys would appear," Eleni continued. "He's been watching her for six months. I called him before I left to come up here, but there was no answer, so I called Emily. She said he'd told her he was going away...would she take care of the cherry tree. Said he gave her a bag of white powder...ground up fish bones...told her to sprinkle it on the earth and water it every other day. Said it would keep the cherry tree strong. For God's sake, the only thing Emily's ever watered is her own body in the shower. She's as unaware as...."

"What cherry tree?"

Eleni flipped the journal open and shoved it across the table. "A few things have happened since you left last night."

Lilli looked down at the floor. "Well, there are two outfits that weren't here before."

"The cherry tree emerged in one of Sophie's dreams right before she reclaimed the ring. In her dream, it was Merlin's gift: a sapling, the earthly embodiment of the east. She planted one in her yard in an attempt to maintain a trail, just like you're talking about. Cherry blossoms were also embroidered on the velvet bag the ring was kept in."

"For the last six months, Emrys has helped care for the tree... and her. He showed up in her life right after she reclaimed the ring...moved in next door to Emily. No one knows where he's from. When Emily said he'd gone, I thought I'd find him here. I thought he'd help us, at the fair, show up, unannounced, like he has from the beginning..."

"Does this Emrys have long black hair?"

Eleni looked up, startled. "Yes."

"I think you need to tell me what Priestesses I missed."

"Do you know where he is?"

"It's possible. Who wore the plain white dress with the red lining?"

"The woman at the fair was Enid. She wore the belt of interlocking circles. I think that the interlocking circles are worn on the part of the body from which the energy emanates, the crown, throat, or pelvic area. They represent mother, sister, and bride. Enid was a bride; the last three priestesses are brides."

She flipped through the journal again and placed it in front of Lilli.

"Read."

JOURNAL ENTRY;

The Story: The Isle of Glass was also known as *Dubhe,* the pivotal star of the Big Dipper. As the constellation traversed the northern hemisphere, its dipper, or cup, would fill with the mystery of the night sky then turn upside down and pour that mystery onto the Isle of Glass. The trees became a conduit, connecting the energies of heaven and underworld via the earth plane. Their wood was filled with wisdom, each tree participating in the story in its own particular way.

The trees that grew in this stellar landscape also had branches that reached out to the earthly directions: north, south, east, and west. The trees, as bearers of wisdom, became the basis for a language known as *Ogham*, the Tree Alphabet. The letters were comprised of lines and notches, like the branches of trees, and became symbols that represented the trees that grew on the Isle of Glass, as well as representing the first letter of that tree.

The men and women that lived in this stellar landscape told stories about the convergence of energies on the Isle of Glass. Thus, man and woman became part of those stories.

The ring is comprised of two interlocking circles or bands, like the *Vesica Piscis*, a symbol that represents the union of opposites. When enlightened man and enlightened woman enter the story, their union creates a third entity, the triangulated stone. This is a union that transcends and opens the door to the wisdom of wood. The ring is inscribed with letters from the Tree Alphabet. The secret to the meaning of the inscription is buried somewhere in the Ogham.

Lilli closed the book. "Arrival of the brides means union is near?"

"My father believed the priestesses represented different aspects of the goddess. The story talks about the convergence of three realms on the Isle of Glass: heaven, earth, and underworld. The goddess is active in all three domains and is described by the various faces of woman: mother, sister, and bride. Guinevere, Enid, and Ragnell are brides. I think my father believed that, if she intends to manifest, she'll need a groom."

Lilli raised the floral silk, now tunic length. "Emrys?"

"It's another name for Merlin. It is possible that Emrys is the physical manifestation of the male enlightenment, taking place in this story. Why else would he have appeared out of nowhere?"

"So… who was here last night?"

"Guinevere."

"What's the message of the brides?"

"My father's notes are scarce at this point. I think he was just beginning to get the measure of it when he died. He says that Guinevere was fated to Lancelot but married Arthur. Lancelot was a spiritual love, and Arthur was an earthly love. Arthur was warned not to marry Guinevere but did it anyway. So, Guinevere pivoted between a spiritual love and an earthly love; they should not be divided. In order for the kind of union this story is implying to take place, spirit must be honored. Arthur didn't, and so his kingdom suffered.

"The simple white dress with the red lining worn by Enid represents royalty beneath a common exterior, spirit within flesh. This kind of love can't be dealt with in human ways. The sovereignty of the goddess must be recognized, no matter what she looks like on the outside."

"And Enid marries?"

"Enid's union was successful. Erec recognized her truth. Despite her peasant clothes, he saw her inner beauty. Erec married her, honoring the queen within…thus the red silk lining. But Erec was so enamored with her that he forgot his own sovereignty, and the knights goaded him for his lovesick ways. His loss of honor instigated years of wandering, in which Erec fought to prove his manhood. Enid went along with him, waiting for the time when he would fulfill that honor and return to their life together, as equals in their own right. He almost dies in battle when she cries out, bringing him back from the dead."

"...A good ending?"

"Yes, but a lesson in the telling. The point is that the three brides will soon merge and become one, if Jack returns in time."

"Who is the final bride?"

"From what I can gather, she is the biggest challenge. Ragnel is like Kundry, ugly to human eyes."

Lilli rubbed her finger in the pool of dried blood on the table. "There is a man in the forest," she whispered, "a great man who dreams within the burned-out trunk of a wizened oak tree. But oak trees don't grow in Campbell River."

Eleni looked down at Jack's blood.

"In his dreams," Lilli continued, "this man is a great stag. I've seen this stag, trapped in a forest without light. And I have seen the man with black hair and the white shadow of a ring on his finger."

"Emrys..."

"He is paralyzed, until Jack returns with the inscription."

"I should have known." Eleni placed her hand on the pile of fabric.

"Do you understand what she's doing?" Lilli asked.

Eleni nodded. "I think so. She's reshaping the energy, cutting the fabric into new clothing. It looks like she's cutting the black leather into patches. The black leather is probably Morgan, female power. Too much power throws life off balance. Sophie realizes she only needs a small portion of leather to access Morgan. She might cut a long strip and use it to tie her jeans around her hips." Eleni began to walk around the room as if in a dream. "She'll transform all these clothes into different kinds of outfits...things to fit our times."

Eleni picked up a piece of floral silk and let go, watching it float to the ground. "Don't you see, Lilli? Don't you see how it all becomes just a parade of cloth? Women acting out Morgan, or Nimue, or even Guinevere? When we don't understand what the myth means, all we do is mirror the surface story; just like Emily. Emily is what every young woman will become if we don't succeed, trapped in the illusion of energies, without ever knowing what they really mean."

Lilli's eyes narrowed into yellow slits. "Whose dream is this, Eleni?"

"It's every woman's dream. Surely you're not immune? How is woman to be reborn but through dream? And this myth is a dream about the rebirth of women."

She folded the floral silk and placed it on Sophie's pile. "I don't want my daughter to die in vain, Lilli. I don't want her twenty-one years of searching to be nothing but a shadow of a life. And she will die if Jack doesn't come back."

"Then maybe you should've never left him," whispered Lilli.

Eleni froze.

"Is that what this is all about, Eleni...your decision from the past? Are you a product of this impotent myth?"

"There are things I don't wish to discuss with you."

"You don't need to; I can smell it. The wound on Jack's hand, the raven's flight, you're all being drawn back together. I'm not blind."

"It's not his fault. He never knew."

"And now he does. And so the wound of enlightenment has spread to his heart. What was your sin, Eleni? What part of this unresolved myth blinded you to leave Jack and not tell him?"

Eleni's knees buckled, and she fell in a heap on top of Igraine's gown. "I didn't think it was him."

"...The immaculate conception?"

"You don't understand!"

"What? That you didn't recognize the sublime in him?"

"You love to challenge, don't you?"

"It's what I do. I'm like Morgan. I stir the pot. Isn't that what this is all about...this myth of yours? Everyone's misunderstood it...relegated all the mystery in life to some place out there in the dark blue beyond. Gods and goddesses touch Earth and then leave for some unknown place. Even heaven is on some cloud in the sky. That's what they're saying, isn't it, Eleni? Even Jesus said that the Kingdom of Heaven is amongst you, but you do not see."

"What are you saying?"

"You reduced Jack to some sort of two-dimensional male and lost the magic."

"You know nothing of us."

"I have eyes, Eleni. But I have something in spades that most other people don't have: animal instinct. When love is really present...in its highest form...something happens. Two people become more than what they were when apart. Something bigger and better is born. You and Jack had a chance. But you fell back on old programming, because you couldn't see the sacred in Jack. You had the chance to anchor all this...to bring heaven to earth through your embrace of each other. Not everyone has that chance. And you threw it away."

"How do you know all this?"

"Why'd you send her here, Eleni?"

"Because I knew he'd understand...be able to help her."

"Not because you knew he was her father?"

Eleni's right hand buried itself in the folds of burgundy brocade.

"For whatever reason, Eleni, you perpetrated the very thing your daughter's trying to heal. That's why this matters so much."

"Sophie's life is bigger than any sum of my transgressions."

"But you'd like to go back and turn the tide."

"Yes! The only way for me to affect the last twenty-two years is to help this myth evolve. Because if that happens..."

"What?"

"It's our only saving grace. I can't go back and change an action that made her life more difficult, but maybe I can help her realize her fate. Yes, I'm biased towards her. She's trying to give birth to something for which there are no rules or regulations. If I could go back in time and change a decision that broke apart what could have been a holy family, I would; my father's gravestone made that blatantly clear. She deserved better. She has the potential to be the embodiment of a greater woman. If she fails, we all fail."

The two women stared at each other. Daylight had long since descended into the sea, leaving only the dim harbor lights cascading ochre shadows into the room. Lilli dropped her head and rested on the table, exhausted.

"We can't afford any more mistakes, Eleni. It's not just about Sophie anymore."

Eleni hunched her shoulders.

"Maybe we should both close our eyes. This story is far from being finished, and Jack's going to need our help."

"What about Sophie?"

Lilli shrugged. "We're both here. One of us will hear her if she awakens."

Eleni struggled up off the floor and collapsed onto the bench. Within five minutes they were fast asleep.

Sophie awoke at midnight. The *Avalon* was rolling in a dark tide. In the galley, she saw both women asleep. She retrieved the scissors, sat on the floor, and grabbed her old white sweatshirt.

She cut the crew neck into a wide ballet neck, almost off the shoulders. She slit the sleeves from shoulder to wrist and removed the banded bottoms from cuff and hem. She opened the side seams from under the arms to the hip and cut a large piece out from each side. She pulled the seams together, tight, to force the shirt to conform in a fitted manner to her torso and hips. Then she set it aside.

Next, she picked up Enid's dress and separated the skirt from the blouse. She turned the skirt inside out and cut out the inner portions of all the pleats in long triangular shapes.

From the pile of remnants, she cut matching triangular pieces from all the other cloth: floral silk, gray wool, burlap, green velvet, burgundy brocade, and black leather. She cut two extra panels of floral silk, as well as two long strips of black leather.

She went to the stove and turned it on, then poured a small amount of water into an iron skillet and placed it on the burner. She disappeared down the hall and returned with a small wheel of bonding tape.

She turned the cut sweatshirt inside out and laid it open on the floor and placed a length of tape against the side seams. She draped Jack's fishy kitchen towel in steam, then hand pressed against the seams to temporarily bond them. When they had adhered, Sophie pressed them with the hot iron skillet, tapering the body till it was form fitting.

She fit the two floral panels in the open sleeves from shoulder to wrist, causing the sleeves to bell open—a sheer expanse of floral silk exposing the length of arm. Next, she turned the skirt inside out, and the cut pleats opened up. One by one, she bonded a panel of fabric to become the inside fold of the pleat. She worked quickly...steaming and ironing with the skillet.

When the skirt was finished, she placed the altered sweatshirt above it, rolled out the bonding tape, and connected the two garments. When it was dry, she turned it right-side out.

She attached the long strips of black leather as a rolled ribbon, one around the hip where the skirt joined the bodice, and one around the neckline. She found a hanger in Jack's closet and hung the gown from a cabinet knob in the kitchen.

From the horsehair pants, Sophie cut a long wide strip that she tied low around the hips and fashioned into a bow. She stopped and looked at her handiwork, lifting the skirt so it fell softly, flashing panels of wizened fabric. Then she wandered around the room.

On the back of Morgan's shimmering black shirt was a large glass button with a silver fluted edge. Sophie removed it. She grabbed the ivory suede ties on Nimue's buckskin pants, undid the knots on the end, and pulled them out of the pants. She threaded the ends through the silver button then continued to hunt through the fabric. The buttons on the back of Igraine's dress were pearl. She removed them and threaded the buttons onto the ends of the suede ribbon. She tied the necklace around her neck like a choker, featuring the silver button at the front of her neck, and allowed the long strands of pearls to fall down the nape of her neck to her lower back, nine in all. She then removed the necklace and draped it across the hangar with the dress.

She went to the bunkroom and came back with the purple scarf and length of auburn hair. She put it on the kitchen counter. Sitting back down on the floor, she quickly cut patches from the remaining garments, folded everything, and stacked them on the table in front of the two sleeping women.

Then, Sophie Alexander went outside, jumped onto the dock, and released the ropes that anchored the boat to the pier. Climbing back on board, she started the motor and slid the *Avalon* silently out of her slip.

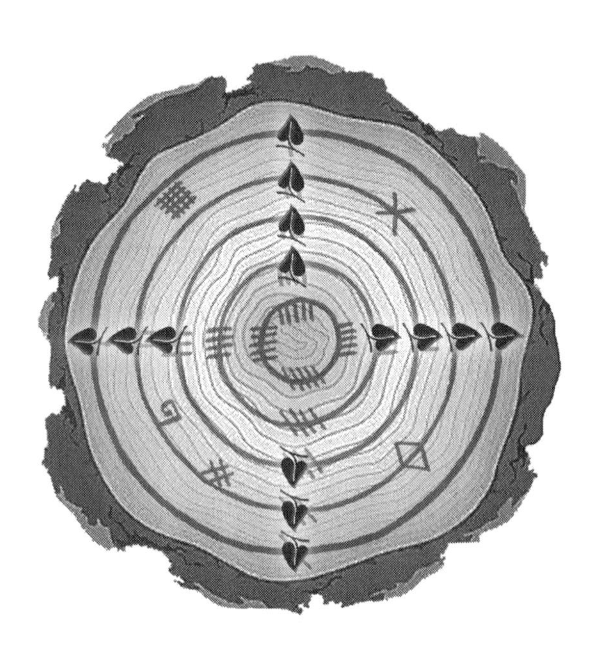

IIII

HAZEL

Creative Essence

IRENE STOOD AT the foot of the bed, studying Jack's comatose form. It was late and Irene was completing her rounds before ending her shift. She retrieved the clipboard and jotted down the stats on Jack's vital signs; not much had changed since he'd been admitted.

Irene examined Jack's face, making note of the recently placed items adorning him. Her hand slid beneath the cross, draped around his neck, as she studied the embroidered cloth wrapped around his bandaged head. She brushed the feather with her fingertips. Irene pulled back the sheets and examined his hand; her trained eye noticed the altered wrap of the bandage. She rubbed the palm lightly, probing the item that had been buried there.

"Looks like someone left you a gift, Jack."

She placed his hand back and pulled the blankets up around his chest. As she did, Irene noticed a tiny flicker of movement beneath Jack's lids; color began to rise in his cheeks, and his breathing accelerated.

"Looks like Lilli's sent you a dream, Jack. Far be it from me to remove her medicine; I've seen it work too many times before." She smoothed the sheets and signed off on the chart. "I'll be back in the morning with the doctor. You've got till then to find your way."

Irene walked to the door and glanced back at Jack, whose only animation was the rapid eye movement of a dreamer. She switched off the lights and headed home for the night.

Jack's heart pounded. It hammered in his chest, pushing the cavity, reverberating in his temples, harder and faster till Jack thought the monitor would blow off the charts.

Then his legs started to move.

They pummeled the earth, ripping a pace frantic enough to match his heart. His thighs strained with exertion, step after step of burning pain...calves climbing, pushing, fighting hard to get away.

His lungs were on fire. He sucked in air, cold as ice, and blew it out in long plumes of white. His hard, shallow breath blasted his head with aching cold, and stinging rain pelted his face and eyes.

Fear. Run!

The world began to close in. Tangled shrubs and thorny branches gripped his arms and knotted round his waist and thighs, as he clamored through forested hills.

Cold...like ice.

Farther up the hill, a white stag broke out of the underbrush. The muscled flanks contracted, powering it off the trail, terror stricken, through the woods. Jack ran after it, reaching wildly to part the wood that was snapped and broken in its path.

Something hissed past, leaving a high-pitched ringing in his head. An arrow lodged in a tree directly in front of him, just as the deep rumble of male voices, barking dogs, and galloping hooves entered his mind.

He pushed past the arrowed tree into a thicket, where he found the stag. Their eyes met, as heated breath rose like frozen plumes of fog.

Suddenly, the stag turned, leapt through the thicket, and disappeared.

Jack followed.

He closed his eyes against the slapping branches and ended up in a thick growth of wood. Flailing around to free himself, Jack stumbled into a large rock that pivoted against the side of a mound of earth. His foot twisted and Jack fell, his forward motion cascading him in a tumbled mass through leaf and limb, onto moist earth, where he rolled downward into a dark cave.

Over and over he rolled...shoulders, back, and hips pressed down into the deep dark cavern. When he finally stopped, Jack listened to the panic in his own breath. But he also heard the breathing of the stag. The soil beneath him was cool and dry; the cave was completely without light.

"You need to get out of here," Jack whispered. "They'll find you...it's a trap!" He heard the stag's hooves as the animal backed away.

"You're safe here," a voice replied.

Jack sat up, startled to hear the voice of another. "The hunters have dogs," he continued. "They'll smell us out. The stag's not safe in here!"

"This place does not exist for them."

"It was easy enough for me to find!"

"They are not of like mind. I assure you, we are safe."

Jack heard the hunters close in, their dogs yipping as they followed a trail that appeared to end in nowhere. Round and round the horses galloped, their riders screaming harsh commands to each other, till they finally retreated down the mountainside. Jack's breathing was shallow, trapped in the upper cavity of his chest. "Why didn't they find us?"

"I told you; this place does not exist for them."

A light began to emanate from the direction of the voice, casting a shadow of a man with the horns of a stag against the cavern wall. He raised a lantern high, exposing tunnels that fed deep into the mountain. "Come," the man said, disappearing into the earth.

Jack scrambled to follow.

As the man walked away, Jack could see by his movements that he was young and powerful. He had a mane of hair that fell like a black waterfall down his back...and he was dressed in opulent robes of gold and silver, the hemline of which was embroidered with moon and stars. The threads captured and reflected the light of the lantern, creating the illusion of a cloak of light. The shadow of the stag's horns flickered on and off throughout the dark chamber.

"Merlin," Jack whispered to himself, following deep into the chasm of the earth.

The tunnel twisted and turned, small channels feeding off in varying directions, leading into an abyss of darkness. White puffs of cold breath and shadows, now man, now animal, appeared and disappeared in the lantern's glow. Suddenly, the man stopped and turned, staring into Jack's eyes. "I believe you have something I need."

Jack staggered to a halt. The man's eyes were mesmerizing, clear and clean as a hawk, blue as ice, and deep as midnight.

"Well?" he continued.

"I don't know what you mean," Jack said.

"I believe it's in the palm of your right hand."

Jack looked down, noticing for the first time that his right hand was bandaged. He looked back up.

"Remove the bandage."

Jack pulled at the tape, slowly unraveling the gauze stuck to his palm. As it pulled back, he felt the movement of a tiny object in the middle of his hand. He dropped the gauze and held up his palm. Sitting in the center, on top of the wound, was a small crystal.

The man reached over and took it from him. "The Record Keeper," he whispered.

"How'd it get there?"

The man held the crystal up to the light, examining the faceted edges, till he saw the etched triangle. "You are about to learn, Raven King, that time is more malleable than it seems." He held the crystal between his thumb and forefinger, twirling it back and forth to catch the light on the etched triangle. "This...Raven King... is a trail...and it's led you back to me."

Jack watched the crystal reflecting prisms of light onto the cavern walls, alleviating some of the darkness. "The crystal cave...?"

"Yes. One piece...one tiny piece of the crystal cave...embedded with all its knowledge...transported through time..."

"Quartz," Jack whispered.

The faceted edge reflected prisms of light into the man's eyes. "Yes...the talking stone. It hasn't taken long. Once it started, it was like wildfire. What do you think...sixty years maybe? The information in this crystal has inflamed your minds with all the knowledge and mystery of life contained in the crystal cave. That which once was only available to the holy few is now rampant in your silicon-enhanced civilization. Quantum theory, subatomic particles...now you see it, now you don't. They chase down the mysteries of life with intelligent machines that increase their ability to think into the beyond...and then it takes them there." He twirled the Record Keeper and looked at it again. "And it all...ends up...right...back...here..."

Jack watched, as the man raised both arms high in the air, the lantern in his left and the crystal in the right. And before Jack could blink, the crystal was thrown with godly force down onto the cavern floor, shattering across the stone in an explosion of blinding light.

"Awaken, Raven King, to God's Universe!"

Jack's eyes closed a second too late. The light burned a searing path through his eyes and into his brain: the light of millennia. He dropped to his knees, arched his back, and cupped his hands over his eyes.

"Oh my God...!" he screamed. And Jack Harrington collapsed onto the cavern floor...blinded by the searing pain of enlightenment.

"I can't see."

"In certain situations, eyes are an impediment."

Jack reached up and felt a cloth tied around his head, covering his eyes.

"Don't remove it."

"Can I see without it?"

"Your vision will be altered. There is no way of undoing what you have experienced. The degree of change is unknown at this moment."

Jack lowered his hands to the floor of the cave, where he sat rigid on cold stone.

"Do you know who you are?" asked the man.

"Who I am?"

"Yes."

"Jack Harrington."

"That is merely a name...a personality you have embraced. It provides walls and defines the parameters of a physical existence."

"It's who I am."

"Is it? Look beyond the name."

Jack's hands inched along, exploring the damp stone beneath his thighs.

"They call you Raven, do they not?"

"It's a recent anomaly."

"Ahh..."

"And from what I can feel of my skin I don't appear to be flaunting feathers."

"Perhaps there is a deeper meaning to the title."

"Is it as dark in here as it feels?"

"For the moment, yes..."

"Why have you blinded me?"

"It is, at times, the only way to see. Did you really think that your current state of consciousness was worthy of the task before you?"

"The inscription..."

"Do you truly believe that something as sacred as that could be discovered by everyday consciousness?"

"I didn't actually apply for the job, you know. It was assigned."

"Yes...many, many years ago."

"Actually, it was rather recent." Jack listened to the rustling of fabric as the man walked up to him.

"Perhaps we should take a different tack. Do you know who I am, Raven?"

The hem of silken robes brushed the floor by Jack's hand. He reached out, gathering folds of cool fabric, rubbing his fingers across embroidered patterns. As he did, the image of a forest clearing and an observatory exploding with inner light entered his mind. "You are Merlin."

"Yes...I am Merlin. But Merlin had many lives. Pray tell, Raven, to which are you speaking...man or myth?"

Jack's hand slid back against the cave wall, the turtle dove bandage tightly wound about his head.

"Does the man beget the legend, or the legend beget the man?" whispered Merlin.

"They are the same..."

"Yes...they are interwoven. Now, tell me what you see." Merlin placed his hand in front of Jack's forehead. A blue light emanated from his palm, onto Jack's brow.

"There was a king..." Jack began.

"Yes, go on."

"A great King and leader...and there was a battle that rained blood upon the earth. The blood was thick with the sorrow of ages, and it created a wound. It was a wound that bled madness...the worst kind of wound. A wound that can't be healed with ointments but which lies unseen in the psyche of man..."

Merlin's eyes flared white, casting an eerie shadow upon Jack's head.

"The king, driven mad from sorrow, left his world and disappeared into the forest...wandering amongst trees and sleeping amongst the animals...learning the blessings and curses of the seasons...hollowed out by pain and longing...trying to heal the wound."

"Man or myth?"

"Both...Eventually his pain became his enlightenment, his madness turned to wisdom...gutted and transformed him..."

"Into what?"

"Prophet."

"Ahh...Three lives...King, Madman, and Prophet."

"Yes." Jack's voice dropped to a whisper, and his head rolled forward onto his chest. He let go the hem of Merlin's robe and raised his hands to his brow, pushing the cloth against his lids. Tears spilled onto the cloth, soaking it, burning his sightless eyes.

"I am sorry," whispered Merlin. "There is no way to enlightenment without pain, Raven..."

The gasps of frigid air that Jack sucked into his lungs were expelled in a haunting wail that echoed down the cavern wall. Pain distorted his face and whitened the knuckles of hands gripped tightly to the cloth around his head. Merlin stood silently and listened to the fading echoes. "Go on."

"His people longed for his return..." Jack continued, "but he was no longer of their world; his old life sloughed off like dead skin.

Even the king's wife could no longer be one with him…unable to go back…outside of time…" Jack took a deep breath and reached again for the robe. "The prophet and seer, now at one with nature and the forest, moved back and forth between two worlds, hoping to guide and inform the people…hoping to teach what he had learned…"

"And then?"

Jack stiffened. "My God…"

"Yes."

"He refused."

"Yes."

"He refused to return to a world that no longer had a place for him. And in his loneliness…he used his understanding of matter and created a spell. He manipulated, took advantage of another's desire, and conjured a way to create a child. The illusion he created was short lived, just long enough for lust and conception."

"And the price?" whispered Merlin.

"The child would be his, to nurture and educate."

"Yes. The child would be mine to raise and teach and send back into the world with all the enlightenment he could possess. Back into the world I could no longer attend. He would return with all my wisdom…in hopes of transformation."

"Arthur?"

"Yes. Arthur, the Raven King."

The cave went very still. Merlin removed his hand, retracting the blue light, and stared down at Jack's motionless body. "Even I had things to learn," he whispered. He turned and walked to the far side of the cave. "The next stage cannot be done alone."

"What are you saying to me?" Jack's voice was dark, hollowed by the cavernous earth surrounding them.

"Our bodies function as vehicles of enlightenment. If I had gone back into the world, who was I to mate with? I wanted a mating of spirit, not just body. And if there was a child of my blood, how

could I stay in that world and teach him the mysteries that belong to the forest? I chose the next best thing. Arthur was the product of another's blood, but the mystery was mine; and the mystery was what mattered...or so I thought. But I was wrong. We can only go so far alone. The next level—the place I was seeking—the state of mind that would heal the kingdom, is one of union. I didn't understand the properties of union within the mystery. The Grail cup cannot be tasted, except with the lips of divine love."

"You hoped Arthur would take the next step."

"The kingdom was dying."

"But why not you?"

"There was no mate my equal."

"Does it matter?"

"Yes, Arthur, it does! I wanted to birth more than flesh."

"What did you just call me?"

"Do you really think this is coincidental?"

"What are you saying?" Jack asked.

"You must not propagate the wound!"

"You called me Arthur!"

"Yes! Arthur, Raven King...man and myth! Jack Harrington is a small chapter at the end of a very long lineage...a lineage of enlightenment. The wisdom contained in the life forces that were Arthur and Merlin is not dead! The energy awaits transformation and rebirth! Look at me! I tried, in all good conscience, to find a way to release the waters of life into the kingdom you ruled. But you were also man...a man of passion. And although I warned you that Guinevere was not fated to you, it mattered not. You were King, and Kings do as they will!

"This union is not just of body, Jack Harrington. Surely you realize that now, with your love for Eleni Alexander. We are all man and myth, but some live more consciously than others. Consciousness is required now! It is essential that we bring this myth into the light of day! We failed before."

Merlin stormed back and forth, batting the darkness with the silken wings of his robes. "This mystery has been buried in centuries of misunderstanding, returning time after time in hopes of being heard. But it is the old story that continues to replay. If the wound is propagated again, we will all slip back into darkness."

"The wound..."

"Yes, the wound. Why did Arthur's Kingdom fail? Why did Nimue garner enough trickery to trap me and send the wisdom back to the wood from whence it came? It wasn't because I tampered with fate. It was because I dishonored the principles of spiritual union. The Priestesses warned me, but I did not listen. And if we don't listen, now, the wisdom will once again sink into its wooden grave. You cannot tell a story that no one wants to hear."

"The wound is the separation of spirit and flesh," Jack whispered. "That's why you need Sophie."

"Yes...Sophie, your daughter. Our destinies are all connected, Arthur, like lightning shattering a night sky. Tell me, do you know the pain of one advancing ahead of the whole? Can you imagine the ache of living as prophet and seer in a landscape of desolation?"

Loneliness seeped into Jack's blood, like some sort of bad overdose. "Stop..." Tears streaked down his cheeks, through dust as rivulets over parched land. "Please stop!" he screamed.

"I am sorry," murmured Merlin. "I am sorry that my pain flows in your blood. I can only say that it is just part of my pain...not all. All would send you back into the darkness I fought so hard to transform."

Gulps of air echoed out of the dark corner where Jack had collapsed. "Please," he pleaded.

"Mankind wasn't ready," Merlin continued. "I manipulated your birth and tried to force an event that would pour enlightenment into the lives of people...to create a world I could walk back into...an enlightened world without desolation. You were to be my beacon, but something went wrong."

"You used me." Jack's voice was tight, strangled with tears.

"Yes. I sent you into the world hoping to create a holy union between you and one of the priestesses—a union of crown and divine love, of land and spirit. I wanted to bring all that I was into the world through you, and have it joined with the high order of priestess. Surely that would heal the Kingdom and spawn enlightenment. Even if I never returned, my work would be done."

"You used me and you used the priestesses."

"To you it would appear so..."

Jack screamed as wrenching pain ripped through his chest.

"All I wanted was to eliminate the darkness," Merlin whispered. "When you've seen as I have seen...when you've looked to the stars and had your mind opened, breaking the shackles that close us in...I wanted, in desperation, to alleviate the ignorance that cloaked the mind of man."

"You are not a god."

"You are correct, Jack Harrington...since it is the man that speaks. But we are sons of God...if we would just let in the light."

"What are you saying?"

"I am saying it is a journey open to all humans, and once you have taken it you cannot look back except in pain for those who chose to ignore and live in darkness. I tried to open a door in the consciousness of mankind, but mankind wasn't ready and so it was flung shut in my face, and I have lain in darkness for centuries too long to count...waiting."

"For what?"

"For what? What is it that you brought me, Arthur?"

"The crystal."

"The Record Keeper. One small piece of the crystal cave...encoded with all knowledge of the universe...sent into the future to prosper and multiply...to educate and force the mind of man to open and expand and understand the miracle of this universe. And it has happened, Arthur! The consciousness has

opened and flowered with such rapidity that now...NOW...the time has come."

"Sophie..."

"The world is ready for my return...for our union."

"Why did she fight it?"

"She is a product of the myth. She has inherited our silence and, thus, resists her own destiny. No one before her has been asked to shift the goddess from nine to ten."

"The Tenth Priestess..."

"Ten is the number of the wizard, of magic and transformation. It is the number of enlightenment. Look to the ones and zeros that comprise your binary code now exploding your universe, Jack Harrington."

"She tried telling me the same thing."

"She is my equal," said Merlin.

"I must get back to her."

"Yes."

"What if she fails?"

"She mustn't."

"The inscription...I need the inscription!"

"Yes. The words that will unlock the ring...the ring she carries alone. It is an untold burden. Do you understand now, Raven King, your duty? Ride your horse, oh noble Arthur. This is the journey you were meant to take. To ride back in time and retrieve the final piece of the puzzle."

"Where is it?"

"Where? Why in the forest, of course."

"The forest?"

"Yes, in the Ogham. You do remember all I taught you, don't you, Arthur?"

"Why do you confound me with all these names?"

"Reach back, Jack Harrington...reach back to another life energy and retrieve what is there to be taken. It's all there inside

you. Everything that Arthur learned from me is within you, as clearly as stars in the universe."

"Why don't you just teach me again before it's too late?"

"And make the mistake I did before? No. I will not interfere with fate again. I believe in you, Jack Harrington. I believe in your nobility. And I believe you carry within you the magic to unearth the wisdom of the Ogham."

"The tree alphabet," said Jack.

"Yes... Ogham...the tree alphabet."

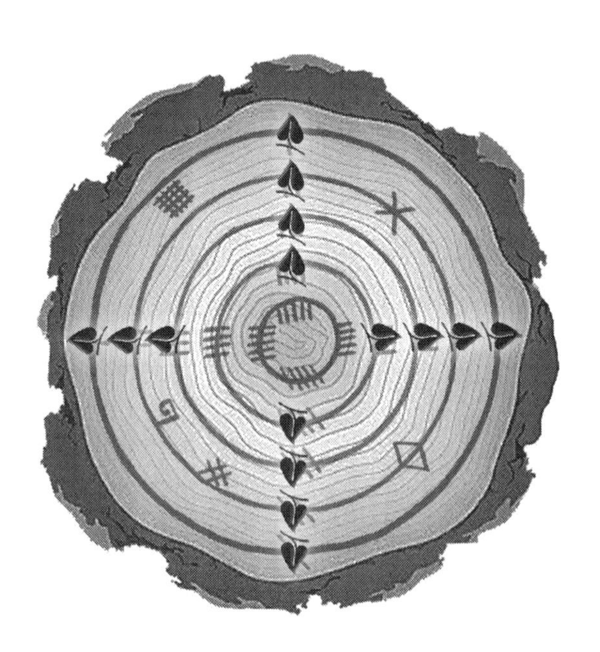

BLACKTHORN

Spiritual Authority

LILLI DIDN'T NEED to open her eyes to know that something was wrong. Even with them closed, she could sense that the world was too dark. Normally, the marina lanterns cast a yellow glow that reflected off water and into the boat. No matter how dark or moonless the night, they were never without light.

There was also a lilt to the boat, a back and forth sashay, like a dance. It wasn't the stable motion of an un-powered vessel being knocked by waves or tides. It was the powered movement of a vessel laboring through quiet waters.

There was, of course, the sound of the motor.

She opened her eyes and looked around; Eleni was sandwiched between the table and the wall, fast asleep. The only thing Lilli could see out the window was the guide light posted on Maude Island, barely visible through a thick fog. They were approaching Seymour Narrows.

She slid off the bench and retrieved Jack's flashlight; the galley clock said it was 3:00 a.m. She fanned light across the room, noting the clothing parceled out and neatly stacked on the table. Hanging from the kitchen cabinet was a gown. She trotted down the hall and checked the duffel bag on Sophie's bunk. Movement in the galley startled her and she returned to find Eleni awake.

"What time is it?" Eleni's eyes were rimmed red and her words slurred.

"Three a.m....we fell asleep," Lilli said.

"Are we moving?"

"Well...Sophie's moving. I think we're just along for the ride."

"She's at the helm?"

"So it would appear."

"Is the boat seaworthy?"

"No."

Eleni pressed her face against the window. "I can't see a thing."

"It's night."

"In case you hadn't noticed, sometimes there's a moon."

"There is a moon, but the fog's so thick you'd never know. Tonight's a black night. I think they call it mutiny."

"What're you talking about?" Eleni swiveled out of her seat and moved quickly towards the galley steps.

"Before you go blasting out, panic ridden, screaming how we're all going to drown...think...and look around."

Eleni looked at the table. "She's folded the clothes."

Lilli used the flashlight to illuminate the dress hanging on the kitchen cabinet. "What about this?" Eleni looked at the gown. "Looks like you were right," said Lilli.

"I'm her mother." She went up to the dress and flared the skirt, revealing the panels beneath the pleats, then ran her fingers down the beaded necklace.

"She thinks she's about to lose herself, Eleni. Look around. Everything's done...organized...ready. She's scared...decided to run."

"How do you know it's not the final priestess?"

"I checked her bag. There's one more outfit."

Eleni looked at the gown. "Why would she complete the gown and leave out a piece of the final priestess?"

"We don't have time to analyze."

"She can't run away."

"She can try."

"No she can't! If she resists she'll be annihilated."

"And you?"

"What is it, Lilli? You think I'm in this for me? I've sweat blood for thirteen years trying to help her find her way! She needs to turn the boat around."

Lilli shined the light into Eleni's face. "The tide's ebbing and we're going with it. That's why it's so quiet. You turn her into the tide now and it'll push our stern in the air like a stinky beetle. Ever see one of those? Shove their ass way up in the air? That's what we'll look like. Flip the stern up and suck the bow down. What're you gonna do? Fight her for the wheel? Piss her off and see if she jumps ship? Right now, she's as unstable as it gets. She doesn't know you, doesn't care what's right or wrong, or whether the boat's capable of making it through the channel. She doesn't care that the fog's obliterating her view of the channel. She's riding the tide, Eleni. Go with it till there's an opportunity to turn her around."

"What're you going to do, go out and offer her a donut?"

"You got a better idea?"

"I can't lose her, not after all these years."

"It's real easy to lose when you're so close to winning."

"I know." Eleni collapsed onto the bench. "That's what I'm afraid of."

"Let me go out and talk to her. We've got about an hour before the tide turns."

Eleni rubbed the calloused leather remnant lying on the table. "You've got twenty minutes, then I'm coming out." She watched Lilli walk to the galley steps and hesitate. An electrical cord squeezed through the bottom of the door hung loosely by the wall. Sophie had unplugged the Christmas lights.

Eleni grabbed the pile of remnants, knocking over a small stack of cut pieces as she did. "Patches..." she whispered. There were ten patches in all, including three cut into circles, three into squares, three pentagrams, and one triangle. The circles were cut from three different fabrics of silver netting, burgundy brocade, and horsehair.

"The circle...or eternity, cut from the fabric of the priestesses representing mother: Argante, Igraine, and Kundry. What are you doing here, Sophie?"

She picked up the square patches. "A square is four. Four represents matter and manifestation...four seasons, four directions...balance and symmetry...cut from black leather, green velvet, and gray wool. The sisters," she said to herself. "Morgan's in the spirit realm, Nimue on earth, and Dindraine—sister to Perceval—in the realm of the holy grail."

She placed the squares on top of the circles. The pentagrams were cut from white cotton, floral silk, and a black and silver cloth. "Enid, Guinevere and Ragnell... the Pentagram...five...is sacred to the goddess...emblematic of the brides."

The triangle had been pieced together with a little bit of everything and bonded to a piece of red silk. "And this one...is the Tenth Priestess."

"It's short hand. You've reduced the active principles to concepts you can understand. The patches can be worn and exchanged according to the energy you're working with."

Eleni spread the patches around on the table. "What're you saying, Sophie?" she whispered. "You've created some sort of symbolic palimpsest here." She turned the pieces over one by one, examining them in detail. On the back of the black leather patch there was a drawing. A quick scan of the others showed nothing. Black leather was Morgan.

The drawing was of a Celtic cross, the circle of time overlaid with the Christian cross. But instead of a circle, Sophie had drawn a spiral.

"According to the journal, this cross is symbolic of the world tree. But you've placed the cross over a spiral instead of the circle...on a patch of Morgan's black leather." Eleni kept turning it over in her hand. "A spiral is a maze...draws you in...it's a different journey than the circle. But, why Morgan?"

She turned off the flashlight and sat in the dark. "You had to embrace wholeness in order to gain access to The Tree of Life. You merged with the dark side of yourself in order to open the gateway to the Tree. I remember seeing him just before I entered the Tree with you. After that, all I can remember are the amazing rings of light: A Tree of Life that grows in rings of wisdom. You entered the Tree and passed through three rings. Between the rings was a river of fog where a boat waited. The boat moved you through the fog, toward your next ring. I was the white shroud draped in silence across the bow of the boat...the beacon of remembrance." Eleni dropped her head. "God, will this never end?"

Muffled voices hammered softly at the galley door. "It's got to have something to do with Morgan. Why do you want me to remember the journey through the fog?" Eleni gazed through the window to the dim light emanating from Maude Island. "Morgan's a challenger, always attempting to break the illusion and force the outcome. She never gives up." Eleni stared, mesmerized by the light breaking through the mist. "You're calling to me, aren't you, Sophie? Part of you doesn't remember who I am, but part of you does."

She fanned the room with the flashlight, lingering on the gown that hung from the kitchen cabinet. Next to it on the counter was the purple scarf containing Sophie's hair.

"Everything's ready. The gown, your hair, it's all ready for the final merging and integration. It's everything you've been working for, Sophie. What would make you run at the last minute and give it all up?"

Across the room, draped over a chair, was the white sheet: Igraine's flag, marked with interlocking circles. "The flag under which the ***Avalon*** is to sail," she whispered. Eleni went over and brushed her hand across the drawing. "Like a white shroud in the fog," she whispered. "There's only one thing that I can think of that would make you run from all this." She grabbed the cloth and disappeared down the hall.

Lilli stepped out into a thick fog that folded round her like a spider's web; it was wet and clouded her vision. Like a dark cloud, it pressed low and heavy upon the deck, muffling the creaking joints of Jack's boat, washing all light out of the night. The hair on her arms stood on end.

Instinct turned her to stern. She took a few steps then stopped, as a shadowy figure emerged at the back of the boat. Its darkness defined it, being blacker than the night, causing Lilli to pull her denim jacket high around her neck and shrink back into its thin folds. Whoever was at the stern bore energy more male than female and caused Lilli's lips to snarl tight against her teeth.

The figure twirled around, its back piled high with heavy cloth that floated and spread like a cloak in slow motion; a swirling cape puffed out, as if the very fog was giving it substance and form, draping from shoulder to foot where it lay heavy upon the protruding toes of Sophie's tennis shoes.

"Sophie?"

The figure's head was wrapped with a thick wool muffler, round the neck and looped over the crown, where it was secured with a fisherman's hat. The fabric stuffed the hat, causing it to crest on the head like a crown. The creature raised its head and stared at Lilli with eyes that glowed searing coals through the mist.

"Ahhh...Coyote. I hoped it might be you."

The voice was raspy. Not a man's voice but neither a woman's, like sandpaper, without color. Lilli's eyes flickered yellow and the blood of animal rose in her throat. She strangled it back and stared at Sophie's feet, knowing they were bare inside the tennis shoes.

"I'm sure Jack's got socks you can borrow...probably smell like fish but what the hell...maybe they'll help you swim faster when we sink." Lilli smiled, hoping her teeth were white enough to deflect the blood gorging her gums.

"I have no intention of sinking."

Lilli took two steps closer. "No one ever does." She reached into her pocket. "Want a Twinkie?"

Sophie looked at Lilli's offering and turned away. "I'm not in the mood for bribes."

Lilli took a deep breath and chuckled. It was dark and low and stayed in the crook of her throat. "I can't imagine anyone ever getting far on a Twinkie bribe." She opened the package and devoured one. "You can't run from this, Sophie."

The only part of Sophie not covered with cloth were her eyes, and they bore no resemblance to anything Lilli had ever seen. This was no Priestess, dark or otherwise. Whoever it was chilled her spine and caused her animal instinct to leap to the fore; she was fighting hard not to shift.

"You are frightened of me, Talapas; I can smell it. Fear sits on your skin like oil, probably thicker and more potent since it belongs to the animal within."

Lilli stared at the shoes. "Funny thing...fear. If you look right at it, it disappears: like mist."

"I'm still here."

"Are you? Or are you just the final vestige, a ghost of what was."

"Looks like I'm back."

"She conquered you," continued Lilli.

"Surely by now you've learned that life is a spiral; it seems to be the common theme. There's always another chance, if you just bide your time; everything comes round again."

"Not everything." Lilli was riveted by the demonic intelligence brimming within Sophie's eyes. "Some things evolve."

"Like Merlin? Tell the old man to go back through his tree to the dust he truly is. He is a weak, ineffectual imbecile, unable to maintain any essence of life on his own...so he reaches for the supple fragrance of woman just to survive."

"You don't seem to be hurting too badly from them."

"The difference, Dog, is that I control them, where he would set them free."

Lilli glanced at the wheel and saw it was locked in position, navigating a steady course up the center of Seymour Narrows. The guiding light on Maude Island barely pierced the dense fog, giving her concern as to their closeness to shore. It was easy to go astray in the channel. Sophie smiled.

"Who are you...?" Lilli's voice was brittle as ice.

"Who am I?" Her arms rose slowly up to the side in a vast arc of thick wool, and as they did, an Island boiled out of the gray water behind the boat. "Why, I am the dark side of the moon, Dog."

Lilli staggered as land billowed out of the sea, breaching like a great whale, forcing water to swell up the ship's sides and spill onto the deck. She slid backwards and crashed onto Jack's fishing nets, where the webbing tangled and bound her feet. Her pupils began to flicker yellow as she tore against the netting, trying to break free.

"Isn't this what you're all looking for: Avalon, the Isle of eternal life?"

"There is no Island in Seymour Narrows!" Lilli screamed into the roar of sea that tossed Jack's boat like a matchstick. "This is an illusion...you have no right to pander with wisdom." Her foot twisted in the net.

"No right? Says who?"

Another arm rose and the sea swelled beneath them. Lilli began to slide uncontrollably towards the edge of the boat. She reached out and grasped the fish net, as the boat lurched, then was tossed back as a wave rose up and crashed down, filling her mouth with briny salt water.

Sophie watched. "You see, Lilli? You're just like all the rest, trapped in a web of your own making. It's easy to control the wisdom of eons, because it's frightened of being free. It's your fear that strangles you."

The net slid back and forth, tangling in Lilli's hair and around her legs. She fought desperately to free herself but the boat corkscrewed, knocking her like a fish out of water; she slithered towards the railing.

"Is this what you learned," Lilli cried out, "to manipulate the energies in a way that serves only you?"

"You mock my abilities?"

"Anything that forces a downward spiral negates ability; you are fear incarnate, nothing more."

Sophie glowered.

"Why, Sophie? Why must you hold yourself back?" Lilli's voice twisted with pain.

"Because...I can."

Lilli stared at the creature, shrouded in wool and mist. "Sophie already redeemed her darkness. You haven't got a chance."

"Why?"

Seawater slopped across the deck, saturating Lilli's hair and stinging her eyes. She stared with blurred vision along the planks of peeled paint and rusted metal at Sophie's feet. A wave rose up and smashed down, slamming her against the sodden deck; she screamed, as her shoulder wrenched further out of its socket; her body went limp. "Because," Lilli whispered, "you've still got your tennis shoes on." But the ocean's roar obliterated her whisperings and no one heard. Lilli's head rolled back and she passed out from pain.

Behind them, the galley door blew open, and a figure emerged wrapped in white. Wind billowed and ripped at the edges of Igraine's flag, filling it with static energy that snapped and coursed fractures of light through the interlocking circles. Sophie stared.

Eleni gripped the garment close to her body as she glanced at Lilli's limp figure rocking back and forth in a pool of dirty brine. Off port side, she saw a feint outline of land awash in mist, and between the land and Jack's boat, there was a river of fog. Then she turned to stern and stared into the face she'd hoped she would never see again. The sheet cloaked her head and shoulders, shadowing the fear that gripped the muscles of her face.

"So," she whispered, "Henri Dumont is back."

The Island was wrapped in fog like a dream...or maybe a nightmare. Eleni looked into her daughter's eyes.

"How dark is your Well..."

"Is that a question or a statement?"

Eleni noticed the tennis shoes. "Funny, isn't it...?"

"What?"

"They don't seem to suit you at all. What is it, I wonder, that keeps you in them? You changed everything else."

Sophie's eyes flared.

"I know you," Eleni continued.

"A rose by any other name..."

"I should have known."

"What? That I would return?"

"No...that you will never be gone. She embraced you. Now you're part of the whole."

"Tsk, tsk, such a pity to have to face the likes of me every five hundred years."

"Not really. Actually, you're an asset." Eleni headed towards the bow. Staggering from the ocean swells she bent down and touched Lilli's neck, confirming a pulse.

"Touching," Sophie whispered.

Eleni listened to the howling screech of wind, whipping through the mast. Sophie followed her as she slid across the slippery deck to the front of the boat.

"Does your Island have a name," Eleni asked.

"Avalon, of course."

"The Isle of women. Yours, however, is an illusion."

"Avalon is an illusion. Didn't you read the journal? Even Samuel knew it was the stuff of myth, born of the pomposity of women."

"Why have you conjured it, then?" Eleni shivered beneath the wet sheet.

"You and your friend seem so intent on seeing its rebirth, I thought I'd leave you there before I depart."

Eleni stared into the hollows of her daughter's eyes. There was no crescent moon on her forehead, and the ring on her hand was as dead as a lump of coal. She grabbed Sophie's hand. "Give me the ring, Sophie." Eleni shoved her paralyzed hand in Sophie's face. "You may not remember, but this is not your journey alone. I've also paid a price." She spat out the words and stepped forward, shoving hard on Sophie's toe. She dug her heel into the shoe and pushed her daughter, forcing her to fall. The muffler slid back from Sophie's head, and she stared down at her shoes, confused.

Eleni towered over her. "You mock and degrade everything the Tenth Priestess is fighting to redeem."

Lilli opened her eyes and listened to Eleni's voice, thick with anger. She dragged herself across the deck and down the galley steps, the fish net binding her feet. Draped across the bottom step was an electrical cord. Lilli grabbed and plugged it in.

"You're nothing but a vehicle of darkness." Eleni whispered.

The Christmas lights woven along the mast of Jack's boat lit up, piercing the night with tiny stars. Eleni and Sophie turned their faces skyward, light filled their eyes, and the ring on Sophie's hand glinted red. Eleni looked back at her daughter then turned and walked to stern. Lilli lay across the galley threshold and watched Eleni tug the rubber dinghy off its hook.

"Eleni..."

The wet sheet clung to Eleni like a second skin.

"What are you doing, Eleni?"

"Creating a trail..."

"You can't throw the dinghy overboard."

"I can, and I will. And then I'll lower myself into it."

"You're out of your mind." Lilli ripped the tangled web of fishing nets off her legs.

"She has to wake up. She has to or we're doomed."

"She has her tennis shoes on. Use that as a trail!"

"This goes too deep, Lilli. The tennis shoes only ground her in this life. There's only one image that might jar her enough. It's the same thing...over and over; it just never ends. She keeps peeling back layer after layer. I thought we were finished, but this reality is just another layer." The ocean swells boiled and receded, like a stewing cauldron tossing the Christmas lights in the wind.

"What does she need to see?"

Eleni dragged the dinghy towards the railing. "The only reason Sophie was able to enter the Tree of Life was because she embraced her darkness. That creature back there is part of her, and it wants to stop her. Every time she faces him, she learns more about her dark side and weakens his power over her. But this time, she's frightened; I have to help her see." Eleni grabbed her left hand and shoved it towards Lilli. "This hand is paralyzed because I put on a ring and took a journey with her into a dream world...Trees that grow with rings of light divided by rivers of fog...I was the beacon...a woman draped in white, lying prone on the bow of a boat floating in a sea of fog! Look around you! It's the same thing all over again!"

Lilli struggled to her knees. "The tree grew in rings of light?"

Eleni hauled at the dinghy. "The rings of light are stages of enlightenment; she passed through three rings. I thought she was finished, but from what I can see, this is just another awakening. Sophie and I are joined by the ring. The pain of that weighs heavy on her, but it's the one thing that continues to reach through, past all fear. To her, I am the image of a soul lost because of her denial to claim her destiny. And without her awakening, I will remain that way. It's the one image that forced her to complete her journey through the Tree. The fear of losing me is greater than that thing you see at the bow of the boat. I have to lower this and get in."

"It's suicide, Eleni. Look behind you...the illusion's fading."

Eleni looked at the Island, merging with the sea and fog. She snapped to attention and clawed at the dinghy with her right arm, forcing it onto the railing. "Help me!" The boat lurched starboard and Lilli slid across the slippery deck to her side.

"Stop! She'll fall asleep and the illusion will fade and we can take the boat back in."

"That's exactly what can't happen!" Eleni screamed into the obliterating roar of the sea.

"Why!"

"If I had done that, she'd still be back in the first ring. She has to wake up! She has to wake up and see what she has the potential to create. It's the only way to move her forward...to break the grasp this fear has on her! If she falls asleep, she'll never know and it will gain strength. Help me!"

Eleni threw the weight of her right shoulder against the dinghy. Lilli looked around frantically, then ran to a coiled rope, grabbed the end, and ran back to Eleni where she tied it around her waist.

"Tie it to the Dinghy. You can haul me in."

"I'll tie one to the Dingy and one to you. There's a good chance it'll tip and you'll be thrown overboard." She found another coiled rope, tied it to the boats eye, and shoved her left shoulder against its rubber flank, heaving it over the edge. Eleni shoved the rope ladder over the side and clawed her way down, lopsided, using only the strength of her right arm.

"Eleni..."

Eleni's wild eyes flickered, as she slid down the ladder and fell into the boat. Within seconds it had disappeared from sight.

Lilli watched the ropes uncoil and snake over the railing, into the sea. She couldn't remember which one was attached to Eleni and which one to the boat. Fool! She could've held the boat steady!

She scanned the masts looking for a searchlight. Jack wouldn't have a boat without a searchlight. There it was, attached to the front mast! She slid across the deck to the galley steps and tumbled inside. On the panel by Jack's desk were a series of switches. She found the one she needed, switched it on, and scrambled back on deck, just as a wave rose out of the sea. It crashed down and hit her broadside, throwing her back into the pile of nets where she hit her head and passed out.

Sophie struggled, weighted down by wool saturated with seawater. She wrenched off the scarf and stared at the Christmas lights shimmering above the boat, creating tiny halos in the fog. The sea continued to boil and swell off starboard where a feint outline of land remained. She scanned the horizon, searching for lost thoughts, when the ship's light cut a channel through the night, illuminating something floating on the water.

Sophie's eyes flickered. Was it a whale? Or maybe some wood adrift? A river of fog wound round then dispersed, opening a window on what looked like a small boat or raft. She clenched the cold metal railing. The searchlight bobbed across the waves, illuminating a tiny boat with intermittent slivers of light. There was a figure, all in white, lying in the boat.

She looked back to stern, up at the Christmas lights, out to the illusive Island receding into fog, and down at her body, heavy with black wool.

A wave rose beneath the dinghy, nearly capsizing it. The figure inside rolled, and the light clung for an instant to the pale skin of a woman's face. Sophie's jaw clenched and blood drained from her skin.

"No...!"

Her scream was drowned in the thick crashing of rolling sea. Water rushed across the bow, corkscrewed Jack's boat, twisting it away from the dinghy. She staggered to the other side, panic gripping the lines of her mouth. Out in the fog, she saw it again, a tiny dark cup of a boat holding the frail form of a woman in white.

"Oh God...it can't be..."

Sophie jerked back from the railing and slid across the deck saturated with salt water toward stern, where she tripped on a pile of tangled fishing nets. In the middle was a figure swathed in black hair and soggy denim. Sophie brushed the wet hair away from the face. She ran her fingers along blue lips and held her finger to the neck, hunting for a pulse. The ring on her finger started to shine. She tugged the nets back, untangling their web, and reached under the arms. Fighting against the jerking torque of Jack's boat, she hauled Lilli across the deck towards the galley steps.

"Grab the rope." Lilli's voice was thick with pain.

"Lilli!"

"You've got to grab the rope."

"Lilli what's happening? Tell me it's not real! Tell me it's a dream!"

"Get used to it, Sophie. It's all a dream."

"It's my Mother!"

She kicked the galley door and dragged Lilli's icy body down the stairs. "What have I done? Why is she out there?" She grabbed a blanket and wrapped it around Lilli just as her head fell back and her eyes closed.

"Lilli!!"

Sophie flew up the steps and out to the railing, where she saw two ropes spiraling over the edge. Which one? She grabbed one and started to haul it in; as she did, the crescent moon began to flicker.

The weight was staggering. As she pulled, ghostly arms appeared around her...linked to her...pulling steadily. She raised her head and stared out to sea. The boat was in sight, and beyond the boat, the diminishing speck of land.

"Avalon is not an illusion to be conjured from the dark side of the moon, Sophie Alexander."

Sophie hauled the rope, its coiled form snaking over the railing, as the crescent moon glimmered. The illusion of arms melded, leaving only hers. Sweat and fog dripped in her eyes, down her chin.

"What you see before you is the price of she who would be free. You will always carry light and dark. Once understood, it can become your ally."

Sophie watched the tiny boat slip across the water, her mother cupped within its hold. Fog trickled streams around her and the Island faded into the sea.

The dinghy bumped up against Jack's boat and a pale hand reached up to grasp the rope ladder. Eleni held on with her right hand, as Sophie pulled, hauling her onto the deck, where they fell in a pile of icy limbs and sodden cloth. Sophie half dragged Eleni down the steps into the galley and wrapped her in blankets next to Lilli. Then she shed the wet wool, wrapped herself in a blanket, and collapsed from shock.

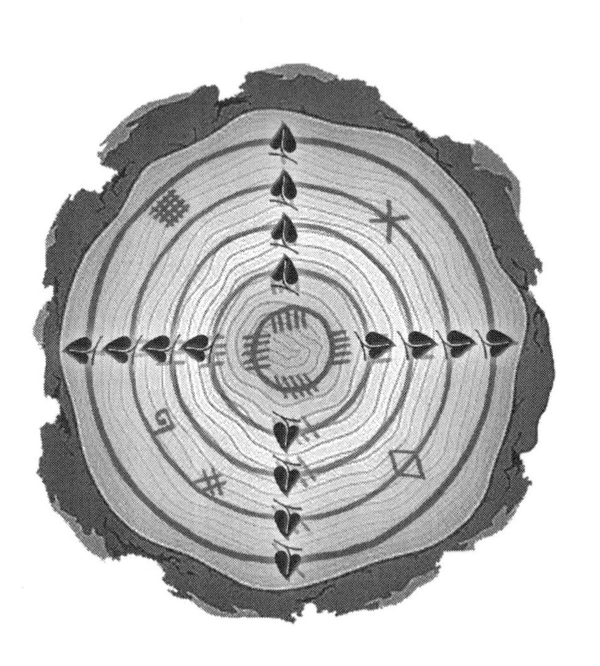

ASPEN

Breath Of Spirit

"YOU MAY REMOVE *the cloth from your eyes."*

Jack untied the mantle, hesitating a moment before opening his eyes. "I can see." His voice was a twist of fear and relief.

"I never said that you couldn't...just that your vision would be altered."

Jack looked into the keen eyes of the legend and felt a spasm in his stomach as the emotions returned.

"There will be echoes...for awhile."

Jack doubled over and retched onto the forest floor. "When did we leave the cave?"

"It matters not. You'll find your answers here."

Jack wiped his mouth with the cloth. "In the forest..."

"Yes."

"The letters for the inscription are in the trees?"

"In a manner of speaking..."

"Well, how am I to decipher them?"

Merlin dropped his head and looked at the cloth in Jack's hand. "You've been given many clues, Jack Harrington. I suggest you pay attention to them. Dig deep. These are not your average woods." Merlin turned and walked away.

"Where are you going?"

"I have an appointment with destiny, for which I have waited far too long. I don't intend to miss it."

"You're leaving me here?"

"That...is your destiny."

"But how in God's name...out of all these trees..."

Merlin spun around, whipping his cloak into a vast arc. "Look at me!"

Jack staggered back from the force of his words.

"Look at me and tell me what you see!"

They stood beneath a wide canopy of leaf and limb, shadowing all in dark and light; Merlin flickered on and off, his form now merging with the light then receding into the shadows. Jack squinted, trying to hold him steady. Then he saw the horns. "I see your shadow in the light."

"What shadow."

"I see the horns of the stag."

"It is one thing to see them in the cavernous earth...quite another in the light of day. This is how your vision has been altered...to see spirit and flesh at once...to see man and myth... and to see, Jack, the mystery of the forest. Trust what you see. Listen to it. And remember what it is that you are seeking."

"The inscription—"

"It is more than an inscription. Words of love alone won't break this spell." Merlin began walking backwards, retreating into the forest. "Think about what you are unlocking. Try...and perhaps you will remember what I taught you when you were just a lad." Merlin stepped back under the gnarled limbs of an aged oak and disappeared.

"God help us," Jack whispered.

The ground at Jack's feet was strewn with forest debris. He walked around, looking for evidence of the language with which he was apparently surrounded. Amongst the fauna was a branch, whose limbs had grown into a parceled bunch of twigs, like a broom. Jack picked it up and swept the earth in front of the old oak. The Ogham was an ancient Celtic alphabet some believed was used originally for purposes of divination. Whether it was or not, its illusive qualities were undisputed. Each letter represented a particular tree and was written in a series of lines above or below a branch. That mark represented the first letter of the tree.

Jack sifted through the leaves, attempting to discern one from the other. The Druids believed there was a difference in communicating with symbols or words. Certain things could not be aptly described with words—mystical things. The Ogham letters could be used to communicate normal daily matters, yet also be saying something else entirely. Eleni had learned about it from her father and shared it with Jack; she had even sent him a few notes to decipher. But that was twenty-two years ago.

Jack grabbed a stick. He remembered that there were four groups of five letters, equaling twenty. He drew a line in the dirt and marked it with the appropriate marking, then straightened up; Samuel's pendant slid out from inside his shirt. Jack cupped his palm beneath the medal he remembered seeing so long ago.

"Well...it's been a long time, Samuel." He rubbed his thumb across the gold. "It's the Celtic cross you always wore. Looks like I had a visitor." He gazed up at the gnarled branches of the oak tree, his mind drifting back twenty-two years. "Did you ever wonder, Samuel...why I suddenly disappeared? I mean, what did she tell you?" He began to circumnavigate the clearing, dragging the stick behind him in the dirt. "So...is the cross the key, Samuel?"

Jack squatted down and quickly drew the interlocking circles and a sketchy figure of a tree growing out of the center with the directions noted in its branches, like he'd seen in the journal.

"It has something to do with the tree..."

He drew a Celtic cross in the dirt next to it, then stood up and studied both drawings. "The tree is the symbol. Samuel described its manifestation in the space/time continuum. But the information that defines the tree is like a seed that grows out of the Vesica Piscis."

He looked back at his drawing of the Celtic cross, then up at his line with the Ogham notches in it. "It looks like a branch. But what's it got to do with the Celtic cross? The cross is another version of the tree. What happens...where the cross conjoins the circle?"

Jack studied the three drawings. "What if...the Ogham letters aren't supposed to be linear? What if the Celtic cross was another version of the information contained within the seed of the tree?"

He grabbed the stick and drew a larger circle with the cross in the center. "Maybe this cross also represents north, south, east, and west. Sophie started in the north," he whispered. "Think, Jack," he said, remembering Merlin's words, "think about what you're unlocking."

"North isn't just a direction. North is a dark wintered night that pulls us down in dreams; we die and are reborn in the north. Come on, Eleni...help me," he whispered.

He grabbed the branch he'd used as a broom and dragged it behind, as he wandered, studying the different trunks and leaves. "Too many trees..." he closed his eyes and breathed deeply. "You wrote me a note once about starting over...after we'd had a fight."

Jack walked back to the circle. "I thought it was a 'T', didn't I. The symbol looked like a 'T'...but it was for...." He looked down at what had become his broom. "Birch—the symbol stood for Birch. You told me that the branches grew in clumps so were used to sweep the houses clean. Birch was symbolic of starting over. Birch must belong in the north because we die and are reborn in the north. We sweep our souls clean."

He made a downward notch off the northern point of the circle. "In the field of time, north represents going within...dying down...sweeping clean...beginning again. Birch must be a description of the energy."

Jack turned quickly towards the east of the circle. "What is east? The sun rises in the east." He looked to the north, then followed the circular route to the east. "Spring. Everything is waking up...budding...flowering. The world dies down in the north...in the winter...hence the downward notch in the line. But in the east...in the spring...life is awakening."

Jack drew a notch outward from the eastern point of the circle, then turned and headed under the canopy of green looking for inspiration. "But what does it stand for?" He raised his head and inhaled. "Spring green. Something about the fragrance makes me think of you, Eleni. Something about the way you smell...in the spring. What is that fragrance?" His cheeks flushed. "A fragrance that smells like the blossom of woman." Jack stopped in front of a tree heavy with flowers. "The maypole tree...the branches were used to celebrate spring and a time of awakening. It's the Hawthorn tree!" He rushed back to the circle and looked at the line representing Hawthorn that branched outward in the east of the circle, expressing the burgeoning force of life. "This is the symbol for the Hawthorn tree."

He faced south.

"Heat...summer...light..." Jack's mood shifted drastically. "Consciousness. Nothing is shadowed in the south. Good and bad, light and dark, are worn like an oppressive crown of thorns." He looked out to the trees and saw a vine tangled in the limbs of a maple. "Bramble is placed in the south. Its energy is neither downward nor uplifting, but crosses worlds. The line crosses through,

but is slanted, because Bramble is humbling." Jack drew the line then turned west. "The sun sets in the west. Day is ending and seasons are pulling life back: autumn, dying down, turning in." He raised his head and looked out to the forest, feeling a breeze ruffle his brow. Directly in front of him was a tall tree that shimmered as the wind blew. "The silver fir...the birth tree joins sea and sand and soil. It grows near the ocean shore and reminds us of the different levels we are supposed to connect...helps move us to the next level."

Jack drew a straight line in the west of the circle, crossing through the base line, pointing inward. "West is the beginning of the movement inward." Sweat trickled down his brow.

"The symbols have a different meaning when combined with space and time. Samuel's other drawing is how the tree manifests. But this one...this one is like entering another dimension."

Color flooded his cheeks. "It's not enough! Four letters are not enough. There's a whole damn alphabet! Where do the other letters go?"

He grabbed the cloth to wipe sweat from his forehead and, as he did, the feather fell to the ground. It fluttered back and forth, sashaying with the breeze, till it reached the center of the cross, where it landed in the dirt. He picked it up, noticing for the first time the imprint of the garment in his hand.

"The turtledove mantle..." He held the feather between his fingers, twirling it back and forth. "I must have had a lot of visitors..." He blew on the feather. "Lilli..."

"The turtledove lives in the center. In Sophie's drawing, it's represented at the junction of the two circles. But this is the Celtic cross..."

"The cross implies the center. The Vesica Piscis implies a place of union...or a womb...as Lilli called it. The cross also represents

the tree. If the letters followed the lines of the cross from outside to inside, they would create a cross of their own. The energy points represented by the trees along the lines of time and space create an inward moving path, like a spiral." He stared again at the cloth in his hand, then took the stick and drew four concentric rings inside the circle, each smaller than the previous. "It's that page in your journal, isn't it, Samuel. The wisdom of the wood is found in the rings of the tree. You have to go within. There are five rings because five is a sacred number to the goddess. That's why Sophie drew her Cherry Tree next to it. She knew she had to enter the Tree to find the ring. And the ring wouldn't be hers, until she achieved a certain level of enlightenment. It's an Ogham Shield."

Jack stepped outside his drawing. Five concentric circles, the outermost one marked with tree symbols on the points allocating north, south, east, and west.

"How do you describe the wisdom of a whole forest?" A breeze whispered across Jack's brow. "It looks like tree rings...which would mean that it represents four dimensions—three spatial, plus time. And if each tree is symbolic of a body of information, then that information will need to manifest." Jack stared inward.

"Son of a bitch." Jack's face blanched, and he started drawing quickly. "All northerly lines point downward. The outer circle has one downward line, the next circle has two, then three, four, and five, all along the northern arm of the cross. He turned east and drew upward lines in the same manner, on each concentric circle, at the conjunction with the eastern arm of the cross. South and west followed.

Jack threw the stick aside and studied his work. "It's a map.... There are twenty letters that represent trees mirroring aspects of evolving consciousness. The fifth ring is the last. When all trees are awakened, they form the Celtic cross, and unlock the ring on Sophie's hand."

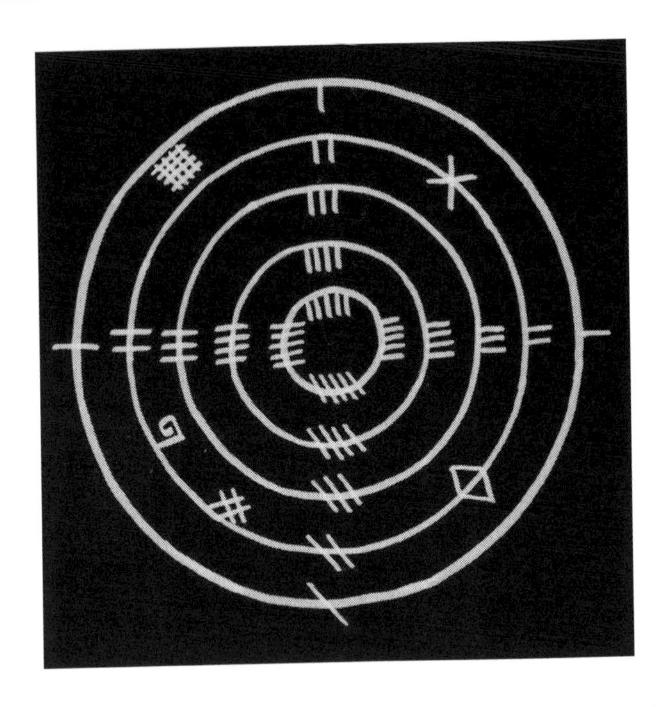

"It's what she said in the journal...that the Tree of Life is reflected in the energy of all trees. This is a map for the progressing stages of consciousness needed to move to the center of the Tree of Life. Samuel's other drawing represented the outer world... and this one...represents the information contained within the Tree of Life. It's the wizard's journey."

"Sophie went through three rings of consciousness. If the letters, or symbols, of the fifth ring unlock the doorway for spiritual union, then what happened to the fourth ring?"

Jack walked the circle. "What are the trees for the fourth ring? I don't remember the symbols!" He bolted into the forest, frantically looking for clues. "I can't work backwards, Merlin! I can't look at the lines and remember what you taught me!" He ran amongst Elm and Holly, Aspen and Heather.

A slight breeze ruffled the branches. "The answers are in the forest, Arthur…they always have been. Look around." Merlin's voice was in the wind. It scattered crackling leaves and petals from spring blossoms. Jack looked down at his feet.

"Everything's here. Spring flowers and autumn leaves and…" He took a step and heard the crunch of frozen leaves beneath his feet. "All seasons are beneath my feet. What does that mean?" He walked around kicking, crunching, and stomping. "It's all right here…"

He stepped on a hard round object, reached down, and picked it up. It was a hazelnut, the last thing he'd had contact with before losing consciousness.

"This is what we've been dealing with, isn't it? But it's not in the north. Hazelnut is women and wisdom…it fell in the river…it's water…rising water and wisdom. It's in the east!"

He ran back and looked down at the fourth circle and the Ogham lines in the east…four outward lines. Then he turned north and looked at the four downward lines of the same ring. "Willow. How do I know that?"

Wind blew through a grove of trees with limbs that bent gracefully, sweeping across the earth. "A cut willow always takes root. It's regenerative, like the moon, and loves water more than any other tree; water…the domain of the feminine." Jack wandered through the trees and continued talking as if they were educating him. "You are the sacred tree of the triple goddess. You will always rise again." He looked back at his drawing in the dirt.

"Son of a bitch…" he whispered…"We're in the fourth ring; Willow and Hazelnut are reenergizing."

He staggered over to the oak tree and collapsed against its massive trunk. "There are twenty letters. Twenty reduces to two. The fifth ring has four letters, each with five cross hatches: ten and ten. Sophie is the Tenth Priestess, and the wizard is numerically one. He's coming out of the tree! Ten reduces to one. They're equals.

Two letters, or trees, or levels of consciousness belong to Sophie, and two belong to Merlin...or Emrys." He took a stick and drew the Ogham symbols for the fifth ring in the dirt.

"Merlin was right...I know these. Ash in the north, apple in the east, elder in the south, and yew in the west; the inherent power in water, immortality, breakdown, and death, and finally, transformation...breakdown leading to transformation."

Jack became very still. His eyes turned inward. Suddenly, he threw the stick violently towards the circle.

"You already know all this, Merlin! You know the final doorway is massive transformation! You know which elements are female and which are male, and you know the symbols on the backs of those rings. You don't need me to tell you!"

Jack hauled himself off the ground and spun towards the Ogham circle. "Why am I here?" He screamed. "There's got to be a missing element. The union of Sophie and Emrys will unlock the fifth ring, but they need to understand the principles of the energies that are unlocking. They need to know these four Ogham symbols. Merlin knows the significance of the four trees in the fifth ring. Emrys is the manifestation of Merlin. He just went into the oak tree and will reappear on the other side as Emrys. He knows the symbols needed to unlock the ring. He's the one who taught me! Why was I sent here?"

Jack's heart blasted against his chest cavity and drummed loudly in his head. The forest had become a vision of light, extending from branch and limb. "There's got to be a missing element."

Suddenly, Jack screamed and grabbed his right hand. The wound on his palm burned bright red, sending a stabbing pain up his arm. He held his wrist and stared at the triangular wound that matched the scar on Sophie's hand.

"Son of a bitch..." he whispered, "...blood."

Lilli rolled over and slammed her shoulder against the floor, grimacing as the joint popped into place. She crawled up the galley steps and looked out to sea. The boat had turned with the tide. Maude Island was behind them, and she could see marina lights in the distance. The fog had cleared, sucking Sophie's nightmare with it. She took the wheel, adjusted the course, and locked it.

Back in the galley, Sophie and Eleni were curled on the floor, their skin blue with cold. Lilli ransacked the closet for more blankets, wincing, as the pain in her shoulder ricocheted down her arm. She slid the white sheet off Eleni and covered her up again, noting the pearl collar still around her neck. She wrapped a blanket around Sophie then started to leave.

"Lilli..."

Lilli glanced at Sophie's heavily lidded eyes, fighting for consciousness. "Don't talk, Sophie. I need to get the boat back."

"Why is Avalon rising out of the myth and into me, Lilli?"

Lilli stared into Sophie's large hazel eyes, sunken into hollows now reddened from cold. "There are places we call sacred, Sophie. Maybe they're sacred, because something happened there, and we honor them for what they remind us of. It seems that Avalon's drawn a lot of sacred myth to it, like a magnet."

"Glastonbury."

"The spring beneath the Tor flows continually," Lilli continued. "It's said that, at one time, some water ran red and some white, and that nine priestesses lived there; but remember, Sophie, it's a myth. There is meaning beneath the story."

"Go on."

"There's a Well known as Bride's Well."

"The ring."

"Yes. But the name itself is revealing, isn't it?"

Sophie swallowed, trying to contain the bile in her convulsing stomach.

"At the base of the hill there's a tree they call the Holy Thorn, a tree found only in the Middle East. It's said that Joseph of Arimathea came to this place after the crucifixion and buried his staff in the ground and that it grew into this tree. The tree blooms every year at Christmas." Lilli looked out the galley hatch to the Christmas lights strung around the boat. "Some say he brought the cup of the last supper and buried it in the Well." She brushed salt off Sophie's brow.

"They also say Arthur made his home there, and that the Knights of the Round Table recognized the kingdom was dying because people had forgotten about this cup. They called it the Holy Grail, and in their chivalric manner began their quest to find it, looking for the object, having forgotten its meaning.

"Avalon has a lot of messages for you, Sophie. But its spiritual identity is where you'll find the key. The priestesses have tried to tell us that we got lost in their imagery and missed the message. Look at it all: one sacred hill with healing waters that flowed freely out of the earth, and upon that canvas you find a holy order of women, the cup of Christ, a sacred tree that blooms at Christmas, and an order of noble men trying to reclaim what was lost.

"Your Avalon isn't just a magical isle that appears out of the mist, whether in Seymour Narrows or some place in England. It's a powerful message that's crying out to be reborn. And you, Sophie Alexander, can help it happen." She tucked the blanket around Sophie's shoulders. "It's in your blood."

"Will I see you again?"

"I need to guide the vessel back to the marina."

"...And after that?"

Lilli winked. "I walk many worlds; I wouldn't be surprised if our paths cross..."

Sophie's head rolled back and her lids closed. "I'll be looking for you..."

Lilli went up on deck, guided the ***Avalon*** into the marina and secured the boat to the dock. She checked the women once more, noting that the color had returned to their cheeks and their fingers weren't so blue. Then she jumped onto the dock and disappeared into the night.

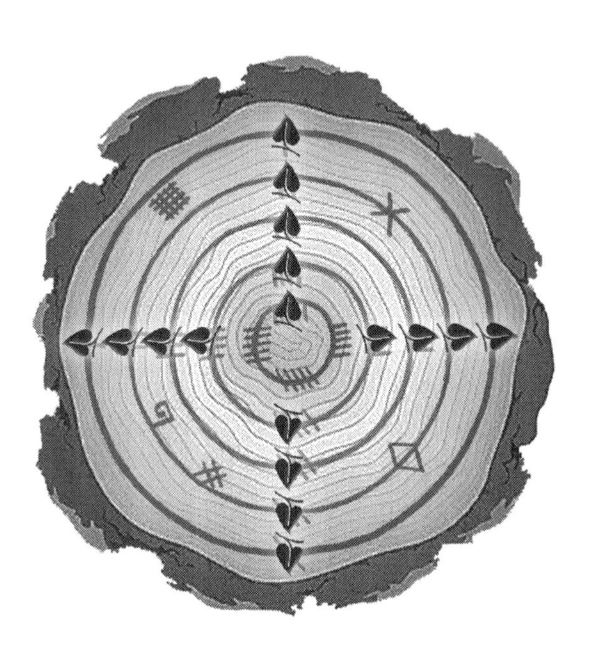

TIIII

ASH

Rebirth

May 7, 2001

JACK AWOKE IN a dark room pulsing with red and green blinking lights, on a hard bed with metal sidings. He jammed his forearm against the barriers, forcing their collapse, and ripped the sensors off his chest. He found the clothes he'd been admitted in, changed quickly and, like a shadow, poured down the corridor of the east wing.

At the front desk sat a spectacled woman with steel-gray hair and countenance. She looked up and saw a man tripping over lace-less tennis shoes, his head wrapped in a scarf with a feather sticking out.

"Call me a cab!" Jack yelled, as he rushed out the hospital door.

The woman picked up the phone to dial, shaking her head in disgust. "It's got to be Jack Harrington."

The cab dropped him off on the south side of the river, near the footbridge. It was pre-dawn. The driver eyed his attire. "You don't look like a man who is going fishing."

Jack grabbed some bills from his pocket and stuffed them in the driver's hand. "Don't believe everything you see." He ran across the footbridge and headed up the path that followed the north side of the river for about a mile then cut off into the trees. The growth was thick and the hill steep. He used limbs for leverage, helping him scramble the rock face. Sweat dripped off his brow, and he breathed deeply from the exertion.

At the top, he followed a path that approached the rear of Lilli's cabin. The river was swollen with spring rain and crashed over the cliff in a thunderous roar. Jack scrambled to the front and stopped short; Coyote was already waiting.

She bared her teeth and growled. Even though Jack knew, it always unnerved him, and he stepped back giving her a wide berth. She stared with yellow slit eyes that Jack thought looked strange, as if she was sick. The coyote leapt away from the door and disappeared down the path. Jack followed.

The grounds were heavily wooded and, normally, it would be easy to lose sight of Coyote. He found it odd that he wasn't having too much difficulty keeping up, till he noticed the animal favoring the front leg, limping and occasionally whimpering.

As they maneuvered through shadowy woods, Jack navigated more by sound than sight, following the snap of broken twigs and crushed leaves. Suddenly, they entered a clearing on the far side of which stood a large tree. Jack watched Coyote sidle up to it. Its trunk was wide and squat, upholding branches that spiraled sinuous limbs through the green canopy overhead.

It was an oak.

It was split through the middle by lightning, cauterized, leaving a gaping hole; it was the same tree that Merlin had disappeared into in Jack's dream. He walked forward into the clearing, encouraged by a pale blue swatch of fabric, extending out from the tree's opening. He focused his eyes, staring into the tree's cavernous womb. There was a body curled up inside.

Coyote sat at the base of the tree looking back at Jack.

"Am I too late, Lilli?" Jack inched closer. Coyote stood up, whimpering from the weight on her leg, then limped off into the forest. Jack stood in silence, wondering if the figure in the tree were dead or alive.

"The Ogham..." Jack began. "The tree alphabet..."

The man in the tree remained motionless.

"It's a secret language. It describes a journey from the outer world to an inner world, using the imagery of the rings of a tree to describe growth..." Jack hesitated, looking for signs of life or awareness or something that would let him know that Emrys was listening. There was nothing.

"The type of tree that best describes a particular type of consciousness is placed upon a point of direction on a circular timeline. The circle and the lines form the Celtic cross; it's a mystic's map." He stopped again, hoping for signs of life. "It's shamanic...going into the world tree via the rings of growth, using awareness of properties inherent in other trees, connecting them with aspects of the four directions. The four directions are used to describe a cyclical psychic process. The tree that's placed on that area of the timeline describes what is being processed...or learned...or assimilated.

"The fact that it's cyclical changes the nature of the symbols, and when viewed in that manner, the alphabet becomes a mystical language. But it can also be used in a linear manner, in which case the symbols, corresponding to the first letter of the tree represented become an alphabet that spells words used in normal communication. But the underlying purpose is mystical."

Nothing moved within the belly of the tree.

"I don't know who invented it," Jack continued, "maybe you...in your forest...when you moved through madness to enlightenment. Since it's a language of trees, mapped out on the rings of a tree, I wouldn't be surprised. But you got stuck in the tree when you realized that you couldn't go any further without merging the principle dualities of life: male and female."

Jack stopped and stared at the burnt-out cave of the old oak. The figure inside sat with knees to chest, head tilted back against the gutted core.

"You're trapped in the fourth ring," Jack whispered. He heard movement and saw the man raise his head.

Jack stared intently, then continued on. "Willow's in the north and Hazelnut's in the east, which represent regeneration and female wisdom. You're in a ring that's divided equally with the female. Blackthorn is in the south and Aspen in the west...coercion, force, and will power. But it's the water that you can't navigate alone. This is Sophie's journey.

"She had to catch up with you; that's why she went back in her dreams and took the journey of the rings. You called her out...went to her in a dream and challenged her. You opened the door to madness, knowing she might not make it through."

"Woman is madness," the voice whispered out from the tree.

Jack stiffened. "The apple tree," he whispered back.

"Yes." The voice was the same as in his dream; it was powerful, dark...commanding. But the biggest thing Jack heard in it was humility. "The poison apple that drives us mad is love...the muse of all creation."

Jack stood anchored to the ground.

"Female energy weaves a silver web through all life, Jack Harrington; entanglement is easy. I wanted to understand it...to harness it. I was on fire with the miracle of the universe and knew that the next door was a transformation like nothing I had ever known..."

"But you couldn't go there alone," Jack whispered.

"No. But neither can she." The man unfolded his legs and spilled out of the oak tree. It was Emrys, the physical manifestation of the myth. "I have been waiting a long...long...time, Mr. Jack Harrington. I have waited for this myth to be woven into the stuff of dreams and for the dream to become reality. And now it is done...and Sophie is the elixir. She is the sweet water that soothes and intoxicates, that heals, and transforms. But her wisdom will not drive this old wizard mad...because now, we are as one."

"You already knew everything I just said," Jack continued.

"Yes."

"I didn't go back for the inscription, did I?"

"Why then?" Emrys looked up. His black hair hung loosely over the same robe of moon and stars.

Jack held up his hand exposing the wound. "Because she carries my blood."

"Yes, you share the same blood. But you also share the same myth. For what is rising in her is also rising in you. You needed to remember, Jack Harrington, the mystery of the forest."

"Why?"

"You have seen the interlocking circles have you not?"

"Yes."

"There is much wisdom that must be carried forward."

"I thought that's what you were for."

"I am a mystery, Raven King. You have seen me as flesh and as spirit. But you carry the blood of all this within you, and it is your duty to uphold and honor that with which you are destined. Arthur represented the nobility of all men...the nobility of action, and the education of a people. He was a great man whose mythic lineage is not dead. You must hold on to what you have learned and help to birth it back into this world."

"The ring would have unlocked without me."

"Would it? Is there not information in blood?"

"Meaning?"

"Her mother has helped to foster the union of nine: It is a female journey. But without the wisdom you have just garnered through the Ogham, the fifth ring could not open. Male and female both must manifest."

Jack looked down at his palm. "Blood."

"It runs in her veins, because it runs in yours. It does not matter what I know, Jack Harrington...but what you know. The letters of the Ogham reflect back the mystery of which we are all a part. Your world has come far from understanding these things. Part of her pain has been to bridge with a reality long gone. She is flesh and spirit...as am I. But she is new, Jack Harrington...where I am old...or have been old and now am growing young again because of her healing waters. But young saplings must have strength within their blood; it is the sap that runs through them like waters rising from a swollen earth. And the strength of her blood lies in the wisdom that runs through yours. You are part of the unlocking of the fifth ring. You are part of the inscription. You are part of the yew tree that grows eternally from within. Do not think you were sent back in vain."

"I'm the missing element."

"Yes. As I said before, time is not linear. Other than that, I can say no more, except that you have fulfilled your destiny, and you have yet to understand what that truly means. We are your future, Raven King. Watch, and remember what you see here today. Remember the journey of the rings and the lessons of the Ogham; it has been buried far too long in darkness."

On the far side of the clearing a branch snapped; Emrys' stance shifted. Jack watched, as color flooded his cheeks and anticipation burned in his eyes. The morning light was a soft haze floating above the ground, bathing the glen with an other-worldly dimension. Out of the shadows emerged a woman on a horse.

The horse glistened, his coat shimmering like the black waters of night. The woman was draped in a cloak of silver fabric that reflected light, and she rode not upon a saddle, but a blanket the color of blood.

The cloak was hooded, cascading over her shoulders in waves of luminous silk, and around her waist was cinched a belt of ebony velvet, clasped with interlocking circles. But the hood draped so low across her brow Jack couldn't see her forehead, nor the crescent moon. He stepped back beneath the branches of the oak and watched as Emrys moved forward. The woman and the man began to circumnavigate the glen...Emrys on foot and the woman on her horse.

"The water is rising. It births out of the mountain and spills across granite cliffs to the sea." The woman's voice was dark and sultry.

"I have seen it, Lady. And at night in the forest, I listen to its song of healing."

"Are you seeking someone, Sir?" The horse's neck arched and his hooves pranced.

Jack watched Emrys' breath quicken, and his eyes fill with love. "I am seeking she that rises out of those very waters," he whispered.

The woman shifted, but Jack still couldn't see her face. The horse continued to paw the ground, and Jack noticed the bridle held lightly in her hands. It was the bridle that had lain on the galley floor.

"Why do you seek her?"

"Because she is my life's breath."

The woman pushed the hood back, off her head and, as she did, Jack gasped; she was hideous. Her hair looked as if it were smeared with thick grease, flattened to her skull. Her eyes bulged from dark hollows, and her skin was more orange than yellow. She smiled, and Jack saw that some of her teeth were missing and those remaining were rotten. "She's like Kundry," he whispered, "woman of enlightenment." He looked quickly at Emrys and was shocked to see that his face was filled with rapture, as if he beheld beauty incarnate.

"...As you sought Nimue?" The woman eased the horse into the light.

"No. When I sought Nimue, I did not understand the principles of union, Lady. To seek with earthly eyes alone blinds us to such things. But I have lain in darkness and learned...and your beauty now is a vision greater than any galaxy that enlivens the night sky. The beauty of all in life that is female is not to be toyed with, but to be honored, as we honor and pay homage to that which gives life...because she is such..."

As the dawn light rose, it slid through the trees and down onto her. It flickered on her face, causing it to alter whether shadow or light rested there. Jack was mesmerized.

"I am weary of falsehoods."

"Surely you can see within my heart these words are true." Emrys stepped forward.

"Do you understand who I am?"

"You are Ragnell, High Priestess of Avalon, the final resurrection of my Bride. There is nothing I wouldn't grant you."

Ragnell watched him, her lids drooping low over yellow eyes. *"You will grant me sovereignty?"*

"Yes. But I need not grant it, as it is yours by the very nature of life. And, in that, I choose to honor life, I honor you, and all that you represent and uphold."

Jack eased closer trying to glimpse the shifting face of Ragnell. Suddenly, light split through the trees hitting her full force. Jack's jaw dropped. The sun had painted her into a ravishing beauty. Matted hair unraveled into a mane of golden red that cascaded over shoulders and arms. Her cheeks were the shade of apricots or peaches, and the hollows of her eyes had softened into cups that held pools of sea green...eyes that stared at Emrys with promises of sensuality and love. Emrys' gaze didn't shift. It was as if this was what he had beheld all along.

"You shall have your bride, Sir. I can hear your words are true. But one more question remains of you."

"Speak and I shall answer."

"You may have me as you see me now, by night or by day. But my beauty is yours for only that, and that alone."

Emrys stared at the woman before him and, for a moment, Jack wondered if he'd even seen the hag at all. There was no lingering concern upon his face, wondering whether he'd want his woman beautiful in his bed at night, yet ugly during the day for others to see, or a beauty to be proud of by day yet ugly in his bed at night. It seemed that for Emrys there was no concern.

"There is no contest, Lady, as I see only beauty. If one or the other must be chosen then the decision is yours to make."

And at that, the flickering shadow of ugliness slipped from her form and fell away into the forest. *"You have broken the spell. By granting me sovereignty over myself, you have freed me from that which nature dictates. Out of the darkness, the prophet has risen. You have earned your sovereignty and now have granted me mine."*

Ragnell nudged the horse forward, till she stood at Emrys' side. The crescent moon shone brilliantly on her forehead, as she leaned down and whispered into his ear, *"She will return."* And with a kick to the side, the horse reared and galloped off into the woods, the silver cape flying behind like starry wings of night.

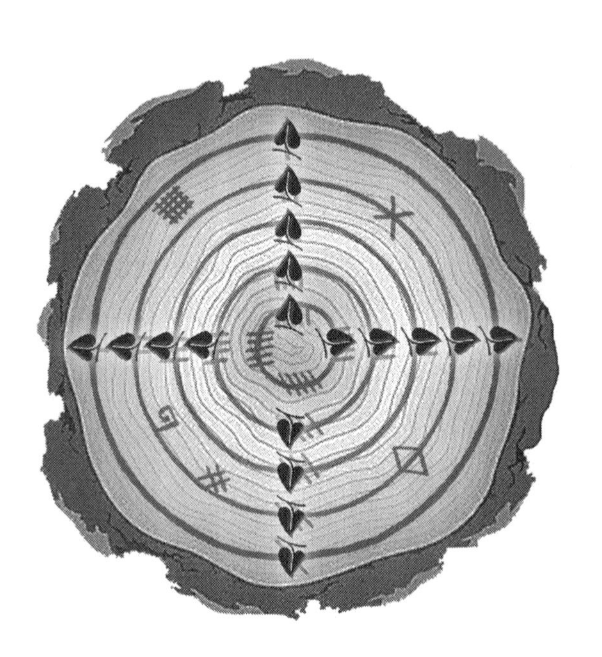

IIIII

APPLE

Immortality

ELENI HAD AWOKEN to see Sophie, dressed in a long silver cloak, disembark the boat and head up the pier; she had the bridle in her hand. Eleni followed behind, along the embankment and up the river. They climbed a steep path that traversed up a hill and opened onto a clearing next to a tiny cabin. But when an ebony horse appeared seemingly out of nowhere, Sophie mounted and galloped into the woods.

Eleni followed as best she could, through a trail of broken limbs and soft dirt, carved into mud divots by pounding hooves. But in the end, it was the voices that guided her. A slight mist blanketed the forest in silence, leaving room for the rising murmur of male voices in the distance. One of them was Jack.

Eleni ran hard, her face slapped by torn branches. Sweat beaded up beneath her pearl collar and dripped down her back. The voices got louder and, suddenly, she broke through onto a ledge above a clearing, where the drama of the final priestess was being enacted.

Sophie was on the horse and Emrys stood at her side, but Jack was nowhere to be seen. She slid down the hill and into the shadows and watched the priestess she knew to be Ragnell transform from hag to beauty. When it was all over and the horse had galloped away, Jack stepped into the clearing at the same moment that a twig snapped behind Eleni. She spun around and stared into Lilli's weary eyes.

"Lilli..."

"You need to go to him, Eleni." Lilli's eyes were yellow and her black hair hung in wet strips down the sides of her face.

"I didn't know where you went. I woke up and she had shifted. I had to follow."

Lilli nodded.

"I had to do what I did, Lilli. I had to. It was the only way."

"I know." Lilli grimaced and rubbed her shoulder.

"Are you all right?"

"I will be. Just need to go away for a while."

"Now?"

"No time like the present, I always say."

Eleni nodded. "Time seems sort of obsolete at the moment."

"It's over, Eleni."

Eleni looked down at her claw hand, hanging limply at her side. "You think she'll come back?"

Lilli looked at Emrys out in the clearing. "Wouldn't you?" She stared for a moment at the two men, her ears alert to their conversation. "He did it, Eleni. Jack did it."

"The inscription?"

"It's much more than an inscription. You have to go to him; let go of your fear and bitterness. You both did it. Despite the loss of years, there was still enough love to span the gap."

Eleni nodded but tears began to trickle down her cheeks. "Too much time has passed, Lilli."

"Not for Jack. For Jack it's always been you. Your love was the spell. Love was the magic that gave birth to Sophie. Love is the mystery, Eleni. It isn't all out there on some cloud. That's what this myth is all about. It's all right here."

Eleni gazed down into the dirt, shivering in the morning cold.

"It takes courage to fly, Eleni...and he flew. Believe me. For Sophie, yes...but mainly for you." Lilli looked down at her hands; they were gray and the nails a dirty shade of yellow. She turned to walk away.

"Where are you going?"

"I need a Twinkie."

"Will I see you again?"

Lilli looked back. "That'll be up to you." The two women stared at each other. Lilli smiled, then walked into the dark forest, where she disappeared beneath the shadowed limbs.

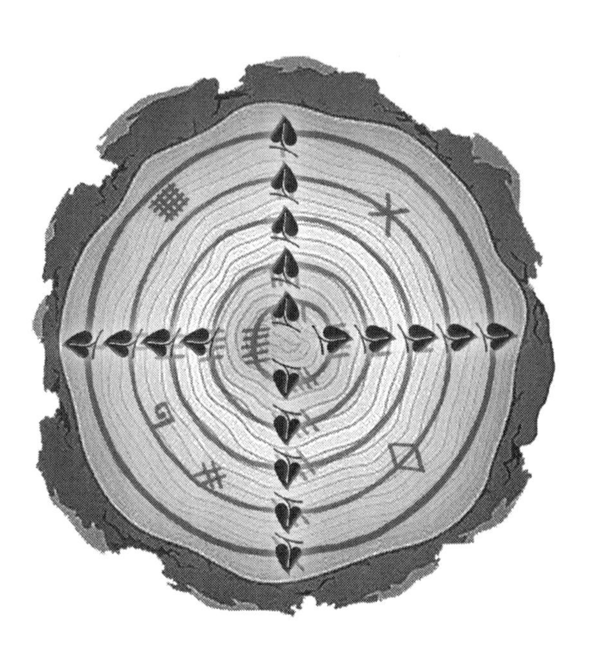

ELDER

Crucifixion

EMRYS STOOD STILL for so long; Jack began to wonder if he'd turned to stone. Finally, Emrys grabbed a stick and walked to the middle of the clearing, where he drew five concentric circles, the outer one five feet in circumference. He raised his head and sniffed the air. "The wind blows from the east this morning."

Jack nodded.

Emrys stepped into the north of the circle. "All things begin and end in the north..." He drew notches, pointing inward, in the northerly direction on each circle. He then stepped into the east and drew notches pointing outward. In the south, he drew diagonal lines, and in the west straight ones that crossed through. "How many would know," he whispered, "the wisdom contained in that one drawing?"

He returned again to the north of the circle, lowered his head, and closed his eyes. "She will be back soon. I suggest you attend to the shadows. Do not try to stop anything...nor speak in any way. We have arrived at something for which there is no map."

Jack looked down at the ground. "You have the map right there."

Emrys remained unmoved. "It is a divine world we enter. The ring she wears will divide and our hearts will merge. We will become the ring. The stone of red triangle is a cup. It is the trinity of blood from which we will drink. But remember, Raven King, that we are flesh. The myth that entered her world through dreams has become flesh. Sophie must walk this world. And I, as man, will walk at her side."

Jack looked up as a raven flew across the clearing.

"There are things within this world that we struggle to understand, Jack Harrington. When all is said and done, all I ask is that you remember what you see here today. Remember, and carry it with you, like a lantern in the night."

Jack stumbled backwards. "Why did you say that?"

"Lantern in the night...?"

"Yes."

"Why do you think?"

"She got sick...they took her away and she died...but I didn't."

"Did she really get sick, Jack? Or did the world just refuse to reflect back her light?"

Jack stared in silence.

"She was your mother. She gave you a gift and asked that you carry it forward...bring light into a dark world."

"Jack O' Lantern..." whispered Jack.

"The great schism...it separates spirit from all life. After a while, the chasm is too great...darkness cloaks us in ignorance, and that which can redeem us is seen as evil...or not even seen at all. Your mother was not ill, nor are you. But you have a responsibility to light the way for others. Become the beacon in the night that she believed you to be, Jack Harrington."

Standing two feet away from the outer circle, in the direction of north, Emrys called out "Birch," the first tree of the first ring. He stood alone with his thoughts, murmuring words strange to Jack's ears. Then he walked east and called out "Hawthorn," then south to Bramble and west to Silver fir. At each point he stopped, and Jack could see that something was happening to him. Pain began to distort Emrys' face.

As he completed a full circle, he stepped in slightly and called out the next tree that resided in the north of the second circle: "Rowan." He moved again through east, south and west...and Jack watched as Emrys relived his very own journey of the rings.

His skin flooded with sorrow and lines began to etch his face. His hair turned gray, then white. The strong muscular frame of the young man withered into a frail old wizard, with hands of knobby knuckles, and pain crippled his spine. Round and round he went, crying out the ancient names, remembering their journey. But when he reached the fourth ring, something changed.

Emrys stood in the north of the forth ring, raised his wizened face to the sky, and whispered, "Willow."

"Water," said Jack under his breath, "the feminine."

A slight rain began to fall. It wet Emrys' hair flat against his scalp and pooled in the hollows of his eyes. He held his arms up and the opulent robes, now faded and worn, began to absorb water. The colors deepened and grew rich, and the moon and stars regained the sparkle of their gold and silver thread.

Jack watched, astounded. "He's reliving the whole damn thing. God help him."

The flesh on his face filled out, and his jaw line firmed with sinew that stretched beneath his neck and shoulders. His spider hair spun into the long black waterfall that swept back from his brow, spilling down his back. But his face remained taut, the muscles pinched from the pain of enlightenment. Then he stepped into the east and cried out, "Hazelnut."

Out from the trees emerged Sophie.

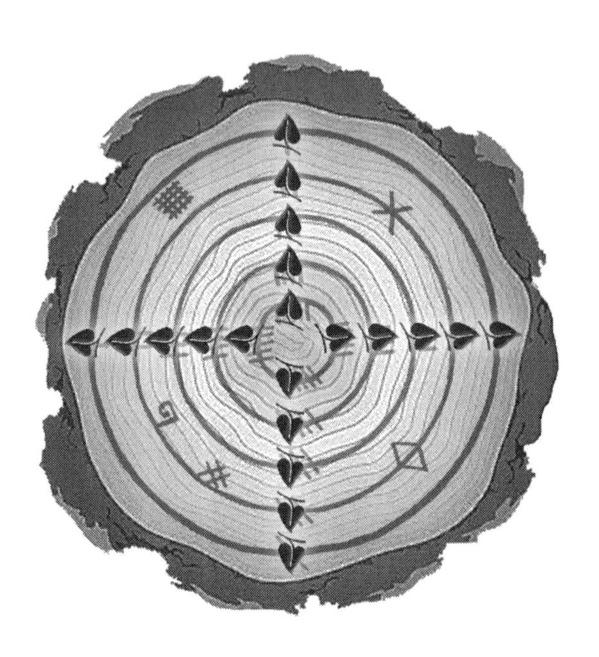

YEW

Transformation

ELENI GASPED.

White silk cascaded from Sophie's shoulders, like gossamer wings, with Ragnell's cloak, inside out, pinned at the throat with a broach of silver and gold interlocking circles. The hood folded back against the nape of her neck, exposing auburn hair, swept up to the crown, where her own mane of cut hair was piled high, loosely wrapped with the purple scarf and secured with a second pin of antiqued gold and silver interlocking circles. She moved slowly, the cloak fluttering away from her shoulders, unveiling her creation, the patchwork bridal gown.

At her hips, braided through the horsehair and leathers ties, was a strip of denim. The woven belt was slung low over her hips and latched in front with a buckle of shimmering gold and silver interlocking circles.

Around her neck was the ivory suede choker, with the silver button at her throat and the pearl buttons spilling down her back. Shining iridescent blue, on the middle of her forehead, was a full moon: the integrated psyche of the Tenth Priestess. She gazed, longingly, across the glen at the man poised in the east.

"Nine hazelnuts fell from the tree into the river and were eaten by the salmon; they are the nine priestesses, imparting their wisdom through the river of life. Yet Avalon, the Isle of Apples, is no more, My Lady," said Emrys.

"But I have seen it," Sophie challenged.

Emrys smiled. "By any other name...?"

"You imply?"

Emrys stared, enamored. "It is known that love of the goddess renders men mad, thus the poison apple. It fell on fallow ground, and your myth turned against you, Lady, as mankind deemed you evil, choosing to not swallow those very seeds wherein lay transformation. I have suffered too long the pain of your loss. I would gladly eat all the apples on your Holy Isle to return to thee and live there with you eternally. But you and I know that the apple is no more."

"Are you denying that Avalon lives?"

"The true spirit of the Isle of healing will resurrect. But the poisoned fruit has been transformed, and you have been reborn. As I have lived in silent abeyance awaiting your return, my eyes see you clearly, one woman who wears the triple-crown. You are the blossom and the fruit of the Cherry Tree, the wood of transformation, the prophecy for which I have waited. If the spirit of Avalon lives on, then it is within this state of grace...and you are her Tenth and only Priestess."

"The fragmentation of the goddess has been healed," Sophie said.

"We have paid the price of enlightenment. Look at me and say that I do not see you," whispered Emrys.

"It is true...Ambrosius Merlinus, Merddin Embrais...Emrys. We are one."

Eleni scrambled through the brush, emerging out of the trees a few feet away from Jack. He turned and stared at her a lingering moment, then shifted his gaze back to Sophie.

"Thank God you're all right," whispered Eleni.

"That's debatable." Jack kept his voice low, watching the two people in the glen.

"I was worried."

Jack raised his hand for her to be still. Eleni walked to his side. "I don't understand, Jack. I don't understand what's happening." Sophie stepped into the west and, with raised hand, made an unusual sign and whispered a word they couldn't quite hear.

"They're stepping into each other's domains," said Jack. "Emrys is in the east of the fourth ring. That's where Hazelnut resides; he's calling to her."

"Why did he age? What made him old then young again?"

"The Seer needs to manifest. Emrys had no option but to relive the tree alphabet."

"The inscription?"

Jack looked at Eleni. "Remember the Ogham?"

"Of course."

"It's not just an alphabet."

"I saw the inscription. Inside each band there were two lines, each marked with five cross-hatches. But I didn't understand."

"They're the marks symbolic of the trees on the innermost circle, the greatest challenge. The ring on Sophie's hand represents the culmination of the Ogham. It's the pinnacle; the wisdom is mapped out when the letters are placed on concentric rings; their meaning changes because of the circuitous timeline. And the directions—north, south, east, and west—become part of the language. It's the story Samuel was about to uncover. Samuel's burial was his way of honoring the goddess, saying that he understood that his lineage was participating in the birth of female wisdom. But it's a wisdom that can't walk alone. Emrys had to reemerge, and together, he and Sophie, will awaken the wisdom in each of the trees. And we're about to watch it happen." Sophie and Emrys continued to move around the circle.

"What are they doing?"

"The interior circle, drawn in the dirt, represents the fifth ring, the innermost point. When the symbols are used linearly, they form an alphabet of letters, but when they're placed on a circular line at the points of the four directions their meaning shifts." Jack pulled out Samuel's Celtic cross from beneath his shirt. "This was the clue: time and space. The Celtic cross is a map."

"Emrys had to bring the mystic in the story to consciousness," Jack continued. "Each tree represents an evolutionary process, a painful one I might add. What you witnessed was Emrys walking all the previous rings of the Ogham and reliving each stage of enlightenment."

"That's why he aged?"

"Yes. But everything changes in the fourth ring. That's where they are now. He has walked three rings, stopping at each point of direction, calling forth from his spirit the energy residing there. Emrys has received the water of life and regeneration from Willow in the north and regained his youth, the water that Sophie's journey released. Now, he's standing in the east where the hazelnut resides. He's honoring female wisdom and fertility, allowing that he cannot be reborn without it. They'll walk the fourth circle...granting each other sovereignty over aspects of creation...male and female...recognizing that each needs the other. The west, where she stands, is represented by Aspen and speaks of willpower and inner strength. The south is Blackthorn, masculine energy and spiritual authority. Sophie is honoring what Emrys brings to this domain."

"Sophie understands all this?"

"Sophie's not just Sophie anymore, Eleni. She's the Tenth Priestess. Look at her."

Eleni watched her daughter walk the fourth ring with Emrys. She carried herself with the nobility of a queen. Her body had filled out...the low cut gown exposing full breasts. "Look...she's wearing the belt of interlocking circles," whispered Eleni. "The priestesses said she was a Queen, harnessing them from above."

"She's their queen, but she's his bride. She's the Bride of Merlin. That's the energy of the myth and the culmination of the fifth ring."

Eleni looked at Jack, his head still bandaged and wrapped with the turtledove sash. "How do you know all this, Jack?"

Jack continued watching the two lovers walk their circle, marking their territory. His cheeks flushed and he looked down at Eleni, her green eyes pulling him in. "I had a dream," Jack smiled. "I guess it runs in the family."

Sophie and Emrys completed their navigation of the fourth ring and stopped, with Emrys in the west and Sophie in the east. As the morning sun climbed out of the east, a ray of light hit the center of the fifth circle and the two of them stepped instantly onto the fifth ring.

Eleni stepped back. "She's barefoot. Should we be watching this, Jack?"

Jack was still staring at Eleni. Perspiration gathered below the bandage at his temples. "Why not? We're her parents."

Eleni turned away, flustered. Out in the glen, Emrys and Sophie raised their right hands and held them forward, almost touching. The ring was hit by light, scattering prismatic color onto the earth. "The right hand..." Eleni tried to regain her composure. "The right hand is the hand of consciousness. The energy of the ring is to be brought into the light."

"The trees of the five rings were also mapped out on the hand, Eleni," said Jack. "It enabled them to use a kind of hand language to pass the story along. But this story was trapped in the third ring; that's where Nimue and Emrys clashed, preventing its culmination. When Sophie went into the Tree of Life, she had to get to the third ring of light, within the Tree, in order to reclaim the ring. That's why it's on her third finger."

Jack's gaze slid down Eleni's neck. "Take off the collar, Eleni."

Her hand fluttered up to the pearls circling her neck.

"You need to take them off."

"They were given to me by Igraine."

"Don't you understand?"

"They were given to me by the priestess that represents the earthly mother...because I am that as well!"

"They were given to you because you need to heed their call."

"You've missed a lot since you fell and hit your head, Jack..."

"Look at me, Eleni."

Eleni turned towards the glen.

"Look at me." Jack cupped Eleni's chin and raised her face towards him. "The message of Igraine's myth is what sent you away from me, Eleni. The message in a lot of mythology, as well as this one, has caused damage because it was misunderstood. It wasn't meant to cause the division of the spiritual and the physical, earthly and divine. It was meant to heal it. Didn't Christ say that the kingdom of heaven was amongst us but we could not see? It's all right here, Eleni. The myth implies that a divine being must be born of earth and spirit...of physical parent and some sort of mystical or divine parent; it's mythology, damn it! It's trying to tell you that we are all body and spirit! It's a divine marriage that gives birth to a divine being. But what is a divine marriage? Merlin manipulated Arthur's birth. He saw a window of opportunity and created a spell that caused a merging of his mysticism with a human woman, hoping to create a noble being that would be the vehicle of his wisdom, carry it out into the world. But it failed." Jack stared into Eleni's eyes, his palm cradled under her chin. "It failed, Eleni, because Merlin disregarded what the priestesses were telling him. There is no greater power than love." Jack dropped his hand. "We wrote those stories, Eleni. In another era, yes, but they were still created by people. And if the people are blind to enlightenment, so is the story."

Jack took her by the shoulders and turned her towards the glen. "Look at them. It's what everyone longs for. Divine union...here, in the body...opening the doorway for the greatest fulfillment of mankind. Let go of the belief that blinded you to me; the collar is a vestige of the past. Let it go, so that we can be transformed along with our daughter."

Eleni's right hand hung onto the pearls as she watched Sophie and Emrys walk the fifth ring. They were using hand signs to speak the language of the trees, giving credence to the belief that there was power in the sound of their words, not meant for ears other than their own.

"What are they saying?" Eleni's voice was tired, with little breath to give it tone.

"Each tree of the fifth ring represents transformation. Ash is in the north and represents the world tree and its connection to all domains. Apple is in the east and stands for eternal creation, the womb, and immortality. Elder is in the south and represents breakdown and massive transition. And in the west is the Yew tree for death and transformation. Emrys and Sophie have each succumbed to massive breakdown in order to be resurrected anew, to harness all domains of the Tree of Life."

"Look at their hands, Jack."

As they walked the fifth ring, Sophie and Emrys held their right hands up, over the center of the circle...touching, as if in prayer. The white stain on the center finger of Emrys' right hand emanated light. The stone began to glow blood red, and the ring shimmered with silver and golden light.

The bands began to separate.

Eleni tugged on the pearl collar, breaking the clasp, spilling pearls onto the earth.

The lovers stepped into the circle, their right palms joined high above their heads. The ring divided, gold to Emrys and silver to Sophie, and the red triangle stone spilled its light down their arms to their lips, where it was drunk as if by one as they consummated their union with a kiss.

And as they did, Emrys gently reached up and untied the purple scarf, letting its silk float to the ground. Sophie's long waves of auburn hair spilled from her crown and tumbled down her back and shoulders, reconnected with its source, the Tenth High Priestess of Avalon.

Jack cradled Eleni into the protective fold of his arms. "We are reborn," he whispered. Eleni succumbed, burying her head in the warmth of his chest.

"Mother of Mercy," she said, "she did it."

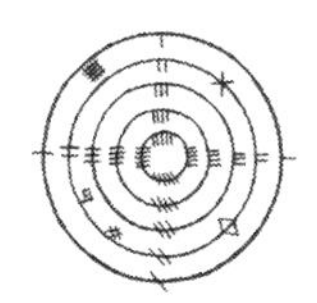

EPILOGUE

MERLIN'S CRYSTAL CAVE on Magdalene Street had been closed for many a long year. The walls had grown damp, and dust carpeted the stone floor. Crystals still cobbled the walls like a great cave, which it was, and they were still brushed regularly with feathers so as to quiet disturbances. The proprietor, Thomas, came in often. He came to tend them, like beloved plants; he came to listen.

In the rear of the shop, an iron bed had been sandwiched between the chaos of books that cluttered the floor, as occasionally he would stay and rest, seeking answers in his dreams.

Thomas had grown old; his broad angular frame was less robust without the sinew of youth, and his black hair was now white. If he stayed overnight, the dust and damp would saturate his lungs, irritating an ongoing condition. When he had trouble breathing, he called Gwyn.

She stood in the doorway, silhouetted by moonlight. Her long hair, now streaked with gray, framed a face as lovely as the first day he saw her. "You should let me call a doctor," she said.

"It will pass, Gwyn. Just sit with me awhile."

"I don't know why you come here. The damp aggravates your lungs. You should sell the crystals and close the shop."

"They are my friends, Gwyn. How do you sell a friend? Besides, they are healing energies."

"They will not heal you forever."

"No...not forever...just long enough to see the prophecy come true."

"It's been over thirty years, Thomas, since the gentleman with the ring was in the shop. We have no way of knowing if the prophecy is being fulfilled, or even if he truly had the ring."

Thomas caressed her cheek. "He had the ring..."

Gwyn got up and walked to the window, drawing back worn drapes, so she could stare down the hillside to the Abbey walls. "You should come home. It's cold in here and the dust is thick."

"I must listen to the crystals, Gwyn."

"Do you really believe they'll tell you where he is?" she snapped.

"Yes. Because he is our son...and because he had the record keeper."

Gwyn continued to gaze through the opaque glass etched with time. "I miss him..."

"You will see Emrys again. But he must find his way back to me on his own. It's the only way, Gwyn. It is the beginning of his journey in discovering who he really is."

"He has no knowledge of you," she whispered softly.

Thomas turned away, looking down the dark corridor to the small front room. "The House of Myrdin has a lineage, Gwyn. It mattered that he not be told from whence he came. If he truly is who I believe him to be, then he will have to harness that which lies within on his own."

"And if he is not who you think he is?"

Thomas sighed. "We have had this discussion many times, Gwyn. The story behind the prophecy is greater than our individual lives; sometimes sacrifice is required. Do you not think I also bear a burden? To live in silence, away from those I hold dear?"

Gwyn turned away from the window. "We have not seen nor heard from him in ten years…ever since you asked me to give him the record keeper on his twenty-first birthday. The power in the crystal is strong, Thomas. What if it led him astray? How do we know he isn't dead?"

"I would know."

"How would you know?"

"The crystals talk. They lived for many years with the record keeper; they hear things that you and I cannot."

"And they speak to you…"

"In a manner…yes. I would know if he were dead, as I will know when the prophecy has begun."

Gwyn turned again to stare blindly upon the cobbled lane that snaked down the hillside.

"As I also know that I will not die without resting my eyes upon our son."

"You have not seen Emrys your entire life but from a distance. How will you even know him after so many years…?"

"Because I have the gift…as you well know. The record keeper will have guided him to the young woman who is meant to be his bride. The young woman who is descended from the gentleman who visited this shop and bought the velvet bag embroidered with cherry blossoms; the woman of prophecy, Gwyn, who will become one with him and reawaken the wisdom of wood."

"When that happens, the crystals will sing. I will hear them, and I will know that our son, Emrys, has merged with the ancient spirit of Merlin, and that he has bonded in love to a young woman who has harnessed the energy of the goddess, and that they have begun the journey prophesied centuries ago. When that happens, he will return to us, with his Bride, to discover his bloodline and spiritual lineage. And we will need to be diligent and listen to the forces that guide, or hinder, his reaching us."

Gwyn dropped her head and started to cry. As she did, an odd murmur emanated from the front room.

Thomas stood up and cocked his head.

It was an eerie elixir of sound, a sweetened discordance, or melodious cacophony that penetrated to the bone. Thomas walked down the hall, like a dead man into the light.

As he entered the dark room filled with crystals, the soft down of hair on his arms bristled, and the back of his parched throat began to open, like a womb, ready for the birth of long awaited cries of exultation.

Thomas dropped to his knees. "They're singing...all of them...singing like choirs of angels..."

Tears welled in Thomas's eyes. "***And their love will open the door for the return of the wisdom of wood...***" he whispered. "They've found each other, Gwyn. The prophecy has begun."

Made in the USA
Lexington, KY
16 November 2011